PRAISE FOR WAR TORN

"*War Torn* might well be destined to be this generation's *All Quiet on the Western Front* or *The Red Badge of Courage*. Jeff Wilson has fashioned a bold and bracing tale that bristles both visually and viscerally with the uneasy juxtaposition between faith and duty. Emotionally riveting, *War Torn* is an angst-riddled tale of combat in which the greatest battle of all is a man at war with his own soul. Powerful, deeply moving, and every bit the equal of the best of Philip Caputo and Tim O'Brien."

—Jon Land, *USA Today* bestselling author

"*War Torn* is an incredible read! An inspiration for war fighters struggling to come home from the fight and an eye-opener for those who want to better understand the devastating effects of war. Written like one of Wilson's bestselling military thrillers, but with an important message buried inside."

—Commander Mark McGinnis, U.S. Navy SEAL,
executive director of the SEAL Legacy Foundation

"Jeffrey Wilson has written a remarkable story about love, friendship and the unmitigated power of faith. If you're a veteran questioning your faith, I want to encourage you to pick up *War Torn*. If you're the spouse of a veteran, I want to encourage you to pick up *War Torn*. And if you're just a person with no ties to the military, but you're looking to be inspired and receive hope, I again encourage you to read this book. Whatever group you're in, you won't regret the read."

—Remi Adeleke, author, actor, speaker,
and former U.S. Navy SEAL

"Jeffrey Wilson has taken his passion for sharing Christ with his fellow military members and the talent that made him a bestselling author and produced an important book that is a must read for combat veterans, their families, and anyone who has struggled with their own crisis of faith. Churches and other Christ-centered missions wishing to minister to these heroes and their families should start by reading this book."

—Pastor Craig Altman, Grace Family Church

"*War Torn* will rip your heart out! Like many combat veterans, Jake experiences the nightmares of combat: heavy gun fights, the death of close friends, and the possibility of killing innocents in the heat of battle. The overwhelming pain is far too common. How does one heal? How does one find hope through all the chaos? *War Torn* reveals God's extraordinary message of hope and ultimately leads to perseverance. A must read!"

—Lt Col F. Damon Friedman, USAF Special Operations, President, SOF Missions, Executive Producer, *Surrender Only to One*

WAR TORN

Other Books by Jeffrey Wilson

The Traiteur's Ring
The Donors
Fade to Black

With coauthor Brian Andrews
Tier One
War Shadows
Crusader One
American Operator

With Brian Andrews, writing as Alex Ryan
Beijing Red
Hong Kong Black

WAR TORN

JEFFREY WILSON

*For my wife and best friend, Wendy, who helped
me find my way home. And for Connor, Jack, Emma,
and Ashley, who make being there worth any price.
And for everyone who has served and understands this story.*

PROLOGUE

Jake stared at the alternating pattern of dark and light brown. The pattern seemed to move on its own, to shimmer and sway. He squinted, then blinked. The colors became solid—became a wall made of plywood. Someone poked and probed him. Metal invaded his ears and nose and light flashed painfully in his eyes, but his body felt as numb as his mind to the intrusive hands and cool instruments.

The doctor standing over him seemed to say something, but his voice sounded far away and tinny, like an old record playing too slowly in another room. Unable to grasp the meaning of the words, Jake absently decided to ignore the voice, and instead continued to watch the projection playing in a loop on the plywood: Cal evaporating in a cloud of blood and bone. One minute Cal was staring into Jake's eyes and motioning him over. And the next—the next moment Cal was gone.

"Cal," he mumbled.

Rachel insisted on calling him Caleb because she loved the biblical story of Caleb, who, along with Joshua, encouraged the Israelites to follow Moses into the Promised Land, believing that God would vanquish the seemingly insurmountable foes they faced. Jake had never understood why that always made Cal smile, until these last few weeks.

And now he was gone.

The explosion hadn't even knocked Jake down. How the hell was that possible—that what was left of Cal could fit in a backpack and Jake hadn't even been knocked to the ground? He watched the horror play out again. And again. Each time, Cal was gone and Jake remained. Maybe it was impossible. Maybe it was just a dream. But he could taste the dirt and blood in the back of his throat. That seemed real enough.

The doctor tugged on his arm, and Jake turned away from the movie, but the images followed him. The doctor was staring at him expectantly.

"Huh?" he heard himself say. The sensation of watching himself from outside of himself—from another, faraway place—made his head swim.

Please, God. Let me be dreaming. Or let me be dead too.

"Your weapon, Sergeant," the tinny voice said. "We need to secure your weapon, son."

The doctor meant him, he realized—he was Sergeant somebody. It was a title from an old World War II movie, a movie where "Sergeant" was a tough son of a bitch and a leader. Jake knew he was neither of those.

A warm hand squeezed his wrist and he looked down at where his white-knuckled fist clung tightly to his M4. The back of his hand, his sleeve, his body armor, even his rifle, were covered in thick dirt mixed with Cal's blood. His throat tightened and he began to sob as strong hands pried his fist from the weapon. He was more than happy to release the gun, but his fingers wouldn't follow the commands that he sent them desperately—commands to let go, let go, let go. When other hands cradled his head and back and gently laid him down, he felt as if he fell a mile into a cavern rather than a foot and half onto the stretcher.

"Stable, but possible TBI. Put him on the urgent bird out to the Cache. What's that make—three?"

"Two," a soft female voice said. "The chest wound died."

"Shit," he heard the doctor hiss. "Two angels at the scene?'

"Yeah."

Angels meant dead soldiers. That, he remembered. Two angels were two dead soldiers—two of his friends. And the voice said another one who'd died here from a chest wound. Cal and two others were dead. Which two? Jake turned and tried to watch the movie again—tried to see which of his other buddies he had let die. All he could see was Cal's face, tight-lipped and motioning him over.

And the boy, right? There'd been a boy. Something about the boy had bothered Jake. A skinny kid, maybe eleven or twelve years old. He had been in a long grey "man dress," as Jake and his buddies had taken to calling the long shirts the locals often wore. The boy's had been bulky—had looked all wrong. And his eyes had been scared—scared and something else, maybe. Someone had shouted at Jake from behind. He couldn't remember who or what, but he thought they were trying to tell him to do something—something important. Then what happened?

He closed his eyes to shut out the scene of Cal exploding all over him, but the movie played relentlessly on the backs of his eyelids now. He felt tears trickle across his cheeks and into his ears and heard himself sob.

Then soft hands touched his arm and something cool wiped across his skin. The coolness was followed by a sharp stab that should have hurt, but instead just felt dull and distant.

A moment later his arm felt hot and he could no longer open his eyes even if he wanted to. He descended into some dark pool from which a voice cried out, "Rachel! Cal!" over and over.

Then he realized the voice was his and he screamed silently inside his mind.

CHAPTER 1

Four Months Earlier

When he was a kid, Jake sat in church beside his parents every week, third pew from the front, left side. There was a smell to the church, not unpleasant and very unique, and even today when he went to a rare service with his mom, that smell made him feel like a kid again. He had no idea if the sermons had been any good. He'd never really listened to them, using the twenty minutes to instead invent stories and imagine scenarios: he was a secret agent, undercover looking for spies; he was hiding from the law, and any minute a SWAT team would crash through the stained glass windows; the entire sanctuary was in fact a spacecraft taking them all to be the first settlers on Mars. As he grew older, the twenty minutes were used for slightly older imaginary stories, which often involved one of the handful of cute girls his age in the congregation. Whatever the minister was saying, it was not really for him. Jake was doing his part already. He never, ever missed a service unless they were out of town as a family.

Today Jake fidgeted quietly beside his wife and tried to follow Pastor Craig's message. He obviously had zoned out, because the preacher was talking about the Church in Acts two, and saying that it wasn't a place but a community of believers. Jake guessed he had missed what tied that in to stuffing ten dollars into the tithe envelope to drop in the bucket. He was still doing his part. He'd been to church close to every Sunday of his life, save the two rebellious years he'd spent at Virginia Tech studying girls and beer. Even then, guilt had driven him to church more than half the time, though he rarely admitted to his friends or roommates where he disappeared to while they all nursed hangovers. While he never really felt that the sermons applied directly to him, he liked how he felt going to church. He liked that it felt like the right thing. And he loved how happy and radiant it made Rachel to have him there with her, holding her hand.

Rachel squeezed his hand now, and he looked over at her and smiled, staring into her beautiful brown eyes, framed by dark hair that she wore long and spent an hour on Sunday mornings blow-drying straight, while those around them spent that same time adding the curls she would naturally have. Rachel positively glowed at church. She loved it here and rarely left with dry eyes, the tears usually beginning during the music when she would sway and sing, her hands lifted up to God. He wondered if that was what kept him coming back more than anything—just watching his wife smile and glow.

"I love you," she said and squeezed his arm with her other hand. He noticed for the first time that Pastor Craig had stopped talking and that folks were gathering their things and heading out of the big auditorium. "Where did you go?"

Jake leaned over and kissed her cheek.

"Just thinking about the sermon," he said.

Rachel volleyed back her best I-know-you-better-than-that smile. "Really?" she said. "And what was your favorite part?"

Jake grinned. "That it made you smile," he said and kissed her cheek a second time, then rose and pulled her to her feet.

They walked together toward the exit, Rachel playfully poking him in the side, making him laugh.

"I know you far too well, Jacob," she said—her name for him on Sundays.

This was the other thing he loved about church and Sundays. Her happiness was infectious and they had fun. It was their day—a day to have brunch with Cal and Kelly. Sometimes they all watched football together or went to the large, nearby county park and rented a canoe. He and Rachel made a real dinner together and watched a movie in the evening. It was their day. When he was a kid, they had checked the church box and then gone to breakfast as a family at IHOP. Then Dad usually worked in the yard, but unlike on Saturdays, Jake was not called on to help him. Sundays with Rachel were far better.

He was having trouble catching his breath and so finally took both of her hands in his and dragged her behind him, saving his ribs. He let go of her hands as they flowed out the double doors in the center of the sea of people, and he pulled down his sunglasses from the top of his head as they entered the bright, sunlit courtyard outside the church.

"Doughnut?" he asked.

"You have an appointment," she chided.

Jake looked over at where Pastor Craig pumped hands with a line of churchgoers.

"Later. I got some time before my going away party," he said and dragged her toward the long line for doughnuts and juice, pulling a dollar bill out of his khakis.

"Jake," Rachel said, her face now serious. "You should really talk to Pastor Craig. I know you think you have me fooled, but it would be weird not to have fears and doubts about this deployment. Maybe he can help you. Maybe he can point you toward scriptures or devotionals that can make it easier for you."

Jake took her hands, his doughnut dollar crumpled between their fingers. He looked at his wife—the love of his life and his true best friend, Cal really being a distant second.

"Rachel, I'm fine," he said. "Sure, I'm nervous. Maybe even a little scared. But I believe in what we're doing, and I believe in the guys in my unit." He flashed her his I'm-cool-with-it smile, the one that had gotten him off the hook when Rachel worried about him after he failed to select for the fire service job. It was the same smile he'd flashed when he told her he wanted to join the National Guard, even though there was a decade-old war going on, and the one he'd used more recently when he had to tell her his unit had been tapped to deploy to Afghanistan. It would give her peace now too, he was sure.

Rachel opened her mouth and then closed it, as if thinking better of whatever had come into her head to say. She did *not* look at peace. He felt an out-of-place irritation rise inside him. Maybe she was the one who needed to spend some time with the pastor. He was about to make the mistake of telling her so, when a slap on the back stopped him.

"Hey, Jake. Wanna chat?"

He looked up to see Pastor Craig's eyes sparkling, and waited for the perfect words to defuse where he was headed with Rachel. The pastor said nothing, which was even better, of course.

Pastor Craig Greene was the reason they had joined Foundations Family Church in the first place. One of Rachel's friends at the day care had told her about the church and its dynamic minister, and they had come to check it out for themselves two years ago, six months after their wedding at John Wesley United Methodist Church. He and Rachel had both grown up at "Wesley UMC," and he even remembered having a little crush on her when he joined the Methodist Youth Fellowship during the awkward year of ninth grade. Rachel had been an eighth grader, so they'd been in different youth groups, but he saw her around a lot and thought she was cuter than any high schooler. He had quit MYF before tenth grade, though, and their paths hadn't crossed again until he came home from his experiment with college, hoping two years of studying environmental science might give him an edge in finding a job as a firefighter, especially with a year as a volunteer with the Blacksburg Fire Department under his belt. If he'd gotten hired by the fire department, he would never have joined the Army National Guard. And then he wouldn't be headed off to an awkward conversation with Pastor Craig—a meeting that seemed weirdly more stressful than deploying to Afghanistan.

Craig looked at him expectantly—his solid jaw carrying a hint of a smile, and his dark eyes reflecting the same good-natured demeanor they always did. He squeezed Jake's shoulder with powerful hands befitting the football player he'd been in his youth. It was rumored that the pastor had once even tried out as a placekicker with the Washington Redskins.

"How are you, Rachel?"

"I'm okay, Pastor Craig. Worried about my husband," she admitted with an ease that always stunned Jake. Truth be told, he always felt a little jealous at how comfortable she was with her feelings—or at least with talking about them, he supposed. He had learned after two decades with his dad how to keep his feelings mostly to himself. He was more open with Rachel than with anyone, but still...

"Jacob will be okay," Craig said and wrapped a bear-like arm around Jake's shoulders. "We're all real proud of him, and this church's prayers will surround him with a shield of God's power, I promise you."

Craig smiled into Jake's eyes, and Jake smiled awkwardly back. "Let's go up to my office for a few minutes, okay?" Craig asked.

"Sure," Jake answered with an enthusiasm he didn't feel. He leaned over and kissed Rachel on the cheek "See you in just a few minutes, baby."

She nodded. "I'll hang out in the courtyard with Kelly," she said, referring to Cal's wife and her best friend.

"Tell Caleb I said 'hey,'" the pastor said, then led Jake toward the glass doors and back inside.

Jake followed, marveling at the self-assurance with which the man engaged his parish—shaking hands, giving hugs, and by some miracle knowing almost everyone's name. Together, they climbed the stairs and then walked down the short hall. The reverend's grandmotherly secretary smiled at them as Craig swept Jake into his modest office.

Jake took a seat in the comfortable chair in front of the large desk. He looked around at walls covered with pictures of church events, inspirational posters with Bible verses, and, of course, a ton of football memorabilia, including a dirty football covered with signatures. Jake had never been to the annual "Man Camp" camping trip that the men's ministry put on, but he had heard that Pastor Craig was fiercely competitive, often coming away from the various events with minor injuries rather than lose. Jake would love to see that side of the man.

"So," Craig said, pulling Jake back to the task at hand. He rested a blue-jean-covered knee on the edge of his desk. Jake shifted nervously. "How are you doing, really?"

"I'm really doing fine," Jake said and tossed in an unconvincing laugh as proof. "Honestly, I'm doing what I feel called to do. I love my country and I'm proud to serve. When I joined the Guard, Rachel and I both knew that this was a possibility. Heck, with all that's going on it was almost a certainty. I want to go. It's the job I signed up for. I'm with some great guys and we're really well trained. The rest is in God's hands."

Jake realized as he said it that there was a part of him that wished like hell he had gotten selected for the fire department job. The chief had told him that the competition was fierce for the two open spots and had encouraged him to keep his application active, implying that he would likely hire Jake next time. Still, had he gotten it the first time, he wouldn't be heading to Afghanistan. He was thrilled by the adventure, but a bigger part of him was nervous—not just about the war, but about such a long time away from Rachel.

Pastor Craig smiled, his feet now comfortably crossed on his desk. He picked up a football from the credenza behind him and began tossing it back and forth between his hands.

"Nothing you're worried about back here?" He was watching Jake closely. "About Rachel?"

It was like the man was a mind reader. Jake had no intention of admitting any real worries. To what end? What could possibly be done about it now? He would go. He would fight with his platoon. He would come back and start his life back up. Simple. Talking about Rachel, though—that was a conversation he could easily have. He knew from talking to the more senior soldiers at the command, those who had been through all of this before, that it was sometimes harder on those left behind to worry. Rachel was strong when she needed to be for herself. She had been a rock after her dad died and been amazing for her mother. But he didn't know how she would do with worrying about *him*.

"I know it'll help her to have the church here. I'm betting she'll get pretty busy with the kids while I'm gone, and I think that'll help a bunch. She's already talked to Diane Barrows about volunteering in the children's ministry for all four services instead of just one on Sundays." Rachel spent one of her two days away from her job at the day care working in the children's ministry at Foundations. Rachel had been an only child, and he knew she wanted a big family with tons of kids—something he would like too, eventually. Once he got the dream job. Maybe it would all come together when he got back.

"I'm sure they could use her," Craig agreed. "She's so great with the kids. And, of course, keeping busy will help make the time go by."

"And she has her women's group on Tuesday nights. And she said she might join the Bible study that Kelly does."

Craig nodded. "We'll keep her busy for you." The pastor dropped the football into his lap. "If you're worried about anything, you can shoot me an email and I'll be sure that someone is there for Rachel. And, of course, you'll be in our prayers too, Jake."

Jake smiled. "That means a lot, Pastor Craig. I really mean it," he said, and he did. But Pastor Craig was still looking at him with that look that said he had more to say. Jake just wanted the meeting to be over. He loved that Rachel was so involved at the church, but it just wasn't his thing.

"What do you know about your namesake, Jacob?"

Jake blinked twice but didn't say anything. God, how he hated this kind of thing. The church he'd grown up in maybe hadn't "fed him spiritually," as Rachel liked to say—whatever that meant—but they didn't have these awkward conversations, at least. His parents had been on the board at their Methodist church—his dad was an usher at times—but they didn't feel the need to get in your head all the time.

"Not much," he finally offered when it was clear the preacher would wait forever for his answer if necessary.

"That's okay," Craig said and opened a large softcover Bible on his desk. He pulled reading glasses out of his pocket. "You can read a lot about Jacob—the original Jake"—he smiled over his glasses, which looked strange on the muscular and vibrant preacher—"in Genesis, especially chapter twenty-five to chapter forty or so." Pastor Craig took off his glasses, and Jake searched for the point. "There are some interesting things in there you would enjoy—like the fact that Jacob's true love was named Rachel, just like yours. I'll let you read about it on your own. What I want you to know, though, is that Jacob was a great leader—leading the people of Israel through some tough times—but he didn't start out that way."

Jake's left foot bounced up and down nervously. Pastor Craig chuckled.

"Relax, Jake," he said. "There's no test after this, and I do have a point." He leaned back in his chair and began tossing the football. "The point is, Jacob became a great leader, but he started out as a schemer—a guy who believed he deserved blessings but was not content to find God's plan for him. Like a lot of people, he figured he had things under control—that he could work things out on his own. He believed maybe that he knew best. Or maybe he just didn't see God as a part of the real, everyday life, you know?" Pastor Craig dropped the football into his lap again, and now held his eyes, and Jake felt even more uneasy. "Eventually, Jacob became a powerful leader and servant of God, but not until he was able to let go of his need to control everything and push his own plan."

Jake felt his throat tighten a little and his face flush. Anger pricked him, but he wasn't sure why. "Are you saying that's what I'm like?"

Jake knew there was truth to some of what Pastor Craig was imply-ing, but that just pissed him off more. Was he supposed to just say a prayer on Sunday mornings and then hope God would do the rest? Wasn't a man supposed to try and control things for himself and his family? He knew he was often short with Rachel when she talked about him "giving things to the Lord" or "surrendering his struggles." Just what the hell did that mean other than doing nothing and hoping God would pick up the slack?

The pastor dropped his feet to the floor and leaned forward on his elbows. His eyes weren't accusing, though; they were warm.

"No, Jake," he said. "What I'm saying is that God has a plan for you, a plan for you and Rachel. You're a good man and you're doing a difficult thing right now, but I want you to be open to God's will and let Him lead you down the path He has for you. Do you think you can do that?"

Jake nodded, unsure why he still felt a little pissed off. He would always work hard to give Rachel, and whatever kids they might have when he got back, a good life. He didn't understand what exactly it meant to let God lead you down a path, but he had no intention of admitting that and spurring a whole new conversation. He somehow mustered at least a portion of the smile that had saved him so often.

"I will definitely pray about that," he said, telling the preacher what he assumed he wanted to hear.

"I've never been a soldier, Jake." The pastor shook his head. "I'm not sure I could do it, really." Jake looked at the tough, powerfully built man and doubted that was true. "A lot can happen in war, I know, and some of those things can make it hard to see God in all of it. I'll be praying that you can see God's plan for you in the stress and fog of war. But the prayers'll mean more to Him coming from you."

Jake nodded and rose, ready for the uncomfortable conversation and strange feelings to be over.

"Thank you very much, Pastor Craig," he said and put out his hand. The preacher stood up and clasped it firmly. "It means a lot that you'll be here for Rachel and that the church is a family for us. I'll be home before you know it." Jake screwed on the full smile he knew he excelled at.

Pastor Craig nodded as they shook, but Jake thought his eyes looked a little sad.

"We're here if you need us, Jake," he said. "Godspeed and safe travels."

Jake let go of the pastor's hand and hustled out of the office, closing the door behind him. The day flew by in a blur, and Jake was grateful for that. By the time he crawled into bed beside Rachel, he felt exhausted, and grateful for the weariness that might actually help him sleep. Breakfast with Cal and Kelly, the farewell cookout with the unit at the picnic grounds on base—a last time all together with their families—and the hour they spent at Rachel's mom's house with Jake's parents had all run together and prevented any prolonged emotional moments. These were the normal things, he thought. He kept coming back to Pastor Craig, though, and his comparing Jake to Jacob in the Bible. He had thought to ask Rachel about it—Lord knew she would know the story the preacher was talking about—but he didn't want to return to talk of God again, even with her. Maybe he would ask Cal about it once they settled in downrange.

Rachel squeezed his arm as she snuggled in close.

"I love you so much, Jake." Her voice sounded tight and Jake felt his own throat grab his voice and make it sound like a stranger's.

"I love you too, baby," he said, as a warm tear rolled down his cheek. He thought he was crying about being away from his wife more than from fear of what he would be asked to do in Afghanistan. The feelings were just a big, unfamiliar mass that blended together in ways impossible to separate. He swallowed hard to keep any other hints out of his voice. "I'll miss you so much, but I'll be back before we even know it." He felt her draw in a shuddering breath. "And we'll have email almost every day, and phone calls and video messages," he continued, now comfortably back in the role of supportive husband.

"I know," she said. "You don't have to worry about me, really. And I know that God will take care of us both."

She pushed her face against his neck and he felt her warm tears on his shoulder. Before he could say anything to comfort her again, her soft hand ran gently across his chest and he lost himself in the feel of her touch. Together they escaped to a much happier place for a while.

Afterward Jake held her tightly.

"I will definitely miss that," he said and kissed her on the top of the head. Rachel giggled and hugged him tightly.

After a few minutes the sex worked together with his exhaustion and he felt his eyes close against his will.

"Will you say a prayer with me, Jake?" Rachel asked softly.

"Of course, baby," he said.

Then, as his wife began to call out softly to God, he drifted away to one of his last deep and dreamless sleeps for a very long time.

CHAPTER 2

Jake stretched his aching back and heaved the lead weight of his duffle bag up onto his shoulders, which did nothing to lessen the crick in his neck. His rifle was slung across his shoulder and low on his right hip, and the heavy bag smashed it painfully against his right butt cheek. He hopped slightly to pop the bag up off his gun, and quickly shifted the rifle farther forward before the bag pulled painfully down on his shoulders again. Then he squatted awkwardly and picked up his second bag by the handle and half stumbled down the ramp that led out the back of the C-130 cargo plane. All the months of training, yet he had never once been asked to practice the awkward art of carrying nine months of gear and personal items into a war zone.

"Jeez, I better use every damn thing in this bag," he mumbled as he shuffled behind Cal.

"Right?" Cal laughed as he struggled with his own load. "I bet we don't use half of what we brought."

"I'm leavin' any shit I don't use at least a hundred times right here in the 'stan when we head home," grumbled Pete Canaday as he fell in beside them. As usual, Pete's gripe was accompanied by a huge grin that made his complaint impossible to take seriously. Next to Cal, Jake figured Pete to be one of his favorite people in the platoon. The kid just seemed happy no matter what was going on. For him, it really was just a big adventure.

"Y'all just have soft lives," joked Shawn Melton. Shawn worked for the fire department—Jake's one-time dream job—and made sure everyone knew how tough that meant he had to be. Jake noticed with some irritation that Shawn had only one duffle bag—a much better explanation for his relative ease.

"One more stop," Cal said, "Then we'll be at our home base and we can drop all of this crap for almost a year."

The thought that they would next pack and carry all their personal gear in nine long months quieted the group and made Jake ache again for Rachel. It had been nearly a week since he had kissed her goodbye in the foyer of their small house, and the thought that he still had nearly the full nine months to go squeezed at his heart.

"This way, girls," TC Morrow said as he slipped ahead of the group with seeming ease, despite his own heavy load. No one knew what "TC" stood for, and all had learned the hard way not to ask. TC had deployed multiple times before this—all while still on active duty—to both Afghanistan and Iraq. Those deployments made the First Sergeant the most valuable man in the platoon as far as Jake was concerned.

"Right behind you, First Sar'n," Jake said and picked up the pace to keep up with their platoon leader.

It seemed a lot colder than he had expected. Their sister guard unit, whom they were now relieving, had spent the brutal summer months in the Afghan lowlands to the south, and their reports had contained more bitching about the heat than anything else. Jake knew the winters were as cold as the summers were hot, but he thought maybe the perception of heat from their reports had stuck with him. In any case, the cool late-autumn air, at least here at the higher elevations of the ISAF base near Kabul, made him chilly without his fleece on, even with the heat-generating work of carrying his half ton of crap across the tarmac.

They had a relatively short walk to the line of waiting CH-47 helicopters, which would haul them on the last leg of their journey to the forward operating base a short hop from Kandahar in the south of the country—a place they would call home, in the center of the violent Helmand province, for a very long time.

TC peeled off and watched from the flight line as Jake and his friends trundled up the ramp into the first helicopter, while the long line of soldiers from their unit filed in behind them and then began filling up the second bird. Jake collapsed into the uncomfortable canvas-and-metal bench seat, kicked his gear roughly under his feet, and shifted his weapon into his lap. He leaned his helmeted head back and panted as his comrades filled the benches around him.

Pete dropped in beside him and Jake shifted left toward Cal.

"God almighty damn!" Pete said. Despite the curse, he still had a cheeriness in his voice that said he was all in for the "long camping trip with his buds," as he had taken to calling the deployment.

"Hey," Cal said and reached around Jake to punch Pete hard in the arm. "What'd I tell you about that crap?" Pete shrugged and Cal raised his fist again. "Don't use the Lord's name in vain—at least not around me."

Cal leaned back in his seat and closed his eyes while Pete rubbed his arm.

"Holy roller," Pete said and rolled his eyes. Then he smiled and winked at Jake.

Jake laughed and leaned his own head back. "So stop pissing him off, then," he said, eyes closed. "Before you lose the use of your arm."

Pete laughed too, but shook his head.

"God loves you anyway, Pete," Cal said with a smile and patted Jake on the leg.

"Yeah?" Pete asked, projecting his voice to be heard over the now-rising whine of the huge helicopters. "If he loves me so much, then why did he damn me to nine months living with you?"

Cal laughed and shook his head. Then they all settled back in silence as a second, duller moan rose under the whine, and the powerful turbine engines began to turn the giant rotors above them. Moments later they lifted slowly into the air and then the nose of the large helicopter dipped slightly and they moved forward and up.

Jake opened his eyes and looked out the small porthole window across from him. He saw the mountains to the east disappear as the helo turned, and then the lower peaks to the west filled the window as they headed south toward their new home. Jake was surprised by the beauty of the country that flashed by until they climbed high enough that all he could see were the peaks of the western mountain range.

"Hard to believe that beautiful countryside hides so much violence and hatred, isn't it?" Cal asked in a hushed tone.

"We'll be okay," Jake said without turning.

When Cal didn't answer, Jake looked over at his friend. Cal stared out the window, his face pensive and a bit sad. Then his eyes closed and his lips moved in a quiet prayer.

Something about his face made Jake shudder.

"We'll be okay," he mumbled again, this time to himself.

He stared out the grimy plastic window and listened with half an ear as Pete told a story about some girl he met the night before they left and how she might be "the one." Pete's laughter was infectious, and he let the pensive mood and worry about the war slip off him and fade away.

The flight was a blur, the bravado punctuated by awkward quiet and then forced laughter. It made time pass with a strange jerkiness. The landing—in the small zone at the edge of the forward operating base, which wasn't even a quarter the size Jake had expected—had a finality about it that made his chest tight. They lined up for a quick muster and then were led by the men from the unit they were replacing to their hut-like living quarters, twisted around inside sandbag walls and concertina wire.

The thin mattress felt ridiculously comfortable to Jake after a week in a sleeping bag on the canvas cots or dirty floors of the transient quarters they'd stayed in along their circuitous route to FOB Douglas. Jake had asked who Douglas had been, but no one seemed to know. He finally found the answer on a hand-painted sign memorializing the first combat death out of the FOB—a Brit, to his surprise. Apparently, the British had operated out of the camp during the early part of the war. Jake realized he had been in high school at the time, which felt bizarre.

Now his aching body melted into the poncho liner he had spread out on his rack, and he sighed away some of his weariness.

"Hey."

Jake opened his eyes to Cal's grinning face staring at him upside down from the bunk bed rack above him.

"Hey," he said. Then he let his eyes close again. "Wanna join the Army?" he asked—a quote from their first conversation about the National Guard a few years ago, and now a running joke.

"Nah," Cal said and swung back up onto his own bunk. "I'd miss Kelly too much," he said, the exact thing he had said that day. Jake laughed.

His bed jostled as Pete squeezed between their bunk beds and the pair across from them in the narrow room, one of four in the hut. Shawn lay on his back on the lower bunk across from Jake, and after being jostled from near sleep, he snapped a quick punch into Pete's thigh, hard enough for Pete to grunt a short "Ahhh shit."

"Watch it, dumbass," Shawn said without any real anger.

"Crap, dude," Pete said, rubbing his thigh, and then tossed a small backpack he pulled out from his larger duffle up onto the bunk above Shawn. "That really hurt, Shawn."

"Great," Shawn said sleepily. "Then it worked."

"You guys wanna find our way to the chow hall?" Pete asked, his bruised thigh apparently forgotten. "They guys from the two-five said they only do dinner from seventeen hundred to eighteen hundred."

"Yes," Shawn said, but lay still with his eyes closed. "Hungry," he said.

Jake looked at his watch and tried to do the calculation in his head. He had not yet reset the time from Germany on the way in. Giving up, he sighed and looked at Pete.

"What the hell time is it?"

Pete laughed. "About seventeen thirty," he said. "You want me to reset your watch?"

"Nah, I got it," Jake said and undid the band. He kicked the bottom of the thin mattress above him with his boot-covered foot, causing the whole frame to shake. "You wanna go get chow?" he said to his best friend.

"Sure," said Cal and slid down into the narrow space between the bunks. He began to button up his shirt.

"No weapon, no chow," Pete said as he slung his rifle over his shoulder.

"What's that mean?" Jake asked with a chuckle as he strapped his watch back on.

"Sign outside the chow hall," Cal answered. "Says *No Weapon, No Chow*. We gotta have our weapons anytime we leave the hut."

Jake felt a somber mood descend on them at the reminder that this was not just another weekend drill. He'd had the same feeling when the helicopters circled the camp for landing and First Sergeant Morrow had instructed them to all go to "condition one," placing magazines in their rifles and loading a round into their chambers. They were now ready for a firefight should something unexpected happen.

Jake pulled on a fleece and then slung his own rifle and followed Pete out of the tight quarters. Cal squeezed his shoulder from behind.

"We're all good, bro," Cal said with a genuine smile as they left the hut. Shawn, in trail, stretched his tall frame and yawned. He, at least, seemed unfazed by the war zone they found themselves in. The group started up the dirt path, just wide enough for a Humvee, between a cluster of four other wooden huts just like theirs. Jake smiled back tightly at Cal. "Romans eight, thirty-one, ya know?" Cal said.

Jake shifted uncomfortably and looked away. He had no idea what Cal was talking about. Cal laughed and slapped him on the back.

"'If God is for us, then who can ever be against us?' Paul said it in his letter to the Romans." Pete looked over his shoulder at Jake and rolled his eyes. Jake actually felt a little better, more from Cal's infectious confidence than from the Bible passage he didn't really understand. "God is with us, bro," Cal assured him.

The camp seemed ridiculously small to Jake. The southern part of Afghanistan was much flatter than the towering mountains they had seen as they flew in and out of Kabul. But FOB Douglas was nestled on the side of a large and rocky rise, looking out over a sprawling swath of gentle hills. The elevation and the rocks surrounding them made the camp much more defensible than if it had been built on the flat lands they overlooked, but Jake still felt terribly naked in the middle of a hostile country. A large and determined force would seem to have a lot on their side if they decided to try and overwhelm the camp.

Above the rocky rise, two wooden towers held soldiers manning fifty-caliber machine guns. The remaining three quarters of the camp's perimeter was a seven-foot cement wall inside a line of cement barricades, inside a line of concertina wire, surrounded by more barricades topped with barbed wire. Within the camp was a maze of ten-foot-tall barricades constructed of metal wire and canvas sacks filled with dirt. Almost anywhere in the camp the men were within a short jog of cover.

The need for such defenses was what made Jake worry.

"I guess we're pretty safe inside the wire, at least," he said to no one in particular.

"Yeah," agreed Shawn. "Unless they sneak close enough to toss in some mortars or rockets or some other indirect fire. I heard they get indirect fire in here a few times a month."

"Awesome," Pete said simply. "So it just comes down to simple luck, huh? Very sweet."

"'Yea, though I walk through the valley,'" said Cal with a shrug.

"Hey, I know that one," Pete said excitedly. "The valley of the shadow of death, right? 'I will fear no evil, for…'"

"I am the baddest son of a bitch in the valley," Shawn finished.

"That ain't it, man," Pete said and slapped at Shawn's head. Shawn laughed and ducked. "Be respectful, dude. That's some Bible shit. Reverend Cal will knot up your arm like he did mine." Pete laughed loudly at his own joke.

"It's from Psalms twenty-three," Cal said. "David is talking about how God is with him even in the most dire places. 'I will fear no evil, for the Lord is with me.'"

"Right," said Shawn with a grin. "I was gonna say that, exactly. Have some respect, Pete."

"No atheists in foxholes," Jake said, but wasn't sure why.

"And no foxholes in Afghanistan, dude," Shawn said.

Jake marveled at the ease with which Cal talked about God and the Bible. It still made him a little uncomfortable, though, because everyone knew they were best friends. He blushed at the thought that he would be embarrassed by anything Cal did. Truth be told, he admired the hell out of him.

The chow hall was a tent over top of a wooden frame. Sure enough, a small sign written in black marker announced *No Weapon, No Chow*, and beneath was cartoon picture of a rifle and a square labeled *MRE* with a red circle and a line through it. Jake chuckled and the three of them pushed aside the double flap of the tent and slipped inside.

A few people, most of them in the worn and dirty cammies of the unit they were relieving, were in line along the short wooden table across from a tiny food preparation area. The man ahead of him looked back and grinned. His weapon was covered with a light coating of dust except around the ejection port and slide, where it looked to have been cleaned meticulously. Riggers' tape was pulled across the muzzle to prevent dirt from getting into the barrel while on long patrols.

"Mmmm," the man said with a crooked grin. "Two meals a day prepared from the finest prepackaged shit-food you can find in the third world." He laughed and then held out his paper tray to the cook, who piled some mashed potatoes and gravy and a large hunk of Salisbury steak onto it. "At least it's hot," the man said. "Make sure and grab a few protein bars at the table on your way out. They're way better than having MREs for lunch every day."

"Thanks," Jake grumbled.

"This doesn't look that bad," Pete said and sniffed the meat on his tray suspiciously. Jake wondered if there was anything that would shake Pete's kid-like optimism.

"Eat it all," they guy ahead of them said. "No seconds."

At the end of the wooden table were small cans of fruit cocktail, which they all grabbed, and then they headed to the first of two long tables bracketed by wooden benches.

The group ate in silence, except for Pete, who dealt with any fears he had by rambling about nothing while the rest just nodded. Jake's mind went to Rachel and he wondered what she was doing right now. He still didn't have the time difference down, but he was pretty sure it was morning, though which hour was math he couldn't quite do. She would probably be up and maybe even at the day care by now. They had been told during the workup for deployment that they would have access to an Internet-and-phone "café," and he had purchased a discount phone card so he could call Rachel as often as possible. He thought maybe after chow he and Cal could check it out and see how the phone thing worked.

"Hey, girls."

Jake looked up from his empty plate and into the grinning face of TC Morrow. "First Sar'n," he said with a nod.

"Unit meeting with the CO at nineteen hundred in the chapel," the First Sergeant announced. "Individual platoon meetings to follow. Second platoon will meet back here in the chow hall. Check?"

"Copy that, First Sar'n," Cal answered for the group.

"See you there, gents," Morrow said. "We start joint patrols tomorrow with the guys heading home in a few days. I volunteered second platoon to go out first. We'll find out which two squads will be going at the meeting tonight. Cool?"

"Hell, yeah, cool," Pete said, but Jake thought his voice sounded tight.

"Let's do the job," the platoon leader said with a nod.

"We're all in, First Sar'n," Shawn said, sounding like the seasoned pro he hoped to be, Jake guessed.

Jake and his friends then sat awhile in silence. Tomorrow their war would begin.

CHAPTER 3

Jake struggled to remember everything he had learned in the last two years in the Army National Guard, and especially since their mobilization to active duty. After a year of doing a weekend a month as a regular reservist, he had been given a full-time position at the unit for a year leading up to the deployment workups. Most of that year, he had done only administrative stuff until they started working up to come to Afghanistan. The training the last three months had been constant and intense, but things that had seemed like second nature—like reflex muscle memory almost—only a couple of weeks ago now seemed so incredibly foreign that he worried he would not even remember how to use his gear, and most importantly his weapon, should the need arise. The men from their sister unit seemed relaxed and strangely unfazed that in a short time they would be outside the wire. Together the units would patrol the small village a few kilometers away in a "show of force" patrol meant to remind the tribal leaders they were here to help them—and remind any Taliban or Al Qaeda sympathizers in the population that they were as lethal as ever. The seasoned veterans joked around and laughed as they checked their gear. The man Jake had been partnered with—Jared something, who lived in Pennsylvania—wrapped green riggers' tape around the tops of his boots. He looked up at Jake, apparently reading his mind.

"Keeps the dirt out, but mostly keeps my boots or laces from hangin' up on shit if I have to jam," he said. "Got it from some Ranger dudes who came through here four or five months ago, but started doin' it after Chuck got a boot hung up on a burned-out car during a firefight and almost got killed." Jared plastered the last piece of tape into place.

"Did he get hurt?" Jake asked. He eyed the tape on the floor between them.

"Nah," Jared said with a shrug and then pulled his body armor on over his head. "Not that time," he added. He looked off into the distance for a moment. "Died in an IED attack about three weeks later." After a moment the soldier shook his head, as if he'd just caught a spider web across his face in the dark, and then looked over at Jake and shrugged again with a crooked smile. "All set?"

"Yeah," Jake said. He looked down at his gear.

Jared slapped him on the back. "You'll be okay," he said. "Stay with me and do what I do."

Jake nodded and they headed over to the rest of the group. His new friend looked back over his shoulder and smiled. "Taliban assholes don't do shit this time of day, anyway. Still hung over from opium and beating their wives. Just a show of force for the poor families in the village."

"Five minutes in the courtyard."

Jake guessed the short, powerful-looking man who'd barked the command was the other unit's platoon leader.

A strong arm bear-hugged him around his neck. "Wanna join the Army?"

Jake tried to smile at his best friend, but his dry lips felt pasted to his teeth. He reached for the tube clipped to his vest and sucked in some warm water from his camelback.

"Will you pray with me real quick?" Cal whispered in his ear.

Jake felt a flash of anger at his friend but didn't really know why.

"Yeah, I guess," he croaked.

Cal squeezed Jake's neck from behind and leaned his head toward Jake's until their helmets touched.

"Father," Cal said in a hushed voice, eyes closed. "Be with us, Lord. Surround us with the power of your spirit. Help us do your work and live by your will. Be with our brothers in arms and keep them surrounded by your light. Help us all to come home safely. Be with Rachel and Kelly, Lord, and help them remember that you are here with us. Your will be done, Lord. In Jesus' name—Amen."

As the prayer unfolded, Jake felt his irritation melt away. He did feel something, he thought—something inside him. A peace spread over him and he felt his breathing slow. At the sound of his wife's name, tears welled up in his eyes, but gratefully they didn't spill over onto his cheeks.

Cal smacked his helmet against Jake's hard enough to hurt a little.

"Let's get this done, bro," he said.

Jake followed him out into the courtyard.

The mixture of the two platoons—the newbies from Jake's unit and the more relaxed veterans only days from redeployment home—rode to the edge of the village in a line of desert-tan, and the occasional green, Army vehicles. Jake sat beside Jared in the back seat of a four-door, up-armored Humvee and tried to look even half as relaxed as the battle-hardened soldier. Jared looked bored at first glance, but after a time Jake noticed that while the Sergeant's body looked relaxed, his eyes darted back and forth in an almost pattern-like fashion, scanning the road ahead and the occasional locals who shuffled along it. Now and again, Jared's body would tense just slightly, and at such times Jake noticed that his trigger finger would tap lightly along the side of the trigger guard of his rifle. Jake wanted almost desperately to know what Jared perceived as a threat at those moments.

His mind was pulled from Jared's thoughts when the Humvee slowed and then pulled off the dirt road behind one of the two enormous MRAP vehicles in the convoy. Jake wondered if the big mine-resistant transport ahead was the one Cal had crawled up into. Their Humvee bounced along the rough terrain, jarring Jake, who reached up and stabilized himself with a hand on the metal roof. After a moment the vehicle turned, and Jake saw that the convoy had formed a loose circle.

"Defensive perimeter," Jared said, motioning with his head for Jake to dismount the Humvee. Jake opened the heavy door to the outside of the circle and slid awkwardly from the vehicle. Just like in convoy training he took a few steps away from the vehicle, then dropped to one knee and began scanning his sector over the sight of his rifle. A moment later he felt Jared kneeling beside him and taking up his own scan while other soldiers piled out of the nearest MRAPs.

"Hold here," someone shouted loudly.

Jake scanned nervously around his sector but saw no movement at all. He glanced over his shoulder and saw for the first time the cluster of low buildings that rose out of the rock-and-dirt landscape—the village they intended to patrol, he assumed. He heard only the rumble of the vehicles and the chatter of what he assumed to be the patrol leaders planning their infil into the village. The loudest sound seemed to be the pulse that pounded in his temple and the impossibly loud sound of his own breathing.

While he scanned, he let his mind rerun the brief they had received what seemed like days ago. The mission, such as it was, was basically just a walk-through of the village, with the two squads split into two groups each that would take different routes, passing through the center of the village at offset times, converging on the far side. They had been told what to look for and had memorized the faces of a few HVTs—high-value targets—but Jake had the sense that no one expected to see any of the notorious bad guys today. The walk-through would simply remind folks that they were still here and planning to protect the good guys and kill the bad guys whenever possible. They'd been briefed on the latest methods Al Qaeda and Taliban fighters had invented to hide IEDs, and then the company Master Sergeant had reviewed the casualty plans and what to do in the event of some "unexpected event." Jake knew the layout of the village, but unlike his well-blooded, veteran mentor, it was all just map drawings and photographs to him.

"Second platoon—huddle up," someone shouted, and Jake rose, but continued his scan of the area around their wagon circle as he followed Jared.

"First squad on me," he heard his First Sergeant holler.

They formed a loose circle, with a small group from third squad still patrolling a perimeter around the vehicles. TC Morrow gave a very short recap of the battle plan, with another NCO watching from the huddle—First Sar'n's own mentor, Jake guessed. Then they split into groups of four and headed on foot into the village from two separate corners. Jake and Jared spread out from Shawn and his mentor on either side of the dirt street and moved slowly toward the center of the cluster of dirty buildings.

Jared seemed relaxed, his shoulders loose and his weapon pointed down, though Jake saw that his head swiveled and his eyes kept moving. He also saw that Jared's finger tapped the side of his trigger guard as he walked.

Jake tried to keep the same vigilant but relaxed look as he scanned the street. He saw very few people about, but now and then a villager—usually a woman, Jake noted—would look out from the doorway of a small house or from between two buildings. They didn't smile, except for one old woman who Jake got the sense smiled at damn near anything, but they didn't frown or look like they hated them or anything either. For the most part, Jake felt they mostly looked bored.

"So do they like us here, or what?" Jake asked Jared, who now and again nodded and smiled at the villagers they saw. Jared shrugged.

"I think they like us, for the most part," he said. "I think they get nervous that if the wrong person sees them being nice to us, they or their families might disappear. Happens all the time. The Taliban are in and out of here, and I think they're just afraid. Probably they would love it if everyone just left them the hell alone to just live their lives." Jared nodded at an old man squatting in front of a house and puffing on a long ceramic pipe. The man nodded back. "The kids love us, though," Jared said.

As if on cue, two little kids—a boy of seven or eight and a younger girl—ran toward them, waving and laughing. Jake watched Jared closely; he raised his rifle a few degrees and scanned the houses and alleyways behind the kids. Jake tensed until whatever Jared was looking for failed to materialize and his shoulders dropped and his finger slipped away from his trigger guard.

"Smile," Jared said as he reached into a cargo pocket with his left hand, his right still on the grip of his rifle. "Hearts and minds, dude," he said and pulled two small Hershey bars out with his gloved hand. "Khosh amadid," he said to the children and handed them the chocolate bars.

"Salam," the boy said and smiled broadly at Jake. "Kheile mamnoon!"

"Kahesh Mikonam," Jared answered and then waved at a woman who watched them closely from a doorway. She smiled and raised a hand in a slight wave.

"Nooshejan," Jared said and patted the boy on the head as he tore open the candy wrapper. "Man bayad, beravam," he said and then waved again at the woman and continued down the road. Jake followed.

"What did they say?" he asked.

"Just thanked me for the candy," Jared said. "I told them to enjoy it. Remind me back at the camp and I'll give you a notebook with a bunch of phrases you can use. Helps out a lot on these meet-and-greet patrols."

Jake saw his new friend was all business again, his head again on a swivel, and Jake concentrated on clearing the roofs and alleys they passed of any threats. He sensed motion behind him, and felt his pulse quicken as he spun around, his finger moving out over the trigger guard of his rifle.

A few yards behind him, the two kids followed, the little girl skipping as she munched on her chocolate bar. Jake pulled his index finger back, his pulse now beating a tempo in his ears at the thought that he had nearly engaged two little kids. The girl laughed and waved, and Jake felt himself relax as he joined her in laughing at himself.

Jake and Jared rounded a corner and merged with Shawn and his partner. They, too, had some followers—in this case four kids, two of them older—munching chocolate and giggling in a line behind them. Jared seemed to relax.

"It's a good sign that the kids are allowed to follow us," he said. "It means their moms don't think there are any bad guys around."

"They know long before we do," Shawn's partner grunted. "If the streets are empty, you're probably already screwed."

In some ways the patrol seemed to take forever, and in others, it went by in a blink. The second half of the patrol was much more of the latter, and after meeting up at the rally point, it seemed like only minutes later they were back in the Humvee and scanning either side of the road during their short convoy back to the FOB.

They didn't talk much on the ride back—Jared's mood seemed strangely somber considering how easy and quiet the mission had been—and Jake was glad to be lost in his own thoughts.

He thought of Rachel and hoped he could call her after they secured from the patrol and debriefed the op. He and Cal had figured out the system for signing up for phone time in the "Internet café," and at a minimum he would get a half hour on the computer to read emails from her and shoot out a few of his own.

Maybe this wouldn't be so bad. If he could get through another hundred or so of these patrols, he would be on his way back home. He chuckled at the thought that he was, technically, now a combat veteran—having survived his first mission in Afghanistan.

For a moment he remembered the story Jared had told him about the friend he lost to an IED three weeks after he'd hung up a boot in a firefight. Jake quickly pulled his mind back to Rachel.

He would get through this tour. No problem.

CHAPTER 4

Ten days flew by, and Jake figured that if the next thirty-five weeks went by at the same clip, he would be home before he even had a chance to get full-blown homesick. His squad, led by either Cal or Shawn, had already fallen into a routine of sorts. They had patrolled the village again the next day, this time their squad joining second squad, with his buddy Mike Patterson in the lead—another fire department hopeful from home. They had also been on two missions deeper in "Indian territory"—as First Sergeant Morrow called the area where the Taliban and the Al Qaeda terrorists they protected moved more freely. Both had required airlift into the area of operation aboard the big CH-47 helicopters. It took no time for Jake and his friends to realize how much they preferred those flights to the high-stress motor convoys fraught with fears of IEDs and ambushes. They all knew stories of helicopter crashes and shootdowns, but they were few and far between compared to the obvious danger on the ground—especially if you weren't one of the lucky ones assigned to the MRAPs, which supposedly could withstand even stacked charges in an IED without anyone inside getting hurt. Even Pete, who had a real fear of flying, preferred the air assault missions, and high-fived his friends when the operation order listed air over ground.

They had been on only one night mission so far. They learned that the special operations forces conducted most of the big hits at night, and when they were called in on such operations they were usually securing a rally point or controlling the perimeter for the SEALs or Army Operators who conducted the capture-or-kill missions on HVTs. "We own the night," one bearded SEAL in unmarked clothes had told him with a wink. That was fine with Jake, as he'd found his single night mission terrifying. The Special Forces guys could keep the night if that's what they liked.

Altogether they had been on six missions since the first patrol through the village, and no one in his platoon had been required to fire a shot. On one of the air assault missions, they had heard the sounds of a short firefight on the other side of the compound they were securing. Two bad guys had been wounded—one of whom they heard had been captured, but none of them ever saw the prisoner—and no Americans had been hurt.

Jake and his squad stuck together in camp. They ate breakfast together every day at six thirty, before morning quarters—where everyone was accounted for and the assignment of work details in the camp occurred. They hung out together in their little hooch, playing cards or video games with the other eight guys from their platoon, who were squeezed into the three other tiny bunk rooms clustered around the small common area of their hut. They ate snacks of fruit cocktail and protein bars and wondered when their first mail packages would come. Every evening they cleaned their weapons after dinner, and at night they joked around in their bunks like teenagers on a camping trip.

Jake had talked to Rachel on the phone four times already, and hearing her voice and her stories from home and church cheered him up, though he found he needed far less cheering up than he had expected. He'd emailed her every day but one—the morning after their night mission he had slept through both breakfast and the Internet time he had signed up for. It had made him moody the whole day to miss reading her words.

Jake slid the receiver back into his rifle, the smell of Hoppe's strong and already familiar. Shawn leaned forward and spit dark brown tobacco juice from his dip of Skoal onto the ground between them, then handed him a soft rag.

"Thanks, dude," Jake said. He felt like a combat veteran already, despite having not yet fired a round except for the hour his squad had spent on the makeshift range set up along the back of the camp earlier that day. Jake wiped the excess Hoppe's and gun oil from his weapon and shivered in the rapidly falling temperature. Across the compound, he saw the brilliant orange-and-pink sky, lit up by the recently set sun.

"Show-of-force patrol," Pete's voice hollered out. Jake looked up and saw Pete and Cal shuffling toward them from the direction of the combat operations center. More of a glorified hut surrounded by satellite dishes, the COC was where the unit leadership planned missions, monitored what was going on in their area of responsibility, and received message traffic about upcoming operations.

"Good," Shawn said with obvious relief.

Jake wasn't so sure. He had decided that if he came home to Rachel having never fired his weapon in combat, he would be quite all right with that. But since that was almost certainly not going to happen, he thought it might better if tomorrow—on their last joint patrol before their sister unit loaded up and headed home—they conducted a real combat operation. Searching for weapons, rooting out bad guys, assaulting a house— something where he could learn one last time from the veteran soldiers they were relieving.

"Up the road?" he asked.

"Nah," Pete answered. "Some new place. Helo infil, so we got that goin' for us," he said, paraphrasing *Caddyshack*.

"Which is nice," Shawn said, finishing the quote.

"Brief is in the morning after quarters," Cal said. "Afternoon kickoff, they think."

Jake nodded. Cal looked relaxed but serious, and he wondered if everything was okay with his friend.

"Wanna go work out?" Shawn asked no one in particular. There was a tent with a bunch of free weights and a couple of machines in the back corner of the camp.

"Not me," Cal said. "I'm gonna skip tonight."

"Me too," Jake said.

"I'll go," Pete said. "You girls stay here and straighten up the house," he added with a grin.

Shawn laughed and slung his rifle casually over his shoulder, where it hung low on his right hip.

Cal slid next to Jake on the wooden bench and watched their friends as they walked off laughing about something. He leaned forward, his elbows on his knees, and sighed.

"You okay?" Jake asked.

Cal smiled. "Yeah, I'm good," he said. "I miss Kelly," he confessed with a weary smile. "It feels like we've been here for a month, but we still have a long way to go." He sighed again and Jake waited, unsure what to say. He missed Rachel more than anything. What was there to say?

Cal turned to him and slapped his shoulder.

"I'm good," he said with a laugh. "Just bein' a baby. You think we could hang out and do a little Bible study later?" he asked.

Jake shifted uncomfortably. He didn't know what reading some passages in the Bible would do to make either of them miss their wives less. Still, his best friend seemed to need him.

"I guess," Jake said. "Where?"

Cal shrugged. "How about out in the back by the berm? We can just sit on the ground and look at a couple of passages and, I don't know, just shoot the breeze or something."

Jake nodded. To his surprise, Cal grinned.

"I thought you might blow me off," he said. "I know you don't really enjoy this kind of thing, though I think you will if you try it. It'll help me to have you at least just sit with me."

"Of course," Jake said, even more surprised now. Cal was the strong one. It felt weird that he needed anything, much less Jake, who they both knew had precious little knowledge of the Bible. "Best friends," he added and offered up his fist for a bump. It felt a little high school, once they had done it. They both laughed.

Dinner came and went—another unremarkable trip to the chow hall just like all the others. They sat in the exact same seats every time now, routine and familiarity a needed comfort. No fresh vegetables or fruit again, despite rumors that they might be getting some any day, which made a running critique of canned fruit and vegetables the predictable theme for dinner conversation. They all grabbed energy bars on their way out and munched them on their ritual walk around the camp—a routine that took all of twenty minutes and required several laps around the tiny perimeter.

Jake and Cal left Pete and Shawn at the "hooch" and then shuffled to the back of the camp, where they sat in the dirt against the rock wall.

Cal pulled out a well-worn black, leather-covered Bible. In the dimming light he read aloud from the New Testament—another letter from the apostle Paul, Jake thought Cal said. The reading was familiar, and Jake thought perhaps Rachel had quoted from the passage before, but he had a hard time paying attention to the words, much less the message. Still, the quiet camaraderie of sitting with Cal alone in the dimming light lifted his spirits. As Cal read, his mind wandered back to the time they had tried to take their wives camping up in the Blue Ridge Parkway—a complete failure, but a wonderful memory. They had sat around a fire they'd built, arms around the girls, and had laughed and talked late into the night. When a rainstorm had rolled in, putting out the fire and soaking every-thing in and out of the tents, Rachel had tried to keep a positive attitude, but even she'd finally given up. It was Kelly who was up before the sun, rallying everyone to pack up the campsite. They'd found a motel not far from the park and stayed one more day for a hike. Jake missed Rachel more than he could have dreamed, but having Cal with him made the distance seem somehow less.

"Jake?"

He realized Cal had asked him something, and he pulled himself back from thoughts of home. "Sorry, Cal. What did you say?"

"I said, can we pray before we go back?" Cal said. The heaviness in Cal's voice had returned and made Jake uneasy.

"Of course," he said and bowed his head. They both knew that Cal would speak for them.

As Cal spoke to God, asking for strength and courage and for peace for their wives, Jake relaxed into the familiar comfort of Cal's voice.

And thought of Rachel.

CHAPTER 5

The pair of huge twin-rotor CH-46 helicopters made one quick turn over the small town and then flared for landing a few seconds and fifty or so yards apart. First squad, with Shawn in charge, piled out the back of the heavy-lift bird, spreading out into a defensive perimeter beside their mentors. Jake realized, with some satisfaction, that he and his teammates had assumed their positions automatically and with little thought, a huge difference from only a week ago. He also realized that he felt not just more confident, but more peaceful and calm. He suspected that the hour at the berm with Cal had done more for him than he would usually like to admit. He was looking forward to doing it again this evening. He smiled as he scanned his sector and thought of telling Cal that the Bible study really made him feel better.

Cal will love hearing that.

With the helicopters now fading into the distance, they fell into two loose groups, which separated and headed toward opposite corners of the village for the same show-of-force patrol that had become routine.

Pete slapped him on the back. "I think I kinda like bein' a badass soldier." Pete's face was all grins.

"Focus, dude," Jake said with a chuckle and shook his head.

Pete rolled his eyes and moved away toward his mentor.

As Jake's squad divided into two smaller groups for entry into the town, he thought again of the thing Cal had said two weeks ago—something that the apostle Paul had told the Romans:

If God is for us, who can stand against us?

Jake realized that Cal's amazing faith was starting to affect him—to awaken something in him. He felt himself begin to slowly, and perhaps tentatively, believe Paul's words. Rachel had that kind of faith—a belief that God's hand was on everything she did. He loved the peace he saw in his wife, and for the first time he thought maybe he was beginning to understand it. He had never thought that anything was missing in his life, but now he wasn't so sure.

No atheists in foxholes.

The cynical words tugged at him, but he knew this was more than that. He was afraid out here, no question about that, but what he felt was more than just fear erased by a desperate need to believe. It was a real peace he felt when he bowed his head with Cal and heard the words his best friend read for them.

Jake and Jared moved to the left side of the street, across from Pete and his mentor, and as he thought of Paul's words to the Romans, Jake felt much more than calm—he felt almost invincible.

Distracted by those thoughts, he nearly walked into Jared, who stopped now and raised a closed fist. Jared scanned slowly across the buildings and rooftops. The combat veteran tapped his finger softly on the side of his trigger guard.

"What is it?" Jake whispered hoarsely.

Jared said nothing at first, just kept scanning. Jake looked over and saw that Pete's mentor had taken a knee and was scanning the rooftops through the sight of his rifle. Beside him, Pete shifted nervously. Maybe for the first time since Jake had met him, Pete had no goofy grin on his face. The four of them were alone on the street, the rest of the two squads divided between a security perimeter around the town and their own show-of-force walk-through.

"Too quiet," Jared breathed over his shoulder.

Jake scanned along the dirt road and saw no movement. Across the street, a young boy looked out through an open doorway. The boy smiled and waved, and Jake smiled back, raising his left hand. As he did, a woman appeared in the doorway, looked up and down the street, fear in her eyes, and then pulled the boy roughly back inside the low brown building. The green door slammed shut as they disappeared.

"Oh, shit," Jared said, and Jake followed the soldier as he moved closer to the buildings on their side of the street. He'd taken only two steps when suddenly the street exploded with gunfire from the roof across the street, and Jake realized in terror that the air all around him was alive with whizzing bullets and brightly lit tracers. "Contact right! Contact right!" Jared hollered. For a moment Jake was unsure what to do, but then his training kicked in and he spun right, aiming over his rifle at the roof across the street as he dropped down on one knee. His right thumb slid the safety on his rifle two clicks and he squeezed the trigger twice—each squeeze letting loose a three-round burst. Chunks of cheap stucco exploded away from the top of the wall just as he saw at least four hooded figures disappear behind the short rise where wall met roof. He scanned for a target, saw two eyes and the top of a black-cloth-covered head pop up for a moment, and squeezed again.

The sound of more gunfire startled him and he scanned, confused for a moment, along the roof again. Then he realized that the bursts had come from just above him on the roof on their side of the street.

"Pete, take cover," he screamed and rose to his feet, pressing himself against the wall.

The ground around the two soldiers across the street exploded in a cloud of dust as they scrambled to their own wall and began to return fire at the roof over Jake's head.

"Heavy contact, heavy contact," Jared was yelling into his radio. "First squad has heavy enemy contact. We are maybe a half block in from our entry point. Multiple shooters on both rooftops."

"RPG!"

Jake pulled his eyes from the rooftop in time to see Pete and the other soldier backpedal toward an alleyway behind them. A moment later they disappeared into a cloud of dust and smoke as the rocket-propelled grenade exploded against the wall where they had been. Jake thought for a moment about the young, smiling boy who had been in the doorway just beside the wall, and then his thoughts pulled back to Pete.

"Pete!" he hollered, peering desperately into the smoke and dust for signs of his friend. The high-pitched whistle of a bullet zipping past his ear made him duck his head as chunks of plaster bounced off his clear Wiley X glasses. He fired another two bursts at the rooftop, and three more hooded figures disappeared just as Jared fired from beside him. He heard a low scream and wondered which of them had shot a bad guy.

The dust and smoke from the RPG explosion wafted painfully slowly down the street, and he saw Pete and his mentor kneeling in the small alleyway, both apparently unhurt. They both aimed and fired at the roof above his head.

Jake pulled back with Jared toward the better cover afforded by the alley between houses behind them. A long rifle barrel appeared over the roof, and he fired again, watching as it pulled back down behind the ledge.

"Man down! Man down!"

The words choked Jake. Across the street, he saw one of the two soldiers collapse against the wall and then slide slowly down into the dirt. Through the smoke and dust, he had no way of telling if the wounded man was Pete or not. The uninjured soldier let go of his rifle and pulled the wounded man deeper into the alley. He then reached down with both hands, holding pressure on the injured man's neck or chest, Jake couldn't be sure which.

Additional bursts of gunfire brought his focus back, but no targets appeared above the rooftop ledge. Jake realized that the gunfire came from the large group of Americans who now approached from down the street at a near sprint. Closing in, the group split into smaller teams, two of which took positions at the corners farther down the road; the others disappeared, no doubt circling around to attack the enemy positions from behind.

"Air support is coming," Jared shouted at him, tapping the side of his helmet where the earpiece from his radio was. Jake felt a burst of hope—coupled with a sudden fear for the family inside the house. What kind of air support? They couldn't bomb the house with the little boy inside, right?

He continued to scan the roof, but no targets appeared. There was an occasional pop of gunfire farther away, and Jake wondered what that meant.

"Squirters out the back of the house. Third squad is engaged," Jared said to him. His mentor stood up. "We're gonna need to clear these two houses."

"Now?" Jake asked. He didn't think the two of them should go bursting into a house that could be filled with bad guys.

Jared shook his head. "When we get some help," he said. He pointed at the radio in the carrier on the outside of Jake's body armor. "Are you up?"

Jake looked down and saw that his radio was indeed on channel three, as they had been briefed. Then he noticed that the power was set to Off. He clicked it on sheepishly with a gloved hand and then winced at the loud and overlapping chatter. An Apache AH-64 attack helicopter roared overhead at a startlingly low altitude.

"All the rooftops are clear," grunted a static-filled voice, which he assumed belonged to the Apache pilot.

"Nightingale three-oh-five. Ten mikes."

That would be the CASEVAC bird on its way to pick up the wounded. Jake resisted the urge to dash across the street and check on Pete. He could still see the wounded soldier in a heap in the dirt, only now three other soldiers surrounded him. One held an IV bag up in the air. Farther away, he heard several more bursts of gunfire. His earpiece filled again with overlapping messages about guys disappearing into a tree line.

Jake closed his eyes for a moment and said a quiet prayer.

God, please let Pete be okay. And Cal—please let Cal be okay too.

He heard a long, deeper burst of gunfire and realized it was the Apache helicopter unleashing its fury into whatever tree line the voices on the radio had talked about.

Moments later four other soldiers joined them at the corner, and Jake felt his shoulders finally drop a few inches at the sight of Cal. His best friend raised his eyebrows and mouthed Pete's name. Jake shrugged and shook his head, and Cal nodded.

TC was barking out the plan to clear the nearby house just as another group huddled around the doorway of the house across the street. Jake thought again of the smiling boy and hoped he would be okay.

Despite the terror Jake felt, the house they searched contained only an older woman huddled in a back room. Jake heard on his radio that the other house was completely empty. He also heard that they had found four dead terrorists in the rows of trees just outside the village and that there appeared to be a lot of blood on the roof. Jake imagined that the woman and her boy must have escaped out the back when the shooting started. He wondered if the blood on the roof meant he had shot someone. As they left the house, a soft voice on the radio made his heart nearly stop in his chest.

"We have one angel."

Jake heard a moan escape his throat. An angel was a dead American, and his mind screamed for Pete.

And then he saw him.

Pete sat in the dirt, his knees up and his left hand loosely holding his helmet. His right hand was on his forehead and he seemed to be shaking uncontrollably. As Jake approached, he saw that Pete's whole right sleeve and the right side of his body armor were soaked in dark blood. His right hand was coated in blood as well, and he seemed oblivious to the fact that as his fingers rubbed circles on his temple and forehead they left bloody streaks on the side of his face. Jake put a hand on his friend's shoulder, and Pete looked up at him, his face full of agony, tears dragging muddy dust down his cheeks and dripping from his chin.

"I couldn't do nothing," he said, his eyes pleading with Jake. Then he began to sob again.

Jake knelt beside him and wrapped his arms around Pete's shoulders, pulling his head against his chest. He found no words to share, just held his friend in the street while he cried.

CHAPTER 6

Jake stared, blank faced, at the maze of barricades and leaned back against the dirt berm. Cal was beside him, but neither had spoken in a while. Jake struggled to come to terms with what he had seen and to shake the images from his mind's eye. No matter how he tried, the picture of the soldier with his throat shot out and of Pete crying in the dirt, his gear covered in someone else's blood, came back to him over and over. He squeezed his eyes shut hard, until white spots appeared in the grey darkness, and then opened them. He felt a hand on his leg and looked over at Cal.

His best friend's eyes were closed as well, but gently, his face slack except for his lips, which moved in cadence to whatever prayer he mouthed silently to God. In that moment Jake filled with envy. Cal didn't look at peace, but he did have someplace to turn in this situation, and that alone was worthy of Jake's jealousy. He watched his friend pray, tears on Cal's dirty cheeks, and wondered if he prayed for the dead soldier, for the family he'd left behind, for Pete and his struggles, or for escape from his own fears. Jake imagined Cal talked to his God about all of those things. He remembered how his best friend had once described his relationship with God as part father-son and part best friends, but one hundred percent someone he could talk to, whatever his thoughts—joy or despair—and God would always answer. Jake didn't know how it was that God could answer, but he decided suddenly that he wanted very much to find out. Was it a voice? A voice in his head? Just a feeling? A sign? He would take any of those things right now.

More tears spilled onto his cheeks, and he realized he was sobbing now. He needed Rachel—to collapse his head into her lap and feel her love for him in his grief. He thought of when her dad had died. She had seemed at peace, or at least in control, until he had held her on her parents' couch. Then she had laid in his lap and cried. He wanted that—not words that would fix anything or platitudes of false comfort. He just wanted to feel unconditional love, like he'd tried to give to Rachel that night.

Her words from that night came to him suddenly. He wasn't one to remember verses—he barely could remember any from his years in Sunday school—but this one came to him so clearly. It was as if…

And so, we know and rely on the love God has for us. God is love. Whoever lives in love lives in God, and God in them.

Had Rachel said that to him? How did he hear it now so clearly in his head?

He looked over and saw Cal's eyes in the dying light as the day shifted to night.

"What does it mean, Cal?" he asked after sharing the verse. "That God can live in us? How does that work?"

Cal smiled.

"You may be thinking of First John four," he said, looking out past him. "It talks about how God is love, and that if you live in that love, you are in God and God is in you." He looked at Jake with clear eyes. "Is that the verse you mean?"

"Yes," Jake said, his voice barely a whisper.

"When you surrender to God—when you ask Jesus to forgive you and to live in you and to guide you in his will for your life—then you are filled with his perfect love for you. The Holy Spirit lives in your heart and, Jake, it's so real. You can feel it—feel his unconditional love for you. It doesn't erase your trials, or take away all your pain. But the comfort of dwelling in his love and having him inside you—it's indescribable. I couldn't do another day here—or anywhere, maybe—without it."

Jake nodded, not even caring to wipe the tears that streamed down his cheeks, dripping off his chin into the dirt.

"How do I do it, Cal? How?"

Cal smiled again.

"Just ask. Ask God and he'll do the rest. John sixteen, twenty-four, says, 'Ask and you will receive, and your joy will be complete.' Jesus says if we knock, the door will be opened. He's waiting for you, Jake. He's waiting today, just as he's always been."

And then Cal's eyes closed, and he again began to mouth a silent prayer.

Jake placed his hand on top of Cal's and bent his head forward, his eyes closed. He sat quietly for a long time, unsure how to start. Then he took a long, shuddering breath.

God...? I don't really know how to start. I really do believe in you, and I think I always have. I just don't know how to be close to you. I don't know how to talk to you or to tell you what I need. I don't know how to thank you for Rachel and Cal and my parents and my friends. I don't know how to ask you to help me with my fears. I guess this is a good start. I hope you hear me, God.

"He hears you, Jake," Cal answered. Jake opened his eyes and felt a warm peace envelop him. His breathing slowed and something inside him changed. He let Cal hug him, something that he normally wouldn't be able to do, and somehow felt God's arms around him also. He cried in both their embraces and knew that something inside him had changed.

He hoped it had changed forever.

"Tell me, Cal," he said. "Tell me how it works. Tell me how to pray."

Cal smiled. "It's like talking to your dad, your best friend, and your favorite teacher all at once. There is no formula. Just talk to him. He already knows you, after all."

Jake leaned back and listened as Cal talked about his own journey. Jake closed his eyes and absorbed the words, but he thought maybe God was talking to him through Cal. He seemed real, for the first time ever.

At that moment, that was more than enough.

CHAPTER 7

A week had passed, and in that time Jake felt he had ascended into infancy. The peace he found in their nightly Bible study and their time spent in prayer was amazing, and had brought Jake to a place he never thought he would be. He had seen in Rachel, and in Cal and Kelly, an enthusiasm that, frankly, had always seemed weird to him. Jake didn't dislike church—not at all—but he'd never understood the passion for it that his wife and friends seemed to have. For them, it seemed like going to a ball game or a concert or a party. They looked forward to it and reveled in it for hours afterward. For Jake, it had always seemed satisfying, but more like finishing a chore or checking a box that needed checking.

But he got it now. He looked forward with real excitement to the things he could learn reading the Bible out loud with Cal and the feeling of peace that he knew would wash over him when he prayed. He really did feel God answering him, in the form of the peace he was asking for, every time he bowed his head.

But he felt like such a damn novice. The more he learned from Cal and their nightly readings, the more he realized how little he knew. He had gone to church almost every Sunday of his life, and believed that he understood the message of the Bible. He had been wrong. Every night brought him a new story he had never heard and verses that, in the context bestowed by his best friend, meant more than the empty words that before had seemed vaguely familiar but not particularly meaningful.

He learned easily to thank God for the things he had. He'd said grace on Sundays at home, of course, and as a kid he thanked God for his family in his nighttime prayers. Now Jake found himself thanking God for the real things in his life—things like Rachel, and his health, and their church—and he quickly got in the habit of thanking God for Cal. He felt certain that God had placed Cal in his life at this time and in this place for a reason. Cal had an amazing way of explaining things. He took verses that seemed confusing and made them so simple and meaningful, Jake found it hard to believe he hadn't seen the simple messages for himself. Part of it was the context—Cal understood the stories and the history and the characters. He made the apostles and Jesus and the people they met along the way real and believable. And part of it was just his knack of boiling a passage down to its message. He helped Jake see the Bible in a way he never had believed possible. For the first time, the Book spoke to him.

"That's the idea, Jake," Cal had said with a gentle laugh. "It's called 'the Word' because it's the Word of God. The Bible is God's way of telling us things we need to know about His love for us, His grace, His plans for our lives. It's also how He teaches us about our responsibilities as Christians. It's all in there. God is speaking to you through His Word—right now, right here, where and when you need Him."

Jake shook his head. "How did you learn all of this, Cal?"

Cal laughed again.

"You gotta read the Word to know the Word," he said with a grin. "And you have to share it with your brothers and sisters in Christ. I've read the Book, but I've also studied it with other Christians. Sometimes just friends at Starbucks, sometimes in formal Bible study at church. At Foundations back home, I go to the Courageous group on Tuesday nights. It's a men's group where we study the Bible and use the Word to help us become all God wants us to be as husbands and fathers. Pastor Craig leads the group and it totally rocks. You would love it. We'll go together when we get home."

Jake had heard of Courageous but had no idea his best friend went every Tuesday, or even what they did there. He had so much to learn. Jake smiled to himself. Rachel would just about jump for joy if he told her he wanted to go to a Bible study at Foundations. He looked suddenly at his watch.

Rachel!

"Dude, our phone time is in like ten minutes."

Cal looked at his own watch and shook his head. "Man, that time went by quickly." He smiled at Jake. "You wanna close us in prayer?"

Jake nodded but still felt uncomfortable praying out loud, even if it was only him and Cal. He bowed his head.

"Thanks, Lord, for letting us share time together in your Word. Help us to learn from what you show us in the Bible. Be with our families and give them peace. Give us your protection and the strength to do your will at all times. In Jesus' name we pray. Amen."

Jake blushed a little that his prayer was almost identical to what Cal usually said, but his best friend didn't criticize him, if he noticed at all. They gathered their things and shoved the notebooks and Cal's worn Bible into Jake's green backpack.

On the short walk to the Internet café in the corner of the camp, Jake and Cal laughed and chatted about regular things—about the guys, about sports. Jake wasn't sure why he'd thought that if he became "super religious" he wouldn't be a regular guy and talk about regular things. He'd had this strange image of people praying every minute and talking about nothing but God. Instead he found he talked with Cal about the same things as always—he just felt way the hell better.

A few minutes later, Jake sat in one of ten plywood cubicles that separated the phones and gave the illusion of privacy, and waited while some computer somewhere processed his calling card numbers and connected him to the phone in his house on the other side of the planet. When it finally rang, Jake was amazed, again, that the ring sounded no different than if he were calling from down the block. Now and again there would be an annoying hum in the background, soft and subtle but very annoying, but tonight he might as well be calling from his mom's house, the call was so clear.

"Hello?" Rachel's voice was breathless and excited. "Jake, is that you?"

Jake closed his eyes and let the confusing mix of joy at the sound of her voice and the pain of separation wash over him. His eyes filled with tears, like they always did, but his cheeks stayed dry.

"Hi, baby," he said. "Guess where I've been?"

"Where?" his wife asked. Her voice was happy.

"Doing a Bible study with Cal," he said. He realized he had unconsciously lowered his voice, and his face flushed with embarrassment.

Sorry, God. I'm new at all of this.

"That's awesome, sweetheart," Rachel said. "How did that go?"

It had been a week since Jake had told her about that night on the berm, the night after the soldier had died. She had cried, first for the soldier, but later he thought maybe tears of happiness at what Jake guessed she must be hearing in her husband's voice. Jake had believed her when she said she believed that God had given them the challenge of this deployment for a reason and that this must be it.

Mike Charlie, God. Mission complete. Feel free to get me home to my wife anytime.

Jake told her about what he had learned reading Romans eight. Well, what he'd learned once he talked about it with Cal and actually understood what the apostle Paul was talking about. Rachel listened and laughed, and now and again said, "Exactly what I think."

Jake looked frequently up at the clock on the wall, where the second hand seemed to speed supernaturally fast around the white face, and before he knew it the call was half over.

"Tell me about your day," he said, wrapping up all the talk about him. "Tell me everything," he added with a smile and closed his eyes. "Start with what you had for breakfast."

"Well, I just finished breakfast a few minutes ago," she said with a laugh. "You just can't quite get this time difference thing straight, can you?"

Jake laughed with her.

"Okay, okay. So, tell me about yesterday, then. You only have a few minutes, but don't leave anything out."

As she began, starting with her breakfast like he asked, Jake leaned his head forward onto the plywood rail of the cubicle and closed his eyes. He let the sound of her voice and the pictures her descriptions put in his mind wash over him. While she talked, he said a short prayer that God would help make the remaining months fly by for her.

After the call ended (with Rachel hollering, "I love you, I love you, I love you," over and over until the connection was broken), Jake sat a moment until the tears dried on his cheeks. Then he collected himself and slipped outside the hut to where Cal waited, wiping his own cheeks but smiling.

"Man, it is really hard, isn't it?" Cal asked.

Jake couldn't think of anything to say, so he said nothing.

CHAPTER 8

Back at their cramped hut, they found things the same as every evening—
a familiarity that Jake had learned was comforting on deployment. Shawn
sat in front of the television that had "conveyed" from the last unit. They
had no satellite TV hookup (though Aaron from first platoon swore he
could figure out a way get it), but the Xbox game system their sister unit
had left worked just fine. Beside Shawn was Brandon—another hutmate
from their squad. Shawn and Brandon had been hanging out a lot—ever
since Pete had become a bit of a loner. That was one change that Jake
hated. He missed the sound of Pete laughing and acting like a goofball.

"Shit! Are you friggin' kidding me?" Brandon shouted, more at the
TV than at Shawn.

Shawn laughed. "Gotta watch for those little bastards. They're small,
but they can still kill your ass." He jerked a thumb at Jake and Cal. "And
watch your mouth—the God squad is here." He winked at Jake, who
smiled and shook his head.

"You don't have to worry about us," Cal said with a chuckle. "If you're
sure God is cool with you, then we definitely are. We love you just the way
you are," he said and gave Shawn a slap on the head. Shawn took a swing
at Cal's leg but missed.

"Dipshit," Shawn said with a laugh.

Jake and Cal leaned their rifles against the wall beside the door that
led into their cramped bunk room. Shawn's rifle was already there—they
had gotten in the habit of each group of four placing their weapons in the
same place so they could always find them quickly should the shit hit the
fan. Jake saw that Pete's weapon was missing.

"Where's Pete?" he asked.

Shawn shrugged. "Not here."

Jake frowned and looked at Cal, who shook his head and raised his eyebrows.

"Oh, you asshole," another laughing voice hollered from one of the bunk rooms. Jake imagined the other guys were lying in their bunks and either watching movies on their laptops or playing games on their hand-held game systems—PS Vita systems for most of them, which was great because they could share games.

Jake looked at Cal again. *I'll go*, his look said, and Cal nodded.

"I'll be right back," Jake announced to no one and slung his rifle over his shoulder again as he headed out the door.

The darkness had come quickly, and he stood a moment outside the hut and wondered where to go. There was a chance that Pete was on the Internet or phone, but if that was the case, then he had no reason to track him down. Maybe he should wait a bit and see if he showed up. Something inside told him that was not the case, however. Besides, he and Cal had just left the café.

A soft noise, like a sigh, drew Jake's attention upward. There was a pretty strict policy against being on the roofs of the huts at any time (one of a myriad of rules they had been briefed on their first day at the FOB), despite the fact that each hut had a narrow outdoor stairway that led to the roof. The rooftops were a maze of wires and cables that connected the small buildings to generators and computer drops, though as far as Jake knew, none of the computer drops worked. He saw a small orange glow, which brightened and then faded—a cigarette.

"Pete?" Jake called in a loud whisper. The glowing ash disappeared, but no one answered.

Jake looked around to be sure no one was watching him and then pushed his rifle behind him so it wouldn't scrape the wall of the hut as he climbed the stairway to the roof.

There was no moon, but the billions of stars in the clear night sky, aided by Jake's now-adapted night vision, allowed him to see the shadows of the empty barrel-like containers on the far side of the roof. To his left, he saw a shadowy shape leaning against the wall. The orange glow flared again, marking the shadow as, if not Pete, then at least as someone.

"Pete? What are you doing, dude?" he whispered again and then moved toward the figure against the wall. He tripped over a bundle of cables and stumbled. "Shit," he muttered.

"Leave me alone, Jake," Pete said from the darkness.

Jake ignored his friend and cautiously found his way over, then slid down the short wall at the roof's edge, landing in a heap beside Pete, his rifle now in his lap. He sighed heavily as Pete took another long, slow drag on his smoke.

"I didn't know you smoked, dude," Jake said, not sure what else to say.

"I do now."

Jake nodded in the darkness. It would have been better if Cal had gone looking for Pete. Jake realized he had no idea what to say. He thought of saying a little prayer, like Cal said he often did, but he didn't know what he would pray for, so he pushed the thought away.

"Dude, what's going on? What the hell are you doing up here?"

"Looking at the stars," Pete mumbled.

Jake looked up. The sky above him was full of more stars than he had ever seen in his life. The total darkness, away from the intrusive light of civilization, unmasked a trillion more stars than were visible at home. He was struck for a moment by the beauty of it.

"Pretty," he whispered, then blushed. What a dumbass thing to say.

"Yeah," Pete said. "I never seen stars like this anywhere." He took another drag on his cigarette and then stripped the ash off the tip and flicked the butt over his head and off the roof.

Jake waited a moment, thinking maybe Pete would say something else. The silence stretched out and he shifted uncomfortably. He turned to his squadmate and tried to make out his features in the dark, but it was impossible.

"Are you doing okay, Pete?" he asked softly. Pete said nothing, though Jake thought he sensed motion that might have been Pete shaking his head—it was very difficult to tell in the dark. "Look, man," Jake started. "The other day—well, the other day was crazy. I know it must have been totally ass for you, dude. I can't even imagine." Jake thought a moment about Pete holding pressure on the soldier's neck and about how blood had sprayed all over him, covering his kit, his clothes—even his weapon.

He really couldn't imagine. "Dude, you did everything right. You took care of business. I think I would have totally freaked out. You were a real pro, Pete."

Pete shifted again beside him, and Jake thought he hung his head now. There was a quiver in his voice when he spoke.

"I never seen a dead person before, Jake. He died right under my hands while I was holding pressure. I could feel the life and blood just rushing out of him between my fingers, and it was—like—shit. There wasn't nothing I could do. His eyes—his eyes looked so scared, like he knew he was dead in a minute. I kept telling him everything would be okay, but, well—it wasn't." Pete sobbed a little and Jake put a hand on his friend's shoulder.

"I know it sucks, man," Jake said. "But we really need you, Pete. We need you to stay strong. We got a long way to go."

"It ain't that. I can do this shit forever. It's just…" Jake could feel Pete's eyes straining to see him in the dark. "It's just, what if it was one of you guys? I know that's totally jacked up to even say. I feel like such an asshole that I'm like—I don't know—happy or something that it was that guy and not Shawn, or Cal, or you, or anyone from our squad or even our platoon. That's so jacked up, right? I mean, that dude—his name was Ryan J. Kindrich, and he was from North Carolina—he was a year younger than me. That dude, like, he had friends. He had parents who loved him and maybe a girlfriend or something. He wasn't married—I checked. But I mean, why is it okay that he's dead? I mean, it's not okay, right?" Pete's voice rose and Jake worried for a moment that someone would find them up here and they would both get in trouble. "Shit, man, like who the hell am I to decide that him getting blown away is okay?"

Jake sure as hell didn't have an answer for that. "Look, Pete. It's not okay that he's dead. Obviously, you're totally not okay with it. It's normal to feel grateful that you and your friends are okay, I think."

"He was supposed to go home the very next day, Jake. The very next day. That is so messed up, man—so messed up."

Jake put his arm around Pete, and he could feel that his friend was shaking. After a moment he felt Pete wipe the tears from his face.

"I got a question for you, Jake." The bitterness in Pete's voice was unmistakable. He was a long way from the happy-go-lucky guy they all knew and loved.

"Sure, Pete. Anything."

"You and Cal," Pete began. "You got your own little thing going on. You go out and pray and read the Bible and shit, right?"

"Right," Jake said. Now he really wished he had let Cal come to find Pete.

"Well, so, like what the hell, man? I mean, you really believe that shit?" Pete almost spit the words out. "You believe that there's a God out there? And if so, what in the hell is He doing? I mean, if there is a God, like you say, He sure don't give a damn about us—at least not about Ryan J. Kindrich from North Carolina, right? Why would He let something like that happen to Kindrich—a soldier on his last day in country, just trying to get home to his friends and family? You guys pray every day and this is the friggin' thanks we get." Pete rattled out a long and wet sigh. "I just don't get you guys, is all."

Jake thought for a long time. Pete didn't pull away from him, despite the anger he had voiced. He knew Pete wasn't really mad at him, but his questions nagged at Jake. They seemed like very good questions, actually, and Jake had no answers for them.

He realized he needed to figure those things out—for himself as well as Pete. He would for sure talk to Cal about it, probably tomorrow evening at the berm.

"I don't know, Pete," he said. "I really don't know."

In the meantime he just sat beside Pete, hoping that the presence of a friend would be enough for now.

CHAPTER 9

Rachel hung up the phone and wiped the tears from her cheeks with the back of her hand. The last couple of calls from Jake had been different, and at first she had been worried sick. She could tell her husband had changed, and so she knew that something must have happened. Typical Jake—he hadn't shared anything with her about what it was. So, she had been forced to rely on her wild imagination and had invented all kinds of terrible scenarios—like he had been injured and he didn't want her to know. That had been the first-place contender in her mind for a couple of days, because he sounded different but not really sad—in fact, not sad at all. If anything, he sounded much calmer and happier—*peaceful*, maybe, was the word. In her military wife's imagination, that all worked out to him being hurt, but happy because maybe that meant he was coming home. She'd decided he hadn't told her only because he wasn't sure if he *would* be sent home or when and didn't want her to worry. It all made perfect sense.

When Jake had finally confided in her what had happened with Cal— that Jake had given his life to Christ—Rachel was embarrassed that the truth should have been her first thought. Jake had been almost giddy with excitement when he described how something had changed inside him when he had said the prayer, asking God to show him how to pray and be thankful. Now, each and every call, Jake spent much of the time talk- ing about what he was learning as he and Cal read the Bible and prayed together. All of that was great, but it was also what made Rachel's happy tears mix with tears of longing. This was what she had always wanted for him—but also for them. She wanted Jake to be more than the perfect partner and spouse he already was—she wanted him to be her partner on her walk in faith, to share the joy and comfort of her relationship with God, which had become the cornerstone of her life.

This is the reason we're apart. This was God's plan for Jake. Perhaps he needed this deployment, with its stress and pain, to make him start his journey.

Rachel knew that, sometimes, it was even harder to find God when life seemed pretty perfect. That's how it had been for her. Like Jake, she had grown up in the church but had never found (or looked for) a real relationship with God. "Religious, but far from God," Pastor Craig had said in the first sermon they had heard at Foundations. In that moment Rachel had known that he was talking to her—or that God was talking through him to her. It was the perfect description of her faith before Foundations Family Church. Rachel had a great life—was very happy and content—and hadn't known before that moment that anything was missing.

You don't know until you know.

She had said that so many times to Kelly, her best friend and an important part of her own journey. It was Kelly who'd taught her that Christianity was never meant to be a religion, but a relationship with God through Christ. Kelly had led her through the early days of her walk, patiently teaching her how to pray and how to find God in His Word.

Rachel looked at the clock—nine fifteen. Her first thought was that Kelly would be here any minute with some Thai food for their indulgent "romantic comedy movie night." Rachel had already scrolled through the new releases on Netflix and "on demand" and found a few good choices—all movies that neither of them would be likely to see if their husbands were home. Not much of a silver lining, but they made the best of it by having a girls' night at least once a week since the boys had left.

Rachel fumbled through the kitchen drawer for a corkscrew (they almost never drank wine when Jake was home, so it was all the way in the back), then struggled to pull the cork from the wine bottle that the manager at the Farm Fresh where she shopped had recommended. She was clueless about wine but really enjoyed it, and knew that Kelly loved it. Another guilty pleasure to go with their movie.

The doorbell rang and Rachel wiped the last of her tears from her cheeks. Cal usually called Kelly at the same time she heard from Jake, so

Rachel figured her best friend would be feeling most of the same emotions that she was. She didn't exactly understand how the phone thing worked for the boys, but they had to sign up or something, and she thought they just always signed up for the same time. Lately it was right after their Bible study—so an early-morning call for her, which she relished—but Jake had emailed to say that he would be up early today and so this call would be in the evening, her time. She refused to let her crazy imagination speculate on what the difference meant.

"Hey, sweetie," Kelly said and wrapped a big hug around her, the plastic bags of Thai food swinging from her wrists. "Did you hear from Jake?"

"Just got off the phone with him," Rachel said and kissed Kelly on the cheek. "Cal?"

Kelly nodded as she came in.

"That's why I'm a few minutes late. I finished up with him in the driveway, actually. I figured you were on the phone with Jake, so whatever. Hope the food's not cold."

They both knew it didn't matter. They had just talked to their husbands, so all was good. Rachel helped her sort the food and then poured them both a glass of wine.

"I hope it's good," she said. "You know me and wine."

Kelly squeezed her arm. "I'm sure it's great," she said.

They sat together and, after a brief blessing from Kelly, began to eat.

"He just seems so much more peaceful," Rachel said, filling Kelly in on Jake's call. "I think, once it's all over and they're home and safe, this will have turned out to be a great thing for Jake—and for our marriage."

"We're all praying for the same things, Rach," Kelly said. "And those prayers are answered, ya know?"

Rachel nodded. "'Where two or more are gathered …'"

They talked for a while about their husbands—recalling stories of the four of them over the last few years. When Rachel looked up, the Styrofoam containers held cold remnants of dinner, their second glasses of wine were half gone, and the clock on the wall showed it was almost ten thirty already—too late for the movie.

"I didn't want to see a movie anyway," Kelly said. "We got enough drama going on, right?"

Rachel laughed. To her, it seemed that Kelly was never really stressed about anything—not even this—but she knew that couldn't be true.

"I don't know how you do it, Kelly," she said and sipped her wine, pulling her legs up under her on the couch. "You always seem so happy. You just deal with things so well."

Kelly looked down, apparently embarrassed. She shrugged, but her face seemed pensive now.

"I wish that were true," she said. "I feel the best when I'm able to give it all over to God, but honestly, it seems like I try and pull it back—to fool myself into thinking I have control—almost right away."

Kelly smoothed a loose lock of hair from where it had fallen across her face. Rachel thought how pretty she looked, but her eyes were not nearly as sparkling with joy as they usually were. Kelly sighed. "I guess we all just do our best."

"Your best seems pretty damn good, honey," Rachel said and grabbed her friend's hand. She was not used to being in this role with Kelly, whose strength and faith were such an inspiration to her—had, in fact, shown her the way to her own faith.

"I do believe that God is with us—with all four of us," Kelly said. Then she looked down at her hand in Rachel's. She looked up. "I do, I just…" A tear spilled onto her cheek, making Rachel's eyes fill as well. "I just love him so much, you know?" Kelly wiped the tear away with some irritation. "Sorry," she said, and then to Rachel's surprise, she let out a laugh and wiped her nose on her sleeve. "Look at me, right? Jake is there with Cal, and here I am whining to you. The nerve."

Rachel hugged her. "Who would better understand? We gotta help each other through this," she said.

In no time they were themselves again—chatting about the kids in the day care where Rachel worked and about Kelly's new job at the church as the small-groups coordinator. Rachel loved hearing the behind-the-scenes drama at the church. They promised to meet again the next night to watch a movie, and by the time they were done laughing, crying, and in the end, praying about their husbands and their friendship, they could have watched the movie and then some.

Alone in bed, the evening turned over in Rachel's head. Strange as it might seem, Kelly's vulnerability was inspiring to her. Sometimes, Kelly's faith—and Cal's, for that matter—seemed so immense as to be unattainable. Seeing Kelly as she had tonight made Rachel feel that her own faith might be enough to see her through, after all. She blushed in the dark at the selfishness of the thought.

Rachel felt that Jake's journey, and hers beside him, had just begun. She knew there would be some bumps yet, but she also knew that together, with God, they could overcome anything. She said a quiet prayer thanking God again for her best friend and for her husband.

"Please keep him safe, Lord," she prayed, and then drifted off to sleep, confident that her prayers would be answered.

CHAPTER 10

Despite the tragic death of Ryan J. Kindrich from somewhere in North Carolina, Jake still felt that, overall, their missions had not gone badly. As the colder weather settled in, there had been a hopeful optimism that things would stay fairly quiet as the "fighting season" wound down with the approach of winter. They all knew that was more of a given in the rugged high mountains to the north and east of them than here in Helmand, but second platoon seemed to be settling into a routine that would only get easier—whether because of less fighting or because they became better at their jobs.

They all agreed that they liked the morning missions best—the show-of-force patrols—because they had all been pretty quiet. Today's mission brought a few elements that made Jake, and he thought maybe the rest of his squad, a little uneasy. First, it was mid-afternoon, and that already meant there was a higher risk of enemy contact. Second, they were heading to a village a helicopter flight away and, worse, one they had not been to before. Third, there had been a lot of chatter around the operations center all morning, and to the soldiers, that could only mean something big—and therefore, bad. The final stressor came when they found that they would be supporting a Special Operations raid. That sure as hell was not a good sign.

"Special Operations teams are conducting a raid at a compound a few clicks away," the company Master Sergeant told them during the brief. "They only go on these raids when they know that some high-value targets are in the area. They do not expect heavy contact in the village that is our objective, but it is very much Indian country, so who the hell knows? Our mission is a high-visibility show of force, and to deny the bad guys this village as a fallback position should the raid go south. We'll need to have our shit together, and I want heads on a swivel. This is not a hearts-and-minds mission—expect to make contact, and then if we don't, well, hallelujah."

Jake had looked at Cal, who grinned back, but his face was serious. He noticed that Pete looked at his boots and shook his head.

Jake pushed thoughts about tonight's Bible study with Cal from his head. He had lots of questions and things he needed to talk about after his time with Pete on the roof last night. Right now, however, he needed to "get his soldier on," as Shawn sometimes said. He focused as best he could on the sketch map of the village, and noticed how very damn close the Special Forces target compound seemed to be. They would infil ahead of the raid, a move meant to ensure that the bad guys didn't think the massive movement was directed at them. It might make them relax a bit while the SEALs or SF guys snuck in on them later from a different direction.

"Or maybe we're just the bait," Dan Manning from third squad had mumbled to him.

Jake chuckled nervously but didn't think that was the case. He doubted that the compound, with a dozen or so guys at most, would be tempted into attacking a well-armed force the size of two full platoons and with obvious air support.

Still, the tension was high as he and the rest of first squad piled into one of the CH-47 helicopters for the hour-long flight to the village. The attack in which Kindrich had been killed had happened so suddenly and unexpectedly, though he supposed they were always expected to be prepared. It had been like a shooting at a mall, almost. This felt like war, for the first time, maybe.

Jake closed his eyes and bowed his head as the huge twin-rotor helicopter skimmed along the rocky terrain, jarring them around now and again with a sudden change of direction when the pilots saw something that made them nervous.

Lord, please help me do my job. Help me to not screw up. And please, keep me and my friends safe.

He added, *Your will be done,* at the end, as he often heard Cal do, but he wasn't sure how much he felt that sentiment. Jake opened his eyes and saw Cal looking at him with a smile. He smiled back and gave Cal a thumbs-up, then watched as his best friend closed his own eyes in prayer.

"Send some of that my way, bro," Shawn called out over the scream of the turbines and rotors.

Cal opened his eyes and smiled at Shawn. "I always do, brother," he said, then returned to his prayer.

Jake watched Shawn nod slightly, then stole a look over at Pete, who sat across from them on the outboard row of canvas bench seats and stared straight ahead at some spot above Shawn's head. His eyes never blinked, his mouth half open and slack. Then his eyes closed and he shuddered, shook his head, and then stared off in another direction. Jake thought how much he missed "old" Pete now that he seemed so different. He didn't think he had ever appreciated how Pete's goofy smile and stupid-ass jokes put them all at ease. He could use some of that upbeat Pete on this mission.

He looked at Cal again, saw his lips move in another prayer, and then watched him slap Shawn on the knee. Shawn nodded and smiled.

No atheists in foxholes.

He chuckled at his own words from another lifetime. He stole one last worried look at Pete and then closed his eyes as the helicopter snaked its way through Helmand and toward their target.

Jake realized just how far second platoon had come as they dismounted the helicopter and assumed a defensive perimeter like they had done it a thousand times. He scanned his sector and coughed out the dust as the helicopters lifted off again and the whine of their engines faded into the distance. A half a kilometer away, two other helicopters infilled at the other corner of the village. For sure, this was the biggest operation, at least in terms of number of friendly fighters, that they had been part of since their arrival.

They had been told to expect the raid to occur within an hour of their arrival in the village, and as Jake followed Pete and Cal—who was squad leader on this mission—he thought how glad he was that Cal had paired up with their somber friend. Jake looked to the west, where the sun still seemed quite high above the horizon. Strange. He'd thought that

Special Operators mostly conducted these raids at night. Jake wondered why they were doing this one in daylight. Maybe the high-value target was only at the compound during the day. Jake shrugged. These were questions above his pay grade.

It took nearly fifteen minutes to reach the edge of the village, a walk that Jake and Shawn, his partner today, made in silence. He felt Shawn's tension, and that made Jake feel tenser as well. As they spread out to opposite sides of the street, twenty or so yards behind Cal and Pete, Jake kept his eyes open but muttered another quiet prayer.

Be with us, Lord. And help me calm the hell down.

Jake hoped God didn't mind the mild swear word, but felt certain He would understand.

The streets were empty, reminding him of the similarly quiet streets just before the firefight that had left Kindrich, with only one day to go on his tour, dead. He remembered the little boy and how his mother had pulled him back and closed the shutters.

Jake scanned the rooftops as well as the windows and doors, his mind full of the rifle flashes from the rooftops a couple of weeks ago. This village was different. It didn't seem so much like the locals were hiding. It felt more like they had left. Jake expected a tumbleweed, like in the old westerns, to roll down the dirt street at any moment.

Shawn looked over at him and gave him an exaggerated shrug and raised an eyebrow. Jake shook his head. Static from his earpiece made him jump a little.

"Where the hell is everyone?" a low voice asked.

No one replied. Up ahead, Cal and Pete had stopped at the corner of a building and were peering cautiously around it, into a side street. Cal raised a closed fist and Jake and Shawn stopped. Jake dropped to one knee and increased his scan, covering his squad leader.

A sudden burst of gunfire startled Jake enough to make him gasp. The fire came from close by, but not close enough to be directed at them, he thought. Cal and Pete pressed against the stone building and scanned around, looking for the source, just as chatter erupted in Jake's ear.

"Contact left! Contact left!"

"Rooftop. Up ahead."

"Contact right, contact right! Zeke, check that doorway."

"I got a flash from a window over there."

Jake remained motionless for a moment, his head on a swivel scanning the rooftops, unsure what to do. He heard more gunfire but saw nothing. It sounded like it was far over to their right.

"Third squad has heavy contact. Three blocks in from our entry point and mostly on the west side of the street. Heavy contact."

"First squad," Cal's voice called out in Jake's earpiece. "We'll come in from the south. On our way." Cal swung his arm over his head at Jake and then he and Pete moved down the street at a fast jog, scanning over their rifles as they went. Jake looked at Shawn, and together they broke into a run behind their squadmates. Jake figured that Cal planned to go a couple of blocks south, then cut over to the right and work back north toward third squad, trapping the enemy between them. He imagined that one block to his left, the rest of first squad was doing the same—or he hoped to hell they were.

"First squad." Cal's voice sounded shockingly calm. "Three blocks south and then work over west toward third squad. Then we'll move north and engage. Watch for good guys—no blue on blue."

The commanding voice that Cal had found somewhere brought calm to Jake as he focused on his job.

The four of them reached the corner of a building and Cal raised a closed fist over his head. Jake and Shawn crowded in on top of Cal and Pete, and both took a knee as Cal peered cautiously around the corner, looking north. The gunfire had seemed to intensify, at least Jake thought it sounded that way, but maybe it was just his fear talking.

"Clear, I think," Cal called over his shoulder. "Pete and I'll take the far side of the street. Let's move up quickly, but at the same pace, okay? Cover the rooftops over each other."

Jake and Shawn nodded and then assumed covering positions as Pete and Cal dashed across the street. Once his teammates were against the wall of the building across from them, Jake stood and rounded the corner, moving forward in a crouch as he hugged the wall. He could hear Shawn's heavy breathing beside him as he scanned through his rifle sight.

Up ahead, only a block and a half away, tracers crisscrossed the street, and rifle flashes lit up from the rooftop on Cal's side of the street, as well as from several second-story windows.

"Holy shit," Jake hissed, but he forced himself to continue to move forward and keep pace with Cal and Pete. He watched their progress with his peripheral vision as he scanned the approaching corner. Jake's finger trembled on his trigger guard and he could taste bile in his throat. For a moment he worried he would have to stop and vomit, but Cal's calm voice in his headset helped him hold everything down.

"Third, we have four guys moving up from a block south. Confirm your position on the east side of the street."

"Copy that … we see you guys. Hurry the fuck up. We're pinned in an alley halfway up the next block. Heavy fire from across the street—west side of the street. Dead-end alley, so we got nowhere to go."

Cal waved a hand at him and Jake met his eyes and nodded. Cal pointed at them and then up at the roof above his head. Jake nodded and stepped out across the intersection, intent on dashing to the far corner for cover before providing covering fire for his friend.

Jake almost fell to the ground when he smashed hard into a figure moving fast down the center of the street. He thought at first that it was someone else from his squad and wondered how the hell they'd gotten to this corner before them.

Then fingers dug painfully into his right biceps and he heard the man scream something at him in Dari. Jake struggled to raise his rifle, but it caught in the man's clothes. Jake looked into dark eyes that peered out from a hood.

"Shawn, Shawn," he screamed, and he felt the movement of the enemy fighter raising his weapon. Jake let go of his forward rifle grip with his left hand and pressed down against the man's arm, which almost certainly was pulling up an AK-47 to kill him.

The explosion from Shawn's weapon beside his head was deafening. One moment he was staring into dark, hate-filled eyes only inches from his own, and the next the face disappeared in a cloud of bone and blood and Jake's ears seemed filled with wet cotton. He realized he was falling backward as the now-dead man's grip on his right arm released.

Jake hit the ground on his left ass cheek, the impact jarring his teeth so that he bit down hard on his tongue. He could hear nothing, but he sensed motion ahead of him and instinctively raised his rifle just as a second hooded figure came into view. He squeezed the trigger twice and the man flew backward, like in a movie.

Jake shook his head to clear it and scrambled to his feet, then felt Shawn's hands pulling on his vest.

"Are you okay?" The voice was dull and muffled, but Jake turned and looked into his friend's face and nodded. Time dragged and the world seemed grey, until his head cleared. He looked down at the dead terrorist at his feet, finding it hard to pull his eyes away from the puddle of gore where one of the man's eyes had been. He felt Shawn shake him hard.

"Are you okay?" Shawn asked again. This time, his voice was clearer but still a bit tinny.

"I'm good," Jake said.

"Then let's go, dude," Shawn said, his voice louder now and trembling.

Jake cast a final look over his shoulder, just long enough to see the man he had killed staring blankly up at the sky. Dark blood spread in an expanding lake around his shoulders and head. Then Jake tore his eyes away and dashed to the corner, pressing himself against the rough wall. He spit blood from his lacerated tongue into the dirt beside him, looked over at Cal, and gave a thumbs-up.

Cal was all business and pointed again at the roof above himself and Pete. Jake nodded.

"Covering fire," he yelled over his shoulder at Shawn.

Jake dropped onto one knee, and together with Shawn began to fire up at the figures on the roof just north of his friends. He tried to concentrate some fire into the open windows as well. As he did, he saw Cal, and then Pete, take two steps out into the street and heave something upward, like tossing a high pop fly at baseball practice.

Grenades.

Jake and Shawn instinctively pulled back around the corner just as three overlapping *whumps* sounded. The air seemed to vibrate. Jake wondered who had thrown the third grenade.

"Move, move," he heard someone shout—not Cal, he didn't think—and he sprinted out into the street, scanning over his rifle at the open windows and rooftop. Jake heard sporadic pops of gunfire and squeezed a few rounds into the open windows as well, though he didn't see any motion or rifle flashes from them anymore. A cloud of dust descended as they ran toward the target building.

Jake and Shawn joined Cal and Pete on the south side of the entrance into the two-story building, just as three guys from third squad arrived on the other side of the doorway. Jake looked across the street at the alley where the soldiers had been pinned moments ago. Two other soldiers knelt there, aiming their rifles up at the windows and roof. One let go a three-round burst, but then the other soldier slapped him on the chest.

"Okay," Cal said, still clearly the most composed, and so in charge by default. "We clear the first floor first, and then join at whatever stairs we find in there. Teams of two, and watch out for each other. We move up to the second floor together only when we know that the first floor is clear. Got it?"

Jake and the other five nodded in unison and then Cal tilted his head toward the radio on his chest.

"First and third are moving into the building to clear it. I repeat, we are *in* the building. Need security outside."

"Copy, Cal. There in like two mikes." Jake was pretty sure it was TC who answered.

Two by two, they entered the doorway, the door itself long gone. Jake and one of the third squad guys—Bill something, he was pretty sure—were the second pair in and moved forward as Cal and the other guy ahead of them cleared the corners. Jake realized that everything had started to take on a dreamlike quality. He felt like he had tunnel vision. As he scanned around, looking for targets to engage, he prayed that he wouldn't find any. He didn't want to shoot anyone else today. The face of the dead man from the corner flashed into his mind, and he forced himself to cycle through a few long, slow breaths—just like they had trained back home.

The first floor was empty, and the six men gathered again at the stairway in the center of the larger of the two rooms they had cleared.

"We got the perimeter secure," TC's voice suddenly crackled in Jake's ears. A long and tinny ringing followed the static-filled voice and Jake took another long, deep breath.

"First floor clear," Cal answered. Weird how his lips moved a second before Jake heard the voice in his headset.

They moved up the stairs two by two.

The second floor was one large room filled with horrible images that Jake suspected would haunt him for a long time. At least one of the grenades had made it through the window, and as he moved left off the top of the stairs, his rifle still up and ready, he stepped with some revulsion over a man's leg, separated from wherever the rest of his body was. A large, dark puddle fanned out from the hip, and Jake couldn't stop himself from marveling that the rest of the leg—and even the pants that still covered it—had not a mark on them.

Blood painted the walls around them like some sort of sick modern art, and pieces of three or more bodies were slumped over beneath the windows. Jake saw then where the leg had come from and realized that at least part of a head must be around somewhere as well. He tasted bile again.

Sensing movement to his left, he swung around just as he heard two loud pops and smelled the familiar sulfur. Blood spattered out from the back of the head of a man slumped against the wall, his rifle clattering to the ground. Jake looked over at Cal, who stared grimly at the now-dead man as smoke rose from the barrel of his M4.

"Clear," Cal said in a voice so steady it gave Jake a chill. He felt suddenly damp and wondered if he might have just pissed himself. "Five—or maybe six—KIA on the second floor," Cal said. "Second floor secure."

"Pull back," TC's voice said to all of them. "We got an Apache gonna clear the roof for you. Call out when you're all clear."

"Copy," Cal answered for all of them. "Come on, guys," he said, this time from the room instead of over the radio. Jake stood a moment, unable to tear his eyes away from the carnage around him. He looked over at Cal finally, and their eyes held each other's. Jake saw that Cal's eyes were wet, despite the commanding voice.

"Come on, Jake," his best friend said softly. "Let's please get the fuck out of here."

Cal's use of the f-word was almost as strange and shocking as everything else around him. Jake nodded and followed Cal out of the room and down the stairs.

CHAPTER 11

The hardest part, for Jake at least, was not leaving right after. Shortly after his team had pulled out of the building and taken up positions at the two corners, the attack helicopter had made three passes over the building. During the first, they reported "activity on the roof" and received confirmation from command elements on the ground that all friendlies were out of the building. During the second, they rained down an unbelievable burst of fire from their guns—the tracers so frequent that to Jake it looked like lasers being fired in some sci-fi film. The loud, belching bursts sent a shower of dust and debris into the street. On the final run, the helicopter passed overhead, then banked and turned north, reporting that the "enemy activity has been neutralized."

Jake was grateful that the First Sergeant had picked another team to clear the building again and secure weapons left by the dead enemy fighters after the helicopters left. He didn't think he could go back in there, though he wasn't sure what he would see that wasn't already burned into his brain.

A slap on his back made him jump.

"You okay, Jake?"

First Sergeant TC Morrow gave him a tight smile. Jake smiled back, surprised Morrow remembered his name. He was pretty sure in the two years he had known him, he had never called him by his actual name.

"Yes, First Sar'n," Jake said, trying to sound tough. He felt disappointed that his voice had a slight tremble to it.

Morrow squeezed his shoulder.

"It gets easier, Jake," he said. For a moment his platoon leader looked off into the distance, remembering something, perhaps. Then he shook his head and smiled again. "Maybe it shouldn't, I don't know, but it does get easier."

Morrow walked off with a nod to Shawn, who moved closer to Jake.

"What the hell was that?" Shawn asked.

Jake just shrugged. His mind filled again and again with the face of the bad guy in the alley. He thought now that the man had maybe looked as scared as Jake had felt, but Jake thought he might be making that up. He had never really seen his face in the moment it took to shoot him dead. The other bad guy, the one whose head Shawn had blown away—now, he had looked scared.

I just killed a man. I may have killed someone on the roof in that village the other day, but I damn sure killed this guy. I just became a Christian— really a Christian—and today I took someone's life. Today I'm a killer. How is this okay?

"Jake!"

He looked up and saw Cal motion him over. His best friend looked tense, but he didn't look as haunted as Jake felt. Cal had shot that guy on the second floor right in the head. To Jake, Cal seemed okay with it.

Man, we got a lot to talk about.

"What's up?" he asked as he approached.

"We gotta patrol these four blocks here," Cal said. "Teams of four, both sides of the street like before."

"We're not done?" Pete asked in a low voice. Jake saw that Pete's face was now a complete mask—almost like a doll's face, he thought. No tension, no fear, no nothing—just flat. He looked like he had been in a thousand firefights before.

"No, we're not done," Cal said. "They think this was a group from whatever bunch of assholes the Special Operations guys were gonna hit, but they don't know. The raid on the compound is happening, like, right now. We patrol here until they clean it up and then head out the way we came to the helicopter pickup. Cool?"

Pete shrugged.

"Cool," Jake said. He thought his voice sounded more solid than he felt. He wanted to get the hell out of here. He wanted to take a shower and wash this whole village off himself. He wanted the face of the dead guy to stop popping into his head.

The hour and a half they patrolled up and down the empty streets felt like days to Jake. He and his friends said little or nothing, but now and again Cal would give him a nod and a thumbs-up. Somehow, Cal being cool with everything made Jake feel like maybe he wasn't going straight to hell.

The Special Operations raid took a few bad guys out of the compound, according to what they heard on the radio, but they had no way of knowing if it was whatever big-deal guys they were looking for. Jake realized it would have been awesome to know that—to know that what he had done had at least mattered somehow, that they had helped take some guys off the battlefield who were real doers—guys planning the killing of Americans or the next 9/11 or something. Instead he got another squeeze from First Sergeant Morrow and a "Great job, second platoon," as he boarded the large, grey helicopter.

The sun set out over the desert as they flew home, and Jake saw Cal's eyes were shut even before the darkness enveloped them. From the way his jaw seemed to tense and relax over and over, Jake doubted he was asleep.

Whether Jake had dozed himself or had just been lost deep in thought, he didn't know, but the flight home went by in a blink. The debrief was cursory at best, and before he knew it, he was shrugging his gear off into a pile in the corner of their room. He grabbed the small backpack where he and Cal kept a Bible and a notebook and slung it over his left shoulder, shrugged his rifle back onto his right, and started back out, eager to find some sort of cleansing at the berm.

"You clean your weapon?" Cal asked softly.

Jake sighed heavily and felt his shoulders sag. Then he set the backpack on his bunk and followed Cal out of the hut to the wooden bench along its front. Several other members of first and third squad were already cleaning their weapons, the smell of Hoppe's less comforting than usual. Jake and Cal joined them, and Jake mindlessly pushed one of the two pins that allowed him to separate his rifle into its components. Instead of completely taking it apart, he flipped the upper receiver forward and pulled a Hoppe's-soaked rag through the barrel, then wiped down the other exposed workings with the same rag. His mind wandered as he worked, and when he snapped the rifle components back together and replaced the pin, he wasn't sure how much of the weapon he had actually cleaned.

He slung the rifle over his shoulder and then slipped back inside and grabbed the backpack. Outside again, he waited patiently at the corner of the building while Cal finished his more professional cleaning job. Jake felt a bit like the teenager he had been only a few years ago, half-assing his chores and then waiting for his ride to the mall.

Finally, Cal slung his weapon and, hand on Jake's shoulder, he led them off toward the berm.

Jake barely heard Cal's prayer asking God to bless their time together and to help them find His will for them in the Word. Then his best friend looked at him with a raised eyebrow. He looked calm and patient, but there was something behind the mask that Jake suspected only he and Kelly, Cal's wife, would even have noticed. It was in his eyes—something dark.

"I got a lot of shit going on in my head," Jake said, then remembered something and stopped. "Hey, that reminds me—I never really heard you swear much before, but you surprised me with a few whoppers today."

Something like annoyance flashed through Cal's eyes before he closed them briefly, but when he opened them he was just the same ol' Cal. He smiled at Jake and looked a little amused.

"Except for taking the Lord's name in vain—which I never do, by the way—there is not a ton in the Word about cussing," Cal said. "I try not to swear much because of Romans fourteen, which I think best sums up what the Word has to say on the subject."

Jake pulled the Bible from the backpack and started flipping through it, looking for the Letter to the Romans. Cal put his hand on the open Bible, stopping him.

"It doesn't say anything about swearing," he said with a chuckle. "What it does say, what Paul is saying to the Church, is that you should never do anything to make a brother or sister stumble. As Christians, we have an obligation to lead by example, because everything we do is a reflection on Christ once we proclaim to be a part of Him. So, me personally, I don't think God really cares that much if I use a strong word to express my feelings in the heat of the moment. But if my language reflects poorly on my faith or on God because people around me think it's 'unchristian' to use that language, then I could be putting a distance between those people and God by my behavior. So, for that reason, I try really hard not to use bad language if I can help it." Cal shrugged. "Today I couldn't help it."

"Shitty day," Jake said.

Cal laughed. "Yeah. Shitty day."

They both laughed.

Jake shivered against the growing cold. He felt unexpected tears in his eyes.

"I never killed anyone before," he said in a trembling voice. "At least, I don't think I did. I dumped a lot of rounds up on that roof the day Kindrich bought it. Maybe I killed someone that day, I don't know." He paused and thought back. He had been scared, but in many ways it had felt like a video game or something. But this…

"Me either, Jake," Cal said, and Jake saw his eyes cloud a bit. "When I shot that guy in the head, the wounded guy in the building, the worse thing I think is that—at first—I didn't feel anything. Later, that felt worse than knowing I had taken someone's life." Cal shifted and leaned back against the berm.

Jake let the silence hover for a moment. He felt relief that Cal had some of the same feelings he did.

"It says, 'Thou shalt not kill,' doesn't it?"

Cal smiled. "As a soldier, I can tell you I have no real conflict with what we do. There are scores of devoted, God-fearing warriors in the Bible. David himself started his rise to God's favor as a soldier, brave enough to trust God to help him defeat an overwhelming enemy. From there he went on to scores of bloody battles, and the Israelites admired him and later followed him as their king because of his often ruthless prowess on the battlefield—slaughtering hundreds, maybe even thousands, of enemies of his people. Later, I can show you a bunch of things in the Bible about faith-based warriors, and as Christian soldiers that's what we are, I think." He looked out over the camp. "The men we're fighting represent a pretty big evil in the world. God has no problem with us combating that, I'm pretty sure. It's just that as a Christian—but also as a human being, I guess—it should never feel good to take another life."

Cal reached over and took the Bible from Jake's lap and began flipping through it.

"For the record, by the way, the original translation of the Ten Commandments says, 'Thou shalt not murder'—the original text uses a word that translates as 'an unjustified killing.' Even in the original text, there was a distinction between murder and justified killing." Cal put a finger in the Bible to mark a page he clearly wanted to share. "Suppose you came across someone about to kill a small child. He's holding him and has a knife to his throat. You have your weapon and a bead on him. Do you think you're wrong to fire—to sacrifice him to save an innocent child?"

"Of course not," Jake said. "I'd smoke the son of a bitch without hesitation."

"So would I," Cal said. "And God would be okay with that, I believe. Being a Christian doesn't mean you have to be a victim. You're allowed to defend yourself. You're allowed to defend the defenseless and your loved ones. As soldiers, we're the defenders of our country and her ideals. We're no different than the warriors of the Old Testament, who God often called to battle against those who would harm his people. We're protectors of our people and our way of life. I happen to believe that America is founded on principles very much in keeping with God's plan for his people. I believe that when I fight for America, I am fighting for God."

Jake thought about it a moment. He hadn't considered it that way at all, and hearing Cal's words was like feeling a weight lifted off him. For a moment the lifeless eyes of the dead man he had shot came back to him and his throat tightened.

"Still hard," he mumbled.

Cal flipped through the Bible, but in the fading light Jake saw a tear run down his best friend's cheek.

"It sure as hell is," Cal said. He looked up and smiled. "Let me start with Jeremiah forty-eight," he said. "Then I'll show you a bunch of other passages I think will help us both."

Jake nodded, ready for the relief he prayed their study would bring him.

"I have some other heavy stuff to talk about too," Jake said and leaned in next to his friend. "Things Pete made me think about—things I didn't have answers for."

Cal squeezed his shoulder. "Maybe tonight we can just get through this—just get through this grieving over what we had to do?" he asked. "We can come back to the other stuff tomorrow, if that's okay?"

Jake nodded. That actually sounded great.

"Let's see what was going on with Jeremiah, and then I have a bunch of stuff to share with you from Psalms," Cal said.

CHAPTER 12

Sleep had been an elusive luxury for months now—first in the terrible, stressful anticipation of Jake's leaving, and now dealing with the emptiness Rachel felt at his absence—and the first part of this night had been no different. Rachel worried about her husband, of course, but more constant was the ache to just be with him. She trusted God to keep him safe, but that did little for her loneliness and desire to be with her husband and best friend. When she did sleep—usually after a couple of hours spent tossing and turning in their bed, which now felt too large and too cold—she slept very deeply. She might wake up during the night, startled by some thought or feeling she usually couldn't remember, and start the long journey to sleep all over again, but when she slept, she slept completely, and it seemed she rarely dreamed.

But Rachel dreamed tonight.

In her dream she sat on a grassy knoll—a real place, and in fact a place where she usually felt nothing but peace and closeness to God. It was where she had gone as a child to play alone. It was where Jake had asked her to marry him. It had been the place where, after the church service with Kelly when Rachel had truly accepted Christ and given her life to God, she had come to sit and contemplate all that had happened. The small hill sat behind her parents' house and was bordered on one side by their home, and on the other by their neighbors. But behind it the hill ran down to the quiet woods where she had played when she was little and had kissed Jake for the first time, years later. At the top, there was a huge, old oak tree that she sat under, both then and now in her dream. It was a place of familiar peace where she went often and always felt close to God. Jake called it her private church.

Tonight, however (in her dream, at least), Rachel felt nothing but anxious. She sat beneath the tree, rocking back and forth, her knees to her chest, and waited for whatever was supposed to happen. It seemed strange to be in her special place of quiet peace and feel fear.

She turned her head when she felt, rather than heard, someone coming up the hill to her left. The man who approached from the path into the woods was in jeans and tennis shoes, the hood from his scarlet sweatshirt bunched around his neck. He had a grey bag slung over his right shoulder and used a tall, thick walking stick. He was young, and he smiled as he came toward her, but Rachel shuddered, though there was nothing at all threatening about him. She was afraid, not of him, she thought, but of what he brought. Still, she sat and waited, unsure what else to do.

"Hello, Rachel."

One moment the man was halfway up the hill, working his walking stick up the path, and then quite suddenly he was beside her, cross-legged, with his walking stick across his lap.

"I'm Luke," the man said. His eyes seemed to glow slightly in the light from the full moon above them. Rachel was certain that a moment ago it had been daytime.

That's just how dreams are.

"Do I know you?"

"Of course," Luke said, but now he was standing beside the tree, his stick leaning against the thick trunk. "I was there that night."

Because it was a dream, Rachel knew he meant the night she had accepted Christ. She nodded, then shivered and looked down to see she was wearing the sundress she had worn to Foundations Family Church that night two years ago.

"Are you an angel?" she asked.

"I'm a messenger," Luke said, and they both knew that didn't answer the question one way or the other.

The cold went away and Rachel saw that she again wore the flannel pajamas she had worn to bed. She turned to Luke, who now sat beside her, his back against the tree.

"Jake is on the path," Luke said, and he looked out over the field beside her parents' house. Then he turned and looked at her, and Rachel couldn't help but feel safe. "His journey will be more difficult," Luke said. "He'll need you, Rachel, and the quiet faith you've found. He'll need you more than ever before, and you must be strong and faithful. God has given you the gifts you will need to help Jake in his time of need, and you'll need to use those gifts."

Rachel felt tears well up in her eyes, though she didn't understand what the angel was trying to tell her.

"Please tell me he'll be okay," she sobbed and put a hand on Luke's arm. She saw that the sweatshirt was gone and Luke's arm was now clad in a shimmering silver cloth. His arm seemed to give off light more than glow. The arm under her hand disappeared, and Luke, back in his scarlet sweatshirt, smiled down at her from a few feet away. "I don't understand," Rachel said, unable to keep the pleading from her voice.

"You will," Luke answered. "And God will be with you to help you. He has given you the gifts, but you must pray for the strength to use them."

Rachel nodded again and felt the tears spill onto her cheeks.

"There is more," Luke continued. "Long before Jake's return, your friend will need you even more. The faith she helped you find, you must now give back to her."

Rachel closed her eyes and said a quiet prayer that Kelly and Cal were okay. When she opened them, Luke was gone.

And so were the hill and her tree.

She sat now in the huge sanctuary at Foundations Family Church. She was alone, seated in the very back row, but up front, on the stage where Pastor Craig gave his sermons, a lone figure rocked back and forth. Rachel knew it was Kelly. Her best friend kneeled, her hands clasped in front of her, and rocked. Rachel rose and went down the aisle toward her.

As she approached, she saw that Kelly wore her wedding dress—the one they had shopped for together. Her head was down and she mumbled what Rachel thought was a prayer, though she couldn't make out the words.

Rachel stopped a few feet away. "Kelly?"

The mumbling stopped, and Kelly stopped rocking but did not look up. Rachel noticed the streaks of blood on the front of the gorgeous wedding dress and wondered how she had not seen them before. She heard her friend sob and then Kelly looked up at her with swollen eyes.

"See?" her friend asked and held her hands out.

Blood ran down Kelly's arms, dripping puddles onto the wood floor of the stage and spattering onto the dress. Rachel covered her mouth with a hand to stifle her cry.

"See what they've done?" Kelly sobbed.

And then she threw her head back and let out a piercing scream.

Rachel sat up in her bed and tore at the sheets and blankets that threatened to smother her. The scream echoed off the walls of the bedroom, and it took her a moment to realize that the scream was actually hers, and not from the Kelly of her dream.

She tried desperately to catch her breath, reaching for the light on her nightstand with a badly shaking hand.

"My God," she mumbled. Finally, her finger found the chain on the lamp and light filled her bedroom, followed by the sound of a thankfully empty water glass falling from her nightstand to the carpeted floor.

Rachel waited for the pounding pulse in her temples to slow and quiet.

What a horrible nightmare.

Something was wrong about that thought, though, and she felt her stomach churn. She realized that she wasn't at all sure that her dream *was* a nightmare. She had read about visions in the Bible—of angels sharing God's plans through dreams. She had never heard of such a thing outside of the Bible, however, and she wasn't at all sure things like that happened in modern times.

Rachel turned and looked at the Bible on her nightstand and bit her lower lip. To her, God spoke to people through his Word, sharing messages through passages in the Bible when they were needed most. At least, that was how it had always been for her.

Rachel pulled the Bible into her lap and closed her eyes, caressing the faux leather cover.

Lord, I am so frightened right now. I'm so scared for Jake and for Kelly. Please help me. Help me know if this was more than a dream.

She slipped a finger between the pages of the Book, her eyes still closed, and then opened the pages and her eyes at the same time. He eyes fell on the passage under her finger.

When the Spirit of truth comes, he will guide you into all the truth, for he will not speak on his own authority, but whatever he hears he will speak, and he will declare to you the things that are to come.

Rachel drew a sharp breath through her pursed lips. The verse was from John, chapter sixteen, verse thirteen. How was this possible? What the hell did the dream mean?

She closed her eyes again, and again mumbled a prayer as she slipped a finger blindly into her Bible. This time the verse was from Isaiah, in the Old Testament:

And your ears shall hear a word behind you, saying, "This is the way, walk in it," when you turn to the right or when you turn to the left.

Chapter thirty, verse twenty-one. Rachel read the verse again, trying to be sure her imagination wasn't making it mean something it never intended. A dark grey circle appeared on the page where a tear dripped from her cheeks.

"God, please don't get mad at me. I'm not testing you, I just need to be sure. I'm testing myself, I think."

She flipped the Bible open a final time.

But it was to us that God revealed these things, by his Spirit. For his Spirit searches out everything and shows us God's deep secrets.

Tears poured down her cheeks now, and she made a mental note to find the verse again in First Corinthians, chapter two.

"God, what does it mean? What am I supposed to do?"

The sound of her cell phone shattered the heavy quiet of the room, and Rachel startled hard enough to drop her Bible to the floor. She reached out a trembling hand for the phone on the nightstand, terrified that it would be a 308 number—a number from the base.

Instead she saw *Kelly* in the middle of the vibrating screen and felt her throat tighten.

Rachel pushed the answer button and brought the phone slowly to her ear.

"Hello?" Her voice cracked and her throat felt as dry as desert sand. On the other end, her friend let out a low sob.

"Rach? Baby, I'm so sorry to call so late…" Her friend sobbed again and Rachel said a silent prayer that she would know how to help her.

"It's okay, Kelly. It's okay. What's wrong, sweetie?"

There was a long pause and she heard Kelly blowing her nose. Then she came back on the line.

"Rachel, I just had the most horrible dream…"

CHAPTER 13

Jake tried to keep his mind on the mission, but he found his thoughts wandering at times to the face of the man he had shot in the alley, and at other times to Pete's questions and how desperately Jake now seemed to need answers to those questions. The night before had been a tremendous help. The passages Cal had found for them said all the right things, and had brought him out of the depression and despair into which he'd felt on the verge of descending. He had truly felt a genuine, warm peace when they prayed together and asked God to help them deal with the things they had been led to do. It felt a lot like the peace he had experienced a few weeks earlier (a few weeks that felt like a lifetime) when he had asked God into his heart for the first time. But today, as they spread out in combat formation to enter the village near their base for a show-of-force patrol, he realized he really needed to know—for himself—the answers to Pete's questions. Where was God in the death of a good man (as far as he knew, he supposed) who died a day before returning home to his family? Why would God let that happen? He wished he'd had a day without a mission to sort out some of that, and to maybe spend time with Pete, whom he worried about now more than ever. He wondered if sharing the things Cal had shared with him might help. Better yet, Cal should talk to him. Jake felt so new and unprepared.

"Heads up, ladies." First Sergeant Morrow slapped Brandon on the back of the helmet as he passed. "Spread out. Act like you done this shit before, guys."

Brandon and his first squad teammate spread out right to enter the village from the northeast corner, while Jake followed Cal, Pete, and Shawn to the left. With the back of his left hand, Jake checked his kit for magazines he already knew were there.

Complacency was the biggest risk as they entered the third month of the deployment, especially in a village they now knew like the backs of their hands. He forced his mind to focus on the job at hand and spread out to the left side of the street with Pete, while Cal and Shawn moved right. He kept his eyes moving across the windows, doors, and rooftops above his squadmates across the street, trusting that Cal and Shawn were scanning just as effectively above his head.

"It's quiet," Pete mumbled nervously.

"Nah, there's kids out," Jake answered. A boy of about four or five waved to him from the open doorway of a low brown house. The woman behind him didn't pull him back inside—a good sign, Jake figured. Her eyes, though—the woman's eyes looked sad somehow. Jake waved to the boy and the woman nodded at him. Then she led her son back into the house.

Guess he didn't want any chocolate. Strange.

It was kind of quiet, Jake realized. But it wasn't the ghost town quiet they had seen before the big firefight. There were plenty of open doors, and now and again he saw kids inside. None of them, however, came running out waving their arms and looking for candy.

Jake tightened his grip on his rifle and began to scan more intently. Pete was right, maybe. This felt wrong.

The dirt street curved gently to the right, and they moved together toward the center of the village, where they would meet up with third squad and the other four guys from first. They would mill around, hand out some chocolate, and then split back into their smaller groups for another pass through the village before heading out.

There was no activity at all on the roofs as they approached the open center of town, where they were told there were sometimes merchants selling stuff, though they had never seen any such thing on their patrols. Brandon and his three teammates were just arriving, and Cal looked over at him and shrugged.

They formed two loose circles in the open square between low, brown buildings, and Jake concentrated on keeping up his scan, though there was no activity other than theirs that he could see.

"Where are the kids?" Pete asked nervously, looking past Cal and Shawn.

Cal shrugged again.

The building behind Cal and Shawn was no different than the other thin brown stucco buildings, but for some reason the bright green door, halfway open into the dimly lit house, seemed out of place in the sea of drab. Jake saw a boy, maybe eleven or twelve years old, and clad in the familiar long grey shirt (a *man dress*, Shawn would call it), peer around the door and then disappear back into the dark house. Jake watched for a minute, expecting the shy boy to reappear, but he didn't. Once more Jake scanned the rooftops and windows on that side of the street. The quiet felt more and more wrong, and his grip on his rifle tightened.

Cal and Shawn were ten or so yards away, too far for a whispered conversation, which for some reason felt appropriate in the quiet. Cal held up two fingers—*two more minutes*, Jake thought he meant—and then motioned him over just as the boy appeared again in the doorway.

At first Jake thought the boy looked ill, and he wondered if perhaps they should call up a medic to have a look at him. The boy's face seemed pale and sweat ran down from his forehead. There was something else, though Jake was not yet sure what, that made him move his finger to the trigger guard and raise his rifle slightly, though he didn't want to scare the kid by bringing his weapon all the way to bear.

Pete's sudden shouts and motion from behind him raised Jake's alarm further and he raised his rifle. The boy moved swiftly now, not quite running but walking very fast.

"Shoot, Jake!" Pete screamed in his ear. "Fuckin' shoot him!"

Jake froze for only a second, but it was a second too long. Shoot what? Shoot the kid? Cal turned and grabbed Shawn by the straps of his kit and lowered a shoulder, pulling Shawn behind him as he spun around.

Jake realized that it was the shirt—the man dress—that was wrong. The thin-faced kid had one hand inside his far-too-bulky shirt. Jake looked through the sight of his rifle, the red dot in the center of the boy's forehead, but his finger would not follow his command to squeeze and send a five-five-six round through the boy's terrified face.

And then it didn't matter. Cal was now between Shawn and the boy, holding Shawn back like a mom protecting her child. Jake was blinded by the bright flash and felt the heat sweep over him, like opening an oven door with your face too close. A split second later he felt the huge *whump* of the concussion, and all the air in his lungs—maybe all the air in the universe—was sucked away. He stumbled backward, almost fell, but managed to regain his balance as he heard a crack that he thought might have been his weapon discharging, though some quiet part of his brain screamed, *Too late, asshole!*

It took a second for his eyes to clear from the bright light, and the burning heat on his cheeks and neck increased, but when his vision returned—an eerie sort of off color, like an old photograph from the eighteen hundreds—there was nothing to see. There was no one standing in front of him anymore. The wall of the brown building was now marred by black, and there were giant holes in the wall, through which he could see only darkness inside the house with the green door. His head felt heavy and his ears seemed to be filled with thick cotton. He heard muffled sounds around him but couldn't make out what they were.

Everything felt like it was moving in slow motion, and Jake realized he had taken a knee. He struggled to clear his head—he needed to know what the sounds were. He felt like there was something he should be doing, and then thought to raise his rifle again and scan for enemy targets.

Jake felt hands on his arms and shoulders just as his hearing cleared and time suddenly sped up to normal pace. His head still felt heavy and he tasted coppery blood in his mouth. As he fought off the hands that pulled at him, he realized that the muffled sounds were coming from him—that he was shouting "Cal!" over and over again.

Cal.

"Lay down, Jake."

The words were far away, but he could understand them now. He looked up into the face of TC, whose strong hands on Jake's shoulders forced him backward onto the ground.

"Where's Cal?" he screamed, over and over.

As he lay back in the dirt, Jake turned his head to the left, searching desperately to find some sign of his best friend. Beside him in the dirt, he saw half of a helmet, the edges ragged and coated in blood. Beside it was what looked like a thumb, the thumbnail dirty but otherwise eerily intact. He closed his eyes and felt himself begin to sob uncontrollably.

He thought of Rachel and then of Kelly. He heard himself scream again for Cal, though he knew he was gone, and his screams seemed to come from far away, from another world almost.

Jake squeezed his eyes tighter, until little fireworks of white light exploded in the red darkness of his eyelids, and tried not to drift off into the warm, dark pool that seemed to pull him under. He was afraid that the darkness was death and worried he would never see Rachel again.

Either way, he knew he would never see Cal.

CHAPTER 14

If he opened his eyes, he would find that he was in a hospital bed some-where, and then he would have no choice but to accept that this was not some horrible nightmare. The time from the explosion until this moment, waking from a terrible, broken sleep, was jarred by fragmented memories. Jake remembered flying in the helicopter and TC squeezing his gloved hand as they loaded him aboard. He remembered the hel-meted and flight-suit-clad medics scurrying around the tight quarters of the UH-60 Black Hawk, and he remembered seeing the red cross on the side of the pilot's door as they slid him in. The medics had looked him over briefly just as they lifted off, and then mouthed something he couldn't understand and patted him on the chest. The rest of the flight, they'd had their backs to him, busy with some other problem toward the rear of the dust-off helo.

He remembered the first stop at some forward area medical place. He had been on a stretcher elevated on sawhorses, he remembered, and he recalled having trouble letting go of his weapon, though he had wanted to let go of it almost desperately. He remembered the doctor talking about a bunch of people dying (though he couldn't remember now how many), and something about a chest wound. Then warm liquid slid through the vein of his arm and he remembered only occasional voices piercing the quiet darkness.

But he remembered every single detail of the explosion that had killed his best friend. He remembered the boy in the man dress and Pete scream-ing something from behind him. He remembered trying to squeeze the trigger of his M4 and shoot the boy in the head before he could do what Jake, and apparently Pete, knew he was about to do. He had no memory of his best friend evaporating in a cloud of blood and bone, but it didn't matter—his mind had filled in the details in such a way that he couldn't separate those images from the real events he remembered.

He remembered that thumb—the bloody fucking thumb with the dirty nail. He obsessed about the thumb—trying desperately to picture Cal's hands. He needed to see Cal's left hand, because if he couldn't be sure whether that thumb was Cal's or not, he was pretty sure he would go completely insane.

Jake squeezed his eyes shut tighter, until white fireworks began to explode behind his lids. It was important, for some damn reason. So important that he could think of nothing else but getting back to the FOB and scrolling through the photos on his laptop. There were dozens of photos of Cal in there. Some of them must show his thumbs, right? Then he could be sure.

"Sir?"

The soft voice and hand on his shoulder jarred Jake, and his eyes sprung open as he scurried to the far side of the bed. His right hand reached for his rifle on his hip but came up with only bare skin.

The young woman, her hair pulled up in a bun, smiled down at him, and he let out a long, rasping breath and tried to uncramp his right elbow. His entire body screamed from the sudden burst of movement. The woman was clad in Air Force BDUs but wore a greenish-blue T-shirt instead of a blouse. She had a stethoscope around her neck.

"Are you my nurse?" Jake asked. His throat felt like sandpaper.

"Oh, no," she answered. "I'm a medic. I need to get your vitals."

Jake pulled the thin sheet up to his chest, fearing he was completely naked under the covers, and stuck out his left arm.

"Where am I?" he asked. His voice sounded gravelly and not his own.

"You're at the Cache level three hospital at Kandahar Airfield. You're in the ICU, but I think you're probably moving to a regular bed today. They just want to get another CT of your head. You know—to be sure." The blood pressure cuff hissed back down while she listened with a stethoscope on the inside of his elbow. The she tore the Velcro sleeve off his arm and smiled. "You were out for a long time, I guess, so they want to be sure."

Jake nodded, but he had no idea what that meant. Sure about what? He had no recollection of getting a first CT.

"What happened?" he asked.

Like you don't know. You choked and let your best friend and God knows how many other squadmates get blown the hell up.

The medic looked uncomfortable and shrugged.

"I don't know. Some kind of a blast injury? Maybe an IED. We see that all the time. I can find someone who can tell you more. Do you remember what happened?"

Jake did, of course, but he shook his head. He turned his head so she wouldn't see his tears.

"Are you having any pain? I can have the nurse get you something for pain."

That sounded great. He needed more of whatever they'd given him at the other place that let him just slip away for God only knew how long. He nodded his head and grunted.

"Where is your pain?" she asked.

"All over," Jake snapped. "I got blown the hell up and guess what? I hurt every damn where."

The medic patted his arm gently but was smart enough not to say anything else. She slipped away before Jake knew she was gone.

His iPod had been in his kit. Jake wondered if they'd brought his kit in with him. A lot of pictures had been transferred onto his iPod, and surely in one of them Jake could see Cal's thumbs.

"Hurting all over?" a voice interrupted his thoughts. "I'm gonna give you a little pain medicine in your IV, okay? It will help with the pain and help you relax while we take you over for a CT. Does that sound okay?"

Jake nodded but didn't look over at the source of the new, older voice. Moments later he felt something warm climb up his arm and then his head felt swimmy and he seemed to float.

He should ask the nurse about his iPod. He would try and find a picture of Cal's thumbs and he could also listen to some music.

Holy shit, he was thirsty. And hungry, maybe.

He would take a nap and then ask about the iPod.

Jake remembered the bumpy ride somewhere and then lying still while he rolled back and forth in some kind of tube. He lay in a hallway for a while, dozing on and off, and decided he would love to have that medicine for the next five months, or whatever was left of his tour. He slept through the next part of his Kandahar Airfield Hospital Tour and woke up in a room with a wall on one side and a curtain on the other. It looked so much like a civilian hospital back in the States that, for a moment, he thought something terrible had happened and he was waking up back home. Then he heard the high-pitched scream of a fighter jet overhead and remembered that something terrible had, in fact, happened, but he was still here in Afghanistan.

"How are you doing, mate?"

Jake looked over at the man in the weird camo surgical scrubs and brown desert boots. He couldn't tell whether he was British or Aussie, but he sure wasn't American.

Cal would know. He could always tell the difference. He could do a great British accent too.

"I'm okay, I guess," Jake said.

The man smiled broadly and ran his hands through curly red hair that was too long for a military cut—U.S. military anyway.

"Yeah, right, right. Helluva coupla days, eh?"

Jake nodded. "How many days?" he asked.

"What—since you came here?"

"Since I got blown up and my best friend got killed in front of me," Jake said, with more acid in his voice than he intended.

"Right," the surgeon said and looked down. "I'm really sorry about that, mate. I really am." He pressed a hand on Jake's shoulder, and Jake believed him. "You've been with us two days. Probably don't remember much from yesterday with all the meds we gave you, but today is a new day. Good news is, you're doing well. CT shows nothing scary. Should be right as rain in no time." He patted Jake's shoulder again. "Just waitin' for your command to decide where to send you."

"What do you mean, where to send me?" Jake asked, genuinely confused. Where in the hell might they send him?

The doctor stroked the two-day stubble on his chin. "You know," he said, but seemed uncomfortable. "Whether to send you back to your unit or back home."

"Home?" Jake sat up in bed, incredulous. Cal was dead. Several more of his friends were dead and he didn't even know who. He had screwed up and people died. And they really thought they could just send him home? "I can't go home," he said, his face full of heat. "How the hell can I go home? I need to get back to my unit. I can't go home while they're still here." The thought of going home—of facing Rachel and, dear God, Kelly—was almost enough to send him crashing over the edge. He had to stay. He had to fight. He had to somehow make things right with whoever was left of his friends.

Jake swung his legs out of bed, no longer caring whether he had clothes on or not. "I gotta get the hell out of here. I gotta get back to my guys."

The doctor put a gentle hand on Jake's back.

"Easy there, mate. What's your hurry?" Jake felt himself calm a bit at the man's soothing voice. "Someone from your command is probably here. I'll go find out for you. I can get them to come by, okay? If you're all good, I'm sure you'll be back with your unit in no time, 'kay?"

Jake nodded and lay back down.

"I just can't go home," he said. "I mean, that's ridiculous."

"Right, right," the doctor said with a smile. "I gotcha, mate. I'll see who's around and have them come back in a jiff, 'kay?"

"Okay," Jake said and felt his breathing slow.

"Cheers, mate," the doctor said, and left.

It would be okay. They couldn't send Jake home just yet.

He closed his eyes and tried desperately to think about anything but Cal and the unanswerable question of who else might be dead.

CHAPTER 15

Rachel tried unsuccessfully to keep her mind from the unanswerable question "why?" as she held her best friend tightly in her arms. Kelly no longer wailed in pain, but her sobbing wracked both their bodies, and Kelly's tears ran in streams down Rachel's chest and neck.

Why?

Her mind drifted again and again to the messages Pastor Craig had delivered on just that subject, usually after some national tragedy, like the school shooting up north, had assaulted the souls of his congregation. She remembered the tearful message he had delivered the Sunday after a two-year-old from their congregation—a little girl Rachel had adored in her Children's Church class—had died suddenly from an illness no one knew she had. Rachel mentally searched for the scriptures in which she had found comfort then. She remembered one from Proverbs—chapter three.

Lean on, trust in, and be confident in the Lord with all you heart and mind and do not rely on your own insight or understanding.

She also thought that she had found strength in John sixteen, verse twenty-two, but she couldn't for the life of her remember what it said.

Kelly's weight grew heavier on Rachel's shoulder and chest, and she felt her grief-stricken friend's breathing slow. She wondered for a moment if Kelly had fallen asleep. Rachel had held her this way for nearly an hour, and her left hand had been all pins and needles for a long time now. Then she heard the whispered mumbling and realized her friend must be praying. Rachel closed her eyes and tried to say her own prayer, but all she could think of was *God, please help us.*

As selfish as it felt, she could do nothing to keep her mind from Jake. She had gotten several calls before the horrible call from Kelly that had sent her racing here to her friend's house. Jake was fine, she had been told. He was injured, but it was not serious, and he was at a military hospital to get checked out. He would call soon, the ombudsman had promised her. A Colonel somebody from base had called as well and made the same promise, but Rachel knew she wouldn't believe it—couldn't let herself, really—until she heard Jake's voice.

"When can he come home?" Rachel had tearfully demanded of both callers. Both told her they had no information other than what they had shared, but promised to call when they knew more. That had been over two hours ago, and she had no idea how long before that everything had actually happened. Rachel squeezed her cell phone to reassure herself that it was still there and that she had not missed any calls.

God, please help us. Please help Kelly, and God, please, please bring Jake home to me.

She held her friend and their tears mixed together on her neck.

CHAPTER 16

Jake had never seen First Sergeant Morrow look in any way uncomfortable, until now. The battle-hardened soldier sat awkwardly in a folding chair beside Jake's bed, his hands in his lap. He looked exhausted and emotionally drained.

"So, anyway, your main doctor—that British dude—says it looks like you're fine. They have to watch you for a day as part of some traumatic-brain-injury protocol, but then you should be done for now."

"For now?" Jake raised an eyebrow.

Morrow scratched the side of his chin.

"Yeah, well, you got blown up, and over the years they've found that some people have delayed symptoms from injuries like that. So, they keep an eye on you on and off for a good while, I guess. But you'll be outta here tomorrow."

"And back to the FOB?" Jake's voice made the question more of a demand.

The First Sergeant sighed heavily and leaned back in the small chair. He held Jake's eyes but seemed to be struggling to decide what to say—or how to say it, anyway. He sighed again and leaned forward, elbows on knees.

"Look, Jake," he said. "They say you're fine, but I mean, come on." He raised an eyebrow. Jake gave him nothing, just held his gaze. "Dude, Cal was your best friend. Shawn was a good friend too, and I know you knew Brandon pretty well also. That kind of loss—it totally screws with you, man. Believe me when I tell you that I know." For a moment Morrow's eyes looked into the distance and saw whatever traumas still haunted him from his previous combat deployments. He shook his head and focused on Jake again. "Maybe you oughta just head home, dude. Get back to Rachel—help her take care of Kelly."

Jake was surprised that the First Sergeant knew Rachel's and Kelly's names, but he shouldn't have been. They were on the casualty report, right? He thought about Rachel and then about Kelly. He missed his wife more than he had ever dreamed possible. But how could it be right between them if he scurried home now, after letting everyone down? And how could he face Kelly so soon? Jake doubted he would ever be able to look her in the eyes.

"How the hell can I go home? I have other friends in the unit, ya know. What am I supposed to do? Run out on them? Leave them over here in this shithole while I sit at home, watch TV, and screw my wife? How could I possibly do that? Could you do that?"

"Pete's going home," Morrow said simply.

"So what?" Jake asked, his jaw clenched. "I'm glad for him, man, but really—so the fuck what?"

Morrow looked at his feet and nodded. He got it, Jake suspected. Maybe he just had to say this shit. Some "you got real jacked up" protocol. Like hell he would go home.

"I know you think it will help, Jake—staying here, fighting your ass off, killing a bunch of Taliban assholes. I know you feel like, somehow, that will make all this right. It won't. You gotta trust me on that, because believe me, I know."

Jake swallowed hard.

Please, God, do not make me go home like this.

His First Sergeant continued. "I won't make you go, Jake. I'll keep you here, if that's what you want. You're a good soldier and we could use you. But this war will go on with or without you. It's bigger than any one of us. Go home to Rachel and get your life together, man."

Morrow stood and put a hand on Jake's shoulder. Jake found he couldn't hold the First Sergeant's sad eyes, and so he looked down at his hands.

"I know you and Cal had a strong faith, Jake." He wondered why those words stung more than a little. "How about you talk to a chaplain before you decide?"

Jake pushed Morrow's hand away roughly, though part of him wondered why.

"I don't need to talk to anyone, First Sar'n," he said coldly. "I'm not scampering home to my wife and leaving my guys here in the 'stan. I'm not that big of a coward. I'm staying." He held Morrow's gaze. "When can I come back to the FOB?" he asked.

"Okay," Morrow said. "As soon as the docs and the psych guys clear you, we'll head back together. Maybe tomorrow, if they get it all done today."

"Perfect," Jake said. He lay back down and felt his pulse slow. Morrow tapped his shoulder and Jake looked over. Morrow held out a bulky satellite phone.

"You need to call Rachel," he said.

Jake felt his throat tighten and there was a burning in his chest. How could he talk to Rachel right now? God, she was probably with Kelly. She would *know*.

"What would I say?" he asked and felt tears spill onto his cheeks. He wiped them away with the back of his hand, angry that they were there at all.

"She's your wife, Jake. She loves you and she's worried sick. Just let her know that you're okay."

He set the phone in Jake's lap and put a hand on his shoulder again.

"Take as long as you need. No time limits here," Morrow said with a smile. "I'll go check with the docs and come back in a little while. I need to check on Pete also.

"The number is punched in already," Morrow added as he left. "Just push Send." The First Sergeant pulled the curtain closed behind him.

Jake sat for a long while, his thumb frozen over the Send button on the satellite phone, tears streaming down his cheeks.

CHAPTER 17

Rachel felt consumed with guilt that her mind drifted over and over to her husband, who was at least alive and well, while her best friend's husband lay in the dark wooden box in front of them. It seemed somehow bizarre that the weather at the cemetery was so nice. It most definitely should be raining. In any good movie it would be a grey, overcast day.

Caleb had been one of her best friends, but she seemed almost incapable of feeling anything but a desperate, longing sadness that Jake remained so far away, and excruciating guilt at how often she thanked God that it was not her husband in that box. The thought of it now brought tears of shame spilling onto her cheeks. The guilt worsened when she realized that anyone looking at her would assume that she wept for Caleb and Kelly instead of for herself.

Kelly's hand squeezed hers, but Rachel could not bring herself to open her eyes and look at her friend—terrified that Kelly would see in her eyes that it was for her own selfish problems that she cried.

Pastor Craig's voice quivered as he delivered the last of his words over the gravesite. Two Army officers had spoken before him—the second a general, she thought, who had handed Kelly a tightly folded flag and whispered something in her ear that made Kelly nod, but sob again. Rachel prayed quietly that she would never know what generals whispered to widows in those moments. Craig had wept openly at the service back at the church. He had quoted Romans eight, but in her grief Rachel had seen no way to apply the words of hope in that chapter to this tragedy that was beyond her spiritual maturity. In fact, she doubted she would ever again read Romans eight after today.

"We know that Caleb is with you, Father. We ask that you hold him tightly and comfort those of us left behind. Help us find peace and meaning in this loss. Be with us, Lord, in our sorrow and remind us of the everlasting joy and peace that awaits us in Your house—peace and joy that we know our brother Caleb now enjoys …"

Rachel faded away from Pastor Craig's words and back to Jake.

The call a week ago—the horrible call from the hospital in Afghanistan—still haunted her. The words—and, worse, the flat voice that had been so not-Jake—seemed so foreign that she had thought for a moment that someone else was on the line with her. She had felt anger that they would try and trick her, make her think this stranger was her husband, when Jake must obviously be dead, just like his best friend. But then something he had said—she couldn't really remember what now—had shocked her into the realization that the voice on the other end of the line really was her husband.

When he'd told her he wasn't coming home, she had burst into tears.

When he got angry that she cried—yelled about how he had a job to do and that people depended on him over there—she had sat in stunned silence and listened to his tirade, a tirade from a complete stranger. He'd then lied to her—she was certain he'd lied—that he had to go, that his time was up. He'd hung up with a mumbled "I love you."

Rachel had cried almost nonstop for the next two days, until the call where he told her he was "safe" back at his FOB. In those two days she had shifted from hurt to worry again. It was obvious that Jake was in pain beyond words. He had lost his best friend and at least two others, including his firefighter friend, Shawn, and she couldn't even imagine what he must be going through. She prayed that others, those with him so far away, would be able to help him in ways she clearly could not. She had brought up how God would take care of Cal and would help Jake with his grief, and was chilled when Jake said nothing. He had gotten off the phone moments later, though her watch said they should have had several minutes left.

"Amen," the somber group around her said in unison, and Rachel realized that the service was over. She opened her eyes, surprised to see that the coffin was gone—that it had been lowered into the ground while she obsessed about her own husband, who was struggling but was at least alive. Her throat tightened at the thought that Caleb was really gone.

She had no choice but to stay with Kelly while they piled dirt on top of her husband. She wanted to run away, but what kind of friend would she be then? So, she stood quietly off to the side and watched Kelly cry and say goodbye to Caleb.

The reception—at the social hall at Foundations Family Church, because Kelly said she could not bear to have everyone in their house, talking about Caleb being gone—was a blur. There were lots of folks in military uniforms—most of whom were total strangers, and only a couple of whom looked vaguely familiar—and an unbelievable number of people from church. To Rachel, it seemed like maybe the whole church had turned out, and she prayed that would give some comfort to Kelly and to Caleb's parents. She stayed close to Kelly but said very little to anyone, and the two hours sped by.

"Can we go to your hill?"

Rachel looked up, jarred from her thoughts about Jake. Her best friend's blue eyes were dry, for perhaps the first time in a week, but still bloodshot and puffy. She clutched the remnants of a tissue in her hands. Rachel thought how Kelly, still a drop-dead-gorgeous blonde, looked years older than she had a week ago.

"To the tree?" Rachel asked, confused. "At my parents' house?"

Kelly nodded. "I know we have to go to Cal's parents', but can I ride with you? We could stop there for a little while, maybe. I just need to get away from all of these people." She whispered the last part like she was confessing to some crime.

"Of course, sweetie," Rachel answered and took both of Kelly's hands in her own, sopping wet tissue and all. The thought of going to her "private church" gave her a chill, and the face of the scarlet-sweatshirt-clad messenger from her dream popped into her head.

Kelly laid her head back and closed her eyes during the drive, and Rachel ran away from her thoughts of Jake and dreams of dead soldiers as best she could.

"I remember when I first met Caleb," Kelly said softly. Rachel glanced over and saw Kelly's eyes were still closed. "I wasn't really looking for anyone, you know?" Kelly continued. "I was young and so new in my faith. I had dated a lot in high school—just silly dating stuff, nothing serious. I thought I was in love with Brad, and did some things—made some mistakes—that I was later ashamed of. It didn't seem like anything terrible—I really did think I was in love with him—but later, when I started to learn more, I felt terrible. Then I met Cal."

There was a long silence, and Rachel felt she should say something, but she had no idea what to add to Kelly's reminiscence of meeting her husband, not even four hours in the ground yet. She was just about to ask God to help her know what to say, when Kelly continued.

"I was so nervous," she said and opened her eyes, staring out the window at the passing houses. "I felt like I had let God down with Brad—like I had failed some test or something—and then there was this new guy who was like, wow!" She smiled over at Rachel. "And he was hot too, let me tell you." Kelly leaned her head back again. "I mean, I was so attracted to him—sexually attracted to him—that it scared the hell out of me. I told him no the first three times he asked me out."

"I didn't know that," Rachel said.

"When we finally went out, all he talked about was his faith. He had been a leader in the Fellowship of Christian Athletes and he loved that group. The more he talked about his church, and the FCA, and God—it was like the hotter it made me. I started to get all nervous and worried I might fail again, and I remember thinking I should cut the evening short—we were at dinner at this little Italian place near campus—and I quietly asked God to help me know what to do." She looked over again with another small smile. "That was new for me then—asking God stuff like that."

There was another uncomfortable silence and Rachel squeezed her friend's leg. Kelly grabbed her hand and held it.

"So, Cal took my hand right at that moment. I looked up and he just looked back at me with that goofy grin he has, you know?" Rachel nodded. Kelly stared out the window again but held her hand more tightly. "I looked in his eyes, all uncomfortable, and there was something—I can't explain it, really. He didn't say anything, but as I looked at him, I just knew."

Rachel felt Kelly's eyes on her and glanced over. Her friend smiled sadly.

"I knew God had chosen him for me—that he was the one God wanted me to share my life with. Later—like much later, after we were already engaged and everything—he brought that up, that same moment, and told me that he was smiling because he knew God had chosen me for him."

Kelly let go of Rachel's hand and wiped her cheeks with her palms.

"And now he's gone and I don't understand what God wants me to do."

Rachel was crying hard enough now to blur her vision, and she thought about pulling off to the side of the road. Then her best friend let out a chuckle.

"We waited, you know—until we were married. Damn, that was hard, but we did it, and I have never been more glad about anything."

Rachel started to say something, but suspected that Kelly might not even be aware anymore that she was there.

"I miss him so much," Kelly said, "and I just don't understand God's plan."

A few minutes later Rachel pulled into her parents' driveway and then drove right across the backyard and stopped Jake's pickup truck at the base of the hill. She turned to say something to Kelly, but her friend was already halfway out of the truck.

They held hands as they climbed the hill. The air was cool—a final goodbye from winter after a warmer-than-usual several weeks of early spring—and Rachel tried to decide whether it was the chilly air or a chill from her dream that made her shiver. She had not been here since the nightmare, but then, a lot had happened in that time. At the top of the hill, Kelly turned and hugged her, choking back another sob. Her best friend let out a long, trembling sigh and then pulled back to face her.

"I just don't want to cry anymore," she said. "At least, not today." The crooked smile was the first Rachel had seen since the news.

Kelly sat down and leaned against the large oak, her knees pulled to her chest and arms wrapped around her knees. "I love it here," she said.

Rachel nodded and sat down beside her, not sure what to say. She looked nervously in the direction of the trail that led to the woods, but no blue-jeans-clad angel materialized. She knew why she shivered that time. Rachel fidgeted with the hem of her dress.

"I love it here too. I came here, you know—that night. The night I gave my life to God, thanks to you."

Kelly smiled and shook her head. "God used me to reach you, Rachel. The journey was yours."

Rachel nodded. She had never needed God more, but for some reason—even here, in her private church—she couldn't find the words to talk to Him. She startled a little when Kelly took her hand. She looked over and saw her friend bow her head.

"Lord, be with us in our sorrow," Kelly began. "Please take care of Caleb and tell him how much I love him and miss him. We know You are with him there and with us, in our hearts, here as we struggle to find meaning, which we probably can never understand. God, please be with Jake and Caleb's other friends in harm's way." Rachel's throat tightened with shame. Even in her deepest sorrow, Kelly prayed for Jake.

Rachel started crying.

Forgive me, Lord. Please forgive me.

Even in the simple prayer, though, she began to feel God's presence. As she repeated the prayer, over and over, she vowed to come here—to her special place with God—again, knowing she would feel something other than loss and fear.

CHAPTER 18

Jake had been back at FOB Douglas for several weeks but had yet to go outside the wire. Truth was, there had been little action for anyone, despite the promises that an early spring "fighting season" should be heating things up in the coming weeks. They had conducted two show-of-force patrols in villages farther afield, plus one in the village where *it* had happened. At the last minute, someone in the head shed wisely passed that patrol to another platoon, but second platoon was mysteriously passed over for both the other patrols as well. Jake had an almost uncontrollable urge to go out on a mission. Not just to go out, but to engage the enemy. He wanted, from some dark and unfamiliar part of his soul, to kill the sick bastards who talked young boys into blowing themselves up, who'd killed Cal and Jake's other friends. He more than wanted it—he needed it in some deep, primitive part of his heart.

On his first morning "home," they had held the ceremony. Jake had been terrified to attend—fearful that he would completely fall apart. The fear had grown to panic by the time the entire FOB had assembled in front of the four pairs of empty boots lined up in front of upside-down rifles with helmets on top—all that was left of Cal, Shawn, Brandon, and a kid named Mike Thomas. It turned out that he was from the helicopter crew—a door gunner who'd thought it would be cool to go on patrol with his infantry colleagues and now had been shipped home ahead of his boots and rifle.

Jake needn't have worried. Instead of grief he felt nothing at first, followed by burning anger. He focused his anger on the enemy, but in his heart he knew there was someone else to blame. His eyes were dry, though he still found it impossible to hold the gazes of the dozens of young men who slapped him on the back or shoulder after they had been dismissed, each with mumbled words meant to comfort. Jake lingered a few moments in front of the makeshift memorial. He looked around to be certain no one was watching, then took the dog tags from where they hung from the butt of Cal's rifle. He closed his eyes, the metal tags cool in his clenched fist, and then slipped them quietly over his head and stuffed them into his shirt beside his own.

A hand on his back made him spin around.

"Sorry," the thin man beside him said. Jake didn't recognize him. "I'm Major Jackson," the grey-eyed man said softly. "I'm the chaplain from regiment."

"What do you want?" Jake asked, his voice sharper than he intended. Something about this soft-looking man just really pissed him off.

"I know that you were close to these men," the chaplain said. "I know you were there, and I wondered if we might talk."

Jake shrugged the officer's hand off his shoulder.

"'These men,'" he said mockingly, "were my family. And just what the hell is there for us to talk about?"

Jackson nodded gently. "I know it's hard, Sergeant," the chaplain said. "It can be difficult to find God in all of this tragedy."

"Haven't you heard, Major?" Jake said and pushed past the man, his fists balled up at his sides. "God isn't here."

That had been nearly a month ago, and the mundane routine of the FOB had done little to change his anger. He needed to go *out*.

Jake avoided the area in the back of the tiny outpost—the berm where he had sat so many evenings with Cal and read the Bible and prayed. He also avoided even touching the backpack they had stuffed the Bible into each night. The raging part of him wanted to toss the whole damn thing into the large bin set aside for the burn pit, but he couldn't quite bring himself to do it. It wasn't because of any feeling of reverence for the Book, which had let him down, it was just that it felt like he would be throwing away a part of Cal, something he could never do.

Jake stretched his back as he leaned against the wall around the edge of the roof of their hut. He didn't care if someone saw him up here—he felt he had earned the right to not be screwed with for minor infractions of largely meaningless rules for at least another few days—but he was getting stiff from sitting on the hard concrete. He rose slowly and then re-slung his rifle before shuffling down the narrow stairway.

"Hey, dude."

Jake nodded at Aaron, formerly of first platoon, but for now assigned to second platoon, first squad, to "fill out" the platoon after the loss. Jake had liked Aaron once, back when he liked anyone.

"Wanna get some chow?" Aaron asked.

Jake hesitated. Hunger gnawed at his belly, but he had not sat to eat with anyone since he had been back. The first few days he had eaten MREs in his tiny room, rather than be around people in the chow hall.

"Sure," he relented.

He walked beside Aaron, who chatted away about some game for his PlayStation Vita that his friend had sent from home. Jake tried to nod at the right times, but had no idea if he succeeded. They grabbed their paper trays as they entered the chow hall, and moments later they sat at the end of a long table that was empty except for two guys in khaki-colored flight suits who belonged to the two combat helicopters that had sat on their tiny tarmac for the last week. They now had their own dedicated air assets apparently, ahead of the fighting season that Jake wished would kick off soon.

He realized that Aaron was looking at him expectantly.

"Huh?" he mumbled.

"I said, did you hear we may go out tomorrow? My buddy works over in admin with the head shed and he heard we were supporting some big thing in that town where them spec ops guys did that hit. Remember that?"

Jake nodded with some irritation. "Yeah, yeah. I remember. So, what does your buddy say we're doing? Is it another special operations thing?"

That sounded good to Jake. If the operators were going in, then there would for sure be some bad guy assholes to shoot. He felt his heart pound in his temple, but there was no fear in his chest this time.

"I dunno," Aaron said. "I asked that too, but he didn't know nothing."

"Well, let's go find out after we eat, 'kay?" Jake said. Suddenly, being around Aaron didn't seem so bad.

"You okay, Sergeant?"

At the hand on his shoulder, Jake looked up. The Major—Major Bowman, Jake remembered, a senior officer from the command element—smiled down at him.

"Yes, sir," Jake answered. "All squared away. Hey, did you hear anything about second platoon going out?"

Aaron's eyes widened at the inappropriate question.

The Major pursed his lips and nodded. "I might have heard something," he said. "I hear you're squad leader now. You all set for that?"

"Yes, sir," Jake answered. "One hundred percent. First squad is your go-to guys, sir."

The Major nodded again. He started to move away toward another table and then paused.

"You calling home, Sergeant? You got a wife back home, right?"

"Yes, sir, I do," Jake answered and glanced at his watch. Shit, he was going to be late for his call to Rachel if he didn't hurry. How the hell did he forget?

"Stay in touch with her, son," Major Bowman said. "Sometimes it's a lot tougher being the one back home."

Jake didn't see any way that was possible, but he nodded anyway. He turned to Aaron as the Major moved toward a table of other officers in the back of the wooden hut.

"Hey, Aaron," he said and piled his trash on his paper tray. "I gotta make a quick call home, but how about trying to find your buddy and get us more gouge? I'll meet you back by my hut?"

"Sure," his new squadmate said, but Jake could tell he wasn't thrilled. He left the younger soldier to finish his meal and hustled off to dump his trash. He would check in with Rachel real quick and then see if he could find out more about a possible mission tomorrow.

CHAPTER 19

Sleep remained elusive, as it often did lately. Jake felt frustration because he was tired, and relief because with sleep came dreams. He knew he would have the bunk room to himself for only a short time—there were two replacements coming to fill the gap left by his three missing friends, and they would certainly bunk here—so he wanted almost desperately to rest while he could. Pete had headed home right from the hospital in Kandahar, and Jake wondered if he had been on the same plane with Cal and Shawn. He hoped so, for some reason. Jake slept now in the top bunk, because when the replacements arrived he knew he wouldn't be able to bear the thought of someone else sleeping in Cal's rack.

He closed his eyes tightly, although the nightmares, when they came, were no worse than the images that flashed on the dark ceiling above him. Over and over he saw the boy in the long grey shirt, and over and over he saw bits of Cal spattered on his gear and the wall beside them. And that damn thumb. Of all the horrible things that day, why the hell could he not shake the image of the thumb?

Jake drifted slowly away from the mind's eye video screen that he had created on the ceiling. Exhaustion collapsed on him like a heavy, warm blanket, and for a while he slept a deep and dreamless sleep.

For a while.

Jake found himself lying on a rooftop, shivering against the cold and not sure how he had fallen asleep. Part of him knew it was a dream, so he didn't worry too much that he had no idea where he was. He heard voices beyond the roof—voices in English, though for some reason he couldn't understand what they were saying. He pulled himself up by the short wall along the roof and peered down.

Pete stood behind another soldier and was screaming at him to shoot, but the soldier just stood there like a dumbass. In front of them, Cal was moving toward Shawn, and a boy walked slowly, dream-like, toward them. He was naked, the grey man dress gone, so that Jake could see the row after row of explosives connected with yellow wires around his chest. From the roof, Jake pulled his rifle up and sighted in, lining the boy's head up in the red dot. He realized now that the dumbass soldier— the one that just stood there while Pete screamed at him—was him. That Jake—the dream Jake—was smiling like an idiot, completely unaware of what was going on.

Jake pulled the trigger.

There was a click, but nothing else. Panicked now, Jake pulled the trigger again and again, each pull followed by the same dull click of an empty weapon. He scrambled to his feet and screamed.

"Cal!"

The explosion should have blown him off his feet, but instead he felt the heat flash past him. When the smoke cleared, he saw nothing but a hole filled with blood. It bubbled like a pot of boiling water, crimson steam rising toward him and obscuring his view. He choked on the thick fumes and waved a hand in front of his face, desperate to see the scene below. As the reddish blood-smoke cleared, he saw the dream Jake standing beside the deep pit and scratching his chin, confused. The dumbass still had his weapon slung low on his hip. Behind dream Jake, Pete lay on his back, staring absently at the sky.

As the blood boiled off, Jake saw what dream Jake stared at in the pit. There was something moving there, and at first Jake felt the thrill of hope that Cal was somehow, impossibly, alive. But as the blood boiled away, he saw that the hole was full of insects, or maybe some sort of lizards. Jake placed both hands on the ledge and leaned forward, peering directly down into the hole.

When he saw the pit was full of squirming, bloody thumbs—alive and crawling over one another—he and dream Jake screamed in unison.

Jake sat bolt upright and clawed at his blankets, but they weren't there. Instead he found himself lying in wet grass, and in a panic, scrambled to his feet. Had he sleepwalked somehow? Might he even be outside the wire?

As his eyes adjusted to the dark, Jake realized that the place was familiar, and in the silvery moonlight he saw the outline of the thick tree just a few feet away. He reached out a shaking hand and touched the rough bark.

I'm still dreaming.

"Are you?"

Jake spun around on a heel and backed away from the voice, his back scraping against the rough tree hard enough to hurt through his green Army T-shirt. There was a young man beside him. The tall grass, wet with dew, shimmered in the moonlight, lighting a wide path down the hill to Rachel's parents' house.

Definitely still dreaming.

Jake realized he was looking at the stranger's thumbs and shook his head, his mouth making a loud *tsk* sound.

"I'm Luke," the young man said. Jake found his voice strangely soothing. The man was clean-cut, but his dark hair was way too long to be Army. He leaned on his thick walking stick and smiled at Jake, the crimson-red hood from his sweatshirt bunched up around his neck.

"Hi, Luke," Jake said, unsure what else to do. He felt peaceful, but there was still an anxious rage just beneath the surface.

"How are you holding up, Jacob?" Luke asked.

Jake wasn't sure when they'd moved, but now they sat beside each other, both leaning back against the big oak.

"I'm angry," Jake said simply.

"I know, Jacob," Luke said and looked sad. "I want you to know that Caleb is safe. He is at peace."

Jake felt the rage bubble to the surface.

"Well, that's just awesome," he said sharply. "But you know what? I'm not at peace. Just who the hell are you, anyway, and why are we here?"

"I'm a messenger," Luke said, and now he stood above Jake, leaning on his walking stick and smiling. "You have to stay on your path, Jacob. The way has become difficult and the other paths seem easier, but only your true path takes you anywhere you'll want to be. Stay on your journey."

As Jake watched, Luke began to shimmer and then the air around him seemed to shimmer as well.

"Your journey has only begun, Jacob, but you have many great things ahead of you. You are tested by these days, but for you and Rachel there is much work ahead. And much joy."

The whole world then seemed to shimmer. It dissolved away, and the cool night air became the stuffy room where he slept. He realized he was propped against the wall in Cal's bunk.

Stay on the path, Jacob.

Jake leaned forward and the tightness in his chest turned to sobs. He began rocking back and forth, the thin metal bunk bed chirping out a *creak, creak* in cadence to his sobbing.

He thought for a moment about the Bible in the backpack by the foot of the bed—Cal's backpack—but he pushed the thought from his head as quickly as it came, another familiar voice whispering in his ear:

Where did that path get you, Jake? Where the hell did it get Cal? All that Bible study and all that prayer and here you are alone, crying in the dark, ten thousand miles from home. Your best friend is rotting in a hole back in the States. Where the hell is God in all of that, Jake?

Jake listened to the voice and let his anger simmer in his stomach. The tears dried on his cheeks as he lay on his back and stared coldly at the ceiling above him.

There are lots of things you can do to feel better.

He had tried it Cal's way, and look where that got him. No, what would make him feel better was going out tomorrow. Going out and finding vengeance.

CHAPTER 20

Anger and an overwhelming need for reckoning had so completely replaced fear for Jake that on the short, bumpy helo ride into the target he felt nothing except a thrilling anticipation. It was like the long drive to Disney World when he was a kid. He checked his gear on the trip in, not out of insecurity or concern about getting hurt, but from a desire to be prepared if his chance to mete out payback presented itself.

Jake did feel some butterflies about being squad leader. He sure as hell didn't want to mess that up. He figured he had enough blue blood on his hands, and he wanted to get his guys back safely beyond anything else. But finding some Taliban or Al Qaeda shitheads was, for sure, a close second.

After the group huddle with their platoon leader, Jake gathered up his guys—Aaron and another guy from first platoon, still on loan, and Terry from third squad.

"All right, guys," he said, trying to sound more confident than he suddenly felt. "Show of force, but you know there's an op going on bigger than that, so let's not be the dudes that jack that up. You heard First Sar'n. I know this is my first time as squad leader, but we all know what to do, so let's just do it. Two by two on the street and cover each other, 'kay?"

His three guys nodded and they headed toward the east side of the small, dirty village. The mission to grab some big-deal HVTs was going to happen on the road out of the other side of the village, and was expected to go down roughly thirty minutes from now. His squad would only get involved if the mission failed, and he figured that was probably unlikely, but you never knew. Jake and his guys would be just a half block away by then and ready to rock if any bad guys squirted past the operators and tried to hide in the village. Jake guessed that the real mission was to create enough of a presence that someone would warn the HVT not to come there, making it easier to pick him up outside of the village, where there was nothing but dirt and rocks and very few places to hide.

A block in, a group of four or five kids laughed and ran toward them. Kids outside and approaching them was a good sign, but the oldest boy—maybe nine or ten, he thought—wore a grey man dress that was disturbingly familiar. Unlike the kid that had killed his friends, this boy laughed and smiled, but Jake couldn't keep his heart from pounding in his chest. He pulled his rifle up and sighted down the iron sights at the kid, who stopped and stared back, the color draining from his face and his arms frozen at his sides. Jake's mind screamed at him to lower his weapon—the boy was scared and clearly no threat, his shirt loose around his thin frame—but his arms and hands ignored him. His right hand squeezed tighter on the grip of his M4, and his index finger slipped inside the trigger guard. Then suddenly his nerves responded to the frantic signals coming to them from his brain and he lowered his rifle at the same time his finger slipped off the trigger. With his left hand, he waved the kid away impatiently, and the boy grabbed two smaller children by their hands and hustled them toward a low, brown house, watching Jake over his shoulder. The little girl waved and smiled, and Jake looked down at the ground, his head shaking and his hands trembling.

"See something?" Aaron asked uncertainly.

Jake swallowed hard and tried to make his voice sound steady.

"Nah," he answered. "Thought I saw movement on the roof," he added, feeling he needed to somehow explain engaging the now-terrified kid. "Just shadows, I guess."

His three squadmates nodded. If they thought he had been inappropriate, their faces concealed it well. He moved with Terry to the right side of the street and scanned over and behind Aaron and his partner.

The rest of the walk to the center of the village was quiet, and Jake and his team arrived a few minutes earlier than planned, so he had them spread out in the small courtyard and maintain a loose perimeter while they waited for the other three groups to arrive. Jake tapped the trigger guard nervously with his shooting finger, the similarity to the last minutes of his final mission with Cal smothering him. He looked again and again in the direction the boy would be coming from—if it was that day, or if they were even in the same friggin' village, which they were not.

"Ten minutes to kickoff," a voice crackled in his earpiece. "Coming up on the center of town."

Jake glanced to his right and saw TC and his team come around a building with a missing front door and no glass left in any windows. Jake wondered why the First Sergeant now felt more like "TC" to him than "First Sergeant Morrow"—perhaps because he was a squad leader? Or maybe he just didn't care about protocol anymore. Jake nodded, and TC nodded back and gave him a thumbs-up. The other team spread out and filled the gaps in the loose perimeter Jake had set up, and then TC walked over to him, wiping sweat from beneath his helmet with the back of his hand.

"Quiet?" he asked, and Jake nodded. "Too quiet?"

Jake thought for a moment and then shrugged. They had seen the kids coming in, but this side of the village was a ghost town. He wondered if that was because word got around the locals that an American soldier had pointed his gun at a kid instead of handing out chocolate.

"We saw a few kids coming in," Jake said.

TC nodded, apparently satisfied, and then looked at his watch.

"Let's get everyone in position on the exfil side. Keep your two-by-two until we know the Operators have mopped up, just in case."

"'Kay," Jake said, hoping he sounded more in control than he felt. Jake had no problem getting shot at, and no longer worried about getting hurt or not making it home—not since Cal and all—but a combination of worry that he might get someone else hurt blended weirdly with an almost desperate need to shoot a bad guy.

He signaled his guys to rally, and they took the left street out of the courtyard while TC and his guys took the right. The other two teams would fan out on the infil side of the courtyard.

Jake scanned the rooftops and windows and glanced at his watch. Just a couple minutes to go, he figured. Halfway down the last block, he took a knee and held a fist over his head. Aaron stepped back against the wall behind them and started a nervous scan, while Terry and his partner did the same on the other side of the street.

A low, far-off *pop* made Jake jump, though he should have been expecting it. It didn't exactly sound like a gunshot, and he wondered if it was the sound of explosives used to stop the bad guys in their vehicles on the road. Whatever the sound, he decided it meant that the Special Operators were now hitting their targets.

"Kickoff." TC's voice crackled in his earpiece, confirming his feeling.

"They're goin'," Jake said to Aaron, stating the rather obvious.

Aaron nodded and they moved together down the street. Jake tightened his grip on his M4 at a second, duller pop that must definitely be the Special Forces shooters. Seconds later he heard the distinct sound of small-arms fire in the distance.

Guess they're not coming along peacefully.

He was turning his head to share the thought with Aaron, when a door burst open to his right at the same time he heard men shouting. Jake spun, raising his rifle as he did.

Two men, both with AK-47s with long, curved magazines slung almost casually over their shoulders, jogged through the door and then stopped, frozen. They stared at the American soldiers for what seemed like forever, but Jake guessed was less than a second. Then the man on the right slowly and deliberately grabbed his rifle. Jake wondered if he intended to drop the weapon in surrender, but then the familiar voice whispered in his ear and he didn't care.

Vengeance—for Cal.

A cold fist squeezed Jake's chest and it felt good in a way that was all wrong. He sighted in on the man on the left, and just as the man's eyes widened, Jake squeezed twice. The first bullet tore through the man's throat, spinning him to his right, and the second blasted through his left temple, exploding out the other side of his head. Just as the body crumpled into the dirt, the man beside him seemed to realize that surrender was not an option and tried desperately to pull his weapon around.

Jake's third bullet tore through the middle of the second fighter's face and pushed him off his feet backward, like something from an action movie.

A faraway voice screamed inside Jake's head, but it was drowned out by the icy voice that whispered in his ear.

Good. An eye for an eye. For Cal and the others.

Aaron had moved to his left and was peering cautiously inside the doorway the men had come through. Jake realized he had best move out of any potential line of fire himself just as TC's voice crackled in his earpiece.

"First squad, is that you? What's going on?"

Jake squeezed his transmit button on his vest, feeling two parts detached and one part satisfied.

"First squad has enemy contact," he said in a calm, even voice. "We got a house to clear, one half block in from the edge of town and the rally point. We have two enemy KIA and an unknown number in the house."

"Copy," TC said, his voice full of relief. Jake listened to him bark orders to the other teams to move to their position.

"What the hell?" Aaron said, and he felt his teammate's eyes on his back. "Dude, that was crazy. You were like *Call of Duty* or some shit."

Jake looked down at the two dead men, both clearly Al Qaeda types from the kits and dress. They sure as hell weren't headed out to do some good deed. Jake figured they were on their way to bail out their buddies at the Special Forces target. He looked at the bodies and felt a cold smile on his face.

Terrorists, three; Jake, two.

A quiet hour later, Jake leaned his head back against the nylon mesh behind his bench seat in the CH-46 helicopter and closed his eyes. The desperate voice—his voice, he felt certain—had grown more distant, and he found the insistent pleas that he re-examine what had happened easier to ignore. The rest of the house had been empty, though they had taken a sizable cache of weapons and a few cell phones out of the back rooms. Some guys in nondescript, unmarked BDUs, with long hair and beards but American flags on their kits, had taken the phones and weapons away with them in a strange-looking vehicle that appeared more like a dune buggy than a military assault vehicle. They had answered questions about the success of their raid with vague mutterings, which sounded like they had probably gotten whatever or whoever they were looking for. The Operators didn't volunteer any more information.

And Jake didn't care. He felt even better than he'd imagined now that he'd evened the score a bit. TC had listened to his brief, about how the armed terrorists had burst out of the house and he had shot them, without questions. If Aaron thought he had done anything wrong, he kept it to himself.

Jake realized he didn't care about that either. It felt good to be in the fight in a personal way. He thought that, maybe, the hatred (and guilt, he reminded himself) that he let drive him had now made him a real soldier for the first time in his life. A strange and sad voice whispered urgently that he *stay on his path*, whatever the hell that meant, but he ignored it.

He chuckled for a moment as he wondered if having voices competing for his attention meant he was losing his mind.

Whatever.

He felt good for the first time in weeks.

CHAPTER 21

Rachel didn't have the emotional strength to wipe away the tears that ran down her cheeks and dripped off her chin into her lap. She set her phone down gently on the kitchen table beside her now-cold coffee and watched the bright screen darken and then turn black. It felt as if Jake was fading away just like that—not gone, just turning dark and distant—and she feared he too would blink away. And she had no idea how to stop it.

Rachel reached for her Bible but found she didn't have the energy to open it and flip through the well-worn pages. She let her hand rest on the cover, then rested her forehead on her other hand and began to sob.

Please, God. Please help him. Help me to know what to do to be there for him. God, whatever dark place he's gone to, I ask that you please be with him and bring him home to me.

She had no strength to ask anything else of God right now, and so she pulled her Bible to her chest and laid her head down on the table while she waited for her breathing to slow and the tears to stop.

She didn't know the Jake who'd called her just now—always careful to steer the conversation to simple questions about her day. The feeling of talking to a stranger unsettled her in a way she doubted she could explain to anyone. It wasn't that she expected him to be "normal," whatever that meant. They had been told in the predeployment groups she'd attended with other wives that their husbands would at times sound different, and she was okay with that. But this was such a change from a month ago— from before the loss of Caleb and Jake's other friends—and, it seemed, even a change from a week ago. She had gotten used to the awkward quiet and the lack of details about his days, but she would still hear, now and again, a glimpse of her husband as he rushed through the call.

But this...

The man on the phone with her had been—*cold*. Not just cold to her, like a marital thing, but coldhearted. Tears filled her eyes again and squeezed between her closed lids onto her Bible. She hated to think of him that way. Jake had always been one of the warmest, kindest people she knew. She had expected that the experience of war, the things he would see and do over there, would change him—maybe even harden him—but not like this.

Rachel sat back up and smoothed her hair out of her face. Then she grabbed a napkin from the table and made a little *tsk* sound as she wiped the snot from her nose.

Maybe she should call someone at the command? She had not attended the spouse support meetings and get-togethers once the deployment had gotten underway, because she'd felt that she had all the support she needed at Foundations and with Kelly. Rachel and Kelly had talked about going to more events, Kelly pointing out that it was a great opportunity to *give* support if they felt they didn't need it for themselves. She had said that God might find an opportunity there for them to help someone in need. Shortly after that conversation, Caleb had been killed and Jake had drifted away. Maybe they should go together on—what was it?—Wednesday night, she thought. Of course, that thought was immediately trumped by guilt at how little support she had given Kelly. She talked to her every few days, but nothing like the daily time together they had once shared. She thought about her dream angel telling her she would be needed by Kelly, and her throat tightened. She had let her best friend down, she supposed, but she was barely holding on herself. How could she possibly help Kelly?

Rachel wondered again if perhaps she should call and tell the command that she was worried about her husband. Might that get him in some kind of trouble? She thought it would for sure make him mad—especially the way he was now—if he were to find out. But what if he was really in trouble and they could help him?

Rachel picked up her phone and scrolled through her contact list. Her finger paused over the Send button and she saw it was shaking. She swallowed hard and closed her eyes.

What should I do, Lord? Please help me know.

She scrolled back up in her contact list and chose a number. She felt her pulse slow and a calm came over her.

"Foundations Family Church—Pastor Craig's office. This is Maggie. How can I help you?"

Rachel hesitated. How could they help her? Great question.

"I think I need to see Pastor Craig," she said with a trembling voice. "As soon as possible, if he can work me in."

Rachel waited as Craig's secretary put her on hold, presumably to check with Craig about a last-minute appointment.

Rachel thought of Kelly and Caleb. She thought of Jake and ached for her life before all of this.

Then she thought, for some reason, about the tree behind her parents' house, and of Luke and the message she had received in her dream.

She decided to call Kelly right after this to check on her.

CHAPTER 22

Jake stared at the computer screen, the corners and edges full of dust and dirt, and tapped his shooting finger nervously on the top of the mouse. Strange that an email in his inbox should make him uncomfortable, but the *Craig FFC* in the sender line filled him with more anxiety than an empty street on a show-of-force patrol. Jake moved the little arrow and clicked to highlight the message, then let the arrow hover a moment over the Delete button. What could Pastor Craig offer him at this point? One more outreach of sympathy that did nothing but take him back to the worst day of his life? Words of encouragement and a quote from an out-dated book, faith in which hadn't done anything to keep Cal alive?

The burning anger felt out of place, like it was staged or misplaced, or more like it had been given to him as baggage to carry by someone else.

What a bizarre thought.

Jake sighed. Craig and Rachel's friends at Foundations might not have done much for him, but they were a comfort that was keeping his wife afloat, something he contributed almost nothing to these days. When he got home, when he left this insane nightmare behind him in this foreign place, he and Rachel would settle back into their marriage, he was sure. There wasn't much he could do about it until then. But in the meantime, the church people were her lifeline. That alone should be enough reason to read Pastor Craig's email.

Jake sighed again and double-clicked on Craig's name.

He scanned the email, as if dancing around the edges of it instead of leaping in would somehow isolate him from whatever it was he was afraid of in Pastor Craig's words—like he could sort of sneak up on the message, take just what he wanted, and slip away before it got a hold of him.

What the hell is there to be afraid of?

Another bizarre thought.

He closed his eyes and read the email:

Jake,

I hope this finds you well and safe. I want to tell you that Rachel is well cared for, and that all of us here at Foundations Family Church are looking after her and helping her through this difficult time of separation. I can only imagine what it is you are going through over there, but you are always in the prayers of our entire congregation. I'm here for you, Jake, as a friend as well as a pastor. Whatever you need, we are here. Please know, in your heart (a place I know you have a hard time looking), that God has a tremendous plan for you and your life. Lean on Him and seek His shelter. Stay on the path, and God will restore and enrich your life.

In Christ,

Craig

PS—Romans 8!

Jake stared at the screen a long moment before clicking Delete and watching the message disappear. A part of him wanted to reply, but just what the hell would he say? He knew that the pastor meant well, but Jake found little comfort in the words, other than those about Rachel being cared for. There was something familiar about Romans eight that seemed important in a far-off sort of way, but Jake chased the thought away. Something Cal had said, probably, and that was somewhere he had no desire to go.

Stay on the path.

That line sent a cool shudder up his neck. A short clip from his dream flashed in his mind and Jake closed his eyes so tightly that he saw stars for a moment.

He closed his email and slid his chair back from the plywood desk with a loud creak. He brushed away an unexpected tear with some annoyance. Jake thought maybe it was just the way the message had made him think of Cal. He looked at his watch and then grabbed his rifle and his small backpack. He was supposed to meet TC in only five minutes.

If he could just get through the next few months, he would be home and his life would be back to normal. There would always be a void where Cal belonged, but Jake's marriage and his life could plod on down the path.

If he took some more bad guys off the planet—revenge for his dead friends—in the time before he left, then that would settle some of his debt and make his life come back together all the more easily.

He headed toward the large hut TC shared with several other senior NCOs, right beside the COC where all the bigwigs planned their missions. The First Sergeant came out of the thin wooden door just as Jake reached for the handle.

"Oh, hey, Jake," TC said, apparently surprised to see him.

"Hey, First Sar'n," Jake said. "Am I early?"

"You're right on time," TC said. He took Jake by the arm and steered him away from the door. "Let's just go for a little stroll, okay?"

Jake suddenly realized that he should, perhaps, have spent a few minutes getting nervous about this meeting. Just what the hell did TC want anyway? It was rare that being called to see your senior enlisted leader was the result of something good. He realized he had been too caught up in his own wallowing to even wonder what TC wanted.

He followed slightly behind the First Sergeant as they walked for a few moments in silence. Jake saw they were headed toward the back of the camp, near the berm where he and Cal had spent every evening for a couple of months, and he felt a band-like tightness in his chest. TC turned toward him and smiled, but the grin seemed forced.

"First off, Jake—and most importantly—you're doing a tremendous job as squad leader."

Jake felt his shoulders sag in relief—just a pep talk.

"Thanks, First Sar'n," he said. "Doin' my best."

TC nodded, and as they reached the berm nestled between the two plywood guard towers, TC stopped and turned to face him.

"I know, Jake. The guys like going out with you. They trust you. In the next day or so, we'll finalize all our shuffling around of replacements and it'll get easier. You'll have the same team mostly, and you guys can get into a flow." TC grinned and shook his head. "My challenge is picking your squad. Everyone wants to be on your team. You've gotten the reputation as quite the badass. Who would have thought, right?"

Jake shrugged uncomfortably and resisted the urge to look down. What should he say to that? He didn't feel like a badass at all. He felt like someone trying to make up for a terrible mistake.

TC nodded like he somehow understood, then continued.

"So here's the thing, Jake," he said. "I think you need to maybe reel it in a little. Being a badass is one thing, but going off the rails is another."

Jake felt his face flush.

"I'm not—"

TC held up a hand. "This is off the record, Jake. Just between you and me—two Army buddies." Jake closed his mouth. "The guys you zapped in that village were hardcore terrorists. No one cares that you smoked them, and they for sure were part of the group the SOF guys were hitting." TC put an arm around Jake's shoulders and started a slow stroll again toward the berm, the last place in the world Jake wanted to be. "I know you're still struggling with what happened to Cal and the others and I get that you need some payback. But I need you to be professional and disciplined out there."

"You said that it was a clean shoot," Jake said, stopping so that TC had to turn toward him again.

TC pursed his lips and nodded. "I actually didn't say that, but we'll just let that conversation go," the First Sergeant said. "What I'm trying to tell you is that we're not at war with the people of Afghanistan, Jake. Those Taliban assholes are the bad guys, and I'm glad you smoked them. But I need you to be a disciplined, professional soldier so that you don't wind up shooting the wrong people next time. Every house in Helmand has an AK-47, so you need more evidence than that. You need to know for sure you're shooting the right people. Do you understand what I'm saying?"

Jake nodded and looked at his feet. He was angry—again—but didn't know why.

TC sighed. "This is not an official counseling, Jake. Like I said—two Army buddies just shooting the shit, okay?" Jake nodded again. "You're a helluva soldier, but you're also a good guy. Please don't let this place— and the bad things that happened here—change that." TC looked off over Jake's shoulder, but Jake sensed that what he was looking for was both miles and years away. "If you do things here that are in conflict with who you are and what you believe, it's a tough journey back—sometimes an impossible journey."

Jake squeezed his eyes shut to clear them and then looked up into the First Sergeant's face.

"Thank you, First Sar'n," he said, more formally than he meant. He held TC's gaze until his NCO frowned and nodded.

"Okay, Jake. Let's just get through the next few months and get the rest of our guys home, okay?"

"No problem," Jake said with more conviction than he felt.

He turned and headed toward his hut, feeling TC's concerned eyes on the back of his head.

He would try and calm down. He would keep his guys safe and maintain fire-control discipline.

But he would be damned if he would stop exacting vengeance on the bad guys who'd taken his friends, when and if the opportunities presented themselves. He would hunt them down and kill as many of them as he could. Then he would head home and put all of this behind him, satisfied he had evened the score. Then he and Rachel could get back to their lives.

CHAPTER 23

Craig stared out the window behind his desk and fought off the urge, almost uncontrollable, to pull the picture of himself and Caleb—together at a beach retreat for the high school students, at which Caleb had volunteered—off the bookshelves that framed the window behind his desk. The last thing he needed was to cradle the picture pensively in his lap, something he had tried desperately to stop doing these past few weeks. The long moments alone with the picture did nothing but elevate his grief and bring back the anger he felt at the loss of the amazing young man who, in so many ways, had become like his third son. Craig had done more than mentor Cal, who had recently professed his dream to become a pastor. He had adored him. Instead Craig picked up the University of Florida game ball, signed by one of their quarterbacks, and dropped it into his lap, where it sat lifelessly.

Craig knew that he and God had a lot more to hash out. The loss of Caleb had not shaken his faith in God, but it had brought up uncomfortable questions—questions that, as a pastor, he knew he would continue to be called on to answer for his congregation. Truth was, Craig didn't have those answers. Caleb's death made no sense to him. He had thought of Romans eight, a New Testament chapter that was often his go-to chapter in his sermons about loss. He knew, academically, that Romans eight in no way promised that everything in the life of a Christian would always be good. No, he understood, in a scholarly way at least, that God, through the apostle scribe Paul, was telling them that even in tragedy God could bring good to their lives.

Craig closed his eyes and felt wetness on his cheeks.

I believe, Lord. I do. I just can't see the good here. I know the hope You're sharing with us in Romans, but I feel so damn hopeless in the face of this loss.

The phone beeped, and the sound made Craig jump.

"Rachel is here for you, Pastor Craig."

Craig sighed and pushed the intercom button on his phone.

"Thanks, Maggie," he said with more cheer than he felt. "Give me two minutes and then send her in, please."

Craig closed his eyes again. This, for him at least, seemed the hardest part of his calling. He needed to help Rachel find peace and hope in her pain. He needed to help her find a way past the grief of her loss and the fear she felt for her husband.

Somehow he had to give her things he still struggled to find for himself.

I love you, God. Please help me. I know you and I have a lot left to sort out. For now, please, Lord, help me speak the words that will comfort Rachel. Speak through me, God, and help her find the peace and hope she needs. Bless our meeting, Lord, and help me be what she needs right now.

And later, I still have so much to ask You, Lord.

In the name of Your Son, Jesus—Amen.

Craig opened his eyes and looked at the football in his lap. For some reason, it brought more tears to his eyes, which he wiped away.

He let out a slow, deep breath and tried to screw a hopeful smile onto his face. He turned again to the picture of Cal, smiling that radiant smile of enthusiastic faith. Then he looked at the pictures on his desk—of his wife, Debbie, and their two boys at various stages of maturity. So many good times, so many blessings. He settled on the pictures of the boys and their wives and his one (so far) granddaughter, taken just two months ago at the beach. He was so proud of everyone in that picture. He pushed away the insistent question of what if it had been one of them.

Craig let out a rattling breath and closed his eyes. He readied himself to pray—but nothing came to him.

Just be still and know that I am God.

He let a sad smile cross his face.

"I'm trying, Lord. I'm trying so hard."

CHAPTER 24

Rachel shifted uncomfortably in the actually quite comfortable chair. She had no real plan for what to say to Pastor Craig, who had hugged her warmly and then stepped out, ostensibly to get them both a soda. In a moment her favorite pastor would return and then he would ask what he could do for her. And just what was it that Rachel hoped he could do?

Pastor Craig was an amazing spiritual leader, but she always felt a little intimidated in his presence. His messages were always so real, and timely, and insightful. Rachel wondered what it was like to have such faith. She worked hard to give everything up to God, to let go of the illusion of control—as Pastor Craig sometimes referred to it in his sermons—and let God take the wheel. But these days, it seemed, she always failed.

So, what did she hope for today?

Perhaps it was just reaffirmation of the things she had learned these last two years. Perhaps it was just a gentle reassurance or pointing to a verse in the Bible that would give her what she needed. Maybe she just needed to talk out loud about her fears for Jake, and she sure couldn't go to her best friend with it as she normally would. How could she lean on Kelly when her friend was still overwhelmed with the loss of her own husband?

As she waited for the soda she didn't want, Rachel realized that what she really needed was direction. She wanted to know how she could help Jake from so far away. She thought about mentioning the dreams—the dreams of her imaginary angel, Luke—but decided she would feel foolish bringing that up.

Maybe when he hears how worried I am about Jake, Pastor Craig can reach out to him on his own. He would do so much better a job. He would know just what to say to help Jake find his way back to the path he had just started on. God, it's so unfair.

Rachel immediately decided that she would most definitely not talk about her feelings of anger and injustice. Craig would surely be disappointed if he saw such weakness in her.

The door creaked open and Rachel put her best "I'm strong and soldiering on" smile on her face. She looked up at Pastor Craig's smiling face and took the Diet Coke from him, committed to looking as strong as she believed she should feel.

"How can I help you today, Rachel?" Craig asked as he opened his own soda and walked around his desk to take a seat. "Are you doing okay?"

"Yes," Rachel lied to her pastor. Then she burst into tears and dropped her face into her hands, her soda falling to her feet, where it bled its bubbly contents onto Pastor Craig's rug.

CHAPTER 25

The nightmares had become such a constant part of Jake's life that he barely ruminated about them anymore. Instead he would lie in his rack, drenched in sweat, and stare into the darkness while doing his four-count tactical breathing. He was generally able to get back to sleep within ten or fifteen minutes instead of the hours it had taken when the dreams had first begun.

Most of the nightmares were tired retreads of the same theme—Jake's failure to prevent Cal's death. The settings would change, the characters would change, but in the end Cal always evaporated in a hot cloud of blood and smoke that covered Jake from head to toe. And then, of course, there were the snippets of amputated thumbs, often mixed with an almost slideshow-like dream of Cal and Shawn blowing up, followed by the faces of the bad guys that Jake had killed. The frozen-in-fear face of the first fighter he had killed in the alley generally made an appearance, but then it was just a parade of dead faces and bodies in an ever-accelerating picture show—the severed leg from the house, the guy Cal had shot in the head, the two assholes Jake smoked during the Special Forces op, and then others that he thought he had just made up. Eventually they came at him so fast that they blurred together, and then Jake would generally wake up panting and sobbing.

Between the nightmares were shorter, tranquil dreams. These always took place at the tree by Rachel's parents' house, and they always involved his imaginary friend, Luke, trying to share with him words of comfort and urging him to stay on some path. Luke seemed to have lots more to say, but with the help of another whispered voice, Jake always managed to shake himself awake before Luke could share whatever it was. Jake woke from these dreams more upset and agitated than from the nightmares. But then his mind always filled with anger and thoughts of vengeance, and sleep would come again.

Jake was tired. He fantasized about a good night's sleep—a dreamless sleep—and imagined it would help him immensely in his effort to shake off the dark cloud of anger and depression that seemed to cling to him no matter what he did or how hard he worked out at the small tent that served as a gym. The ops tempo had been slow. They'd had a steady stream of missions, usually low intensity and boring, with a rare burst of excitement that Jake had been remote from, much to his frustration and the relief (he suspected) of his team.

Jake's squad had remained unchanged for a few weeks now, including Aaron, who had permanently changed platoons, and two replacements they had received shortly after Jake's conversation with TC. The two new guys were complete opposites. Reed was quiet—almost brooding—but he never complained and Jake had never seen him get riled up about much of anything. He did his job with a quiet cool that Jake appreciated. Reed talked about himself almost not at all, but Jake felt certain this was not his first deployment.

Mike Swanson couldn't be more different than Reed. Like Jake, Mike had dreamed of becoming a firefighter, and by coincidence had moved to a town just forty-five minutes from Jake's home, shortly before deployment. Mike had two big dogs and had broken up with his girlfriend just before they shipped over. He had a cousin who was a firefighter in Chicago. Jake knew all of this because, unlike Reed, Mike talked almost constantly about himself. A part of Jake understood it was just nerves, but a bigger part found it irritating as hell. On a mission Mike was always wound tight, and seemed to spend more time looking at Jake for direction than he did scanning windows and rooftops to clear for bad guys.

Overall, though, Jake had a good team for clearing streets and showing American power. They were, as a team, a little untested yet, but they just needed to see some real action. The lull was putting them at risk of complacency.

Something that Jake hoped to change today.

They (whoever the hell "they" were) had learned that there was a sizable weapons cache surprisingly close to their FOB. Not only was the cache thought to be in a cluster of buildings a short convoy from their outpost—maybe fifteen minutes beyond the nearby village—but it was thought that the bulk of the force that safeguarded and distributed the weapons would be off-site, likely delivering guns and explosives to other bad guys so they could kill more Americans. Jake thought of the boy in his bulky grey man dress and wondered if the explosives had come from this very cache. Jake realized the fingers on his right hand had turned numb from the tightening grip he had on his rifle.

"Hey, Sar'n."

The high-pitched voice made Jake jump a little. Mike Swanson joined stride beside him.

"Mike," Jake answered curtly. Mike didn't get the clue.

"Headin' to the brief?"

Jake choked down his irritation. He really needed to relax around his new squadmate.

"No, dude, I'm headin' to the mall. Whadya think?" He shook his head and rolled his eyes.

"Right," Mike said with a nervous laugh. "Sorry."

They walked together in silence to the long plywood hut that served as their briefing room. Most of first platoon and at least half of second platoon was crammed into the room already. There were never enough of the folding metal chairs, and most of the soldiers stood along the walls, chatting and ass grabbing like a high school sports team. Jake and Mike joined Aaron and Reed in the far back corner. Reed raised an eyebrow— an unspoken request for some information—but Jake just shrugged and shook his head.

"Find out in a minute," he mumbled.

Reed nodded, leaned back against the wall, and stared at a spot on the ceiling.

Strange friggin' guy.

"Gentlemen," a voice boomed, and the Major walked to the front, TC in tow. The room quieted. Mike was whispering something to Aaron, so Jake elbowed him roughly in the side and pointed to where TC was loading images onto a laptop that were then projected onto a dust-covered sheet that had been nailed to the wall. "Most of you already know what we're up to, since y'all gossip like a bunch of eighth grade girls." The chuckles in the room dissipated quickly, and TC began pointing out things on the relief map and satellite image projected on the wall.

"There are three buildings in this area that can't really even be called a compound. There is a low retaining wall around about a third of the area, and a slight rise to the rear that's a little rocky. We'll come from front and back, so we'll need time to circle around and get second platoon into position without making a big stir to announce our presence. The weapons are in here"—TC directed a laser pointer at the center one of the three long rectangular buildings—"and the bad guys, if they're there at all, will be in the other two buildings. They usually have a couple of guys on the roofs of both buildings, but we'll get an overfly apparently, so we'll know if there are guys up there. I don't know the source, so don't ask, but we will apparently also get a pretty accurate head count of bad guys in the buildings just before we kick off, so we'll have that going for us ..."

"Which is nice," most of the men in the room said in unison, quoting the *Caddyshack* line. Jake was surprised. They rarely got such great real-time intelligence for a mission. But then they rarely, in Jake's view anyway, did much of any importance.

"Pretty straightforward profile," TC continued. "Come in from front and back, second perimeter of guys in reserve for support and to grab any squirters, and then we take down all the bad guys. Once they're all controlled, we bring up our EOD buddies to check the target building for booby traps, then we inventory the cache and pat ourselves on the back."

"EOD coming in with us or do we wait around?" Jake looked over at Reed, a little surprised he'd interrupted the platoon leader with his question.

"Good question," the First Sergeant said. "We got a couple of EOD riding in with us, so we won't have to wait around on target forever for them to get there. I hate that shit as much as you guys do. So, coupla things, and then we'll break into our teams for details. First, a lot of these guys keep their families with them—because they are cowardly assholes—so watch for women and kids. Fire-control discipline, guys."

Jake had a flash of the kid in the grey man dress and shook his head. "Second, watch your step, because these jackasses do indeed booby-trap their stuff. Don't get in a rush and get any of us hurt, 'kay?" There were nods around the room. "Last, for all you John Waynes from over in second platoon"—Jake felt several sets of eyes on him, though it could have been his imagination—"the head shed really does want these guys for intel, so have a little self-control. Take some guys off of the X if we can, 'cause they can't ask nobody questions if you smoke 'em all."

There was a moment of quiet while TC scanned the room.

"All right, second platoon, sit tight—we got this room. First platoon, get with your First Sergeant in the yard and we'll get y'all split up into sticks, 'kay?"

There was shuffling and banter as first platoon left the room and Jake and his squad leaned against the wall and watched them go.

"Guess we'll start calling you Duke," Aaron said and slapped Jake on the back. Jake felt his face flush and said nothing. Then he and his squad joined TC and the others in a tight circle.

Jake felt pretty certain he would feed his hunger for vengeance today.

CHAPTER 26

It seemed impossible that they had moved thirty guys into position completely undetected, and Jake worried that they might be in some pretty bad shit in a minute. He waited for the "go" call in his headset, and tried not to wonder if the bad guys had spotters out or, worse, if they all had night vision goggles and could see his team crouched in the big stretch of nothing right now. Not much to do about it at this point, he figured, and tried to get his "it is what it is" attitude on.

When he heard the crackling "Go!" in his earpiece, he raised a hand and his team rose behind him and fanned out a little as they crossed the seventy-five or so yards to the cluster of buildings. A few yards to his left, third squad spread out similarly, the men crouched forward, peering over their gun sights at the eerie green low-resolution world the NVGs revealed. Jake saw no movement, and scanned repeatedly up at the roof, where fighters seemed most likely to appear. He saw no movement there or through the dark windows on either side of the door. But the terrorists, knowing full well about the American night vision technology, frequently boarded up windows and doors to prevent light escaping, so he refused to allow himself to be comforted by the lack of light.

Jake and his team spread out beneath the window to the right of the door as third squad did the same to the left. Crouching beside the door, Jake tried to calm himself—to slow the pounding pulse in his temple and the slight tremor he felt in his right hand, squeezed around the grip of his rifle. His finger tapped along the trigger guard with a mind of its own.

Jake raised a closed left fist above his head—an unnecessary signal to hold until the second "go" came, but he needed some sort of movement or he felt he might explode. He couldn't decide whether his tremor and raspy breathing were from fear or excitement. For a moment he considered a brief prayer, but then clenched his jaw and shook his head in annoyance, his lips sucking against his teeth.

Like that'll help.

"Go!"

The voice in his headset shut out the debate, and Jake, Aaron, and Reed rose and crowded beside the door as three of the four men from third squad did the same on the other side. Mike remained in reserve beneath the window, like his counterpart on the other side. Jake chopped his left hand in the direction of the door.

Aaron and Ben, from third, simultaneously smashed against the door, knocking it from its hinges into the house. Jake and Dave Munn— the third squad leader—pushed past the two of them as Aaron regrouped to follow Reed through the door after them.

Jake and Munn moved right and left, respectively, clearing the blind spots in the corners and behind them as the next two in line moved deeper into the room, clearing ahead and the far corners. Jake heard the loud *pop* of someone—Munn, he thought—firing their weapon, and fought the overwhelming urge to look in that direction. Instead he cleared his side of the room and then moved right to make space for the men behind him to enter, shouting, "Clear," as he did.

"Clear," he heard Munn shout back and then, "One tango down."

Reed and his counterpart surged forward deep into the room, ready to push on to clear the next room, and Jake dipped his rifle downward so he wouldn't tag them as they became lead.

"Contact, contact!"

At first Jake was confused, not sure if the call had come perhaps from his headset, because he saw no movement. Then Reed took a knee and squeezed off two controlled rounds, just as his partner from third squad dropped to his belly and slithered across the floor in a panic, clear of the wide, arched doorway into the back room. Jake moved against the wall as Reed rose to a crouch, fired again, and then moved past Jake and pressed himself against the wall beside him.

"I think I saw five, maybe six," Reed said in a steady voice that seemed out of place. Then chunks of wall exploded out and away beside him, someone on the other side firing blindly through the wall, hoping to kill Jake and his team. "I think I hit one guy."

"Shit," Jake hissed and dropped to a crouch, trying to make himself small. "Covering fire," he shouted, and immediately Reed dropped to the ground by Jake's feet and pushed his rifle barrel around the corner of the arched doorway and squeezed off a couple of rounds. Jake stepped over him into the doorway, leaning forward and scanning for a target.

The other room was chaos, several fighters crouched against the walls near old furniture, firing rapidly at Jake and his team. Jake centered the red dot from his sight on the forehead of an older man with an AK-47, but before he could squeeze the trigger the man's head exploded in a red-and-grey puff. Jake pulled his sights to the right, where another jihadist stood in a combat crouch, his rifle pointed at Jake, and Jake pulled twice—one round hitting the man center mass in his bare chest and the other missing him completely and shattering the already-broken bannister beside him. Jake re-aimed and fired again as the man fell, the third round penetrating the top of his balding head as the man pitched forward.

Jake saw a blur of movement farther up the stairs and fired two more rounds just as a boy, barefoot in a grey man dress, registered in his mind. It was too late to take the rounds back, and the boy screamed as his back arched and he tumbled down the stairs. For a moment Jake saw the other boy—the boy who had killed his friends—exploding, and a smile crept onto his face. Then he saw the boy he'd just shot—no more than twelve or thirteen years old—lying prone, eyes open in shock and fear, with no weapon beside him, and Jake felt a wave of nausea sweep over him.

The wall beside him exploded and bits of cheap wood splintered and tore at the side of his face just as one of the third squad guys shouted, "Left, Left." Jake dropped to a knee and spun left. He saw the two shooters, one already covered in blood, and flipped his rifle to a three-round burst as he squeezed twice on the trigger. He heard the loud *pop* of several other rifles firing and both of the terrorists jerked back and forth like something from a bad action movie, then crumpled to the ground.

There was a long silence, broken only by the tinkle of the last two pieces of spent brass bouncing across the floor and a soft moan from Jake's right. After what seemed like minutes, Jake cleared his throat.

"Clear," he half mumbled, his voice shaking. Then he looked around the room at his men. "Everyone okay?"

"Yeah," someone said.

"I'm good."

"All good for third squad," Munn said.

Jake heard a commotion behind him and spun around, raising his rifle, then lowered it quickly at the site of Mike coming through the door. Mike looked past Jake at the five dead men in the room behind him.

"Holy shit," Mike breathed.

"Dude, you're bleeding," Reed's calm voice said from beside him, just as Jake noticed the warm trickle down his chin. Several crimson drops spattered onto the floor between his feet.

"Is it bad?" Jake realized his voice was flat and even—nothing like how he felt. Reed dabbed at Jake's cheekbone with his sleeve.

"Nah," he said. "Ricochet or some shit, I think. Can't see bone, at least. Coupla stitches, maybe." He handed Jake a clean bandana and Jake held it against the gash, which now began to burn.

"Second platoon, what the hell's up?"

The voice in his earpiece was TC's and sounded worried. Jake realized he should have checked in already, as the other team would certainly have heard the gunfire. He tilted his head to press the cut on his face against his shoulder.

"First and third are okay," he said into the radio on his chest. "Heavy contact, five KIA, no blue casualties."

"Six," Reed said and jerked a thumb over his shoulder toward the front room where he had capped the first bad buy. Jake nodded and then pointed at the staircase with his rifle barrel and spoke to the room. "We gotta clear the upstairs, like, right now." Then he spoke into his radio. "House not yet secure."

"Hey, this kid is alive," someone said. The word *kid* made Jake's chest burn and he tasted bile in the back of his throat. He looked over to see Aaron kneeling beside the boy, who Jake now thought might be only ten or eleven. Another voice whispered in his ear, calming him.

No different than the kid who killed Cal. If he's innocent, what is he doing here? Send him straight to hell—for Cal and Shawn.

Jake felt another wave of nausea. For some reason Rachel's face popped into his head. Her beautiful brown eyes looked up at him from a smiling face, and then she frowned and was gone.

"Clear the upstairs, guys," he barked. "Two by two." Jake keyed his radio again. "Make that five KIA and we may have a medevac," he said calmly. "Not a blue force—I say again, not a good guy."

"Christ, he's just a kid," Aaron said and his voice cracked. "Jeez, he's like eight or something." He looked up at Jake with tears in his eyes. "Do you think I shot him, Jake?"

Jake felt his face flush.

"Who cares who shot the little asshole? Clear the upstairs—*now*," he shouted at his squadmate. Aaron rose on wobbly legs and seemed to get his act together. Jake joined him at the stairs, unable to resist casting a glance at the boy's pale face. He and Aaron followed Reed and Munn up the stairs.

"I'll stay with the kid," someone said from below him. He heard the tearing sound of someone opening a blowout kit—the small bag of medical supplies they all carried in their cargo pockets.

"First platoon, all clear … second, you cool?" he heard in his earpiece.

"Clearing the upstairs," Jake said into his radio. He would give just about anything if they would just stop calling the wounded boy "kid."

"Copy. Heading to the main building. Clear your house and rally outside. Advise status of your medical."

"Urgent," Jake said softly. "Urgent surgical."

The familiar voice tried to whisper something to him again, but he squeezed it out of his head.

CHAPTER 27

Jake lay on his back and stared at nothing but dark. He guessed it would be about midday by now, but with all the windows blacked out for light discipline it might have been the middle of the night. A thin sliver of light snuck in from beneath the cheap door that wouldn't close completely, and made his world more grey than black. The occasional laugh or shout from his roommates—hard at work on some Xbox game in the common room—kept him from drifting to sleep.

Not that he had any desire at all to descend into that trap. He knew the images that waited for him on the other side of sleep. He had no doubt he had added some faces to the slideshow of death he watched every night now, but that didn't bother him, really. He found his way to calm much more quickly recently, having acclimated in some sick way to the nightmares.

What kept Jake awake more than anything were thoughts of the boy. No one had said anything about it—not TC or the First Sergeant from first platoon. He wondered if that meant it was okay somehow—okay that he had shot a kid. How was that possible?

A single sharp rap on the door made his pulse quicken for a moment.

"Shit," he breathed, then, "Come."

The sliver of light grew into a long panel, followed by a head-shaped shadow and a soft whisper.

"Sar'n?"

Aaron.

"Yeah, dude," Jake said, unable to keep the heaviness from his voice.

"Talk a minute?"

Jake sat up in his bunk and dangled his legs over the edge. He leaned forward to rub his face with both hands. He figured whatever Aaron needed was part of his job as squad leader, but he just wasn't feeling it right now.

"Come on in, dude," he said, almost against his will.

Aaron shuffled in and sat precariously on the edge of the bottom bunk across from him, his head bent forward in the low space. Jake hoped he wouldn't turn on the light.

"You hear anything about the kid?" Aaron asked, but he was staring at the ground, apparently unable to look at Jake.

Jake sighed heavily. He was so not the right guy for this—not right now.

"Anything like what?" he asked. "It ain't like they carry some kinda terrorist ID card, you know." What the hell did Aaron want him to say? Jake figured he could just tell Aaron that it wasn't him who shot the boy— that Jake had fired the rounds that dropped the boy down the stairs. Then he suddenly realized that he didn't know that, not for sure. If Aaron thought it might be him, then he must have fired some rounds that way, right? Maybe Jake hadn't shot the boy at all.

"It ain't that, Sar'n," Aaron said, and Jake could hear the quiver in his voice. "I just wondered if he, you know, made it."

"You mean, like, did he die?" Jake asked. All of a sudden that mattered more than anything to Jake. He wondered why he hadn't asked that himself yet. The boy had been alive when the medevac helicopter had flown him off the X. Jake felt pressure lift off him—he might not have shot the kid at all, and maybe the kid hadn't even died.

"Does it matter so much?"

Jake looked toward the voice from the doorway and saw Reed leaning against the frame, his hands in his pockets and his blouse untucked and unbuttoned.

"Sar'n," Reed said with a nod.

"What's up, dude?" Jake answered. Aaron looked at his feet, uncomfortable.

"Seems to me," Reed said, and rubbed his chin as if in thought, "the kid Aaron's talking about was at a terrorist safe house that was also a gigantic weapons cache, right?" Neither Jake nor Aaron said anything. "Right," Reed answered for them and then continued. "This wasn't like some big village full of families—hell, he was the only one there except for shooters, as I recall. Learnin' the trade, maybe? No one likes to see a kid killed—don't get me wrong—but seems to me this guy was a bad guy already or would be eventually. Maybe we saved some future American from being shot by this guy in a year or two, did ya ever think about that?"

Jake opened his mouth to say something, but closed it again.

"Maybe he was just a kid hanging out with his dad," Aaron said by way of objection.

"And learning all about the family business and how Americans are the great devil, right?" Reed asked. Then he looked hard at Jake, his eyes dark and full of something. "You guys lost a squad to a kid, didn't ya?"

Jake felt a belt tighten around his throat and the familiar whisper returned, telling him how this was war and just another eye for an eye. Another voice screamed protest from the back of his mind. It sounded like his voice, but he thought it might be Rachel's.

Reed straightened and took a step back. "Anyway," Reed said to Aaron, "I'm sure your squad leader was gonna tell ya kind of the same thing—right, Jake?" Jake held Reed's cold eyes and said nothing. "See you guys at chow." He spun on a heel and disappeared from the doorway.

Jake felt Aaron's eyes on him, but his mind was a swirling cloud of competing emotions.

"Jake?" Aaron's voice was almost pleading.

Jake looked down at him from his bunk, and for a minute he hated Aaron a little.

"War is a shitfest, dude," he said. "Shake it off and keep doing your job."

Aaron wiped a tear from his cheek and started to say something, but caught the words in his throat with a grunt, apparently thinking better of it. Then he rose and looked at his feet as he shuffled out.

"Thanks, Sar'n," he mumbled. And he was gone.

Jake lay back on his bunk and crossed his arms over his eyes. Only a handful of weeks left to go. He just had to get through them and then he would go home to Rachel. He would pick up his life and forget all about this place. He would put this whole nightmare behind him.

He thought about maybe heading over to sign up for phone time to call Rachel.

He couldn't remember if he had called her yesterday or not.

CHAPTER 28

The crazy late-spring heat wave had finally moved away—north or south or wherever the weather lady on the local news said such things went—and Rachel felt relief and gratitude. The heat was uncomfortable, of course, but more importantly it made it really hard to look as stunning as possible for Jake, which Rachel felt was the one thing about their reunion over which she had some sort of control. She wanted to look beautiful, and sexy, and (somehow) not so damn nervous.

Rachel had no idea why Jake was coming home a week or so ahead of the rest of his unit, but right now she didn't really care. She had gotten over the initial dread that the email brought her—that he must be hurt or sick or in trouble or something, right? On the follow-up phone call, Haunted Jake (as she had come to think of her husband's hollow voice at times) had reassured her that everything was fine and that some of the unit always came back early to get things ready for the main body's return. Rachel had no idea what the hell that meant, and didn't care. She had prayed so hard that Jake would come home safely, and for the last few weeks had felt almost panic-level fear that something terrible would happen right at the end. Now, save some highly unlikely commercial aircraft crash (she bowed her head and said a little prayer now about that too), Jake would be safely home with her in—she looked at her delicate watch, which was hard to read but matched her earrings perfectly—five minutes.

Rachel shifted in her red dress a little, trying to be sure she had no panty lines showing, and looked around at the rather small crowd in the foyer-like atrium where the hallways from the three arrival and departure gate areas converged at the commercial airport. She didn't see anyone who seemed anxious enough to be waiting, like her, for someone coming home from war. Of course, Jake's flight was arriving from Atlanta, not right from Afghanistan. Still, she thought maybe someone else from the unit would be with him. He had said several people were coming in early.

Once she was certain no one was looking at her, she looked down and adjusted her neckline self-consciously. The plunging neckline made her feel sexy, but was it too much? She would never have worn such a low-cut dress to the day care, or to Foundations Family Church—or almost anywhere—and now she was having second thoughts. Of course, there was no way she could possibly get an opinion from her best friend, now could she?

She pursed her lips at the thought. It had taken her days to tell Kelly that Jake would be home a little early. The guilt she felt over the relief and joy that accompanied Jake's return was almost unbearable. Rachel had worked so hard to not let those feelings keep her from Kelly, who needed her now more than ever, but it had been a struggle. Maybe she should have let Kelly come with her to the airport. Kelly had offered to be there, to hold her hand while she waited and support her. She had even offered to just drive her and wait in the car, so Rachel wouldn't have to worry about driving while she was distracted about Jake's arrival.

Rachel had graciously refused, halfway convincing herself that being there would be far too painful for Kelly. But a part of her wondered if her reluctance was more about her fear that Kelly, with all her pain and loss, would somehow ruin this reunion she had prayed about for almost a year now. God, she hoped that wasn't it—that she wasn't that selfish.

Motion to her left caused her to turn, and her heart almost leapt from her chest at the sight of a man in digital Army BDUs, a duffle over his shoulder, coming from the hallway to the other gates. Had she been looking the wrong way? But no, it wasn't Jake at all. At the sight of a woman in a yellow dress (also with a plunging neckline, she noticed with some relief) and a toddler beside her, he dropped his bag, then swept them both up in his arms. Rachel watched the family for a moment, too many emotions swirling inside for her to get a handle on any of them. She rummaged in her purse for a tissue when she felt the tears trickle onto her cheeks.

A strong hand appeared from her right, holding out a bandana, and her breath stuck in her chest.

She looked up at Jake—his face so thin, but his crooked smile the same one that had grabbed her the first time they met again a few years after high school—and her purse crashed to the floor as she wrapped her arms around her husband's neck.

"Jake, oh, Jake," she breathed. "Oh God, Jake." She couldn't stop her sobbing. This was nothing like the sexy, confident woman she wanted Jake to find waiting for him.

He didn't seem to mind. The rose in his hand floated to the ground beside the scattered contents of her purse and he took her face in his hands. He smelled like something—something mechanical and not at all Jake—but she didn't care. Her mouth found his and she kissed him almost furiously as their tears mixed together on their faces. She felt her nose begin to run and realized with some horror that she was about to drip snot on her husband. She pulled away from their kiss into a hug, her body shaking as she cried.

"I love you so much, Rachel," Jake breathed into her ear with a shaking voice. "Oh my God, you feel so good. You look so beautiful." She squeezed him tighter as he began to sob as well. "Oh, Rachel. I missed you, baby."

She became aware of the sound of applause around them. She had no idea if it was for them—bystanders caught up in the emotion of their embrace—or if some rock star had just arrived. Her eyes were squeezed too tightly shut to look.

They stood there a long time, crying and clutching at each other. The commotion around them dissipated and she felt herself grow weak with relief and love—and lust, she suddenly realized. She needed to get her husband home and all to herself immediately.

Rachel finally pulled away from his embrace and looked at Jake's tear-covered face and red eyes.

"Let's go home, baby," she said. "Please."

Jake nodded and looked down. His eyes seemed dark.

"Yes," he said softly. "Let's go home."

She let Jake scoop the mess on the floor back into her purse, keeping both arms wrapped tightly around his biceps—afraid if she let go for even a moment, her husband would fade away from her.

She let Jake carry her purse, the damaged rose, and his own large backpack as they headed to the door—away from the worst year of their life, and forward toward the parking lot and home.

CHAPTER 29

Jake sensed that Rachel needed him to talk, but he decided that she needed him to be normal even more. Inside him was an anger—not at Rachel, or even at anyone in particular—and he was terrified that if he tried to engage in small talk right now that anger would boil to the surface. So, he gripped the steering wheel tighter than he needed to and drove them to Rachel's parents' house.

Jake understood that their families wanted to celebrate his safe return, but how could they possibly understand that the last thing he wanted was to be around a bunch of people—any people, really, other than Rachel—who would slap him on the back and try and talk about things they couldn't possibly understand? Jake had suggested that maybe they wait until everyone else was home—just another few days, after all—and then celebrate with the men from the unit. Rachel told him she thought that was a great idea, that in fact the ombudsman had emailed her about a big welcome-home celebration for all the families, but had explained that this was just close friends and family. With some difficult prodding, he had convinced her to keep it to just immediate family, but even so he felt nothing but dread at being in a room with happy people celebrating his return. He had decided not to try and explain it to Rachel, since he didn't in any way understand it himself.

"You okay?"

Her touch on his arm made him unconsciously jump and he tried to give her his best crooked smile. Her eyes were soft and happy, but also had that look of concern that should have made him feel good, but instead sort of pissed him off a little.

"Yeah, good," he said and forced out a laugh he hoped sounded better than it felt. He put his hand on top of hers, aware that his was unexpectedly damp with sweat. "Just kind of nervous about being around everyone—like I told you."

She leaned her head on his shoulder for a moment and then looked up at him.

"I'm sorry, Jake. It's just too soon, isn't it?" He hated the pained look in her eyes. "Do you want me to call and tell them we can't come?"

"And tell them what?" Jake asked, more sharply than he meant to. "Everybody is already there."

Rachel looked uncomfortable at the short flash of temper, and Jake felt terrible about the look on her face.

"I could just tell them I got sick, maybe?"

Jake tried to do his four-count tactical breathing to calm himself and then screwed on his smile again.

"You know what?" he said and squeezed her hand. "I'm being stupid. I think I just want to hide away with my beautiful wife for a while, but it'll actually be great to see everyone." She looked at him—studied him was how it felt—and pursed her lips. Jake forced another laugh and kissed her cheek, his eyes sideways on the road ahead of them. "I mean it, Rach," he said. "Don't pay me any mind." She smiled a little. "Thanks for setting this up."

"I love you, baby," Rachel said and sighed.

"Another few days and I'll be right as rain, I promise," he said, pained that he had almost made her sad.

Rachel laughed and Jake raised his eyebrows.

"I've never heard you say that before," she said. "Where did that come from? 'Right as rain'?"

Jake thought for a moment, unsure. Then he saw, clear as day, the Australian surgeon, promising Jake would be okay. He had just figured out which of his friends were dead. He shook his head to chase the memory away, and smiled at Rachel and shrugged. Rachel smiled back but looked away, unsure.

He just wanted to push the stupid thoughts and fears out of his head and get back to their life. Maybe this, a "normal" evening with family that used to be a twice-a-month-or-so thing, would help him get there.

If he could just stop the damn dreams. The dreams themselves, plus how tired he was all the time, were probably the biggest issue. They would go away soon, he felt sure.

Jake tried to unclench the cramp in his neck as he made the final turn onto the pretty country road where his wife had grown up. All around them, planned communities and complexes and shopping centers had sprung up in the once-small-and-quiet town, but this street had somehow been spared the sprawl. The houses were far apart on yards measured in acres instead of fractions, with real driveways that took you more than ten feet from the road. Jim and Becca, Rachel's parents, had always had the best front yard of all. After Jim had passed, Becca had decided that one way to honor her husband was to keep that up—though now it was a paid lawn service that made it happen. The yard sprawled on either side of a winding gravel drive that went a good fifty yards and then took a dogleg to the right before arriving at a low, ranch-style house with a huge, wraparound porch. As Jake made the turn into the drive, the big oak tree on the hill—Rachel's church tree, he called it—waved at him before disappearing behind the house as they approached. The tree—or maybe the whole hill with its path diving down to the glen of trees beyond it—made Jake's stomach flip. The face of the young man in the red sweatshirt, with his old-fashioned walking stick, flashed into his mind and he felt something—not fear; more like nervousness, like when you were a teenager and you thought your parents might have discovered you'd snuck out with friends to TP the neighbors' houses. As he swung into the circle of gravel in front of the house, Jake made a conscious effort to not look back at the tree, a part of him sure that his imaginary friend, Luke, would be there on the hill, his cheek resting against his staff, staring at Jake sadly. Jake sighed and tried to shake off the "just got caught" feeling.

"You okay?"

Jake closed his eyes as he shut off the motor. "You gotta stop asking me that, babe," he said, his voice soft. Then he opened his eyes and leaned over to kiss his wife. "I'm great, Rachel," he said and touched her cheek. "I just gotta settle in to being at home."

Rachel nodded and smiled. "Sorry," she said nervously.

"For what?" he said and smiled.

Jake held Rachel's hand in his and carried a six-pack of her dad's favorite beer in the other—a heavy, dark beer that Jake always pretended to love when they were over. Truth was, he was more of a light beer guy, but it had seemed early on like a way to bond with his then-fiancée's dad, and ever since, there seemed to be no way to renege on his white lie. Now that Jim was gone, he still drank the beer whenever they visited Rachel's mom, and the emotional energy of the gesture actually made him enjoy it more than he used to. The strong smell of the grill out back filled his nose and then his soul, and he smiled a real smile and realized he could eat his father-in-law's famous mixed grill—which Becca now manned up and made on weekends, almost as well as Jim had—just about until he burst today. Rachel had fed him like a recovering anorexic for the last few days, but the smell of the backyard cookout was most definitely the smell of home. Jake saw that, other than the king cab pickup truck Becca still drove, the circle drive in front of the house was empty.

Cool. Maybe I can ease into this a little. It would be so totally different if we were meeting Cal and Kelly here.

Jake's heart skipped a beat at the thought.

"Jake!" Becca crashed through the front door as they arrived on the porch and wrapped her arms around Jake in a way that his own mother would never have found comfortable. Jake wrapped his beer hand around his mother-in-law's waist and tried not to drop the six-pack as Becca bounced up and down in his awkward embrace.

Becca kissed Jake on the chin and then split Jake apart from his wife, taking each of their hands in her own, and practically dragged them into the cool house. Jake felt himself begin to relax at the familiar feelings. Everything was just as it had been the evening they'd spent here a few days before he had left. That was less than a year ago, so why did it feel like a lifetime?

"Emma and Shayne are running late," Becca said as the three of them maneuvered through the screen door. "Emma was bringing dessert, but they got running late and so they're stopping at the Farm Fresh for something." Jake smiled. Emma—Rachel's younger sister—had not been on time to anything Jake could remember since he had married into the family. He liked her boyfriend, Shayne, who was totally laidback, which was probably the reason they were still dating after four years and not something more. "Your parents won't be here until almost three, you know." They both knew her statement was more a question. Jake's parents were not the best communicators, to be sure. Rachel's open, warm family—full of jokes and hugs and laughter—had been an adjustment for Jake those first couple of years.

"Yeah, they called and told me," Jake said. He no longer felt embarrassed by his parents and how distant they must seem to outsiders. He loved them and he knew they loved him. He had stopped wishing for them to be something else. He knew he would never live up to their expectations—or his mom's anyway—and he was fine with that now, too.

Becca nodded, kissed his cheek again, and almost skipped to the kitchen.

"I'll be right back," she hollered over her shoulder, "with wine for my daughter, a beer for Jake, and some meat for the grill."

Jake scanned the pictures on the long, wide mantel over the fireplace and saw only two new pictures: one of Rachel holding hands with her mom in front of Foundations Family Church, and the other of Jake in BDUs and his full "battle rattle"—all of his gear and weapons—taken on a training evolution just before they had left. He was smiling in the picture, but Jake couldn't imagine why, and for a moment that goofy, naïve smile made him feel a surge of irritation. He turned away from the picture and squinted instead at the picture of Rachel and Becca.

In the picture Rachel wore a pretty, dark-colored dress. Jake felt himself suddenly consumed with suspicion that the picture had been taken at Cal's funeral. But then why in the hell were they smiling? Why would anyone even take a picture on such a day? Rachel looked pensive and maybe a little sad in the picture, but for God's sake, their best friend—her best friend's husband—was being buried. How could she have even the hint of a smile on her face? What an insanely inappropriate time for a picture. He could think of no reason why anyone would want to record such a black day.

As he stared at the picture, he tried to imagine where he would have been that day. Rachel had never written or spoken to him about the funeral, something for which he had been grateful at the time. But now he felt oddly displaced and left out, even if it was from such a terrible thing. He wondered if it had happened before or after the memorial ceremony at the FOB. It must take some time to get the bodies home and through the whole process, right? It had taken over a week for them to get to their FOB on the way into the deployment, so probably the funeral had been after the service downrange and his terrible encounter with that dumbass chaplain. He tried to juggle the time difference in his head for the two thousandth time, attempting to picture where, exactly, he would have been.

A hand on his arm made him spin around, his right hand reaching behind him for—for what? For his rifle?

Rachel pulled her hand away as if from fire.

"I'm ... I'm sorry, Jake," she stammered. "Are you okay?"

Jake looked around, grateful no one was there to see him but his wife, though Becca was just disappearing into the kitchen.

"You were staring," Rachel said softly. "I tried to get your attention."

"What the hell is this?" Jake asked and jerked a thumb toward the picture on the mantel.

Rachel looked confused, and maybe something else.

"What?" she asked. "I don't understand, sweetie." Her voice cracked a little.

"This picture," Jake continued, feeling anger rise up from his chest, crawling up his neck like smoke—or something equally impossible to contain. "Why the hell would you take this picture?"

Rachel shifted nervously and twisted her hands together.

"I don't understand, Jake," she said again, and Jake felt more irritated still. "That's my dad," she said softly. "It's me and my mom."

"I know who the hell it is, Rachel," he said and heard his voice rising, but from far away—in another room or something. "Why on earth would you take this picture?"

"It's my mom," Rachel said again, and a tear cascaded onto her cheek. "It was the last day of the Christmas youth program."

Jake felt his breath pulled away and a band tighten around his throat. He saw Becca looking at them from the kitchen door, then pull back when he glanced at her. For a moment he felt panicked, as if he were being smothered. What the hell was he doing?

"I'm so sorry, Rachel," he mumbled and took her hands in his. Rachel wrapped her arms around his neck. Her sobs drove more daggers into his heart. "I'm sorry. I thought…" He thought what? What on earth would have made him think that the picture must somehow be linked to Cal's funeral? What in the holy hell was wrong with him?

"I'm sorry, Jake," Rachel sobbed. "You weren't ready. You tried to tell me. I shouldn't have made you come."

Jake felt a new anger well up inside him, but again he had no idea what it was he was angry about, and he swallowed it back down.

"No, no," he stammered and held his wife. "No, baby. I'm sorry. Everything is fine. I just—I just—well, never mind. It's so stupid." Jake tilted Rachel's head up by the chin so he could look into her tear-filled eyes. He realized when her face blurred that his own eyes had also filled with tears. "I'm glad we're here, sweetie," he said, but the anxious pounding of his pulse in his temple reminded him that was a lie. "Please, let's just forget it and have fun, okay?"

Rachel nodded and tried to smile.

"Tell your mom she's looking so young I thought I caught my wife out partying with the girls," Jake joked, and Rachel coughed a half laugh, but her smile became more genuine.

"Okay," she said and wiped her nose on the back of her hand. For a moment she looked almost childlike, and Jake loved her even more. He hugged her again and looked toward the kitchen, smiling at Becca, who smiled back but blushed to be caught spying.

Jake broke the embrace and kissed Rachel's cheek. Then he took her hand and led her to the kitchen.

The hours slowly erased Jake's horror at how the celebration had started. Becca had made the afternoon easy—somehow understanding Jake's need to talk, but not about anything real. They chatted about Jake missing the hunting season, though both knew he was no real hunter. They chatted about the baseball season, well underway and seeming to arrive earlier every year. Becca was a die-hard Orioles fan and watched baseball more than her husband had. Jake knew he was supposed to be a Baltimore fan—his folks were from eastern Baltimore originally, though Jake had never lived there—but he'd always liked the Braves. He had been to tons of games for their farm team in Richmond during his college "experiment" and just never stopped liking them. In any case, he wasn't a die-hard fan like Becca, and had made no effort to keep up with the early season from Afghanistan.

I had a lot of shit going on.

He let Becca catch him up and tried to seem interested. Jake was grateful that Rachel hovered, constantly touching his shoulder or arm, holding his hand, kissing his cheek, or squeezing his leg. Just the smell of her approaching—and he could smell the scent of her shampoo or body spray from across the room since he got back—made him feel more at peace, separating him from the confusing anxiety that seemed never far below the surface.

The arrival of his parents, about a half hour after Emma and Shayne arrived, made things worse.

Jake was already feeling anxious to leave not long after Rachel's sister's arrival. He got the impression that he made Emma uncomfortable—almost as uncomfortable as Jake felt about Shayne's constant questions. Her boyfriend stopped short of asking if he had killed anyone, but he clearly wanted some stories—some violence-packed combat action tales—that Jake had no interest in sharing. Rachel sat on Jake's leg on the long bench seat built into the deck and rubbed his arm gently, no doubt feeling him tense at each of Shayne's questions about what the bad guys were like, what kind of weapons did they have, did he ride in helicopters. Shayne seemed oblivious to Rachel's, Jake's, and eventually even Becca's attempts to change the subject. Finally, Rachel bailed him out.

"That's enough soldier talk, huh, Jake?" Rachel looked sternly at Emma's boyfriend to make her point. "Jake has had nothing but soldier time for almost a year. I know I've had enough of it for sure. Let's have some family time."

Jake had nodded, unsure what else to say. When he felt tears lightly rim his eyes, he felt angry, confused about why he was tearing up. And at first his parents had saved the day.

"Welcome home, son."

His dad's voice filled the room just as his presence always seemed to do. The words were flat, and Jake knew only he would be able to sense the emotion behind them—subtle but there. As usual, his mother said nothing, but as he turned to greet them, she wiped a tear from her eye, her expression annoyed at her loss of control. Jake felt joy at seeing them, followed by fear and guilt—though about what, he had no earthly idea. In any case, it made his tear-filled eyes more appropriate, should anyone have even noticed.

His mother hugged him and patted him gently on the back of the neck. His father stuck out his hand and Jake shook it firmly, just as he knew his dad would expect.

"Dad," Jake said with a nod.

"Jake," his dad said, softer than Jake expected. "We're glad you're home, son." He held Jake's hand longer than usual and then he really surprised Jake with "We missed you, Jake." He qualified it quickly with "Your mother, especially."

"I missed you too." And then the moment was gone and his dad turned to Becca, thanking her for having them over.

Jake's hands were shaking when he sat back down, and he thrust them between his knees, hoping no one else would notice.

"You okay, baby?"

Jake relaxed at Rachel's touch as she slipped onto the bench beside him.

"Great," he said. "It's awesome to see everyone."

He ignored the concern on his wife's face and then accepted a second beer from Shayne.

"Didn't get any of this in Afghanistan, right?"

"Right," Jake acknowledged. He was having a lot of trouble trying to figure out why he suddenly wanted to punch Shayne in the face. Even though they were outside, Jake felt suddenly claustrophobic. He stood up more abruptly then he meant to and felt cold beer slosh onto the back of his hand. "Excuse me," he said to Shayne without looking at him. "Gotta hit the bathroom." He squeezed Rachel's arm.

"Get rid of some of that beer," Emma's boyfriend hollered after him and Jake imagined what it would be like to choke him. There was no way in hell he would have that kid on his squad—not even in a training situation, much less outside the wire. He was way more irritating than Mike Swanson.

Jake set his beer on the side of the sink and forced himself to pee, just in case someone might be listening at the door. Then he washed his hands and splashed some cool water on his face. He leaned over the sink, water dripping from his nose and chin, and sobbed softly.

What in the hell is wrong with me?

He was so flooded with competing emotions that for a moment the dizziness of them made him nauseated and he thought he might throw up. Then the feeling ebbed away and he whistled out a long, slow breath, swallowing hard on the taste of beer and the chips he had been snacking on. Composed, Jake sipped water out of the sink from cupped hands, then dried his face and arms with the hand towel on the sink. He grabbed his beer, refused to look at his reflection in the mirror, and slipped out of the bathroom.

His dad stood just outside the door, between him and the open sliding-glass door leading onto the deck. Jake felt his pulse quicken, wondering what his dad might say that would piss him off.

"Doing okay, Jake?" his dad asked, his grey eyes holding Jake's—of course.

"Fine, sir," Jake said. "Thanks so much for making the drive."

His dad nodded and pursed his lips. "Listen, Jake," he began.

Here it comes.

His dad clasped his hands in front of him and leaned back on his heels. For a moment Jake thought he looked like a kid about to recite something at a school play—a seven-year-old, searching for his lines.

"Jake, I just wanted to say that your mother and I . . . well, we're real proud of you, son."

"Thanks, Dad," Jake said.

God, please let this be over.

"Of course," his dad said, "I know you had a tough time over there. I know it was tough, and well, I'm real sorry for that."

Jake felt his face flush in anger. He squeezed his hands into fists, struggling to swallow it all down. He had hurt Rachel once today already; he didn't want to cause a scene and embarrass her.

"I'm fine, Dad. I'm sure that you're surprised to find your soft son was a damn fine soldier—a real killer."

Jake's father's eyes widened. Jake couldn't remember him ever looking genuinely surprised, and it made him feel good in a cruel sort of way.

"I didn't mean that at all," his dad said, his voice much more controlled than his face suggested.

"I'm good at this, Dad. I was a squad leader and everything. I killed a lot of bad guys and saved a lot of lives." Jake saw Rachel look over at him curiously, but he doubted she could hear them from out on the deck. "Look, let's just get back to the party. You can tell Mom you delivered her message of how surprisingly proud she was."

Jake walked past his dad and joined Rachel, slipping his arm around his gorgeous wife. At the feel of her, his breathing slowed and his face cooled.

He has no idea what I did or what it cost me.

"You okay?" Rachel asked and squeezed his arm.

Jake choked down his irritation and smiled, then kissed her on the cheek. "Baby," he said. "You gotta stop asking me that."

Jake quietly sipped a few more beers, ate some great food, and waited for things to get back to normal. He figured in a few weeks, once he was formally released from active duty, things would go back to the way they used to be.

CHAPTER 30

Rachel watched the shadows from the trees outside their bedroom window as they danced their ballet across the walls and ceiling. The little bit of light didn't bother her, and she usually found the movement of the shadows relaxing—her version of counting sheep. Tonight she found herself unmoved by the shadow dance, her thoughts and emotions so conflicting and changing that she could barely keep up. The more her mind wandered, the more she lost control of where her thoughts took her.

Jake's arm across her waist was comforting—it was what she had prayed for every day for so long—but it was also weirdly foreign. Rachel imagined that was normal after sleeping alone in their bed for over nine months, but it was still disconcerting. Jake breathed heavily in her ear, having had way more beer at her parents' than he usually did—and she realized, with some guilt, that she was a bit relieved that they had not made love tonight after he had drank so much. It was the first night they had not been intimate in the four days since he had come home.

Jake twitched beside her and mumbled something she couldn't understand. The room was too dark to see his face, but she knew it would be his new, tense face, and she could hear his teeth grinding together. His arm twitched again and Rachel felt his hand ball up into a fist.

Gently, she stroked his cheek and his forehead, hoping her touch might lure him back from whatever bad dream he was having, but Jake pulled away from her and mumbled again. Rachel sighed and then slipped from beneath his arm and out of their bed. She kissed him, felt his jaw tighten as she did, and then tiptoed quietly out their bedroom.

She had learned to be quite comfortable on their oversized sectional sofa, falling asleep there when she'd tossed and turned in their bed while he was gone. She'd felt less lonely curling up on the couch with a big blanket than she had lying alone in the middle of their bed. Rachel pulled her favorite fluffy blanket out of the bench storage beneath the TV, snuggled beneath it on the couch, and then reached for the remote.

Two AM television was no better tonight than it had been over the last nine months, but Rachel scrolled through the channels anyway, barely paying attention to what the info guide said. She wanted, more than anything, to know just what it was she felt so worried about. Jake was different, but of course he was. He had been in combat in a horrible place, experiencing things she couldn't—and didn't want to—imagine. He had been there, in battle, only days ago. Surely he just needed time. The thought that the sullen, jumpy man from her parents' house might stay forever was frightening, but also, perhaps, silly. She wished she had attended some of the command-sponsored support groups. Maybe they had talked about what to expect and she might have found comfort in knowing this was all completely normal and short-lived. She closed her eyes and sighed. Maybe her stress was just the uncertainty.

I just want my husband back. I want Jake.

She saw plenty of glimmers of her old Jake, but there seemed so much darkness on top of him that she could only now and again catch a glimpse of him. Those glimpses gave her hope, of course. He was still in there somewhere.

Rachel clicked off the TV and closed her eyes again. She needed to give this to God. In her meeting with Pastor Craig, they had approached the idea of surrender from several angles. Her pastor had told her that true surrender required trust—trust that God would be in control if she asked and trust that while He didn't promise freedom from struggles, He did promise freedom from worry and guidance on how to navigate those struggles. She needed guidance for sure. But surrender was proving difficult. And she had a sense that Pastor Craig, normally so animated and passionate and real, might well be struggling himself. That scared her to death. If Pastor Craig was having trouble finding peace, what hope was there for her?

She needed to pray for Jake and to pray for strength, but more importantly the wisdom to know how to help him. She wanted desperately for

Luke, in his hooded sweatshirt (how could that be real?), to be more than a dream and to come again and help her. Just some support and maybe a little advice, some encouragement, was all she needed.

Rachel clasped her hands in her lap and began to pray.

Dear God …

The scream shattered the calm silence of her prayer and she jumped and gasped, looking around in a panic. The scream sounded so close, she thought someone had snuck up on her when her eyes were closed, but when second scream came, she realized it came from the bedroom.

Rachel closed her eyes briefly again, her prayer now short and to the point.

"Please help me, Lord. Please help me help him."

Then she rose from the couch, anxious to help her husband, but without a clue what that might mean.

CHAPTER 31

The heaviness in Jake's head and the dry burning of his throat were easy to incorporate into the familiar dream, making it all the more vivid and real. Jake peered around the corner, wondering where the hell everyone was. The dusty street was empty, but that wasn't right somehow. Across the street, at a forty-five degree angle from where he peered from the relative safety of the alley, the light breeze blew clouds of dust into the open doorway of the two-story brown building.

Jake stepped cautiously from the alley, scanning up and down the street, but saw nothing. The sun was low, which made the shadows at the edges of the building a great place for someone to hide, but there was no movement he could detect.

Jake keyed the mike on the shoulder strap of his kit.

"First squad in position at the target building."

He waited for what seemed like forever, but no answer came. Jake checked to see that the green power light was on at the top of his radio, and it glowed back at him in the dying light.

Let me just get this done.

He moved across the street quickly and deliberately, his head swinging back and forth as he scanned windows, alleys, and door-ways around the sight of his rifle. He arrived at the open doorway and peered quickly inside, then pulled his head back as he absorbed what he saw—nothing.

"Should we go in?"

Jake turned, startled by the voice. Beside him stood Shayne, his sister-in-law's boyfriend, in full battle gear.

"What the hell are you doing here?" Jake asked. A faraway part of him felt a weird and inappropriate comfort at the change in the dream. Maybe it wasn't a death dream at all.

"Right," Shayne laughed back at him. "Come on, dude. Let's kill some bad guys." Then he slipped into the building through the dark doorway, smiling over his shoulder. "Let's make some war stories."

"Wait," Jake called after him in a harsh whisper, but Shayne was already gone. Jake keyed his mike again. "First squad is in the target building. We need a perimeter. We need security here." Then he followed Shayne into the shadowy room.

A dim light filtered into the large front room from deeper in the building. Jake recognized the inside immediately, though the building had been all wrong from the outside. As he moved left to clear his corner, he saw Shayne take a knee.

"Contact!" Jake heard his dream partner shout, and Shayne began firing before Jake could stop him.

"Wait," Jake hollered over the deafening roar of Shayne's M4.

There had been three or four three-round bursts from the rifle while Shayne screamed "Woo-hoo" in delight. Then he turned to Jake and rose, a huge smile on his face.

"Oh my God, that was awesome!" Shayne said and slapped Jake on the back. "This is so cool, dude. I totally just blew away that guy. Did you see it? Did you see all the blood?"

Jake pushed past Shayne into the back room.

The kid lay facedown by the bottom of the stairs. Unlike last time, there was no doubt about whether he was dead or not. Half his head, from his left eyebrow up, was completely gone. His right arm lay in a tangled and bloody mess beside him, connected to his shoulder by a thin strip of grey skin.

Jake spun around in anger, grabbing Shayne by the front of his body armor.

"What the hell is wrong with you? He was just a kid."

Shayne continued to smile back idiotically.

"Oh my God, that was so friggin' cool, dude." He began to laugh.

Jake yanked him closer. Just before he readjusted so he could slap the shit out of him, a deafening gunshot echoed in the room and Shayne's head evaporated completely, leaving only his neck, which sprayed blood across Jake's face. Jake let go and watched the body crumple to the floor. Then he spun, painfully slowly, raising his rifle as he did.

He saw just the bare feet as they dashed up the stairs, then disappeared. Jake dashed up the stairs in pursuit, his rifle up and ready and his finger inside the trigger guard. As he topped the stairs, he heard the distinctive double pop of an M4 followed by a thump. Slowly he scanned the room.

Cal stood in a half crouch, smoke coming from the barrel of his rifle like in an old western movie. Jake looked where Cal aimed, and saw the barefoot man against the wall, blood dripping to the floor behind him—just as he remembered it. He looked down, but the strangely intact, amputated leg was not at his feet where it should have been.

"Emma is going to be so pissed," Cal said. "You were supposed to watch Shayne's back. You guys were supposed to come back together."

"I'm sorry," Jake said and felt tears fill his eyes.

"Don't tell me," Cal said and shook his head. "Tell Kelly."

Then white heat from the explosion engulfed Jake as Cal exploded yet again, spraying him with gore as he did almost every night. When the smoke cleared, Jake looked down and saw only a bloody thumb where his best friend had been.

He screamed.

Jake grabbed at the hands that seemed to claw at him and wondered why in the hell one of the guys would be grappling with him. Had he screamed that loudly? For a moment he had a panicked fear that perhaps the FOB was being overrun—maybe this wasn't Reed or Mike Swanson at all. Maybe someone was going to try and saw off his head. He squeezed tighter on the wrist he had grabbed.

And Rachel winced in pain.

Jake recognized immediately where he was and what he was doing. He released his grip on Rachel's wrist and reached gently for her. His gut tightened when she pulled away. Then she seemed to realize he was back from his nightmare and she collapsed on top of him, her arms around his neck and her voice coming in pained sobs.

"I'm so sorry, Jake," she wailed. He felt her tears, warm on his neck. "What is it, baby? What is going on? How can I help you?"

Jake had no answers to any of her questions, so he just held her and let his own tears mix with hers as he rocked her and made a sad "shhh" sound in her ear.

He had nothing else to give.

CHAPTER 32

Craig knew there was no reason in the world why he should be a part of the homecoming for Caleb's friends, due back in town later today. He had scanned the list Maggie had found for him, hoping he might find a name—any name—of someone from his congregation. There was no one there.

Except Jake and Rachel.

Craig rationalized that since Jake had been home for nearly a week, it would be inappropriate for Craig to show up at the homecoming for him, especially since he had not called on the young couple yet. He pressed his thumbs into his temples and let out a trembling sigh.

That wasn't the reason. He couldn't explain his anxiety at attending the homecoming any more than he could explain why he had not yet visited Jake. He'd convinced himself that Jake needed time to settle in, but in truth Craig knew it was he who needed more time. Why in hell was he having such difficulty with this?

A soothing voice pulled him from his thoughts with a start. "How are you doin', boss?"

Craig smiled at his friend and colleague as best he could. Chris had an easy way about him, a casual style that belied the staggering smarts and insight his associate pastor had. Unlike Craig, who when he looked in the mirror saw anything but a confident evangelical pastor, Chris *looked* like a pastor—a younger, good-looking southern pastor.

"Good, Chris," Craig answered and leaned back in his chair, reaching almost unconsciously for his University of Florida football—his security blanket of late, it seemed. "What's up?"

"Takin' a break," Chris said and plopped down in an oversized chair beside Craig's desk. "You wouldn't even have hired an associate pastor if you didn't hate the business stuff so much."

Craig laughed at the running joke. It was true—he hated the number crunching with a passion rivaling his love of preaching. But Chris balanced his ministry in a million ways more important than his ability to manage the business side of things. Often when Craig found himself stuck, it was Chris who so easily found the theological connection he needed to polish a message, or an emotional answer to a problem for a parishioner, one that Craig would later find so obvious he would wonder why he hadn't seen it himself. Chris also had a relaxed style of preaching that Craig often envied.

"Yeah, well, the more we grow, the more secure your job becomes."

They laughed together.

"Seen Jacob and Rachel yet?"

Always to the heart of the matter, his partner. Craig looked at the football he was spinning over and over in his hand.

"Not yet," he said. "Letting him settle in."

Chris nodded but pursed his lips.

"I know you're struggling with this, Craig," Chris said, and his blue eyes looked right through all of Craig's armor. "There's no shame if you need me to make the call. I can touch base and then you can follow up later."

"You think I'm waiting too long?" Craig asked.

Chris shrugged, but his eyes reflected the answer they both knew.

"Your call, boss," his friend said softly.

Craig nodded.

"I'll have Maggie set something up. Maybe I can see them tomorrow." Now that he knew what he should do, he felt he should see them before the homecoming event for the unit that was only a few days away. If they couldn't work that out, he would try and meet with the couple as soon as possible after the Saturday event.

Chris rose and put a hand on his shoulder.

Taking a break, my ass.

"Want me to come along?"

Craig's ego screamed a resounding "no" in his head. But was that the best thing for the young couple he was supposed to be serving? Craig sighed heavily.

"That would be awesome, Chris," he said and looked at his friend. The blue eyes held no judgment, only compassion. "What the hell is wrong with me, man?"

Chris smiled.

"You're human," Chris said with a wink. "Doesn't that suck?"

They both laughed. Craig had no doubt God had sent Chris to him and their church. His friend squeezed his shoulder and left through the side door that connected their offices. Craig's phone chirped and he pressed the intercom button.

"Hey, Maggie," he said and realized he felt so much better. He looked at the door between his and Chris' office and smiled. "What's up?"

"Kelly stopped by and dropped off an invitation for you," his assistant answered through the speaker on the phone. "I asked her if she wanted to see you, but she just asked me to pass on the invite. It's for the unit homecoming."

Craig felt an ache in his chest at the same time.

As always, the Lord was a hundred steps ahead of him.

"Thanks, Maggie," he said with a resigned smile. "Put it on my calendar and remind me to call her later. Can you also try and set up a meeting for me?"

Craig passed on his request to meet with Jake and Rachel and then Maggie clicked off. He leaned back in his chair and tossed the football back and forth between his hands. He had a lot of work to do on the message for this week's sermon, but for the moment he allowed his mind to stay where it had drifted, and to think about how he could comfort Jake and Rachel.

CHAPTER 33

"I think you'll like Reed. I like that dude a lot, but just know he is, like, really quiet and hard to read. Mike is totally a loser, but you know, back here I might even like him. Not everyone's a soldier, but maybe he's not such a tool back at home."

Jake was talking a mile a minute, almost manic in his demeanor, and Rachel struggled to keep up with all he was saying. She saw that he tapped his right index finger on the side of the gearshift almost constantly—a nervous tic he had developed somewhere and that he now seemed to do mostly when his eyes glazed over and he stared away at nothing. She was having a hard time reading whether Jake was nervous or just excited, or maybe something else altogether. She had never seen him quite like this, but she would take this over the sullen, withdrawn man she'd lived with the last few days. She would take it a thousand times and Sunday over the man who tossed and turned, and sometimes screamed in terror, in her bed at night. She put her hand on his leg and squeezed.

"I'm just so excited to meet all of your friends. I know that I kinda know some of them already, but not really." She stopped herself from continuing down that road. She had only really ever known Shawn, who was dead, and Pete, who Jake had not said a word about since he got back.

And Cal, of course.

As Jake continued with his rapid-fire descriptions of people she didn't know and things she didn't completely understand, her thoughts drifted again to Kelly. Since Jake had returned, she'd spoken to Kelly only once, and that had been yesterday. She loved her friend for giving her space right now and hated herself for needing it. She couldn't imagine what the homecoming would conjure up for Kelly. She was glad when, on their brief call yesterday—which Rachel had conducted in hushed tones, somehow afraid of Jake knowing they were speaking—Kelly had told her that Pastor Craig had agreed to accompany her to the homecoming.

Jake's leg jumping up and down jerked her back to the cab of his truck and away from the soul-crushing guilt about Kelly. Her husband looked at her with arched eyebrows.

"Huh?" she said.

To her relief, Jake laughed—a nervous laugh, but no flash of temper, at least.

"Where'd you go?" he asked, and she shrugged nervously. "Guess I'm kind of rambling, aren't I?"

Rachel smiled and shook her head.

"I think once everyone is home …" Jake's eyes drifted off and then he jerked his head back to her again. "Once everyone is home, it'll finally be over, Rach. I'll really be home and we can be back to who we were, you know? We can pick our life back up."

Rachel felt a wave of hope and smiled for real.

"I want that so much, Jake." She felt tears in her eyes, and Jake's strong hand on her thigh, which made her shudder a bit. "I love you."

"I love you too, baby," he said in a pained voice. "Everything's going to be okay really soon."

"I know," she said.

God, please let that be true. Please, Lord, let me find my husband again.

The National Guard base was fairly small, so the public park, with its shady trees, picnic tables, and lake, was much better, and happier, for the homecoming party. As they pulled into the parking lot, Rachel was shocked at the number of vehicles. She'd always thought of his unit as just Jake and his friends, though of course she knew it was much larger than that. Still, the lot, overflowing with double-parked vehicles, shocked her. She had asked about inviting their families, but Jake's face had clouded and she hadn't brought it up again. She wondered if it would have helped her to have someone with her, then remembered Kelly and Pastor Craig would be there, though she felt little comfort at that thought.

They parked and headed over to the enormous crowd scattered about the open field and clustered in the covered shelters at three of the four corners. Everyone was in casual civilian clothes, but it became easy to tell who the service members were. Not just because of the short hair—it was something in their eyes, something she was painfully familiar with seeing in Jake's eyes. The distant look and awkward gaze that pulled away. She saw immediately, however, that the look disappeared when they spoke to each other.

Jake pulled her by the hand toward the concrete slab and tin roof sheltering a dozen picnic tables by the lake.

"There's someone you have to meet," he said. Rachel liked that his voice sounded more like—well, more like Jake.

"Jake," a muscular, dark-skinned man called out when they were close. The man bear-hugged Jake, lifting him up off the ground. Then he set him down and clapped both of his shoulders in his powerful hands. "Surprised you could find the place. Seemed to have trouble finding your way around Helmand." Her husband laughed at whatever the joke meant, and then both men turned to her. Jake's friend, his kind eyes in contrast to the intimidating rest of him, reached out a hand. "You must be Rachel," he said and took her small hand in both of his. "It's awesome to finally meet you. We missed each other at the predeployment picnic." There was something familiar about the voice that brought a strange anxiety that seemed out of place.

"Nice to meet you, too," she said and realized that, whoever he was, she meant it. "We didn't stay long at that picnic. We had a family thing."

"Rachel, this is First Sar'n Morrow—my platoon leader," Jake said.

"TC," the man corrected him. He held her eyes a moment and then added, "We spoke on the phone once."

And it all came back. The platoon leader's kindness on one of the worst days of her life. He had spoken with her before and after she spoke with Jake. After ... after all that had happened. She felt immediately connected to the man, but fought the waterfall of conflicting emotions just the same.

"Of course," she said and regained her smile as TC released her hand. "Of course. You have no idea how you helped me that night, sir," she added.

Jake and TC laughed, but Rachel missed the joke. The First Sergeant patted her back.

"We're not laughing at you," he promised. "It's TC to you, First Sar'n to Jake and the men, and it ain't 'sir' to no one." Both men laughed again. TC smiled warmly. "Pete was right," he added. "You're way too good for this clown."

Rachel smiled politely. Her stomach churned, not just at the mention of Pete, but at the dark look the name brought to Jake's face, though the look disappeared as quickly as it came. "I'm lucky to have him," she assured TC. She rubbed her husband's arm and he took her hand. "And so grateful to everyone to have him back. And thankful to God, of course."

Jake let go of her hand, a flash of something on his face as he turned away, pretending to scan the crowd.

"Of course," TC said. He slapped Jake on the back. "Jake here is one of the best squad leaders I ever had," he said. "A real badass and a helluva soldier."

"Squad leader?" she asked, before she could stop herself. She knew what that was—Caleb had been a squad leader. This was the first she had heard that Jake had led men in the war, though now her mind clicked to something she had overheard between Jake and his dad at her parents' house. Her husband shrugged uncomfortably and she let it go.

"Find me in a little while, bro," TC said to Jake and man-hugged him again. "Gonna work the room," he said to Rachel with a wink. She wondered if she had treaded on some unspoken tension, and she felt bad. She loved seeing Jake excited to talk to someone—anyone. He seemed like the old Jake.

Rachel took Jake's hands in hers. "You didn't tell me you were a squad leader, baby. That's awesome," she said, wondering if it was. "That's, like, a big deal, right? Like a promotion?"

Jake shrugged again. "Not a promotion, really. Just a job that needed doing." His jaw twitched. They both knew why.

"I'm proud of you," Rachel said, fighting the wave of nausea and dizziness, unsure if it was prompted by thoughts of Cal or by Jake not telling her about something she thought was a big deal. Before his deployment, he had often talked about making squad leader. Apparently he had not only made it and had led men in combat, but had been really good at it.

"Let's get a beer," Jake said, changing the subject and leading her away. "I have to find Reed so you can meet him. I think he might be married too."

Might be married?

It seemed bizarre that Jake wouldn't know for sure. This was someone he had lived with in close quarters for months. In fact, now that she thought about it, it seemed even more bizarre that she had never heard Reed's name until the drive over today, despite their (admittedly strained) phone calls several times a week.

Her husband was a quiet rock star. Every few minutes another young man would come and slap him on the back, or occasionally embrace him in the classic back-pat, hips-out man hug of athletes and soldiers. Some of the men seemed in awe of him and others greeted him like a casual friend, but all seemed to admire him. There were constant references to things she didn't understand—the military had such a slang- and acronym-filled language. It made Rachel feel awkward, like she had crashed a party she wasn't invited to. Not that she minded. She loved seeing Jake with his friends—though that word seemed out of place, maybe—and had no problem being the third wheel. No, what bothered her was the discovery that there was so much she didn't know about her husband. It felt stupid—being bothered by that, especially when there were rules about how much he could say from a war zone—but she and Jake had always shared so freely. She had always felt that no one on earth knew her better than Jake, and vice versa. He felt like a stranger now, and she hated that feeling.

"They didn't even have a friggin' chance to surrender, I heard." A young man laughed and looked expectantly at Jake, who was smiling, but the smile hadn't reached his eyes. "Doubt they had time to think anything but *oh, shit!*"

"I engaged the enemy using escalating force as outlined in the rules of engagement for our AOR," Jake said stiffly, then sucked down a long swallow of beer.

"Well, you smoked 'em both so fast they got buried with surprised looks on their faces."

Another round of laughter from the group.

"Dead men tell no tales," another soldier said with a chuckle.

"They can never be dead enough," Jake said, and his ice-cold voice gave Rachel a chill. He was looking off, past the group, with his faraway-and-elsewhere stare that she hated so much. Were these men talking about some people Jake had shot? People he had killed? She knew what happened in war, but the idea of her husband shooting two men dead seemed almost impossible. The idea that he was now laughing about it was something even worse than impossible.

"Rachel!"

She turned with a start away from Jake, and Kelly wrapped her arms around Rachel's neck. Rachel hugged her back, breathing in the warm comfort of the familiar scent of her best friend. Kelly pulled away and held her at arm's length. Rachel felt tears in her eyes and desperately willed them back. Kelly's smile was warm, but her eyes had the slightest cloud in them.

This must be so hard for her.

"Rachel, you look so awesome. I am so happy that Jake is home and safe. You look so much better," she said and then laughed and covered her mouth. "You know what I mean."

"Thank you, sweetie. Are you…" Rachel swallowed hard. What did one say? For Kelly, this must be like a wake. "Are you all right?"

"I'm better every day," she whispered into Rachel's ear. "It's been a struggle, but God has never left me." She smiled like someone with an awkward secret. "I'm not mad at Him anymore," she said with a shrug.

"Mad at who?" Rachel's voice and throat tightened. Was she mad at Jake? Were they going to have this conversation right here? Now? Kelly squeezed her shoulder and smiled again.

"I never blamed anyone," she said, apparently reading Rachel's mind, "but I was pretty mad at God for a little while."

Rachel looked down at her feet, unsure what to say. Then she glanced over at her husband, still deep in animated conversation with people she didn't know and gratefully unaware that Kelly was here. Rachel was unsure how that would affect him, and he seemed so happy right now. So like Jake. She became aware that she'd unconsciously shifted herself between Jake and Kelly.

"Where's Pastor Craig?" she asked and realized she was speaking in a hushed voice. She glanced nervously at Jake again.

"Talking to his fans," Kelly said, gesturing over her shoulder. Rachel saw the pastor, in his blue jeans and a loud, colorful shirt, gesturing madly with his arms to make some point, surrounded by a small group of men. She smiled. "He'll be over in a minute."

Rachel felt anxious at the thought of the pastor joining them. Not for herself, but for Jake, who she had no doubt would be uncomfortable with Craig being there. She realized how absurd that thought was, but that made her no less certain it was true. She was suddenly overwhelmed trying to guess what went on in Jake's head and what had happened to the new faith he had seemed so excited about.

"I'm gonna grab another beer. You want anything?"

Rachel felt herself start at Jake's touch and then her pulse quickened as she looked over at Kelly, nervous for both of them.

"Hi, Kelly," Jake said, as naturally and comfortably as if they were in the courtyard after church a year ago. Her husband hugged her best friend easily. "It's so great to see you."

"It's great to see you too, Jake," Kelly answered, though Rachel thought her cheer sounded a little forced. "I'm so glad you're home."

Jake looked at Rachel and raised an eyebrow. Rachel felt for a moment as if she were caught in some weird dream. She raised an eyebrow back.

"Something to drink?" Jake repeated with a smile. His gaze looked distant, unless that was just her imagination.

Rachel shook her head and Jake kissed her cheek and headed off with the small group of men he had been talking to. "Be right back," he hollered over his shoulder.

Rachel let out a trembling sigh.

"He seems like he's doing great," Kelly said and squeezed her arm. "I know you were worried."

Rachel nodded. "Yeah, he's great," she said, praying there was no hint otherwise in her voice. "I'm so glad he's home." She tried to take the last sentence back in her head, suddenly terrified of how selfish it must sound to her widowed friend.

"Yes" was all Kelly said, and Rachel tried to read nothing into the single word. Then her friend waved as Pastor Craig approached.

Rachel summoned her brave and happy face for the pastor and tried to chase off the words of death and killing that had come so easily from the husband she thought she knew.

CHAPTER 34

Jake hoped that he had contained his shock at turning and seeing Cal's wife—no, his *widow*—standing beside Rachel and smiling at him as if nothing at all had happened. For a moment he felt anger bordering on rage that she was there at all. Then he realized with anguish that his anger was at himself. She was there alone because he had not saved Cal. Then he had seen that damn pastor heading over. What could possibly ruin this day more?

"What kind ya want?" one of the first-platoon guys—he couldn't remember the guy's name, though he had patrolled with him dozens of times—asked as he flipped the lid up on an enormous cooler.

"Full," Jake answered, and the young man laughed and fished out a beer for him.

The cold beer felt good on his throat, which for some reason seemed to have that same burning dryness he'd often felt outside the wire. Given a choice between heading out on one more show-of-force patrol or hanging with his dead friend's wife and the pastor who had adored Cal—well, he had no doubt how easy that choice would be.

They blame you, of course. They would never blame everyone's favorite guy for dashing in front of a suicide bomber like a dumbass.

The voice in Jake's head was familiar but not his own. For a moment he felt the heat of the explosion and the warm, wet paste of Cal's blood drying on his cheeks beneath his combat goggles. Jake squeezed his hands into fists, cold beer spilling onto the back of his left hand, and choked down a sob.

"Dude, I totally remember that! We were back at the FOB but heard all about it. You capped two shitheads that day, didn't you, Jake?"

Jake couldn't place the voice and couldn't look over, because the world seemed to be spinning around. He forced out a laugh and raised his beer over his head as he turned away, terrified the others would see the tears in his eyes.

"Gotta find a lav," he called over his shoulder, trying desperately to sound in control. "Back after I dump some beer."

Jake weaved through the crowd around the coolers, trying to remember which way the long line of Porta-Johns was. He needed to find Rachel, to just hold her for a minute and let her touch pull him back to the here and now, but then he remembered she was with the pastor and the widow. He felt certain that joining them would send him spiraling out of control. Maybe he just needed a couple of minutes alone.

And more beer. That will numb the pain, the familiar voice almost hissed into his ear.

Jake veered away from the crowd lined up in front of the blue plastic portable toilets and headed toward the woods at the edge of the lake. His bladder screamed out that, hey, it really did need to take a leak.

I'll piss in the woods. I gotta get away from all of these people and get my shit back together.

Jake walked a short distance down a dirt path, then left the path and moved deeper into the trees. He chugged what was left of his beer, then dropped the bottle to the ground at his feet, pulled down his fly, and sighed as he relieved himself, his head leaned against the bark of the tree in front of him. He shuddered, feeling tears on his left cheek.

"Oh, my God," he said aloud. "What do I do to make this shit stop?"

He needed to find Rachel and then get the hell out of here and go home.

Find your way back to your path, Jake. The answers are there.

Have another beer. That will chase away your demons.

"Both of you shut the hell up," he mumbled to the familiar voice and the voice from his dream.

Jake zipped up and squatted down on his heels, his face in his hands. The last thing he needed was more beer—his head was swimmy enough. He rubbed his temples and spent a few minutes doing his four-count tactical breathing until his pulse finally slowed and his breathing no longer seemed raspy and loud. Then he let out a long, whistling sigh and got slowly to his feet, steadying himself on the tree before remembering he had peed on it and pulling his hand back.

He felt better. He had no desire at all to talk to the pastor or the widow, but maybe he could chat with some guys for a few minutes and then Rachel would find him. She would sense his need to be away from Kelly and Pastor Craig, right? She would find him and they could slip away. Everyone was home safe now—except the dead guys—so he would slap a few backs and then put this whole life behind him.

"Time to get back to the real world," he mumbled and strode back out of the woods.

"Couldn't take the line, huh?"

The laughing voice jerked him back. TC grinned at him, hands in his pockets.

"Too much beer," Jake said, trying to sound normal, or happy, or drunk—anything but crazy.

TC smiled again.

"Been there," he said and joined stride with Jake, who realized he hadn't even paused to talk to his First Sar'n. "You okay, buddy?" TC asked.

Jake frowned. Weird enough that his First Sergeant had started calling him Jake after they lost Cal and Shawn, instead of "young lady" or "jerk-off." If he was now "buddy," something was clearly wrong in the universe.

"Yeah, I'm good," he said. "Just gotta find my wife. Might be time to head home. She hates these things," he added, thinking how brilliantly that would explain everything.

TC nodded. "Supposed to be an awards ceremony late this afternoon," he said, halting, which forced Jake to do the same. "Didn't figure you would want to be there, actually." He fished in his pocket and came out with a small blue case. "Hate those things myself," he added with a shrug and a smile, "but what're ya gonna do, right?"

Jake's throat tightened, but he nodded. "What the hell is that?"

The thought that there was some medal—an *award*, for God's sake—that they would present him after his failures in Afghanistan made a wave of nausea sweep over him that he couldn't blame on the beer.

TC nodded like he had read his thoughts.

"Purple Heart," he said. "For your injuries that day."

Jake said nothing, but stared at the blue box like it might contain a scorpion that would attack him if he touched it. TC tapped the side of the box with his index finger.

"You're in for a commendation medal too. End-of-tour award. You really cowboyed up, and your leadership with your squad got a lot of guys home. That award will come later." He held out the box to Jake, who felt himself shaking his head. "Take it, Jake," his First Sergeant said softly. "You're an amazing soldier, but this medal is just for the beating you took."

Jake reached out and took the box, which felt cold in his hand, and slipped it into his jeans pocket and out of sight quickly. How could he possibly be expected to wear a medal that would also be awarded to Cal—and to Shawn? Again TC seemed to read his mind, and Jake figured clair-voyance must come with being a platoon leader.

"It hasn't been announced yet, but it sounds like Cal will get a Silver Star for what he did that day for sure—maybe even the Distinguished Service Cross." TC looked down at his hands. "If it was up to me, he would get the Medal of Honor, but I guess he went to the wrong war."

Jake felt his head swim. *I just want to stop thinking about that day—about all of this shit.*

TC put his arm around Jake and started to lead them back toward the cookout.

"You have another week before you have to come back to work," he said. "And then you'll have a lot of decisions to make." Part of Jake knew TC was referring to career decisions, but another part felt such a conver-sation was inconceivable. Jake nodded. "Any chance you can come by on Monday or Tuesday anyway? Just a short chat—two Army buddies, nothing formal."

The last time the First Sergeant had talked to him as an "Army buddy," it wasn't all that friggin' awesome. He nodded anyway.

"Sure, First Sar'n," he said. "I'll come by Monday morning."

"Great," TC said and seemed relieved, as if there was any chance Jake could say no to the invitation. "I'll buy ya breakfast," he added.

Jake walked quietly beside him for a moment and then peeled off when it was obvious that TC was headed back toward the shelter by the lake.

"Better go find the wife," he said, certain his smile and casual wave had fooled his platoon leader. "I'll call before I come over Monday morning."

TC smiled and waved back. Jake could feel his eyes on the back of his head and struggled with the now-familiar feeling of anger. He walked slowly, scanning the scattered clusters of people spread out over the park. He wanted to find someone to hang with just long enough for the horrible feelings to go away and for Rachel to find him. As much as he needed to leave, he needed to avoid Kelly and the pastor more. He heard a burst of familiar laughter and looked right toward the smaller shelter near the entrance to the park.

Pete stood in a small group of second-platoon guys, all of whom Jake knew. The desire to be with friends was overshadowed by the fear of facing Pete. How could he? Pete had been right about everything and Jake had been an idiot. He had let his fear about the war drive him to the fantasy Cal had been selling about God, believing that reading the Bible and saying a prayer would make the war easier—that it might even keep them all safe. Jake realized he was angry about that—angry at Cal. Angry at Cal for dying and proving himself wrong. And Jake had been wrong along with him until that day. It had taken Pete getting hurt and their friends getting killed for Jake to see it. What the hell do you say to that guy?

Pete laughed again and turned his way, and for a moment their eyes met. Then Pete grinned broadly and waved Jake over. For a moment Jake considered pretending he hadn't seen Pete, but that opportunity had passed, so he screwed a smile on his face and waved back, walking toward Pete, who now headed his way. They met halfway, and Pete, still grinning, wrapped him up in a huge bear hug.

"Dude!"

Even a few beers in himself, Jake could smell the brewery on his former friend.

"Holy shit, dude," Pete continued, his words just slightly slurred. "Holy shit, how are you, man?"

"I'm great," Jake said. Pete showed only smiles, and Jake figured he had worried for nothing. Pete didn't seem to hate him at all. In fact, Jake felt some comfort that the smile was the same goofy smile that Pete'd had before the deployment. Maybe he was that same fun guy again, and if so, there might yet be hope for Jake.

"Glad to be home."

"Right?" Pete said, a little louder than was probably necessary. "Shoulda come home with me, dude."

Jake nodded, not sure what else to say. That would have been completely impossible for him, of course.

"I hated leaving you guys," Pete continued. His gaze seemed far away. "I didn't even get to see you or talk to you after—well, after everything happened." He glanced up at Jake and then looked away. "I was surprised they didn't make you come home with me." He took a long pull on his beer and Jake suddenly wished he had his own beer to drink. "Not that they made me come home, I guess," Pete continued in a weird voice. "But my back was all jacked up in the explosion. They asked if I wanted to go home, and I didn't want to leave you guys, but I was, like, you know—not wanting to stay and not be able to perform and all. I didn't want to slack off and get someone else hurt."

Jake shifted uncomfortably. "Everybody missed you, Pete, but we knew you got hurt. We were all just glad you were okay." Jake realized that for most of the last couple of months he had actually not thought about Pete at all, and remembered no real conversations about him. Jake wasn't sure he had even heard Pete had hurt his back. Once Pete headed home, it was kind of like he didn't even exist anymore, at least to the men still in Afghanistan. He had disappeared that day with the others. And now—despite the goofy grin—Jake realized he was talking to a stranger. Was it Pete who was different or was it both of them?

"Yeah, well, I would much rather have been in the fight with you guys," Pete continued, but still he didn't look Jake in the eyes. "They had me driving a desk, doing a bunch of admin bullshit for the unit. You wouldn't believe how much work there is to do to support the unit when they're deployed."

Jake nodded uncomfortably again. Who the hell was this guy? He was struck with the realization that his friendship with Pete was changed forever. After today he'd believed the rest of his life would go back to normal—especially his relationship with Rachel—but things with Pete would never be the same.

He didn't even reach out to you, did he? Not even an email. He just sat back here, had fun, drank beer, and forgot about the friends he left behind in that shithole. Too busy to email or send a care package to the guys still ass-deep in the suck while he lived the good life.

With some effort, Jake shook away the whispering voice.

"We need to get together, dude," he said to Pete, forcing his best former-Jake grin. "I gotta go run and find Rachel before she gets pissed."

"Yeah," Pete said. "I owe you like a thousand beers or something. Let's get together this week."

Jake had no idea why the hell Pete would think that he owed Jake anything. To Jake, it would certainly seem the other way around, and that debt was the only thing that could make Jake endure more of the awkward time with his former friend.

"You working on base next week?" he asked Pete. Jake realized he had taken a step back from his friend for some reason.

"Nah," Pete said and chugged more beer. "I was supposed to work to catch up on all the admin stuff we got going on with everyone getting back." He looked down at his feet. "But my back is still all jacked up and it's been killing me lately," he continued, his voice small. "So I took leave next week."

Jake nodded. "Well, just call me, I guess," he said.

"Definitely," Pete said. "You still got the same cell number?"

"Same number."

"I'll call ya this week," Pete said and waved over his shoulder.

Jake watched Pete stagger away while a chorus of off-key thoughts competed in his head. He ignored them all.

"There you are."

At the unexpected hand on his arm, Jake jumped, reaching for the weapon he no longer carried.

Rachel pulled her hand away and grimaced.

"Sorry, baby," she said, her voice full of pain. "I'm sorry. I forgot."

She forgot her husband is crazy now.

With some struggle, he found his Jake-grin again.

"Don't be silly," he said and took her hand. He scanned quickly around and felt relief that neither Kelly nor the pastor was with her. "Just didn't hear you come up. Great soldier, huh?" he asked with a forced laugh. Rachel smiled politely and rubbed the back of his hand.

"Weren't there some other people you wanted me to meet?" she asked.

Jake loved her so much in that moment. He suspected Rachel had no desire to talk to any more soldiers today. He knew for sure he didn't.

"Nah," he said. "Everyone's pretty much lit. That's what happens when you have free beer for guys who have been in a beer-free war zone for almost a year." He smiled at his wife. "We can go whenever you want."

He thought Rachel's face showed relief.

"I think there's supposed to be some kind of award ceremony or something," she said. "You don't want to miss that, do you?"

Jake tapped the cold blue box in his back pocket with a finger. He had no desire to hear the bigwigs tell them how great they had done and hand out medals and give speeches. They were home. Time to move on.

"I'm fine to miss that," he said. "We can stay if you want, but I'm pretty much done."

"Let's head home, then," Rachel said and kissed his cheek.

"Do you need to say goodbye to anyone?" Jake asked, though he dreaded having to stop by and see Kelly and the pastor. He and Rachel used to joke about the hour it took them to leave a party while his wife said goodbye to everyone. He'd tell her she should start saying goodbye when they walked in, and then the timing would work out about right. He wondered if Rachel could read his thoughts, though, because she shook her head.

"No, I already said goodbye," she said and wrapped her arms around him. "Let's get home."

Jake sighed with relief and hugged her. He looked over at where Pete was weaving back and forth, his arms flailing while he told a story to a group of guys.

"I'm in," he told his wife and kissed her cheek. "Now I'm really home," he said.

Rachel smiled as they headed across the field to the crowded parking lot, but Jake couldn't shake the worry that she looked unconvinced.

CHAPTER 35

Jake stared at the ceiling. The morning light snuck in through the heavy curtains and painted a weird pattern that he tried to concentrate on to keep his mind from the disturbing parade of dreams he'd had. His left hand unconsciously caressed the cooling sheets on Rachel's side of the bed, while his right fingers caressed his cheek and temple—the site of the cuts and scrapes that had long ago healed after the explosion. Rachel had slipped from the room as quietly as possible and gotten dressed and done her makeup in the half bath off their family room, trying not to wake Jake up as she got ready for church.

He knew he should go with her. They had been apart for so long that a trip to church should hardly keep him from her side for even a short time. They had not even discussed Jake going the evening before, and Rachel had told him only that she would bring home some Starbucks coffee on her way back from church. Jake wondered if that had been a hint, but he had not taken the bait, instead telling her how awesome it would be to sleep in.

Not that he had any desire these days to spend more time with his eyes closed than was absolutely necessary.

"No sleeping in in the 'stan," he had told her. "Every day is Monday, and anyway, the shitty little racks are so uncomfortable you can't wait for morning to get the hell out of them, even to go to muster and have a terrible breakfast."

Rachel had squeezed his hand and changed the subject.

The evening had been great and filled Jake with hope that he was on track to get his life back. By evening he had more than recovered from his afternoon beer buzz, and they had laughed together about things

Jake couldn't even remember. They ordered a pizza and watched an old Will Ferrell movie on Netflix, holding hands and giggling together. They made love at bedtime. Jake fell asleep feeling almost like life was normal.

The dreams had dampened his optimism only slightly. Jake figured that they would also disappear quickly, now that things were getting normal again. He stared at the ceiling, enjoying the feel of their bed, and sighed heavily. He'd forced his thoughts away from the nightmares, but his mind instead found its way to the questions that TC would no doubt have for him tomorrow. Was he going to stay in the unit? If so, would he try and stay full-time, or was it time to get a civilian job and just do the weekend-warrior National Guard deal like most of his platoonmates? He had no idea what else was on the agenda, but he suspected there was more.

The harsh reality of those questions that needed answers made the luxury of lying in bed fade, so he swung his legs out from under the sheets.

Rachel had left coffee warming in the pot, with a note that she loved him and a reminder that she would be bringing home Starbucks. Jake glanced at the time on the microwave oven clock—probably another forty-five minutes until she got home. He would have a short cup now and still be able to enjoy whatever she brought him. A half cup of black coffee in hand, Jake plopped down on the couch and turned on the TV.

In what felt like only minutes, his empty cup was on the coffee table and he half-consciously clicked the remote on his third or fourth trip around the circle of the guide channel. Again he failed to register what the choices were, his mind instead seducing him into thoughts about Cal and Afghanistan and images from his nightmares. Then the scrolling screen jumped to the right again and there was a whole new list of two hundred or so choices of TV shows to watch.

Jake sighed, clicked the TV off, and dropped the remote on the couch beside him. He was surprised at how much time the cable box clock told him had slipped by. He wanted almost desperately for Rachel to come in the door and rescue him from his damn mind.

Images of Kelly, his best friend's widow, now replaced the barrage of nightmare pictures. He saw her in her Sunday best, waiting for "the boys" to go to breakfast after church. He saw her at their small kitchen table, laughing, a plastic band on her head holding a card with the word she was supposed to guess from their clues. Her hand was on Cal's arm. Then his mind invented a picture of her standing beside an open grave, dressed all in black, as they lowered a flag-draped coffin into the dark hole. In his made-up daydream, she stood alone until Jake came over in full-dress uniform and handed her a flag.

On behalf of a grateful nation. I'm so sorry, Kelly.

But she wouldn't look up at him.

"Oh, holy shit," he exclaimed, and snatched the remote from the couch and turned the TV back on, clicking over to Sports Center and turning up the volume, as if the noise could drown out the pictures in his head.

He didn't hear the door open, but he heard Rachel's keys rattle onto the table by the front door. He straightened himself up a little on the couch.

"Hey, baby," he called. "I'm in here."

"So I hear," she hollered. "Why is the TV so loud?"

Rachel kissed his cheek from behind the couch and handed him a big cup of steaming coffee. Then he heard her high heels clatter to the floor and she came around the couch and plopped down beside him. Jake accepted her light kiss and took her free hand after lowering the volume on the television with the remote.

"Glad you're home," he said, hoping she didn't sense the real reason behind his relief.

Rachel smiled and said nothing, maybe not sure what to say and feeling that talking about church might be a mistake. Still, Jake sensed she had something to say.

"Everything okay?" he asked. He couldn't be sure why he felt so anxious. He knew he wasn't quite his old self, but surely she saw he was well on his way.

"Jake," she said softly.

Uh-oh. That doesn't sound good.

"What's up?" he asked, ignoring the ache in his stomach.

"Please don't be mad, baby," Rachel said, then set her coffee down and took his free hand in both of hers. Jake hoped he looked cool and understanding, though he felt neither. "Pastor Craig asked about coming by this afternoon." She squeezed his hand gently. "His secretary left a few messages about it late last week, but I never got back to her. He asked me personally this morning at church. I know you feel funny talking to him right now, for some reason ..."

For some reason? How can I explain how betrayed I feel? I did the God thing, and where was God on the day Cal died? Where was God anywhere in Afghanistan—a place he has clearly forsaken? And where was God in my pain and loss?

"... but he really wants to check on us and welcome you home."

Jake leaned forward on one elbow but kept his hand in hers, despite the urge to pull it away. He struggled with competing feelings of anger and guilt, so he said nothing.

Rachel caressed his arm.

"Jake," she pleaded. He looked up at her and tried to smile, but he suspected his face showed nothing but stress. She continued, obviously with some difficulty. "Baby, when you found Christ over there, when you and ..." She paused, choking up. "When the two of you started praying together and reading together—it's just that you sounded so much happier than I'd ever heard you before. You seemed so excited." Rachel looked down, and the tear that trickled down her cheek calmed Jake's rising anger. He waited for her to continue, but it was pretty obvious where she was going. Rachel wiped her cheek. She looked Jake in the eyes. "You need Him now more than ever, baby. I don't understand."

At that, Jake did pull his hand away. He stood up and paced away from his crying wife.

"You don't understand? Really?" He tried to shove his hands into his pockets and then felt idiotic when both fists slid along the legs of his pocketless sweats. "What's to understand? I tried it Cal's way, didn't I? I said the prayers and believed God would be with us and keep us safe. I read the damn Book and tried to see how it fit into everything I was doing. I even let myself feel those things—those feelings inside that you always talk about. What did that get us? Just where the hell was God that day, Rachel?" He stared at his crying wife, his hands now on his hips. He realized he was towering over her and stepped back a bit, but the rage in him kept growing. A part of him felt relief that he wasn't close enough to grab her by the shoulders. Jake heard his voice rise into a raging scream that frightened even him. "Cal is dead, Rachel. Cal is dead, Shawn is dead, Pete is totally screwed up, and hell, I'm not much better. Just where in the hell is your God in all that?"

Jake felt himself shaking and knew he had to get away, like, right now. He feared that she would follow him into the bedroom, so he stormed to the front door and nearly pulled his shoulder out of joint yanking against the dead-bolted lock.

"Shit," he hollered.

Then he spun the lock, pulled open the door, and stormed out. Jake did manage to choke out an "I'll be back in a few minutes" over his shoulder, and to control the urge to slam the door.

He walked down the sidewalk, frustrated again by his lack of pockets and his fists bouncing against his thighs, and did his best four-count tactical breathing. He stepped on a stone and then stubbed a toe on the uneven sidewalk. He swore under his breath and wished he had thought to bring shoes.

I just need to calm down. I need to get my shit together and get back to check on Rachel. None of this is her fault.

Rachel had never discouraged him from joining the National Guard, even with the war going on. She had gently shared her fears, but never once tried to talk him out of anything. Cal and he had made the decision to do it with the support, but not any real enthusiasm, from their wives.

Jake also knew he would never survive what he was going through without his wife. Rachel was the best thing that had ever happened to him and he needed her more than ever. It occurred to him that she had suffered loss and pain too, and maybe she needed him as much as he needed her. Some husband he was turning out to be.

Jake sighed and looked back at their house. He remembered when they had moved in, how excited and in love they had been. It all seemed so far away, like in a story someone had made up and then convinced him was true.

Jake took a few more deep breaths and walked slowly back home. He would apologize and try to make everything all right. He owed her that for sticking with him through this. He would meet the damn pastor and listen to his bullshit about how everything is good for people who love God. He would do his best to bite his tongue and be polite. Maybe in a few months he would even be able to BS his way through church sometimes if it made Rachel happy.

Jake shook out his hands like a swimmer taking the blocks. Then he reached for the door with a quivering hand and opened it.

"Rachel?" he called into the quiet house. "Baby, I'm so sorry."

CHAPTER 36

As he turned his truck onto Jake and Rachel's quiet street, Craig had no real expectation that this afternoon would be easy. That had been confirmed around lunch when Rachel called, her voice full of tears, and cancelled the meeting. She had called back only a half hour later, the tears gone but her voice still strained, and apologized and asked if Craig could still come by for a short visit. The use of the word "short" was in no way lost on him.

"You okay?"

Craig looked over at the calm face of his associate pastor.

"You looked like you went to the Bahamas for a minute," Chris said with his patented boyish grin. Chris always had an infectious ease about him, and Craig—the "serious" one—found himself smiling back.

"I'm good," he said. He mentally checked the address and then pulled into the third driveway from the corner. "It's not like I'm in charge anyway, right?"

Chris' smile broadened.

"Giving up the control you never had anyway?" he asked with a chuckle, paraphrasing one of Craig's favorite lines.

"Right," Craig said with a laugh and pulled the keys from the ignition. Then he sighed. He looked more closely at Chris, comforted by the wisdom and seriousness he saw in his blue eyes, despite the boyish smile. "Will you?"

Chris nodded and bowed his head.

"Lord, be with us as we meet with Jake and Rachel. Please allow us to release our own barriers and egos to You and be vessels of Your plan for these two. Speak through Craig and comfort him in his own pain and doubt."

Craig winced, but nodded his bowed head at that.

"Bless this meeting and soften Jake's heart that he may hear and accept Your words and Your plan for him and his marriage. In Jesus' name we ask these things—Amen."

"Amen," Craig replied and slapped Chris on the knee. "Thanks, dude."

Chris nodded. "Got your back, man," he said.

Craig felt better and more confident as he walked with Chris to the front door.

Rachel answered the door after only a moment. Her face seemed tense, but her eyes were dry and her smile real enough.

"Thanks so much for coming, Pastor Craig," she said. "And I'm so glad to see you, Pastor Chris. I didn't know you were coming, but I'm glad you're here." She led them from the foyer to the adjoining family room and gestured to the couch. As they sat, she clasped her hands nervously. "Jake will be out in a just a minute," she said. "Can I get you guys anything?"

Craig had long ago realized that the imposition of accepting something, sometimes from people with very little to share, was vastly outweighed by his parishioners' universal need to do something, to offer something, when the pastor came to call.

"I'd love a glass of water," he said.

As expected, Rachel looked relieved to have something to do. "Pastor Chris?" she said.

"Whatever you're having is great," Craig's partner said.

Rachel headed to the adjoining kitchen.

"Jake will be right out," she repeated, and Craig wondered if that was more hope than fact.

He looked around the comfortable family room for clues to the couple. He knew from experience that people were often different at home than the folks he spoke with after church. Not intentionally—at least, not usually—but he was often surprised how different people he thought he knew were, once they were in the comfort of their own homes.

Not much evidence of that here. The pictures of Jake and Rachel were spread about the room and showed the happy couple he knew from Foundations Family Church. He knew Rachel much better, of course—she was very active in the children's program and had been part of the young women's group in the past. He was struck by the number of pictures of the couple together with Caleb and Kelly, though he knew they'd all been the best of friends. He felt his heart ache at Cal's smile and piercing, confident eyes.

An elbow in the side brought him back and he looked up at Chris, who gestured with his head toward the kitchen. Craig realized Rachel had asked him something.

"I'm sorry, Rachel," he said. "What was that?"

Rachel stuck her head in from the kitchen.

"I asked if you would prefer some iced tea."

"Sweet tea?" he asked, ignoring the concern on Chris' face.

"Of course," she said with a laugh, her voice sounding more like the Rachel he knew. "Some of us are *from* Virginia."

"Tea sounds great," he said. He smiled at what Debbie would say about all that sugar.

Rachel returned with two tall glasses of tea, which she handed out, and then jogged back to the kitchen, returning moments later with two more glasses, which she set on the coffee table. Then she sat down on the L-section of the couch beyond them, smoothing her dress and crossing her legs.

"Jake will be out in a minute," she said.

Craig nodded and sipped his tea.

"Awesome tea, thank you," he said. "Don't go tellin' Debbie I had this tall glass of sweet tea," he added with a wink. Rachel laughed, an easy comfortable laugh, but then glanced behind her at what Craig guessed to be the bedroom door. She touched her watch but resisted looking at it. "So how are you doing, Rachel?" he asked. "Must be great to have Jake home."

Rachel's face clouded for a moment and Craig worried what that meant.

"It is," she said, her smile back. "I missed him so much. It felt like five years, though nearly ten months is sure too long anyway."

"You take your time getting back to the children's program, Rachel," Chris chimed in. "You spend as much time together as you two need until Jake is all settled, okay?" One of Chris' many jobs was to oversee all the youth programs, though they had two youth pastors that did the actual hands-on ministry.

"Thank you," Rachel said, and her eyes ticked toward the bedroom door again. "It's an adjustment, of course. I love him being home, but it takes time for him to, I don't know, get all the way here or something."

That sounded odd. Craig realized that he had not had much experience working with veterans and their families. They weren't really a military town, except for the National Guard base not too far away. There were plenty of veterans in the congregation, but not any "fresh" veterans—until now. He suddenly felt a little overwhelmed again.

"What do you mean?" he asked, trying to sound as casual as possible.

As if on cue—or maybe because he'd been listening at the door—Jake appeared from the bedroom, the big teenage smile Craig remembered on his face.

"Hi, Pastor Craig," he said and reached out a hand from behind the couch. Craig twisted awkwardly to accept the firm handshake. "Pastor Chris," Jake said with a nod.

"Great to see you, Jake," Chris said. "Welcome home, bud."

"Thanks a lot," Jake said. For a moment something a little like anger flashed in Jake's eyes and Craig felt underqualified again.

God is here, and He's fully qualified.

He felt better at the mental reminder.

Jake sat beside his wife and took her hand in his. Rachel leaned over and grabbed Jake's tea, which she handed to him.

"Thanks, baby," Jake said and kissed her cheek. Then he took a sip and held Craig's gaze. There was that look in his eyes again, and Craig shifted uncomfortably.

Small talk proved difficult, since Jake had been completely out of touch for nearly a year. They chatted a little about his plans with the Guard, but Jake had little to say. It seemed he hadn't made any decisions and Craig got the impression he was supposed to talk with people in the Army later in the week. Chris talked with Rachel about a few of the youth program kids, none of whom Craig could place by name, and they made the obligate queries about the couple's parents. Craig realized quickly that he probably needed to either leave or dive in.

"Well, Jake," he said and leaned forward, placing his tea on the table. "We're sure glad you're back. I know you've been through a lot the last few months, and Chris and I just wanted to see that you were doing okay and see what we might be able to do to help you and Rachel."

Jake raised an eyebrow.

"We're doing okay," he said, his voice flat. He looked over at Rachel, who smiled but looked down at her tea. "It's been tough, I guess, but we're doing. Right, sweetheart?"

"Right," Rachel said.

Craig nodded.

Jake continued. "Look, it's been tough on Rachel, and I know the last week has not been what she hoped for"—Jake looked genuinely pained and Rachel seemed to physically wince at the comment—"but I do feel we're better every day. We're putting it slowly behind us and moving on. I feel like our marriage will be back to normal in a few more days, once I get this all behind me at work, if that's what you're worried about."

Craig sipped his tea and tried to look relaxed.

"I'm not worried about anything," he said. "I just want to be sure that you guys know that Foundations, and especially Chris and I, are here for you if you need anything."

"Anything like what?" Jake asked, and again held Craig's eyes in an uncomfortable way. There was a coldness there that he had never seen in Jake—maybe had never seen in anyone.

"Jake, you've experienced things over there that I'm sure I could never even imagine. I know, of course, that you suffered terrible loss, but I'm guessing you also saw and experienced things that are difficult. We want to help you if we can."

To Craig's surprise, Jake rose.

"What will you do, Craig?" he asked hotly. "Will you pray for me? Will you read me some scriptures—tell me how God will make every-thing better?"

Craig opened his mouth to answer, but Jake continued over top of him.

"All due respect," Jake said, which Craig had long ago learned usually meant just the opposite, "I'm grateful that Rachel had the church to lean on while I was gone. I'm thankful for everything you guys did for her while I was thousands of miles away in the suck, but do you really think coming here and reading me Romans eight will make everything all better? Do think your prayers and encouragement will allow me to unsee the shit I saw and the things I did over there? Don't you think that's awfully naïve?"

"There's some really good stuff in Romans, actually," Craig began, and set his tea on the table again. "But I'm in no way trying to trivialize what you went through, Jake. I can't even imagine, and I doubt I could have done it. But, that being said, wouldn't it stand to reason you could use some comfort and some prayer to deal with those things?"

"I tried that," Jake said and paced behind the couch, his hands in his pockets. "Believe me, I'm not trying to be rude. I know you want to help, but Cal and I spent hours in the 'stan talking about that kind of shit. I know Romans eight—it was one of Cal's favorites, probably because he said it was one of your favorites."

Craig's chest ached at that and he closed his eyes for a moment. When he opened them, Jake had already paced the length of the couch.

"I know verse twenty-eight. Where is all that 'good,' Pastor Craig? We prayed for peace and protection, and for the 'good' your Romans eight promises, and what did I get? My best friend blew up all over me. I lost two other friends that day too. Cal believed God had a plan for him, and guess what? That hope is spattered over a dirty wall in some nameless little shithole village in Afghanistan, isn't it?"

There were tears streaming down Jake's face now, and his voice was quivering. He looked over at Rachel and his face filled with pain.

"I'm so sorry, baby," he said, and Rachel looked down at her hands. Jake turned back to Craig. "You see, I promised my wife I would be nice," he said. "I love her more than anything, and so I'm going to excuse myself. I've already broken that promise and probably her heart, and it's best if I just excuse myself."

Craig searched desperately for the words, the inspired words that would stop Jake in his tracks and bring him back to the couch so that he and Chris could try and help him. He found nothing and so mumbled, "I'm so sorry, Jake. We didn't come here to upset you."

Jake stopped at the bedroom door and sighed a heavy, tearful sigh and looked at his feet, his hand on the doorknob.

"I know that, Pastor," he said. "I really do. But what you have to offer has more questions than answers for me." He turned and looked at his now-crying wife. When Jake looked back at him, for a moment Craig saw a scared young boy, but the image was quickly replaced by an angry man, full of pain and regret. "Pray with my wife," Jake said, and there was no sarcasm in his words. "I know that will help her feel better."

Then he disappeared into the bedroom and closed the door behind him.

Craig looked at Chris, his best friend's boyish grin completely erased.

Then he moved over to Rachel and put his arm around her.

"I'm sorry, Rachel," he said and felt his own tears fall. "I wanted to help, but I feel I made things worse."

"It's okay," Rachel said. "It's just too soon."

"Can we pray together?"

She rose and straightened her pretty dress. "Pray for us, of course, but right now I think I should go check on my husband."

"Of course," Craig said and rose again. "Is there anything we can do? Are you going to be all right?" He was suddenly filled with images of the violent, crazed war veterans depicted in films when he had been young. Might Rachel be in danger?

"I'm fine," Rachel said. "He's just a little jaded after ... everything."

"Are you safe?" Chris asked, perhaps reading Craig's mind.

Rachel looked shocked.

"Of course," she said. "Oh my God, of course. It's still Jake. We're doing fine. Just—he just needs a little time for the church stuff, I think." She forced a smile. "It's not even been quite a week," she added. "We're better every day."

Craig wasn't sure if she meant it or was mocking what Jake had said, but he left it alone. Rachel walked them to the door and hugged them both.

"Thank you both so much for coming."

Craig stood a moment by the closed door before looking at Chris. His friend shook his head and raised his eyebrows.

"We're gonna have to pray hard about this one," Chris said.

Craig nodded. He wondered if they needed more help than that—professional help of some sort.

They drove away, Craig fighting the pain in his stomach.

CHAPTER 37

Jake spent the rest of their Sunday apologizing to his wife. He had never intended to lose it like that, but what the hell did the two pastors know about his experiences? They had been here, safe and comfortable, while he had been over there. They had been praying for him and then going to lunch while he was fighting for his life, killing human beings, and losing his friends. In what universe could they possibly understand him enough to help him?

Still, he knew he had crossed the line and it was Rachel, the only thing that mattered to him in the world, who had paid the price. She had told him again and again—each and every time he apologized and asked for her forgiveness—that she understood, but how could she? She hadn't been there either.

"I should have known you weren't ready," she said, tears dripping off her chin. "I am so sorry, baby."

After what a total and complete asshole he had been, she had apologized to him. That she somehow blamed herself hurt worse than anything.

Jake forced the thoughts of yesterday's painful afternoon from his mind as he showed his military ID at the main gate to the base, preferring instead to think about the nice, though strained, dinner they had enjoyed together and the way Rachel had fallen asleep on the couch while they watched some silly sci-fi movie. He had felt so totally normal during those couple of hours. Jake remembered little of the movie but loved the way she had cuddled close to him and dozed off with his arms around her. They used to laugh that a movie on the couch was all the sleeping medicine she ever needed. He had always loved that, actually. Last night he had stared at her for an hour, stroking her hair and listening to her soft, feminine snoring with a smile on his face.

Jake pulled his truck into one of the many open spots beside the building that housed his unit and sighed as he switched off the motor. The lot was nothing like on a drill weekend, when if you didn't get there early you might have to park several buildings away. Today the lot was nearly empty, though he saw TC's truck near the entrance in a reserved spot—a perk of being a senior NCO.

Jake was in uniform. The clean, pressed BDUs felt odd after nearly a year in a war zone, where faded-and-dusty cammies were the norm. It felt stranger still to not have his weapon slung over his shoulder with an extra magazine in a Velcro pouch on the stock.

No Weapon, No Chow.

Jake smiled at the memory. They had still been so green when Pete had told them about the sign that first day, and he remembered now how it had sunk in where they were.

Jake straightened his uniform blouse and gently fingered the combat infantry badge he now wore on his left chest—the mark of a combat veteran. Another change since he had last entered this building.

Jake shook his head and made an unconscious *tsk* sound, then pushed through the double glass doors into the building. He refused to be that guy—the vet that lived in the past. He walked past the row of pictures of the commanding officer and NCO staff and then entered the first door on the right—the main admin office for his platoon.

"Hey," he said after a moment, when neither of the two young men tapping on computers looked up.

"Hey," the closer man—almost a boy, really—said, raising his gaze. His eyes fell on the rank insignia on the tab in the center of Jake's chest and then the combat infantry badge above his left chest pocket. His eyes widened a bit. "Oh, sorry, Sar'n," he said, a little flustered. "Thought you were Masterson from medical. We're a little swamped with all the guys coming back. Help you?"

"Sergeant Harris—Jake Harris—for First Sar'n Morrow," Jake said. "He's expecting me."

"Yes, sir—I mean, yes, Sergeant Harris. Sorry about that, Sar'n. Let me find the First Sergeant."

Jake chuckled and tried to remember feeling as flustered as the young man was. His insignia said he was a corporal, but the badge was pretty new and Jake figured he had not been here long. He had probably come aboard recently, and was clearly not prior active duty. Jake remembered feeling less of a soldier because he had not been a prior-active-duty guy when he had joined. Hell, he'd felt that way until a year ago. He figured he wouldn't feel that way again ever, not after this past year.

"He's coming up to get you, Sar'n," the young man said. Jake nodded and felt the boy staring at his combat insignia again. "You just getting back from Afghanistan?" His voice was soft, almost reverent.

"Yeah."

"How was it?" the soldier asked, his eyes wide.

"Sucked, for the most part," Jake said. He was relieved by the sound of the familiar, booming voice.

"Jake," TC said as he wrapped an arm around Jake's shoulders. He turned to the two young soldiers. "You guys met Sar'n Harris? Best damn squad leader in the platoon," he said. "A real badass," he added with a laugh. "Right, Jake?"

"If you say so, First Sar'n," he said uncomfortably.

"Come on," TC said and ushered him out of the small front office. "I promised you breakfast."

They small-talked about nothing on their way over to the cantina that served as a lunch place and coffee shop for the handful of full-time staff in the unit. Jake had been one of the full-timers, and had been grateful for the job as he waited for an opening at the fire department. It seemed weird to think about that now. It seemed like a million years ago, and more like someone else's life. He realized suddenly that he couldn't remember what it was like to not be a soldier who had fought in Afghanistan.

Jake ordered a cup of black coffee and a bacon-and-egg sandwich. He noticed that TC closed his eyes quietly for a moment, and Jake wondered with some surprise if he was saying a blessing. Then the moment was gone and TC dug into his steaming plate of bacon and eggs while Jake picked at his food.

"So how's Rachel?" TC asked. Jake figured that was an obligatory question.

"She's great," Jake answered. "Glad I'm home, of course."

"Of course," TC agreed over a huge forkful of hash browns. Then he set his fork down and leaned back. "So, Jake," he began. "You interested in staying in a full-time support job?"

Jake knew the question would be coming, but he still had no idea what the answer was.

"Is my job still available?" He had worked in the training department for just over a year before being deployed.

"Of course," TC said. "You'll make Staff Sergeant in another year or so with this deployment. You could run the training department after that. The question is more if you want to stay full-time. You were trying to get on with the fire department, as I recall."

Jake nodded. For a moment he saw Shawn's face smiling at him, as real as if he were sitting across from him instead of TC. He closed his eyes and squeezed the image away. He wondered if he could ever think about the fire department without being haunted by Shawn's death.

"Honestly, I don't really know what I want to do, First Sar'n," he said. "I barely even feel home yet. I wake up and still feel like I should grab my rifle and hustle over to muster."

TC nodded. "I get that," he said. "It takes a while for that to go away. I feel the same way, and this was my fifth deployment."

Jake felt his eyebrows arch in surprise. Five deployments? Jake could scarcely imagine.

"You must like it, I guess," he said.

TC shrugged. "I don't know how to do anything else," he said simply. Then he sighed. "No decisions have to be made right now," he said. "You got some time. For now, you're right back in your old job until you say otherwise. You got a couple of weeks of postdeployment leave coming to you. Add some regular leave to it if you need to, until you feel settled in at home. We can do without you for thirty days if you want."

Jake wondered what the hell he would do all day for a whole month.

"Won't need that much time, First Sar'n," he said.

TC nodded again. "So, later today you gotta do some paperwork. You gotta fill out your postdeployment PTSD questionnaire, and whether you stay or go, you still have to do your medical to assess you for benefits based on the deployment. Be honest on that damn thing, okay, Jake? Once you say *no* to everything there is no going back, and it can cost you some benefits."

Jake nodded and shrugged. Hearing *PTSD* didn't sound all that great, and the thought of answering a bunch of headshrinker questions written by people who had never killed anyone or been shot at sounded really painful.

"I also want you to do me a favor," TC said and reached into his pocket. He seemed uncomfortable. He handed the card to Jake. Jake flipped it over in his hand. The front had the emblems for the four armed services on it, and on the back it said simply, *Veteran Support Activity East.* There was a local number underneath.

"What the hell is this?" Jake asked. He was unsure why he felt irritated.

"It takes a lot of time to in-process to the VA system," TC said. "The active military system is almost as bad. These guys are just sort of a bridge for guys who are home from deployment. It's all informal and they can help a lot while you do paperwork or even just decide if you want to, or need to, get help from the military or VA."

Jake tapped his finger on the side of the card and pursed his lips. He had a sudden vision of long-haired, bearded guys in wheelchairs wearing sleeveless black leather vests and chanting something angry. Was that how his First Sergeant saw him?

"What do I need this for?" This time the anger in his voice didn't seem out of place at all.

"Maybe you don't," TC said and leaned his elbows on the small table between them. "When I came back from Iraq my third time, I sure as hell needed them, though. They were great. There's no docs. Just a bunch of other guys who have seen and done the kinds of things you have. They're all vets. Some are older guys from wars gone by, and lots are from Iraq and Afghanistan. The best part is that they're outside the system, so everything is private and doesn't find its way into a service record, you know what I mean?"

Jake nodded. "But why do I need them?"

"Look, Jake," TC said and leaned in even further. "Don't you feel like you can't really talk to Rachel or your other friends because they can't possibly understand what you've been through? Don't you worry that if you talk to the VA or military, it can label you or affect your career?"

Jake shrugged.

"Well, I did, I can tell you," TC said. "All I'm asking you to do is call and go to one meeting. See if you think it'll help you. See if it clears your head so you can make better decisions about what to do next." He leaned back and crossed his arms. "I can't make you go, because it's not an official thing. If I could make you, I wouldn't. You gotta decide on your own."

Jake stared back at him and felt kind of far away. He had no idea what to say.

"One meeting as a favor to me. Just some guys to chat with about what you've been through, or just listen if you prefer."

Jake nodded. "Okay," he said. "I'll drop in on one meeting as personal favor." He tried to screw a Jake-grin onto his face. "If for no other reason than to show you I'm fine and don't need anything, okay?"

"Fair enough," TC said, seeming satisfied. "Let's finish up breakfast, fill out your leave chits and your questionnaires, and get you back to your beautiful wife."

Jake chewed a bite of his sandwich and felt his gut tighten.

He wondered what the hell kind of crap would be on this PTSD questionnaire.

CHAPTER 38

Jake sat in his truck, the motor running, and tapped the steering wheel, unsure what to do. His mind raged with images and thoughts unloosed by that stupid questionnaire. Knowing the right answers to put to not seem crazy had been ridiculously easy, but it had not sheltered him from the slideshow of horrible images the questions had unleashed. His heart still beat too fast in his chest, a full half hour later, but he was at least grateful that filling the frigging thing out had been his last task of the day.

He missed Rachel terribly. The thought of the collapsing into her arms pulled at him like a drug. Unfortunately, with her embrace would come questions about his day. What had happened, what had he decided to do about the Guard? Jake didn't think he could handle that yet. He needed some time to push the images and memories back into their box first.

He looked at his watch.

It was almost sixteen hundred—four PM. Jake pulled out his cell phone and scrolled through it looking for Pete's number in his contacts. He pushed the call button.

"Yeah?"

"Hey, dude," Jake said as casually as possible.

The silence on the phone was uncomfortable.

"It's Jake," he added.

"Jake!" Pete's voice was now more what he had expected. "What's up, bro? Whatcha doing?"

What the hell am *I doing? Go home to Rachel, you idiot.*

"I just have a little time—maybe an hour—to kill. Thought I might swing by and catch up."

Pete's laugh unnerved Jake for some reason.

"You'll have to swing by the Tap House," he said, referring to a local bar packed on the weekends, but that Jake imagined would be near empty on a Monday afternoon. "'Cause that's where I am."

Jake hesitated a moment, but the familiar voice whispered reassurance.

Just a quick drink—a drink with a friend who was there, who gets it. A drink will help you relax before you go home to Rachel.

"Sounds good," Jake said. "See you in like ten minutes."

The drive gave Jake nothing but time to think about what the hell he should do next with his life. A huge part of him wanted to put the Army behind him completely. How else could he ever begin to forget? Another part wondered just what the hell he could possibly do now. He didn't think the fire department was an option, and anyway, that just filled him with guilt about Shawn. He had proven once already that he was no college guy, and what would he even study? Once you were a killer, once you went down that road, maybe you couldn't really be anything else.

He had some time. His physical was next week. His postdeployment physical could as easily be a separation physical if he chose. The wars in the Middle East showed no signs of wrapping up, so staying would likely mean another deployment eventually. Jake wondered what kinds of questions those damn doctors would ask.

For a moment the boy in the grey man dress, his face pale and bathed in nervous sweat, popped so realistically into his vision that Jake swerved the truck a little to avoid hitting him. He was rewarded by a long horn blast and a middle finger from the woman in the Lexus beside him. He waved and smiled.

Jake could smell it now. He could actually smell the small village. He had become so accustomed to Afghanistan, he didn't think he'd realized that it had a distinctive smell until just that moment. He heard a sob escape from his throat.

After he pulled into a spot at the Tap House, Jake leaned his forehead against the steering wheel and wiped his eyes. He felt for the card in his pocket and shuddered. How could TC think that telling a bunch of vets about these dreams or images or whatever the hell they were could possibly help? How was he supposed to talk about any of this?

I promised him. I'll go and listen and then leave.

Jake slid from his truck and realized his hand was trembling as he pushed the button on his key fob to lock the door. He hesitated at the door to the bar. He had to tell Rachel something, right? He couldn't just let her wait and worry. He pulled out his cell phone.

"Hey, baby," she said after only the first ring. Jake pictured her sitting on the couch, anxiously waiting to hear about his meetings on base. The thought of her asking about everything made him need a drink even more. "Are you on your way?"

"Almost," he answered, trying to sound as normal and cheerful as possible. "Pete just called me and asked if I could meet up with him for a few minutes. I guess he's having a hard time or something."

There was a pause, and in his mind Jake could see her pursing her lips like she did when she was worried.

"Of course," she said softly. "Is he okay?"

"I think so," he said. He was already in the lie with both feet, so what the hell? "Just needs a friend, I think."

Another long pause. "Are you okay?"

"I'm fine, baby," he said and tried to sound reassuring. "I'm great."

"Did everything go all right on base?"

"Yeah, of course," he said through gritted teeth. "Just some admin stuff to get done." Jake closed his eyes again and let the guilt consume him. "I'll be home as quick as I can, okay? I just need to make sure he's all right."

"Okay," Rachel said. "Take all the time you need. I love you."

"I love you too," he said. For a moment he thought his voice might crack, but it didn't. "See you real soon."

Jake clicked off after she said goodbye. Then he slid his phone into his back pocket and pushed through the door.

"Jake!"

He saw Pete at the bar and slid onto the bar stool beside him, where a frosty mug of beer already waited for him.

"How are you, dude?" Pete asked. Jake saw that his friend's eyes were already red and there was a slight slur in his voice.

"Great," Jake said and took a big swallow of beer. "Shitty day is all."

"I have a lot of those," Pete said in an eerie, flat voice that gave Jake a chill. "To our brothers in arms," Pete hollered in a louder and more animated voice as he raised his glass. Jake clinked his mug against Pete's nearly empty glass.

He took a long pull on his cold beer—big enough to give him a slight brain freeze—as Pete emptied his own glass.

The bartender slid two more beers in front of them.

"From the guys at the end of the bar," he said.

Jake nodded at the middle-aged men and took another swallow of the beer he was still working on.

"Works every time," Pete whispered and then laughed. He raised the new beer to the men at the end of the bar, who gave a small salute back. Then he tipped back the glass and took three big chugs.

Jake laughed softly with his friend, though he didn't see what was so funny.

CHAPTER 39

Rachel didn't remember falling asleep, but she knew that she was. Part of her felt the uncomfortable crick in her neck from the awkward position of her head on the small throw pillow of their couch, and another felt the cool night air on her cheeks as she leaned back against her tree. She pulled her legs up to her chest and shivered, her mind telling her the chill was from the thin blanket she'd used to only partially cover herself on the couch, but it didn't matter—either way she was cold. She also knew that it wasn't just the cold that made her shiver.

She waited, unsure what she was waiting for.

The last time she'd had this dream, it had seemed so real, and in her heart she truly believed she had been visited by a messenger of God. This felt much more like what, perhaps, that night with Luke and all that followed had been—just a dream.

What about the Bible verses after I woke up? How can I explain that as a dream?

You saw what you your mind wanted to see in those passages, nothing more.

Rachel shook her head. She didn't believe that. She had faith that God had found a way to reach her in her need. Dream, vision, messenger—whatever it was didn't matter. She knew God had spoken to her that night.

And so, dream or not, she waited, full of hope and expectation.

And guilt.

Rachel saw—or maybe just sort of sensed—movement at the edge of the woods where they opened onto the path up to her tree, the path itself almost shimmering in the moonlight. It occurred to her that, later, when she was awake, she should check if the "real" moon was the same three-quarter moon that hung over her tree in this dream, or vision, or whatever.

I wonder what that would mean.

She saw the outline, a silhouette, materialize from the shadows. She thought the figure wore a red hooded sweatshirt, but it could just be wishful imagination. Before the figure could come fully into view, she was jarred by an animal-like shriek.

Rachel sat up on the couch, tilting precariously to the left, where one hip had slid partway off the narrow sofa cushion. She barely caught herself with an outstretched hand on the coffee table before she toppled to floor. She looked around the dim room, confused. Had the sound been real or from her dream?

Then the scream came again and she knew.

From the bedroom, Rachel heard Jake holler out a third time, this time screaming words that didn't make sense to her, but that she imagined had something to do with a terrible battle going on in his nightmare.

She had fallen asleep waiting for Jake to come home and was surprised that he had somehow slipped into the house and then to bed without waking her. She wrapped the blanket around her, noticed that it was a fleece throw they kept in the bedroom, which Jake must have covered her with, and hurried toward the bedroom.

She could smell his stale beer odor from the bedroom door and worried for a minute that he might have gotten sick. The smell was that of a drunk, rather than of puke, but she would have hurried to his side either way.

Rachel clicked on the light on her nightstand.

Jake was writhing back and forth, his face bathed in sweat and his features contorted in pain, or anguish, or maybe both. He mumbled something about a thumb, she thought, and she reached a hand gently toward him.

Inches from Jake's shoulder she pulled her hand back, unsure. She still had some bruises from the last time she had touched him in the middle of a nightmare, and wondered now if she should let him be until it passed. Then he began to sob and she felt her heart ache.

Rachel sat beside him on the bed and caressed his bare shoulder, pulling her hand away quickly, just in case.

His eyes didn't open, but Jake's face softened and he stopped writhing.

"Rachel?" he mumbled and reached for her, found only air, and wrapped his arm around his own waist instead.

"I'm here, baby," she whispered and placed her hand on his cheek.

Jake covered her hand with his and then his eyes opened slowly. He smiled for a moment and she smiled back. Then he squeezed his eyes shut again.

"I'm sorry," he choked out and then sobbed again.

"For what?" she asked and rubbed his bare chest, still moist with sweat from whatever horror tortured him in his sleep.

Jake opened his tear-filled eyes and looked at her.

"For everything," he said and kissed her palm. "For getting drinks with Pete instead of coming home to you. For being distant. For Cal. For the war. For everything."

Rachel slipped beside him in the bed, wrapping her arms around him as he buried his face against her.

"For not being me anymore," he said and began to cry a little harder.

Rachel felt tears on her cheeks. "You're still you, Jake," she said. "I love you, so I know. You've been through so much. Please, Jake. Please just let me help you. Let God help you."

"I can't," he sobbed. "I'm just so pissed off."

Rachel felt her eyebrows arch in surprise. Was he mad at her?

"Who are you mad at, Jake?" she asked softly and kissed the top of his head.

"Me," he answered and he began to cry harder. "And Cal," he added.

Then he wrapped his arms around her and cried. His cries were that of an inconsolable child, and Rachel cried with him.

She had so many questions. She wanted to know about his anger. What was it that made it so hard for him to turn to God? She had learned early from Kelly, and more recently from Pastor Craig, that Christianity was never meant to be a religion—it was a relationship. It was an intimacy with a real, loving, present God. How could she have made it through so far without Him to walk beside her? She could feel Him beside her, and inside her heart. She wanted that for Jake. It was the help she couldn't give him. Proverbs came to her, from somewhere in chapter three, she thought:

When you lie down, you will not be afraid, when you lie down your sleep will be sweet.

She was far from perfect in her ability to surrender her fear to God, but that passage that came to her described perfectly why Jake needed God right now. She wanted to tell him, but she was so content to hold him, and she was afraid that it would drive him away again.

She also wanted to know where he had been so late with Pete. She wanted, almost desperately, to know about his day and what had happened on base. She needed to know what their future was.

There would be time for that later.

She held him and cried with him. She prayed a short prayer for him and for their marriage. She held him and eventually fell asleep, tangled around him.

CHAPTER 40

The late-morning sun streamed across the wood desk and Craig laid his head back on the soft, faux-leather cushion of the couch in his home office. He wished he had his football to toss back and forth. He didn't really have any work to do in his home office, he just needed the sanctuary of his space—the place he was left alone. His youngest son, Matthew, would be home from school soon with the typical Wednesday homework push for tests on Friday. His wife was in the other room, working on something for one of the women's groups she led. Truth was, he could probably be pretty much alone with his thoughts anywhere right now, but this was the only really private space. He was worried that in his current state of mind he might snap at his wife and son, neither of whom bore any blame for his depressed mood and feelings of professional impotence.

A knock on the door pulled Craig away from his wallowing.

"Yes?" he called out without getting up, and without much luck at keeping the inappropriate irritation from his voice.

The door opened and the sight of his beautiful wife's smile and eyes softened his heart for a moment.

"Sorry, sweetie," she said. She always understood him, even when he didn't understand himself. "Chris stopped by to see you."

Craig sat up with a groan—the once-foreign sound now common since he had hit the big five-oh.

"Cool," he said. "Tell him to come on in." Craig sat up and stretched out the ache in his neck from the awkward angle he'd let the stiff pillow put his head in.

The door opened wider and his associate pastor came in with a smile.

"Thanks so much, Debbie," Chris said as he entered.

"I'll get you guys some tea," Craig's wife said as she closed the door. Neither of them objected, the years having taught them that the tea would be coming whether they declined or not. They smiled and nodded at each other at the unspoken, running joke. That and Deb's love of thank-you notes. Chris sat down in the easy chair beside the couch and crossed his blue-jean-clad legs, hands in his lap, and smiled that comforting, but sometimes annoying, all-knowing smile.

"What's up?" Craig asked, pretending not to know.

"Just wanted to drop by and see how you're doing," Chris said.

"Great," Craig said and then sighed heavily at the lie. "I don't know," he confessed. "You know what the hardest part of this job is?"

Chris nodded—this was a conversation they'd had many times—but he still read his lines. "Tell me," he said.

"Giving comfort and peace and hope to people in situations where I've been unable to find it myself," Craig said.

"Yeah, that part sucks," Chris agreed.

The study door opened and Chris took his tea from Debbie. "Thanks, Deb. This is the only reason I ever come here."

Debbie smiled and shook her head. She knew the joke. She put Craig's tea on the coffee table.

"You guys are jerks," she said with a laugh.

"I love you," Craig said and grabbed at her hip. Debbie shifted to avoid the pinch.

"I love you too, baby," she said with a wink and then she closed the study door behind her as she left.

They sat in quiet for a time and then Chris sipped his tea and dove in.

"How do ya think yesterday went?" he asked. Typical Chris. Why beat around the bush?

Craig leaned forward, his elbows on his knees.

"About like I thought it would," he said. "Jake is hurting and I'm not sure I can help him." The admission was a crushing pain in his heart. It wasn't just his bruised ego. He liked Jake and understood his pain, but he also knew that Jake was struggling with demons from more than Cal's death. That had been pretty clear in the young man's eyes. But the truth was, Craig was still working out Cal's loss for himself, and this might just be too hard for him right now. "Jake needs answers that I don't think I have yet," he confessed. "He needs some answers and some guidance, and this time I think I'm just not the guy."

Craig looked at Chris—his associate pastor, but also his own spiritual counselor and, these last few years, his very best friend after Debbie. Through Craig's tears, his friend's face blurred.

"Hey," Craig said and wiped a stray tear from his cheek. "That's why there's two of us, right? Isn't that what we always say?"

Chris nodded, but Craig doubted it was a nod of agreement.

"Maybe his questions are different from what you think," Chris said softly. "Is that possible?"

Craig was struck by the enormity of the simple statement and let it turn over in his head. Was he projecting his own questions and doubts onto Jake? How the hell selfish would that be? Maybe he was missing Jake's needs altogether. He looked up into the patient eyes of his best friend.

"You said that Jake just found Christ, really, right?" Chris asked. "That he gave his life to Christ just a short time before it happened?"

Craig nodded. Cal had emailed him about Jake maybe a few weeks before the tragedy.

"So," Chris went on, leaning forward in his chair, "were the questions you had about God and tragedy the same a month after Debbie dragged you kicking and screaming to God as they are now?"

Craig thought a moment.

"No," he said. "No, I suppose not."

So, what are the questions I failed to find in Jake?

He looked expectantly at Chris.

"Do you remember eighteen years ago, when Jeremy got sick?"

Craig nodded at the painful memory. The church had been much, much smaller then and Chris had only joined his ministry a year before. Chris' then five-year-old son was diagnosed, and for more than a year the struggle in Chris had been terrible to watch. It had all turned out okay, and in fact Chris now claimed the entire thing had strengthened his faith immeasurably, even with the permanent disability his son lived with. His son was now an amazing young man of faith, serving in the church beside his dad.

Chris continued. "I never stopped believing in God during that time." He still smiled, but his eyes seemed far away for a moment. "I didn't question my faith in God, but I was angry and confused. Now I see how God made so much good from that, but at the time, well, it was just impossible."

"I remember," Craig said. He had found Chris' strength during that time an unbelievable inspiration, but had no doubt the struggle had been difficult.

"I don't know that Jake is at that point in his faith," Chris continued. "His doubts are more fundamental, I would think."

Of course. Craig realized that in the midst of his own struggles and anger he had not allowed for Jake's younger and more fragile faith. How could he not have thought of that?

Chris squeezed his arm. "It sucks being human, huh?"

They both laughed. That was exactly what Craig had said to him during one of their many late-night talks about Jeremy, when Chris still struggled with his anger toward God.

"Early on in that mess, you told me about hope dying at the cross. Do you remember that?"

Craig nodded again. "I remember that very well. God spoke through me that night for sure." Craig doubted he had nearly enough wisdom to have come up with that analogy on his own. He had thought of it many times since, but had never used it with anyone else.

"I think maybe that's something Jake needs to hear," Chris said.

Craig leaned back and ran both hands through his short hair.

"You may be right," he said, though he was actually positive Chris was right. Maybe God was calling Chris to take the lead here. "I don't know when I might get a chance to share it with him, though. He seems pretty angry with me and Foundations right now. Do you think maybe you should take the lead on this one for now?" Craig heard the childlike hope in his voice.

Chris laughed and shook his head. "I don't think so. I think Jake needs you right now, just like I did eighteen years ago." He rose, sipped a little more tea, and then put a comforting hand on Craig's shoulder. "And I think maybe you need Jake."

Craig knew he was right. Stupid damn wisdom. He rose too. "Be praying I get that chance," he said.

Chris smiled again. "Way ahead of you," he said.

Craig watched his friend go, heard him call out a goodbye to Debbie as he went down the hall, and then Craig sat heavily back on his couch. He closed his eyes.

Lord, please help me find another chance. Help me be Your vessel to reach out to Jake. God, help me do a better job and please, please, make another opportunity for me.

Craig opened his eyes and looked up into the smiling face of his wife of nearly thirty years. This time his smile felt a bit more real.

"You okay?" she asked. She sat beside him and took his hand.

Craig nodded. "Better," he said.

He put his arm around her and held her, his thoughts again on Jake and Rachel.

CHAPTER 41

Jake felt his leg bouncing up and down but had absolutely no ability to make it stop. He supposed he had been lucky that when he called the number TC had given him, the next meeting was the following day. No need to wait around and worry. He could just get it over with and tell TC he had gone, and thanks a bunch for the tip. Then he would never, ever put himself through this again.

Jake looked around the mostly empty circle of chairs in the meeting room of the rec center. He returned the nod of another guy who looked about as excited as Jake felt. The guy rolled his eyes and then looked at the floor.

Jake doubted he would be here at all if not for Rachel. After passing out drunk at home instead of coming home for dinner and discussing their future like an adult, how could he deny her the simple request? His own damn fault for even telling her about the meeting, though he wasn't sure how he would have otherwise explained the card she found in his uniform shirt. Jake figured he would do just about anything to stop hurting Rachel.

"Hi," a voice said, snapping him back to the present. Instead of a long-haired guy with a beard and a sleeveless black leather vest, Jake looked up to see a clean-shaven man in khakis and a button-down, his hand extended. Jake guessed him to be about thirty-five, maybe forty. Jake shook the hand, which was firm, and nodded at the stranger. "I'm Hank," the man said and then slipped into the chair beside him.

"Jake," he replied. "You run the group?"

The man laughed. "Not hardly," he said. "The group is run by Adrian. He gets some help from Tom Black—Dr. Black, I guess, but he seems way to cool to be a doctor, much less a psychologist. He sits in and makes a comment or two, but the group is really Adrian's baby." The man crossed his legs at the knees and dropped a cell phone into his lap. "And ours, of course."

"What's your role here?" Jake asked, curious now. The dude looked like a banker or an insurance salesman or something.

"Same as yours, I imagine," he said with a genuine smile. Jake noticed there was something about his eyes, though. A flicker of something. Hank watched Jake a moment and then laughed and shook his head. "Bosnia," he said with one eyebrow raised. "Then Iraq later on. Fifth Ranger Battalion."

"You were a Ranger?" Jake asked before he could stop himself.

"Always a Ranger," the man answered. "And you? What is your role here?"

"Afghanistan," Jake said. The word stuck in his throat a little. "Like, last week."

The man nodded. "Welcome to the group, Jake," he said and clapped him on the arm. "And thank you for your service."

Before Jake could say anything else, he followed Hank's eyes as the doors opened again.

"Hey, guys," the young man said, one hand waving while the other dragged the left wheel of his wheelchair, causing it to turn in that direction. Jake guessed him to be around his age. He looked a little like Cal, actually, except for the black cargo pants folded at mid-thigh over what must be very short stumps. As the young man rolled closer, Jake saw thick scars on the right side of his neck and face, though they did little to detract from the smile and piercing blue eyes.

"Hey, Adrian," Hank called with a nod. "Sup, brother?"

"That's Adrian?" Jake whispered.

"Yep," Hank said. He waved Adrian over. "Adrian, this is Jake."

Jake shook the strong hand, covered in a fingerless black glove.

"Great to meet you, Jake," Adrian said. Jake had seen the sparkle in those eyes somewhere before. He found it impossible not to smile back. "TC's friend, right?"

Jake raised his eyebrows in surprise. "You know TC?"

Adrian laughed and released Jake's hand, then slipped his wheelchair between Jake and the chair beside him with ease.

"You might say that." He gestured at the stumps spread out in front of him in the wheelchair. "Guess I'm the reason he has to wear that damn Silver Star."

"Silver Star?" Jake suddenly realized he knew very little about his First Sergeant. He thought maybe he had only ever seen him in BDUs. For sure, he had no idea TC had a Silver Star.

Adrian nodded. "Iraq, almost five years ago now." There was no far-off look in the young man's eyes and no sadness in his voice. "TC was my squad leader—thank God. And I mean that literally, of course."

Jake wondered if Adrian referred to the squad leader part or the God part. He flashed on an image of Cal beside the berm, his Bible in his lap. He realized where he had seen the spark in Adrian's eyes before.

"Hey, Todd," Adrian said with a wave at the sullen man slouched down in the chair across from Jake. The man raised a halfhearted wave. "How you doin', brother?" The man shrugged. "How's Kathy? Still running your platoon?"

At that, the man smiled and sat up a little. "Yeah," Todd said. "Still driving our bus, thanks to you. Kids are great. I'm better too, I guess."

"Cool, dude," Adrian said. "One mission at a time, right?"

The man's smile broadened. "One mission at a time," he agreed.

Two other men, both older than Jake, Adrian, and Todd—maybe older than Hank, even—walked in and took seats.

"Hey, guys," Adrian said.

Jake felt his stomach tighten. He guessed they were about to get started.

They did, but it was nothing like what he expected. Jake had imagined some sort of group therapy session—talking about their "feelings" and their mothers and stuff like that. Instead it felt more like hanging out with buddies from high school. They talked about sports (mostly about the "damn Washington Redskins," as Hank kept calling them) and about wives and kids. Todd talked a little bit about some job interview he'd had. Everyone seemed to know about it, but Jake wasn't sure what it was all about. Hank's wife was pregnant (a chorus of "Again?" and laughter).

After a short while Jake realized they were swapping war stories. There was no weirdness, no analysis, just telling stories like they were reminiscing about being on a baseball team together. One of the guys, Jake didn't catch his name, told a story about falling down a stairwell during an assault on a small house in Iraq. He had twisted his ankle pretty bad, but had been more worried about getting shot by one of his teammates as they came through the front door. He had waved a Cyalume light stick madly over his head, screaming, "American, American," as other soldiers stormed the room. Jake imagined it had been terrifying at the time, but telling it, the man laughed until tears came down his cheeks. Jake thought briefly about the dash up the stairs the day Cal had shot the wounded terrorist in the head, but didn't find anything funny in that story to relate.

They talked about food. Some guys bragged about how crappy their food had been at some small FOB in western Afghanistan, while Adrian bragged about the amazing chow they had been served at a large base in Fallujah, Iraq.

"We actually got steak and lobster like once a month," he taunted.

"Bullshit," one of the two latecomers said.

"All true," Hank shot back. "And wasn't there a salad bar?"

"There was," Adrian said, laughing. "And made-to-order omelets. Gotta love KBR."

"Soft-ass Army guys." The other man laughed. "We Marines don't need that Marriott-style living."

"Yeah, well, you can bet your ass I would have taken it," the other Marine said.

The time flew by with only a few somber moments, mostly when the men became quiet after telling a story about a friend from the war. Jake could always tell when those stories were about brothers left behind.

He didn't know why he felt better, but he did. Maybe it was just laughing about things no one would think was funny unless they had been there themselves. Maybe it was the—admittedly artificial—sense of camaraderie. The ease he felt was offset by the moments that he flashed to Cal and Shawn and the occasional images of death and gore, but even those moments felt less dirty or sick or something—at least less so than they did at home while holding hands with his wife.

In what felt like minutes, the hour and a half was gone. Jake had sat down terrified that he wouldn't make it through a full hour, and now he found himself wishing for just a little more time.

"Good to meet you, Jake."

He looked up at Hank and shook the man's hand as he rose.

"Hey, you too," Jake said.

"See you in two weeks?"

Jake frowned. This had been nice. He had enjoyed the familiar feeling of men who knew where he had come from and what he had done. He felt better, that was undeniable. But wasn't this just a Band-Aid for the short term while he made his adjustment to home? If he was to let go of the horrors of the last ten months, he couldn't come reminisce about them every two weeks, right? Clinging to the past—to his year of war—would make it impossible to move forward. He needed to forget all about Afghanistan if he wanted his old life back.

"Yeah, maybe," he said. He watched Adrian as he laughed with the two latecomers across the room. "So what's the story with Adrian?" he asked. "What happened?"

Hank smiled. "I don't know. He doesn't really talk about it that much. IED, I think, but I don't really know."

"How the hell is he so happy all the time? God, I don't think I could stand it. Losing my legs, I mean, shit."

"Yeah," Hank said with a somber nod. "Amazing. A couple years ago, when I was struggling again with, well, you know, with the things we struggle with." Hank shook his head, chasing away some demon. "Anyway, back then, I would think about Adrian and how happy and positive he always was. How he talked about life like it was the greatest gift ever. I would think about that and I would get embarrassed, I think. I lost some friends and—other things—but look at him. He lost friends, his legs, the life he knew..." Hank sighed and then looked back at Jake and smiled again. "I guess I figured I kind of owed him, you know? Like if he could go through all of that and still be the guy he is, then maybe I needed to get my act together." Hank wiped a tear from his cheek with some annoyance. "Anyway, great to meet you, Jake," he said with a wave and then hustled off.

Jake followed him out a moment later. Part of him wanted to talk more to Adrian—find out about the connection to TC and maybe more about how the hell he was so damn cheerful. But a bigger part wanted to get out of there, away from the past and the memories.

That part won.

He snuck out the door and headed for his truck. He wasn't sorry he had come, but he didn't see how he could possibly return and still leave Afghanistan behind him for good. Hank had been coming for *years* it sounded like. Jake couldn't stand the thought that he would still be here two years from now, thinking about that day and wiping tears from his eyes.

As he passed the small table by the door, he did pick up a card from the pile—the card with Adrian's name and number on it. He thought he might have thrown the one TC gave him away, already committed to this being a one-time thing. Jake tucked the new card into the back pocket of his jeans.

You never knew.

CHAPTER 42

The modest calm Jake felt after the meeting didn't last long, but it did make for a great evening with Rachel. He picked up some Thai food take-out (her favorite, and he could at least tolerate the pad Thai) and they ate on the couch. She wanted to know all about the meeting, and he felt bad that there wasn't really that much he could tell her. She told him he seemed more relaxed and that he should go again.

"I might," he said, but he knew it was a lie. He knew he had to do this on his own, that he had no chance if he was with guys who kept reminding him about the things that haunted him. He wanted to get away from all of that—away from the horrible images and the guilt. Guilt about Cal and Shawn. Guilt about the boy he had maybe killed in that house.

I have to do it on my own or I won't be able to do it all.

They talked a little about what he should do about the Guard—at least enough for him to share with her that he had no idea what he should do next. She told him she would support whatever he wanted, and he believed her.

They held hands, watched some show he had a lot of trouble focusing on—something about a guy who was supposed to be a bad guy but for some reason helped the FBI—and later, they made love for the first time in a week. They fell asleep wrapped around each other in bed.

And then the fantasy of a normal life was over.

The smells were so real and thick that he knew where he was before he opened his eyes. The smell of the village was a mixture of dirt—Afghanistan dirt that smelled very different than American dirt—and garbage and spices from food cooking in the stucco-walled homes around him. It would not have been an unpleasant smell had it not meant he was back in Helmand province.

Jake wiped the sweat from his neck and followed Cal through the darkening street.

"It's just a little farther, I think," Cal said. His voiced was strained and Jake thought he sounded like he was in pain. He started to ask, but then they left the alley and spread out on their side of the street, and Jake took up his scan of the rooftops and windows of the low buildings across from them.

Cal moved quickly—more quickly than Jake thought was safe, actually—and Jake had trouble keeping up while also scanning for enemies across the street. Worse, there were no American soldiers on the far side of street scanning the roof above his head or the alleys and doorways behind him. Jake felt certain that any moment he would feel the blast of a bullet shatter the back of his head.

"Slow down, dude," Jake whispered harshly to Cal, but Cal looked over his shoulder, a grimace on his face, and then broke left and dashed across the street.

"Shit," Jake muttered, but turned to follow his friend.

Cal sprinted across the dirty street like a man possessed. As he moved up the block, three men suddenly appeared along the wall just before the familiar doorway into the two-story building. The men sat in the dirt, their backs against the cracked wall and their AK-47s in their laps. They had not been there a moment ago, but Jake accepted that dreams had their own rules. Cal stopped in front of the first man, who did nothing but raise his eyes, and squeezed off two rounds into the man's face. Blood, bone, and grey gore spattered the wall behind the man. Cal moved to the next man and did the same, with the same gory result. Then he turned to Jake.

"This one is yours," he said with a sad smile.

Then he moved to the doorway and peered cautiously in.

Jake hesitated in front of the third man. For a moment the man smiled up, his curly hair protruding from beneath a red hooded sweatshirt. He held a staff in his lap—an old-fashioned walking stick. Jake lowered his weapon as the man raised the staff. Then the polished walking stick became a rifle and Jake didn't hesitate, firing twice in to the black-hooded, middle-aged man on the ground. The man let out a child-like scream and then rolled to the right, writhing in pain and hissing out a last breath as he came to a stop at Jake's feet.

Jake stared down at the lifeless eyes of a boy—perhaps eight or nine years old. What had once been a red hood and then a black hood was now an Atlanta Braves baseball hat. The rifle was now a baseball bat, which rolled out of the boy's dead hands and spun a half arc around Jake's left boot. One dead eye stare up at Jake. The other stared toward the ground, where a dark pool of blood spread from beneath the dead child's disfigured head. Jake sobbed and stepped back.

"Come on, Jake! Hurry before they kill me!"

Jake followed Cal's voice into the dark house, his eyes still on the dead boy. He didn't see the sea of bloody thumbs in the doorway, and his feet slipped out from underneath him in the slick blood trails they left as they writhed across the floor. He landed hard on his right hip and let out a little grunt.

Jake looked up at the silhouette of Cal, his arms stretched out crucifix style, lit from behind by an eerie light. He was naked from the waist up, his torso bathed in sweat that ran in little streams between the bricks of C-4 and wires strapped to his chest.

"Where the hell were you, Jake?" Cal's trembling voice pleaded. Then the boy standing beside Cal, barefoot beneath his grey man dress, squeezed the trigger in his right hand, and he and Cal disappeared in a cloud of smoke and blood.

The blood spattered Jake's goggles, and he tore them from his face. Though he felt the heat of the explosion, the force didn't even make him sway. As the smoke cleared, he backed up, his boots pushing though the ankle-deep pool of severed, squirming thumbs.

He almost lost his balance, and he screamed at the thought of falling into the horrible mass of moving digits. He pedaled backward and instead landed on his ass in the dirt outside the building, right beside the dead boy.

Red smoke poured out of the doorway and Jake pushed himself farther backward with his hands and feet, afraid the thumbs would come pouring out of the doorway like—well, like rats from a burning building. But they didn't.

"Where the hell were you, man?"

Jake looked up at Pete, who stood over the body of the dead boy Jake had shot. Pete wore jeans and a Metallica T-shirt and shook his head at Jake. Then he took a long, slow pull on the beer in his hand.

"It happened so fast," Jake sobbed up at his friend. "I didn't know."

Pete shook his head again. Then he pulled a Beretta nine-millimeter pistol from a drop holster on his right thigh and tipped it up to his lips like a beer, before squeezing the trigger and adding his brains and blood to the already gory wall behind him.

Jake stumbled to his feet as Pete's body collapsed on top of the dead boy's. He was too weary to run, so he stumbled down the center of the dark street, tears flooding his face. As he walked, he pulled his rifle harness up over his head and let his M4 drop into the dirt. Then he stripped his body armor off and dropped it as well. He felt the eyes of the Taliban fighters on him from the rooftops all around, and he began to mumble a quiet prayer that they would just shoot him in the head and make all the madness stop.

Jake stopped and tilted his head back, eyes clothes, and stretched out his arms. He turned in a slow circle in the middle of the street, waiting for the relief the torrent of terrorist bullets would bring.

"Jake."

Jake stopped his slow circle and opened his eyes.

Luke stood before him, the red hood of his sweatshirt bunched around his neck, and his sad face leaning on his hands that still clutched the polished walking stick. Behind the angel was a gentle glow. Though Jake was still in the dirty street in Afghanistan, the glow seemed to come from the large tree on the hill beside Rachel's parents' house.

"Leave me alone," Jake screamed at the messenger. His hands pulled at his hair and then covered his sobbing face. "Please, just leave me the hell alone—all of you." Jake drew in a long, rattling breath and then dropped his hands and opened his eyes, fully expecting Luke to have been replaced by another horrible apparition.

Instead Luke smiled sadly back at him. Together they stood beside Rachel's church tree. The village in Afghanistan had evaporated entirely now. The air was cooler and Jake shivered.

"You can do this, Jake. You can do this, but you must stay on your path. I wish there was an easier way, but there isn't. So many great things are ahead for you both, if you can just let go."

"You're not real," Jake hissed at the messenger. "Part of me wished you were—if only to get some answers to Pete's questions—but I know you're just something from my mind."

Luke smiled. "Your mind belongs to the Lord, Jake, so maybe that's true. Your heart belonged to him also. Do you remember the peace that brought? Do you remember?"

"I remember Cal exploding all over me after I prayed to your God," Jake replied in a low, flat voice. "Leave me alone."

"Of course, Jake," Luke said, but frowned. "But what about her?"

As Luke shimmered and then disappeared, Jake saw Rachel. She sat beside the tree, her knees pulled up to her chest. She rocked back and forth, sobbing, and Jake saw that she clutched something tightly to her chest. He took a step toward her.

"Rachel," he whispered and reached for her.

"Jake!" Rachel screamed his name in anguish, her head back, and Jake saw that she held a tightly folded, triangle-shaped American flag to her chest.

Jake sat up in bed crying and pulled his knees to his chest, just as dream Rachel had done.

Stay on the path, Jake, a voice whispered from somewhere far away.

Jake stifled another sob and looked at Rachel's sleeping face in the dim light. It was hard to tell in the shadows of their bedroom, but her face looked sad. Jake wondered what she dreamed about.

You need to get away from all this shit for a while. That dream messenger is just you losing your mind. You need to get away from that too. Rachel can't understand, because she hasn't seen what you have seen. Get some time for yourself before you lose the rest of your mind.

As the oily voice whispered to him, Jake slipped quietly out of their bed. He grabbed his jeans and a black T-shirt from the dresser and closed the bedroom door quietly behind him as he left.

He just needed a little time to himself—some time away from the lies of his nightmares.

CHAPTER 43

Jake kept his phone beside him on the table in the corner so he would see it light up if Rachel called. He was pretty sure he wouldn't hear it over the din of the loud bar crowd. He had not been at all surprised to find Pete at the Tap House, but his friend had left to take a leak a good while ago and Jake hadn't seen him since. He looked at the clock on his phone—almost two in the morning.

I need to get home before Rachel wakes up.

He had spent just over an hour with Pete. The hour was the least satisfying of his life. Pete tried to talk about the war, but every time he would tell a story, all Jake could think about was how Pete had left, how he had left Jake and everyone else to fight it out in Afghanistan while he drank beer and tried to get laid at this very bar. Jake knew the anger he felt toward Pete was unfair. Some part of him even wondered if he was really just angry at himself and taking it out on Pete, but the more beer he drank, the more he resented Pete, and he'd been glad when his friend left for a bathroom break.

Jake sighed and tipped the beer back, enjoying the coolness in his throat. Some part of him was still surprised to enjoy something as much as he enjoyed this beer—the part of him that was not yet home from Afghanistan, he imagined. For a second Jake felt himself missing the war. There was such a structure to it. A simplicity. You passed the time, you ate your meals, and you learned to not think—much less worry—about things you couldn't control. You hoped every day you would be going out on the next mission, and then the moment you stepped out of the helo or your Humvee pulled outside the wire, you spent every minute praying that you could just turn around and go back to the FOB.

People you knew died. You did terrible things that would haunt you forever. You saw horrible things you could never unsee.

How crazy was it to miss something like that?

Jake looked at his phone again. He was surprised that Rachel had not called already. Perhaps she was awake and wanted to leave him be. Or maybe she woke up and just assumed he was in the living room again, as he had been so many nights the last week.

Jake looked around the bar for Pete but wasn't surprised when he still didn't see him.

Left me again. What's new?

"You the other one?"

Jake looked up at two guys who stood beside the table with their hands on their hips. Both, from their age and dress, looked to be college kids. The Tap House was more of a local bar then a college hangout, but there were at least a handful of students at any bar in town. Jake guessed the bigger one was an athlete of some sort. Both had red, glazed eyes and were clearly well into their night of partying.

"Other what?" he asked. Behind the two, a small group of other guys whispered and giggled. A girl in a green sweatshirt waved at him and then laughed.

"Other soldier boy," the bigger kid said.

Jake shook his head and turned away. "Whatever, man," he said. But he felt a familiar heat begin to rise in his chest. What the hell did these assholes know about soldiers or sacrifice?

The bigger guy put a hand on his shoulder. "Hey, you a tough guy?" he asked. "You a tough guy like your friend?"

Jake looked up at the two again and heard their friends laugh.

"You ever kill anybody, soldier boy?" the smaller guy asked and giggled like a girl.

"Yeah, did you?" the bigger guy asked and looked at his friends, who egged him on. "'Cause we got a bet that rugby players are way tougher than you Army pussies. Definitely tougher than your friend. So much for 'leave no man behind,' dude. That guy done left you behind."

"Left you behind," the smaller kid slurred and then giggled again.

Jake swallowed the rage as best he could. He just wanted to get home to Rachel now. He should never have left her. Coming here had been a mistake.

"Look, dude. I'm definitely not as tough as a rugby player, that's for sure."

The man turned to his group of friends. "See, girls?" he hollered. Then he put his hand on Jake's shoulder again and Jake felt the heat rise past his neck to his face.

"How many little kids you kill over there, tough guy?"

The rage exploded out of him like a white light, and Jake was only barely aware of the room around him. He reached across his chest with his left hand and grabbed the wrist of the hand on his shoulder. Jake pulled down sharply and twisted at the same time, hearing a scream of pain that made a grin spread across his face. As he rose, he pulled down on the rugby player's arm and heard a satisfying thud as his face crunched into the wooden table.

Jake leaned close to the boy's ear and saw with some satisfaction the small pool of blood spreading out on the tabletop from a split lip.

"I've killed so many people that one more won't make any difference," he whispered. Then he slammed his forearm across the boy's face and heard him scream again before he slid, sobbing, to the floor.

Jake looked up and saw the crowd of college kids spread out in all directions.

"I'm calling the cops," the rugby player's partner hollered over his shoulder as he bolted for the door.

"Hey, what the hell, man?"

The voice came from a large man behind the bar who had a phone in his hand.

Jake wondered for a moment what would happen if he just left. The kid on the floor was pedaling backward and crying, the blood on his chin and cheek now dripping onto his fraternity sweatshirt. He had a split lip, but he was obviously fine.

Jake saw his phone light up and heard it vibrate on the table. *Home* flashed across the screen. He reached for the phone, unsure whether he should answer it. Maybe he should step outside so it would be quiet.

"You saw that guy started it, right?" he shouted to the bartender and scooped up his phone.

"Maybe," the bartender said, "but I don't give a shit. You need to wait and talk to the cops, man. You know I can find you. It ain't a big town and I know you're friends with Pete. I can find you at the base, you know."

Jake slid his phone into his pocket and headed for the door.

"Fine. I'll talk to them," he said. "I just gotta call my wife first. I'll be right outside."

"You wait right here," the man shouted at Jake's back.

The rugby player was holding some bunched-up napkins to his lip, and when he saw Jake he scurried away, his eyes widening in fear. Jake shook his head in frustration and walked past him. The crowd parted like the Red Sea.

Jake walked out the entrance and nearly collided with a cop who was just reaching for the door handle.

"Whoa there, son," the officer said. "What's the hurry?"

"Gotta get home to my wife," Jake said. He realized how drunk he felt and wondered if he had slurred his words.

"In a minute, maybe," the officer said. "Come on back inside with me first."

Jake sighed. The phone in his back pocket vibrated again as he followed the police officer into the bar.

CHAPTER 44

Rachel found herself praying in her sleep. She was aware of the dream-like smell of her church tree, but also of the soft sheets of their bed. She prayed that she would dream about Luke and that maybe he could tell her what to do. She prayed that she would then wake up and open her Bible and that the passage she turned to would show her how to help her husband. She wondered if that had truly happened before, or if in her fear and stress she had made it all up. Maybe she'd just taken random passages and twisted them so they seemed like they were meant for her.

"Rachel," the soft voice urged. "Open your eyes."

"Not yet," she whispered back. She needed another minute of dream-prayer before she could face any more nightmares about Jake or Cal. Then she realized where she knew the voice from and opened her eyes. "Luke?"

Luke leaned his chin on his arm, which was wrapped around the thick walking stick. There was a glow about him that made him easier to see in the dim light of the quarter moon, which was low behind the woods down the hill from her tree.

"Yes, Rachel. It's me." The messenger smiled at her more with his eyes than his mouth.

"Are you real?" she asked, realizing immediately how like a child she must sound.

"Of course," he said. "Everything you imagine is real."

The paradox confused her, but she decided not to think about it. She needed Luke's comfort before she woke up to find her husband's side of the bed empty and cold. Her non-dream hand reached out even now across the empty pillow where his face should have been.

"Can you help him?" she asked Luke and then felt tears on her cheeks. The tears felt real, like they were on her real cheeks back home in bed.

"He has to choose, Rachel." Luke looked sad. "That freedom is the greatest gift and the greatest curse. The Father loves you too much to take it from any of you, though it sometimes breaks His heart more than you know."

Rachel looked down at her feet. She wiggled her bare toes in the wet grass and felt the cool sheets on her heels. She wiped a tear from the side of her nose.

"I chose badly," she whispered. "You told me Kelly would need me and she did. You showed me what would happen and asked me to help her, but I didn't."

She felt Luke's eyes on her.

"It's a gift and a curse."

Rachel nodded.

"Now she can be there for you," Luke said.

Rachel lifted her head. For a moment Luke seemed more like a ball of light than a man, but then the light fused together and he was the same sweatshirt-clad man as before—neither young nor old, not quite happy and not really sad.

"How could I ask that of her?" Rachel asked. Tears dripped off her face onto both the wet ground and her cool, dry sheets. "I failed her so terribly. How can I ask for her help?"

"Because she wants to give it. She needs to be there for you." Luke smiled again. "And because there is no scorecard, Rachel. If there were, it would be very lonely up there." He gestured upward with his eyes.

Rachel nodded. She opened her mouth to ask a question, but then Luke was gone. She was alone by her tree and forgot the question she wanted to ask.

The chirping of her phone made her open her eyes, though they hadn't actually felt closed. The soft moon-glow of her tree hill became the glow of her ringing cell phone on her nightstand. She looked over at Jake's empty side of the bed as she reached for the phone. Rachel had the distinct feeling that something was going to happen, and in her mind she saw Luke's eyes—both happy and sad. She wondered if what would happen would be good or bad. Then she remembered that it would be their choice—hers and Jake's. She swiped the screen of her phone and put it to her ear.

"Hello?"

"Rachel?" Kelly's voice was soft but urgent. "Sweetie, I'm sorry to call so late. Did I wake you? I just—I don't know, I just felt like I needed to call. Is everything all right?"

Rachel looked again at Jake's cold, empty side of the bed. She started to cry.

"Oh, Kelly, I don't know," she sobbed. "I'm so sorry, Kelly. I'm so sorry for everything. Please. Please can you come over? I need you."

"I'll be right there, Rachel," her friend said. "I think I knew you needed me tonight. Is Jake all right?"

Rachel sobbed harder. Then she thought of Cal, and the guilt simmered up in her again. She saw Luke's eyes and she wrestled it back down.

"I don't know, Kelly. Please hurry."

The phone clicked off and she knew her friend was on the way. She dialed Jake's phone. For a moment she wondered if he was in the other room, maybe even asleep on the couch. But when the chirping sound of the phone ringing in her ear wasn't joined by a corresponding ring from the living room, she knew.

He wasn't here.

The phone clicked over to voice mail and she listened to Jake's greeting—a happier Jake from a million years ago. Rachel hung up and stared at the wall. Where was he? Was he okay? Luke would have told her if Jake was hurt, right?

Rachel shook her head. How silly to expect a warning from a dream.

She slipped out of bed and wrapped herself in the big fuzzy robe Jake had given her for Christmas two years ago—an inside lover's joke about how cold she seemed always to be. Then she headed for the kitchen to make tea for herself and Kelly. Time was like a liquid sloshing in a bucket, and it seemed like both minutes and hours before Kelly knocked on their door.

They sat together on the couch, Rachel unsure what to share about her strange dreams, but her worry for Jake came spilling out in choppy sentences and then sobs. She told Kelly about his distance, his anger, and his nightmares. Rachel laid her head against Kelly's shoulder and wiped the snot from her nose with a tissue, then tossed it to the floor with the nest of others.

"I called twice, but he didn't answer," she said. "He might be out driving around or something. I know he has these terrible dreams. But why won't he answer? Doesn't he know how worried I am?"

Kelly said nothing, but rubbed Rachel on the back gently.

"I had no idea you guys were having such a hard time," she whispered finally. Rachel thought there was a sadness in her voice from more than her concern for Rachel and her husband. The guilt bubbled up again.

"I know," she said. "I didn't want to bother you," she said and immediately regretted it.

"Bother me?" Kelly pulled away to look Rachel in the face. Rachel looked down in shame. "Sweetie, you're my best friend. You're like family to me and Cal." The mention of Cal's name made Rachel's chest hurt. "How can you ever be bothering me?"

"When you needed me, I wasn't there," Rachel said, her voice quivering with the pain she felt in her throat. "I was so selfish, Kelly. I am so, so sorry."

Rachel couldn't hold it back anymore and the tears now came in shaking sobs.

Kelly held her for a minute and then straightened Rachel up by her shoulders and tipped her face up by the chin.

"I miss you, Rachel," Kelly said. She firmed her jaw. "And I won't lie to you—I missed you during that time. But sweetie, I understood. Jake was still gone and he was struggling with Cal leaving, just as we all were. I missed you, but I rarely called you either, did I? If I had needed you, I know I could have called and you would have come." Kelly hugged her. "I had Romans eight and I got through it."

Rachel felt herself flush with something like anger, though that was not really the right word.

"I don't know how you can turn to Romans eight," she said and looked down. "I've come to hate that verse. I hate how Pastor Craig always quotes it. Cal is gone. Shawn is gone. I feel like my husband is all but gone and I'm worried near to death about him. I let myself drift from my best friend in her time of need." Another sob escaped and she felt herself shake again. "I just can't see the good in any of that."

Kelly sighed, her hands folded now in her lap.

"I've sure been there," she said. "After Cal died I was so angry at God. I didn't understand how he could let that happen. Cal was such a good man, such a loving and devoted Christian. It seemed so unfair."

"It is unfair," Rachel wailed. "I miss him so much. I loved Cal so much and it's so unfair. And now I'm losing Jake too." She leaned against Kelly's arm. The anguish she had not even known was there enveloped her.

"I don't know that it's supposed to be fair," Kelly said.

Rachel pulled away and looked at her.

Kelly continued. "I spent a lot of time with Pastor Craig and Debbie in the weeks after it happened. I think Craig and I struggled with some of the same questions. He and Cal were so close, you know, and he was hurting too. But he told me that there was never any promise of fair."

"What do you mean?"

Kelly sighed again. "For the longest time I thought that Romans eight meant that if we trusted God, if we followed Him and worshipped Him and praised Him, our lives would be good and we would be blessed. With Craig's help, I think I understand now that God is not promising that."

Rachel felt her last lifeline pulling away from her. "Are you saying God won't help us—that we're on our own?"

The thought almost made Rachel's heart burst.

"No," Kelly said softly and smiled at her. "No, not at all. I think He's promising something even larger than what I thought, though at times maybe much harder. God's promise is that He'll always be there for us— no matter what. You see, Romans eight, twenty-eight, doesn't say that there will always be good in our lives. It says that He will help us find good in all things. The promise of Romans eight is that no matter how bad things seem, no matter how broken our hearts feel and no matter how lost and in pain we become, if we put our faith in Him, He will help bring good to our lives—and the world around us—despite the hardships and tragedies."

Kelly paused and Rachel let her words swim around in her head for a moment.

"It's hard to see any good in Cal's death—for me especially, I assure you." Kelly's voice broke a little and she dabbed at her eyes with her sleeve. "But I'm no longer mad at God. I trust Him to help me make my life into something good, even if I have to do it without Cal."

Kelly covered her eyes with her hand now as tears escaped onto her cheeks. Rachel wrapped her arms around her friend.

"I'm not mad at God, because God didn't kill Cal," Kelly whispered from her embrace. "I will never understand why I have to live without him, but there is evil in the world, Rachel. There is war, and hatred, and cruelty, and none of that was God's plan for His children. But when we suffer at the hands of this world that we're in, God is still there to lift us up."

Kelly leaned back and grabbed her own tissue. She dabbed at her eyes and then blew her nose. "Excuse me," she said with an embarrassed grin.

Rachel hugged her again.

"I am so sorry, Kelly," she said. "I've been such a bad friend."

"No, Rachel," Kelly answered in her ear. "You're my friend and you'll always be my sister." She touched Rachel's cheek and Rachel looked again into her eyes. "How can I help you and Jake?" Kelly asked. "If I can help you to bring Jake back to the path he started on with Cal—if we can help Cal's best friend together—then we can make Cal's life, and maybe even his death, mean something even more."

Their embrace was interrupted by the ringing of Rachel's phone on the table, and they both jumped at the noise.

Rachel picked up the phone but stared at a number she had never seen before.

Her eyes closed as she swiped the phone to answer. "Hello?" she said tentatively.

"Rachel? It's TC Morrow—from Jake's unit."

Rachel felt her breath disappear from her chest in a rush. The room seemed to somehow get smaller.

"Is Jake okay?" she asked. Kelly's hand squeezed her arm harder.

"Yes, yes," TC said. "Oh God, Rachel, I'm sorry. Yes, Jake's fine. We have a bit of a situation, but Jake is fine. I'm headed to him now. I want to make a suggestion, though, if you're agreeable."

"What happened?" she asked, able to breathe again now that she knew her husband was in some sort of trouble, but not dead or hurt.

She held hands with Kelly and listened as TC told her what had happened and what he recommended they do next.

CHAPTER 45

Jake dropped his forehead into his palms, his elbows on the metal surface of the police officer's desk. He should call Rachel. TC had promised to call her, but Jake needed to hear her voice and tell her how sorry he was. He thought he might be allowed to call soon. He seemed to remember something about one phone call when you went to jail, but maybe that was just in the movies.

I should have called my wife.

He had rationalized that he didn't want Rachel to suffer the humiliation of coming to pick her husband up from jail, but he knew he was just a coward who didn't want to hear the pain in his wife's voice—pain that he had caused, again.

"You want a coffee?"

The hand on his shoulder startled him and he looked up at the police officer who had brought him to the station from the bar.

"I'm okay," Jake said. He swallowed hard. "Is that kid okay?"

The officer chuckled. "The drunk rugby player? Yeah, he's fine. After talking to all the witnesses, it sounds like he had that and more coming. You're lucky that everyone saw him grab you. That makes what you did self-defense, and from what I hear that jackass needed an ass whipping, so you're good there. We still got the drunk-and-disorderly charge to consider, but let's see what your platoon leader says first."

The officer patted him twice on the shoulder and smiled again. Then he leaned in, a conspiratorial look on his face.

"Take the coffee," he said softly. "It'll help you sober up a little and mask the beer smell some. I wouldn't have wanted my First Sar'n to bail me out, but I sure as hell wouldn't have wanted to smell like you do if he did."

Jake looked at the officer closer. "Army?"

The officer nodded. "Tenth Mountain Division," he said. "Two tours in Iraq. I know how you might be feeling, but it does get better."

Jake felt tears well in his eyes, and for a terrifying moment thought they might spill out onto his cheeks.

"I'll take that coffee, I guess," he said with a smile.

The officer patted his shoulder again. "Good call," he said. Then, over his shoulder as he shuffled off, he added, "From the sound of his voice, your First Sar'n Morrow is a big, mean guy. Very good call indeed."

A few minutes later Jake sat beside the officer, who tapped with two fingers on a computer keyboard to finish up his report. Jake had a strong suspicion that the rules were being bent, and he was grateful. He remembered the boy's hand on his shoulder, but he didn't recall anyone "grabbing" him. He wondered if asking to call Rachel would be pushing his luck. Before he could ask, his thought was interrupted by an unexpected voice, and Jake almost choked on his coffee.

"Hello, Jake," the voice said. "How's your night going?"

Jake turned in his chair and wiped coffee from his chin as he looked up into Pastor Craig's serious face.

"Pastor Craig," Jake said. "What are you... how did you know? Did... did First Sar'n Morrow call you?" He felt at once worried about how angry Rachel would be that their pastor—their *church*—would know what happened. And he was angry at TC. How dare he call the pastor without asking? There must be some rules or something against that, right?

"No," Craig said. "I called TC to see what was going on with you, but it was Rachel who called to tell me what was going on. She's fine, by the way. You've scared the hell out of her again, but she's fine."

"You called TC?" Jake said. He must have heard wrong. "You know him?"

"Kind of," Craig said. "I've met him, but he's more a friend of a friend. He runs a men's group at Heritage Baptist Church and I'm pretty good friends with Pastor Davidson over there. He talked to Rachel before I did, and then he and I agreed I should be the one to come get you. I hope I might be able to help. He says to tell you he'll need to talk to you in the morning, by the way."

WAR TORN

Jake's swallowed hard at that—not a meeting he would relish.

Craig reached his hand out toward the cop, who rose now. "I'm Craig," he said and shook the officer's hand. Jake sat between them feeling like a kid whose dad had to come get him from the principal's office.

"I've heard of you, Pastor Craig," the officer said. "Thanks for coming. Jake seems like a good guy. I'm glad he has you for a friend."

Craig looked down at Jake and smiled.

"We'll see about that," he said, "but I sure hope that proves to be true. Is there anything you need me to do? Anything I have to sign or something?"

"Nah," the officer said. He reached into his desk drawer and grabbed Jake's cell phone and keys, which he handed to Jake. "Like I told Jake, the prosecutor will decide about the drunk and disorderly. I'll give my two cents, so I doubt there will be any charges. This time ..." he added with a stern look at Jake.

Jake shook the officer's hand and slipped his phone and keys into a back pocket. "Thank you so much."

"Thank your preacher here," the officer said. "Thanks to him, I don't have to hold you in the drunk tank until morning. Like I said—I been there and it does get easier."

Jake nodded uncomfortably. Then he followed Craig out of the large room full of empty desks.

"You gonna take me home?" Jake asked as they walked out into the dark street.

"Not yet," Craig said as he pulled out keys and pressed the fob, making a pickup truck in front of the police station light up with an accompanying chirp. Jake raised his eyebrows in surprise. He had expected a grey Camry or maybe a Lincoln—certainly not a gorgeous king cab pickup. "I have pretty vivid memories of how you're feeling right now," Craig said as he opened the passenger door for Jake, "so grabbing a beer is out of the question." He closed the door and then walked around and slid into the driver's seat. "Nothing better for the hangover that's waiting for you than a big, greasy breakfast, lots of water, and another cup of coffee. I know just the place."

Jake looked at the pastor. How the hell did a preacher know what he was feeling like? Craig seemed to read his thoughts and laughed.

"I wasn't born a pastor, Jake," he said. Craig put the big truck in Drive and pulled away from the curb. "I was a mess when Debbie met me, I can tell you that. I'm not proud of my youth, but it does make me understand certain things better, I guess."

Jake shook his head. He thought of the officer and how cool he had been. "Guess I'm pretty lucky that cop was Army, huh?" he said softly.

"I don't believe much in luck," Craig said. "But it does seem like someone is watching out for you, doesn't it? Like maybe there's a plan for you, huh?"

Jake sat in silence. He felt anger rise at the suggestions of some master frigging plan, but his relief and gratitude seemed able to tamp it down. If listening to a sermon was the price of getting off so easy, Jake figured he could take that.

"I guess so," he said. "Maybe," he added. He didn't want to give the impression he was all in for the inevitable message, however. He looked over at the pastor, his strong hands on the wheel of the truck. "Did you say TC leads a men's group?" he asked.

"Does that surprise you?" Pastor Craig asked, looking over with a smile. Jake said nothing, but realized it did surprise him, though it shouldn't.

Minutes later they were seated at the diner, and Jake felt his head clear once he shook off the wave of nausea that accompanied the first whiff of the eggs, sausage, and hash browns the waitress slid in front of him. She placed a similarly huge plate of food in front of Craig. The pastor shrugged sheepishly.

"I'm out with you at four o'clock in the morning," he said and scooped up a big bite. "I'm cheating on the diet, 'kay? Our secret," he added with a wink.

Jake was amazed at how easy it was to be with the pastor, who he remembered as so larger-than-life from the stage at Foundations Family Church. He thought of TC being a men's group leader at the other big church in town. He thought of Rachel and the peaceful look on her face, which almost glowed when they bowed their heads at church. He thought of Cal and his humor and faith, even in Afghanistan. Then he saw his friend evaporating in a cloud of bloody fire and thought of Pete's questions on the dark roof in Afghanistan, after he had held a dying soldier.

Jake sighed the confusing and competing feelings away and took a big bite of eggs and meat and then washed it down with coffee. After the second wave of nausea ebbed, he realized the greasy food was making him feel better. Who'd have thought to ask Pastor Craig for the best hangover cure?

"So, Jake," the pastor began after his own big bite. "What's going on with you, man?"

Time to pay for breakfast.

"I'm still struggling a bit," Jake confessed, "but I'm getting better, I think."

"Yeah, I see that," Craig said with a hearty laugh. "What were you doin' last week? Knocking over liquor stores?"

Jake shrugged sheepishly.

"Anyway, that's not what I'm talking about, Jake. But I think you know that."

Jake wasn't exactly sure what Craig meant, though he suspected. He figured that Rachel had shared her excitement with the pastor after Jake told her he had given his life to Christ. Maybe Cal had even emailed about it—he and Pastor Craig had been close.

"You and Cal were doing a Bible study together, weren't you? He said you were really passionate about it. This was just before …" To Jake's surprise, Pastor Craig's voice cracked. Craig cleared his throat and continued. "Sorry, Jake. I'm still struggling with things myself, I guess."

Jake's eyebrows rose. He couldn't imagine Pastor Craig struggling with anything. On stage he was so strong and confident. He was funny at times and clever and so in control. Jake found this side strange—and a little uncomfortable.

"I know you were close to Cal," he mumbled. "I'm sorry for everything that happened."

This time the tears did spill over and Jake wiped them away with an irritated swipe of his palm.

"Anyway, I know where this going and I appreciate it, but I'm really not your guy for this."

The pastor nodded. "It sounds like you were on the way to being that guy. From what I hear."

"Yeah, well, that was before everything, you know."

"I *don't* know, Jake. I've never been to war. I can guess a little at what hell you must have been through, but I don't know, not really. I can't even imagine. But that seems like it would make you need Christ even more once you found him."

"Look," Jake said, his voice quivering now. He swallowed hard and wished some of the anger away. "I appreciate all you've done for Rachel and what you want to do here, but you're right—you don't get it." He pushed his plate away and reached for a napkin to wipe his tears.

Craig nodded. "That's fair," he said. "So tell me, then—make me understand what I'm missing. I'm not here to talk you into or out of anything. I like you and I would love to help you and Rachel while you're 'struggling,' as you call it. So, help me understand."

Jake shifted in discomfort and irritation.

"It's just you and me, Jake. You don't have to worry about hurting Rachel or about pissing me off. Tell me what you're thinking."

"Okay, I will," Jake said. His anger had settled but most surely had not disappeared. "I prayed every day, Pastor Craig. I read the Bible with Cal. I prayed for our safety. I prayed for our wives and that we would do the right things, do them well, and come safely home. I prayed He would keep us safe just hours before Cal was blown up in that damn village. Where was God? Why would He let that happen? Where's the great life you get following Christ? I lost my best friend, who loved God more than anyone I have ever met. I killed people and had people try to kill me. I prayed I would do the right thing, and guess what? I let down two of my friends and now they're dead. I did things—maybe did some really bad things. Where the hell was God in all that? You want me to just forget all that injustice and start singing in the choir now?"

Jake's voice had risen, and the waitress was looking at them nervously from the counter. He realized his fists were balled so tightly that they made his hands and forearms ache.

"You want answers to those questions, and that's fair," Craig said sadly. "But I don't have those answers. None of us does. I do know that nothing in the Bible says that if you follow Christ your life will be easy—or fair, for that matter. For the early Christians, it meant a life of persecution and even death. Sunshine, rainbows, and unicorns is not the promise of a life with Christ, Jake."

"Yeah?" Jake challenged. "Then what the hell is?"

"God promises the greatest gift of all—the opportunity to have a relationship with Him. That relationship is possible because of all that Jesus sacrificed on the cross for us—the ultimate gift of love."

"I know the story of the cross, Pastor Craig," Jake said with new irritation. Was that all the pastor had to offer?

"I don't think you do," Craig said. "Do you think that day was sunshine and rainbows? When they nailed our Savior to that cross after savagely beating Him, and then raised Him up to suffocate and bleed to death, do you think there was a whole bunch of high-fiving that day?"

Jake shifted in his seat, unsure what to say.

"Jesus had a close team of disciples and scores of followers, Jake. What do you think was their mood that day? Do you think they were grinning that—yes, finally—let's get this crucifixion going and have our sins forgiven? Hell, no." Craig pounded the table with his palm, making Jake's fork fall to the floor. "Hope died that day, Jake. The story of the cross is the story of hopelessness, of loss, of pain, of suffering and guilt. It's your story, Jake. I've never been to war, that's true, but do you really think that Jesus and His followers, on that day, didn't share a little of what you went through?"

Craig let out a trembling sigh and lowered his head. Jake stared at him, feeling something shift inside him. He had never thought about it that way.

"The hope we find in Christ did not happen at the cross, Jake. That was a day of horror, loss, betrayal, anger—you name it. The message of hope we find in Christianity came when Jesus could not be defeated by death. It came in His resurrection three days later and His promise that through Him, and through His death on the cross, we could have an eternal relationship with God."

Jake sat up in his seat as Craig paused. He realized he almost desperately wanted Craig to continue.

"The things you experienced in war—especially the loss of Cal that day—that's *your* cross, Jake." Craig wiped his eyes with his napkin. "And mine," he whispered. "Now we need to decide where we will find our hope after all that. I let you down when we met a few days ago. I was going through the motions and doing my job, but honestly, I wasn't feeling very Christlike that day. Losing Cal hurts me too. I'm sorry I wasn't better for you then."

"What's different now?" Jake asked.

Craig smiled. "A friend helped me see things differently, I think. And now I'm trying to do the same for you."

"But why?" Jake asked in a quivering voice. Didn't Craig know Cal was dead partly because of him?

"Someone loved you enough to die for you, Jake."

Jake's heart stopped in his chest and he felt cold on his neck.

My God, he does know. How can he sit here with me, knowing Cal and Shawn are dead because of me?

"He shouldn't have died," Jake sobbed and laid his head on his hands on the table. He felt Craig's strong hand on his shoulder.

"I'm not talking about Cal, Jake," he said softly. He paused a moment and let out his own shaky breath. "Jesus Christ hung on a cross, battered and bleeding, because He loved you enough to suffer so that you could be close to God. If He finds you worthy—if you're good enough for Him— then you're sure as hell good enough for me. He died for your forgiveness, son. How dare you refuse to forgive yourself, no matter what happened over in Afghanistan? How dare you refuse that gift when you know what it cost on that day?"

Craig's words unfroze something in Jake. Something Cal had said, but he couldn't quite find it. He raised his head and wiped his eyes, looking at Craig's red eyes for the first time.

"How do I do that?" he asked. He thought of Rachel, home alone and worried, and felt ashamed. "I want to get there, but how do I do that?"

Craig smiled wryly. "I told you I don't have all the answers, Jake, and I don't. I don't know how to get you all the way where you want to be—where God wants you to be. But I know how to get you started. You have to turn back to God, not away from Him. You have to let some of these things go, and you do that by giving them to Him. He told us that no burden is so heavy that He can't bear it for us when we need Him, and that has been true so many times for me—most recently when we all lost Cal."

Jake nodded. He thought maybe the pastor was right, but saying it and doing it, well…

"You don't feel worthy of Him right now. I get that, Jake. Here's a news flash—none of us deserve the love He gave us when He died so we could be with God. None of us. The very definition of grace is kindness and forgiveness that you don't deserve. It can't be earned because all of us fall short. Every one of us. You'll get better with it over time. For now, ask yourself this: If what you're saying about Cal dying for you and the other men is true—if that is what you believe really happened—then don't you owe it to him to find your way back to God? He loved you so much and it was so important to him that you find Christ. Can't you honor him by living your life, to the best of your ability, in a way that honors his life and faith?"

"I don't know, Pastor Craig. I don't know if I can. I think I want to, but…"

Craig smiled at Jake with eyes both sad and hopeful. "It just takes that first step, Jake. He's always ready, and I'm here when you need me."

"It would help me to know why," Jake said, remembering Pete's questions on the roof that night, questions Jake had planned to ask Cal after the mission. He looked out the large plate-glass window, but his hazy reflection was all he saw. "If I could just understand why this could happen to Cal and to Kelly—to all of us. If I could somehow make sense of all of it, you know?"

"I hear you, brother," Pastor Craig said. "Free will—what a bitch, huh? You see, none of this was ever God's plan for us. We live in a fallen world because of choices made not just by us, but by others—all the way back to Adam and Eve's first rebellion against God's will. That's about all the 'why' I have, Jake, and I know that doesn't help much. In the end you just have to surrender it to Him, be still, and know that He is God."

Jake nodded, but he wasn't sure he understood what the pastor meant. He had a feeling, though, that Cal might have said something similar if they'd had a chance to talk. "I think I need to go home to my wife," Jake said. "She must be worried sick."

Craig smiled and waved at the waitress. "Yeah," he agreed. "And I'm getting too old for these middle-of-the-night breakfasts."

They rode in Craig's truck in silence, and Jake adored how Craig seemed to know when not to talk. His words from breakfast swirled around in Jake's head and mixed with so many things Cal had said.

Jake didn't know if he could do it—if he could find his way back to that faith he had started to feel along the berm in Afghanistan with his best friend. There was so much pain associated it with it now—so much loss and guilt that seemed woven with the faith Craig talked about. His words made sense, but there was so much Jake would have to let go of for the words to feel real or possible.

At the curb he looked down in his lap and then over at Craig.

"Thank you, Pastor Craig," he said.

"I was up anyway and it was on my way," Craig joked, and they both chuckled.

"I didn't mean for the ride," Jake said.

Craig reached over and hugged him awkwardly. Then he shook his hand firmly. "I know, Jake. I'm here anytime."

Jake nodded and slipped out of the truck. Then he walked slowly to the door. The lights were on in his house and he saw movement in the windows. Feeling lighter than he had in months, Jake opened the door to Rachel.

CHAPTER 46

It was the heat that drove Rachel from their bed. The sun was streaming in through the breaks in the curtains, and even though they had only slept a few hours, her body told her it was way past time to get out of bed. She guessed it had only been the complete emotional and physical exhaustion that had let her fall asleep at all. The only blessing of the night had been the sense that she and Kelly were reconnected. The lingering guilt had nearly dissipated and she felt she had her sister back. All of that was, of course, overpowered by the horrible anxiety of all that was going on with Jake.

With some difficulty, she untangled herself from Jake's embrace and padded into the kitchen. She had not programmed the coffee maker before bed, hopeful as she was that they might both sleep in quite late. Rachel sighed heavily and dropped a filter into the machine, then spooned dark coffee in after it and shuffled to the sink to fill the water tank.

She wished she knew more about Jake's night. How could she help her husband—be the wife God called her to be, as Kelly would put it—if she didn't know what the hell was going on? Jake had seemed better, other than reeking of beer again, once he came home. His platoon leader hadn't even come to the door with him, so she hadn't been able to ask him what had happened.

The coffee maker made a long, whistling sigh, and then the life-giving dark liquid began dribbling into the carafe. Rachel tapped her fingers impatiently on the side of her mug after adding a splash of cream. She glanced at the clock. It was almost ten o'clock. Normally plenty late enough to give the First Sergeant a quick call before Jake woke up, but what if he'd slept in too?

Rachel collapsed slowly onto the couch with her coffee and the phone. A long sip of coffee did more for her than two more hours of sleep would have done. She looked at the phone. She would wait until ten thirty, maybe. With the amount of beer Jake had consumed, maybe he would sleep until at least then, but she deserved to be armed with a little knowledge before they talked.

"Baby?"

Rachel started, coffee sloshing into her lap.

"Shit," she said and then blushed. "Sorry," she said and looked up at Jake's haggard face, which had appeared in the doorway to their bedroom. "Did I wake you? I wanted you to sleep in."

Jake shuffled over and kissed her on the head.

"Wish I could have," he mumbled. "You deserve sleep way more than I do, though."

Rachel resisted the urge to tell him how much she agreed with that. She said a short prayer for patience.

"Can I get you coffee?" she asked instead.

"I'll get it," he said and squeezed her shoulder before heading into the kitchen at a snail's pace. "Who you calling?" he asked.

"No one," Rachel lied and then felt guilty. "Didn't want the phone to wake you if it rang. You must be exhausted."

"No more than you," he called out from the kitchen, his voice a little stronger. There was something else in his voice, something hard to pinpoint, but it gave her a surge of hope.

Not too much hope, girl. You can't afford more disappointment. Long slow distance.

"I'm really sorry about that, Rachel," Jake said as he walked back in with his own, oversized cup of coffee. "Do you need a refill?"

"I'm good," she said softly.

Jake joined her on the couch—not too close, but not too far either.

"Where did you go last night?" she asked. "I mean, I guess I know where you went. Why did you leave me in the middle of the night? And why didn't you tell me you were going?" She heard the anger in her voice and wished she had asked the question differently.

Jake looked down at his hands. "I don't know," he said and his voice cracked. "I'm really sorry, baby. I think I didn't want to wake you." His eyes got that far-off look she hated now more than anything, and then he continued. "I had a dream—a nightmare, you know—and I guess...I don't know, I just wanted to get away for a little while." Jake sighed heavily. Rachel thought there were tears in his normally happy and strong eyes, but he turned away and she wasn't sure.

Rachel put a hand on his shoulder. She didn't want him to hurt. She thought maybe she wasn't mad, actually—just so damn worried. "What happened, though? You didn't tell me much last night. You just kept saying you were sorry and then you fell asleep. TC didn't tell me much either. He told me you weren't in an accident or anything, so I at least knew you weren't hurt."

Jake let out another rattling sigh.

"I got in a fight," he said. He still didn't look at her.

Rachel felt her maternal worries surge back in full force. "You what? A fight? Oh my God, Jake. Are you okay, baby? What happened?" Despite her promise to herself to be calm—that Jake needed her to be calm and patient—she realized she was crying again.

"No, no, Rachel," he said and wrapped an arm around her shoulders and pulled her head onto his chest. She wondered if that was just so she couldn't see the tears in his eyes. She cradled her coffee cup in her lap and let herself be held. "I'm fine, I'm totally fine. It was so stupid. This guy was—he was just ..." He sighed again and his voiced cracked. "It's so stupid. It doesn't matter."

"Did you hurt someone?" Rachel asked in a low whisper, her chest tight.

"No, sweetie, no," he said and pulled her closer. "Everything's fine. I'm just so damn sorry that I worried you."

Rachel shifted her coffee to one hand and hugged him back.

"It's okay, Jake." She pulled away slightly and looked up at him. "Please, don't do that to me again, though, okay?" she sobbed. Then she hugged him again. "I was so worried."

"I know. I'm sorry, Rachel. Never again." The pain in his voice was very real, whether Rachel could believe his words or not.

They held each other for a minute and then she straightened, sliding her mug onto the coffee table and wiping the tears from her cheeks. She tried to put a smile on her face as she set her hand on her husband's leg.

"So what did you guys talk about?" she asked, trying to keep her hope that something might have shifted for Jake out of her voice. "You were out awhile after I talked to TC. And you should know"—she bit her lip, not wanting to see Jake mad again, but she had to be honest—"well, I called Pastor Craig to tell him what was going on."

Jake shook his head, but his face wore a grin of sorts that was hard to read. "Oh I know. I'm sure you're excited that I got a sermon, huh? I deserved it, I guess—needed it, even."

"Sermon?" she asked, confused. "What kind of sermon?"

Jake chuckled. "Well, you know—Pastor Craig always sounds like he's giving a sermon."

"Pastor Craig?" Rachel was unable to cover her surprise. Anything to do with Foundations Family Church got nothing but a scowl since Jake returned. "What are you talking about, Jake? Did you call him? You talked to him?"

He looked confused now as well. "He took me out to breakfast after he picked me up at the …" His face flushed and he looked at his coffee cup. "You know—at the jail."

"TC took you to breakfast? Pastor Craig was there?" His words sunk in. "Wait—you were in jail?"

"No," Jake said and looked at her funny. "Pastor Craig took me to breakfast. I thought TC told you about jail. I mean, I wasn't in jail. I just— you didn't know I was with Pastor Craig? He was the one who picked me up. TC wasn't there."

Rachel pushed away a bit so she could see her husband's face more clearly.

"Pastor Craig picked you up at jail?" she said. She felt how wide her eyes had gotten. She didn't know whether to feel relieved that the pastor had taken him to breakfast or mortified that the church knew Jake had been arrested. Now she understood why TC had insisted she call Pastor Craig to let him know what was going on. She decided that Jake spending time with the pastor far outweighed any embarrassment about the circumstances, and then chided herself for even worrying about appearances. But Jake was still staring at her, confused. "Why did Pastor Craig pick you up?"

"I guess TC asked him to, if you didn't," Jake answered. "Didn't he tell you?"

Rachel felt an inappropriate laugh escape her throat.

"No," she said and made a note to give TC a piece of her mind if she ever saw him again. That bit of knowledge might have helped her find another hour of sleep. "No, he did not tell me our pastor took you to breakfast." She looked at her husband and gave him her best smile. "So how did that go?"

To her surprise, Jake took her hand.

"Actually, it went well," he said. "Way better than you would think. He said some cool things." Jake's voice cracked again and he closed his eyes. "He sounded a lot like Cal."

Her husband began to sob and she pulled his head into her lap and smoothed his hair. Tears streaked freely down her face, but there was relief in them. She had not heard him say anything about Cal—especially about his faith—since he'd been home, except to yell at Pastor Craig and Pastor Chris when they'd called on them. That had to be a good sign, right? She dared not let herself get too far ahead of things.

She stroked Jake's rough, unshaven face.

"Will you be talking with him again?" she asked. She closed her eyes and grimaced. She shouldn't push it.

"I don't know, baby," he mumbled. "I know you want me to. I think about what he said, and I think about how I felt before everything happened, and I want to, but..." She felt him sob again. "I don't know."

Jake sat up and looked at her, holding her gaze. Rachel felt a shudder. He hadn't looked at her like that since before he left for Afghanistan. She saw the real, loving Jake in his stare.

"I have to go talk to someone else first," he said softly.

"Who?" she asked, then a dismaying thought struck her. "Not Pete again? I'm sorry, Jake." She put a hand over her eyes. "I can't take you going drinking with him again."

"No," he said and took her hand and squeezed it gently in his own. "Not Pete. Just a new friend I made. I have some questions I have to ask him. Then we'll see, okay?"

"Where did you meet him?" Rachel blurted, unable to control her worries. "Not at that bar?"

Jake smiled at that. "No, Rach," he said. "It's a guy I met at that damn meeting TC made me go to. His name's Adrian."

She leaned against him and closed her eyes. Just the short burst of emotion had sucked all the energy out of her and she felt completely exhausted.

"I'll call him in just a little bit, okay?"

"Okay," she mumbled.

What else could she say?

CHAPTER 47

Jake sat at the small table in the back of the Starbucks, nursing both a huge coffee and his hangover. He glanced up again as another member of the long stream of the "coffee generation" paraded through the line. He usually preferred just black coffee—and he hated ordering using all the foo-foo words—but he figured some extra sugar and caffeine would help him get through whatever this day held. There was something hanging in the air that he truly felt couldn't continue to suspend itself over him, and it seemed today was going to be the day, whatever the hell that might mean. So, Jake ordered exactly the same drink as the business-woman ahead of him in line, blushed when the barista called out, "Venti skinny double-shot caramel macchiato for Jake," and now sat sipping the hot (and actually delicious—damn it) drink and waiting patiently to see where exactly his life would head.

The door opened again and Jake saw no one at first, then adjusted his gaze downward and saw the top of Adrian's head. He knew it was Adrian not just because of the height, but because of the scarred and mangled ear. He stood up slightly and waved, and Adrian lifted one hand off the wheels of his chair and waved back. Then he wheeled himself over, his scarred face all smiles, matched only by the peaceful smile that was no less concealed in his piercing blue eyes.

"What's up, Jake?" he said, as if they had been friends for years instead of having met only a few days ago.

"Can I get you a coffee?" Jake said after shaking the strong, gloved hand.

"Ah, no," Adrian answered with a wave. "One more coffee and my kidneys will explode." He laughed. "Been that kind of day."

Adrian pulled out a sports bottle, which Jake assumed contained water, and took a long pull. Jake sipped again on his new favorite coffee.

"So what's up, man?" Adrian asked again. "You sounded a little distracted on the phone. Everything okay? Rachel all right?"

Jake raised his eyebrows, amazed that Adrian would remember his wife's name.

"Yeah, yeah," he said with a confidence he didn't feel. "Everything's cool. Are you crazy busy? We can get together another time." The rising discomfort was making Jake wish he had maybe waited on this until he felt a lot better. Still, there was a powerful sense of urgency that he couldn't understand.

Find your way back to your path, Jake—for everyone.

Jake felt certain that, this time, anyway, the voice was just his own mind talking to him. Either way, he needed to find his path forward—for Rachel if not for himself.

Adrian just waited expectantly.

"Actually," Jake began, and found it hard to look at Adrian's eyes and smiling face, "things aren't really that great. I'm struggling with some things, and after meeting you the other day I thought, I don't know, maybe you might be able to help me."

"Of course," Adrian said, his voice now quite serious and his eyes full of concern. Jake hesitated and looked down at his hands. "Look, dude, whatever it is, there is a pretty fair chance that I'll get it." Adrian gestured at his face with one hand and his wheelchair with the other. "Been there, same as you, ya know?"

Jake nodded. "That's kind of it, actually," he said. "I look at you and imagine what you've been through. I don't know, I guess I'm kind of ashamed to be having such a hard time?"

Adrian leaned into the table. "Why on earth would that be?" he asked.

Jake shrugged. "I don't know," he said. "I mean, you've clearly been through some wicked-ass bad shit, you know? I've had my stuff—I lost my best friend over there ..." Jake hesitated. Should he add that he thought that might be his fault? Should he mention how much he came to love the feeling of revenge he got from the killing? He decided there was nothing he could add that would total up to what Adrian had survived. "But, I mean, nothing like what you must have been through, and look at me. I'm a total mess, ya know? You seem to be doing so great."

Adrian leaned back and smiled.

"Yeah, ain't I amazing?" he said with a laugh. Then he grew serious again and leaned onto the table. "I wasn't always like this, Jake. I had some incredibly low times. There were times when, honest to God, I thought it would be easier to just check out. It's a process—a long one for me, I promise you, but a process."

Adrian took another long pull on his water bottle. Jake marveled at how easily he talked about this—even thoughts of "checking out." Had Jake thought of that himself? He didn't think so, at least not yet.

"And anyway," Adrian continued, "my struggles are no more than yours. You can't compare loss and pain. Your struggles are your struggles, whatever they are. It's not a contest—it doesn't work like that. Whatever I went through doesn't change the reality of your loss or guilt or anger. Hell, you weren't there. And I wasn't there for your shit either."

Jake nodded. That made sense. He thought he could maybe let go of the feelings of guilt related to others having it worse than him, if he tried. But still…

"So how do you do it?" Jake asked. "I can do the work—the 'process' or whatever—but how do I know what to do? What's your secret?"

Adrian's eyes sparkled with a confidence that Jake envied above anything right now.

"It's not a secret," Adrian said. "It's one of the oldest and most well-publicized tricks in the Book. Hey, that's a good one, actually," Adrian added with a chuckle. "I gotta remember that. The Book, get it?" He laughed again and then shook his head when Jake stared at him, confused. "Sorry," Adrian added. "Let me read you something."

The young man rummaged in a sort of saddlebag that hung from the front of his chair where his legs should have been. He pulled a worn Bible from the bag, full of dog-ears and bookmarks and folded sheets of paper.

"You ready for this?" he asked.

Jake nodded.

More than you know—or maybe not, I guess.

Adrian cleared his throat and read:

"'Therefore, since we are surrounded by such a great cloud of witnesses, let us throw off everything that hinders us and the sin that so easily entangles. And let us run with perseverance the race marked out for us, fixing our eyes on Jesus, the pioneer and perfecter of our faith. For the joy set before him, he endured the cross, scorning its shame, and sat down at the right hand of the throne of God.'"

Adrian looked up at Jake and smiled.

"That simple verse saved my life, Jake. I don't know what it says to you, but to me, it says that if I can turn to Christ, if I can 'throw off' what hinders me and entangles me, then I can run the race He planned for me—I can live the life that God wants for me. I think of Him—up on that cross, bleeding and dying, not for His sins but for *my* sins, and I'm shamed by my own struggles. It says that He scorned the shame of that crucifixion—and that He did it for me."

Jake stared at Adrian's smiling, confident, scarred face, and for a moment saw Cal, as clear as day, sitting beside him, nodding.

"So you're saying that's why you're so happy all the time?"

"No," Adrian said. "You don't get it. I'm not even saying that I *am* happy all the time. God never promises us that. Being a Christian doesn't mean being happy all the time. It doesn't mean there are no tribulations or struggles. I have good days and bad days. I'm still pissed off sometimes, even now. What I mean is that my relationship with God gives me the strength to deal with whatever crap comes my way. I don't believe that God caused my pain. I don't think God took my legs and burned me over half of my body—He's a loving God who would never do that. That was other forces—evil forces, or the dark side of man, or the devil, or whatever you want to call it—but not God. And I'll tell you this for certain," he said, and there was fire in his eyes. "Without God—without Jesus as my savior—I would have given up long ago. I would have quit and lost everything, probably even my life. Now, I thank God for the life I have. I thank Him every day for the good things I get to do."

Jake frowned. "So you're telling me that this was God's plan for my life—for your life?"

"No," Adrian said, and he seemed frustrated. "Not even close. I don't believe that this was God's best purpose for me, any more than I believe that war and crime and destruction and the Holocaust, or any of the billions of examples of evil in the world, are even close to God's perfect plan for any of His children. What I am saying"—the frustration was gone and the fire was back—"is that God has given me real purpose in my life anyway. And real joy. Despite living in a fallen world, Jesus walks through it all with us. That's the secret to joy."

Jake felt a stirring again. It was at once familiar and frightening. He looked at Adrian and smiled. Adrian's eyebrows rose.

"You remind me of someone," Jake said. It had been a while since thoughts of Cal made him smile.

"Extra-short, legless guy—bad hair—worse skin?" Adrian said and laughed.

"No." Jake laughed too, not at all uncomfortable by the sick joke for some reason. "Big heart," he said.

"Well, thanks," Adrian said and blushed a little. "The verse I read you goes on," he said. It basically says, 'Consider him who endures … so that you will not grow weary and lose heart.'"

Jake felt a warmth flood over him at the words.

"Kind of like He wrote it just for us, huh?"

Jake nodded.

"Can I share some other things with you, Jake? Some other things that have helped me over the last three years, four months, and seventeen days?"

Jake nodded again.

"Please," he said.

CHAPTER 48

"It's a good thing women bear the babies, 'cause you would suck at waiting in the waiting room. For goodness' sake, girl, sit down here with me."

Rachel smiled at Kelly, who sipped her tea on Rachel's couch.

"They let the husbands into the delivery room now, in case you never heard," she quipped back. "What are you, from nineteen fifty-five?" She smiled at Kelly but kept up her pacing by the window. A car turned the corner and she pulled back the blinds, but it was a minivan belonging to the neighbors up the street instead of Jake's truck. "Damn it," she said and then turned. "Sorry," she added.

"No need, sweetie," Kelly said and calmly sipped her tea. "I get it. So, who is this guy?"

Rachel sighed and dropped onto the couch beside her, leaning her head back.

"I don't even know. He didn't really say and I didn't want to push. Adrian something, I think he said."

Kelly nodded gently and smiled at her.

Rachel let out her fears. If not to Kelly, then to who, right?

"He's got to be some other guy from the war, right? I mean, why else would he be at the group? Is that even a good idea? Maybe he has the same crap going on as Jake. Maybe they're in a bar right now, doing tequila shots and waiting for that damn Pete to show up."

She hated how she referred to Pete. A million years ago she remembered liking Pete a whole lot. He was fun and always goofing around. She knew he must be struggling with his own demons, just like Jake. It wasn't very Christlike to make him the enemy. She vowed to find more Christian charity.

"We don't, I guess," Kelly said and took her hand. "You said Jake seemed so much better though, right? After he met with Pastor Craig?"

"I guess." Rachel sighed. Had he been? She wondered if that had just been the bottomless bottle of wishful thinking she'd carried around regarding Jake this past month. "But he always seems to run away from God. Maybe this Adrian dude is who will help him run this time."

"Or maybe not, Rachel," Kelly said soothingly. "Besides, we both know you can't really run from God."

Rachel nodded, but she wasn't very sure she knew that at all. Not anymore, and not when it came to Jake.

"You want to say a prayer about it?"

Rachel rubbed her face and hopped to her feet to resume her pacing.

"Sure, I guess," she said. She believed with all her heart in prayer, but if the first five hundred prayers didn't do it...

She walked over to her friend anyway and plopped down next to her, then reached out both her hands, somewhat half-heartedly.

The sound of a car made her jump to her feet, leaving Kelly's hands empty. Her friend patiently reached again for her tea.

Rachel pulled back the blinds and looked out on the street in time to see Jake's truck pull into the driveway.

"It's him," she said and looked over at Kelly. "It's him," she said again, her voice full of both relief and anxiety.

"Do you want me to go?" Kelly asked and started to get up.

"No, no, no, no," Rachel stuttered, her free hand gesturing for Kelly to sit down.

Rachel watched her husband as he sat a moment in the cab of the pickup truck. The tinted windows kept her from seeing him as clearly as she needed to. When he leaned his head forward, she nearly moaned— he could be doing anything from crying to praying, though the latter seemed very unlikely from the Jake she knew. Then he slipped out of the truck. He tossed his keys in the air again and dropped them when he tried to catch them. To her relief, he laughed at himself and shook his head, then scooped up his keys and headed toward the house.

"He's laughing," Rachel said as she sprinted over to the couch and sat down. She smoothed her shirt where she had been twisting the bottom of it to calm her nerves, and then tried to look calm. "He's laughing," she whispered again to her friend.

Kelly patted her on the leg and chuckled. "Yes," she whispered back. "I heard."

The door opened and Jake walked in.

Rachel popped back to her feet, giving up on the looking-casual ruse. She hurried to her husband and hugged him.

Jake hugged her back. "I missed you too," he said with a good-natured laugh she had not heard in a long time. Tears filled her eyes, yet again. "You know I was only gone for, like, two hours, right?"

"I missed you," Rachel breathed into his chest. She pulled back and searched his eyes for some clue as to how he was, where he had been, who the hell Adrian was, and just what he and Jake had been doing. Her face must have asked all those questions, because Jake kissed her gently and smiled.

"I'm fine, Rachel," he said. Then he shook his head ruefully. "Okay, I have a ways to go to get to fine, but I feel a lot better, okay?"

"Okay," she said and hugged him again to hide her tears.

"Hi, Kelly," Jake said over her shoulder. There was a hint of the pain in his voice, which made Rachel nervous all over again. "Thanks for coming over to be with her. Today and last night, I guess," he added sheepishly, evoking that little-boy Jake Rachel had fallen in love with. "I'm sorry about last night," he added. "I'm sorry about everything." Again, the tightness in his voice made Rachel anxious.

And then Kelly was beside them, hugging them both.

"Welcome home, Jake," Kelly said. "I didn't get to tell you that yet."

It sounded like Jake tried to say something, but then he didn't. He pulled back from Rachel and looked her in the eyes again, both of her hands in his.

"Can we go for a drive? I want to talk to you about some things."

Jake looked at her as if she might say no. She smiled him and hugged her husband tightly.

"Of course," she said. "I would like that."

CHAPTER 49

Jake felt Rachel's hand tighten in his as he made the turn onto Centerville Road, which would lead them to the neighborhood where Rachel's parents lived. He looked over at her and she stared back, confused.

"I want to talk somewhere special," he said.

Jake knew how special the church tree was to Rachel. He knew it was where she'd found her faith. It was why a couple of years ago he had chosen that spot to ask her to marry him. They had enjoyed a "surprise" party (Jake always suspected Rachel had known exactly what was going on) with her family afterward.

He had a strong sense that he might be able to close some sort of circle by talking with her there. That tree had been in a lot of his dreams the last several months, beginning in Afghanistan and continuing on until as recently as last night. He in no way expected to see Luke, the messenger who had nagged him in his dreams, but he wondered if he might feel his presence there.

Once he'd put the truck in Park and shut off the engine, he came around to Rachel's side and opened her door—not in an attempt to be chivalrous, but because it appeared she would just sit there with her mouth open otherwise. Jake took her hand and led her slowly up the hill to her tree.

He sat with her in the grass beside the tree and took both of her hands in his.

"Rachel," he said and felt his throat tighten. He looked at her wet eyes.

"I'm here, Jake," she said. "I'm not going anywhere."

"I know," he said and squeezed her hands. "I want you to help me with something, baby." Her eyes almost pleaded with him to let her. "But I need you to understand that this is just a beginning. I need you to understand that there will be ups and downs and that I'll jack things up, more than once probably," he said.

"I love you so much, Jake," she said and tears streamed down her cheeks. "Anything," she added with a nod. "For better or for worse, until death do us part..."

Jake smiled and then looked at his hands a moment. This was the "worse," he supposed. He loved her so much. He summoned his courage and looked up again at her.

"I miss Cal," Jake said and his throat tightened over the name. "I feel so guilty and ashamed of so many things, some I don't know if I can ever tell you. But I think I'm most ashamed that I ran away from all the things Cal gave me—ran like a coward—at the first sign of trouble."

Jake let out a long, whistling breath and cleared his throat. For a moment he was back in Afghanistan, but the feeling was one of joy, not pain. He saw Cal's face in the dimming light of the setting sun—that smile; those eyes filled with strength and confidence and love.

You wanna close us in prayer, Jake?

His throat relaxed and his breath came back. He smiled now as he thought of Cal, sitting in the dirt by the berm. He thought of that amazing peace he'd felt in prayer with his best friend—and his newfound savior. Then he thought of Rachel and the amazing peace—almost a literal glow—he would see on Rachel's face when she would close her eyes in prayer at Foundations Family Church on Sundays. God, how he wanted that. For himself and for them together, as husband and wife.

"Will you pray with me, Rachel?" he asked.

"Oh yes, Jake," she sobbed. "Yes, baby, of course. It's what I always wanted for us. I love you so much, Jake."

He hugged her tightly and then bowed his head, ready to take the first step on his long road.

Stay on the path.

Jake smiled at the image of Luke in his mind.

He closed his eyes and prayed out loud—not at all unaware that he chose the exact same words Cal had taught him in the dirt beside a berm in Afghanistan.

They stayed on the hill beneath the tree—Rachel's tree—until the sky turned dark and the air became chilly. Then they walked down the hill, hand in hand, along the narrow path that led back to their truck.

And home.

EPILOGUE

Six months later

Jake's leg bobbed up and down almost painfully, no matter how much he commanded it to stop. He heard Rachel giggle, shot her a dirty look, and then laughed at himself.

"Shut up," he said, but chuckled when he did. Then he sighed. "How many people are in there?"

Rachel looked through the narrow rectangle of glass in the wooden door that led into the adjoining room.

"I don't know. Just a few."

Jake heard a muffled voice and then an explosion of laughter. His eyebrows rose and his leg resumed its bounce.

"A few? That sounded like a thousand people," he said. "Baby, I don't know if I can do this."

She kissed his cheek.

"You can do this," she said and hugged him. "There's not that many people, and remember, they're all just like you. They're like the guys you lived with every day. They came to see what this is gonna be all about, just like you."

Jake sighed. He supposed she was right. Anyway, this was the next mission. No turning back now. They were almost on the X.

The door cracked and Pastor Chris stuck his head in. "Ready?"

Jake sighed and held up a finger. Rachel took his hand and bowed her head with him.

Jake closed his eyes in prayer. "For you, Lord," he said. "And for Cal."

He opened his eyes and nodded at Pastor Chris. "Okay."

JEFFREY WILSON

Jake stood by the door as Chris gave him a short introduction. He shot another dirty look at Rachel when he saw that there were at least a couple dozen people sitting in the chairs in the meeting room above the chapel. She giggled and gave him a thumbs-up. Jake sighed and walked over to the podium.

"Hey, guys," he said and cleared his throat. "Sorry, I'm a little nervous."

A soft wave of laughter swept the room and Jake swept his eyes across the crowd with it—mostly men, he saw, but a few women as well.

"Thanks so much for coming. My name's Jake. I'm Army."

There was a collective "hooah" from the group, followed by some good-natured "boos" and then more laughter. Jake nodded and smiled. And then he relaxed at the comfort of the camaraderie and the knowledge he was finally back on the path.

"Go Army," he said. He looked out at the group again. "Afghanistan. I got back a while ago, but really just got home in my head more recently." The room quieted. "Like many of us, I saw things that shook my faith in myself and in God. I did things I'm proud of and others that I'm not as sure of. I lost people close to me." Jake's voice cracked and he gripped the podium. "I'm really home now, but a part of me will always be over there—in Helmand province—with the ones I lost. I want to tell you about my cross—about the death of my hope. And then I want to tell you about my journey back, about the resurrection I found and the hope I have now, thanks to my relationship with God."

And then the words and feelings poured out from him like he had told the story a thousand times, though as he talked he realized this was the first time he had shared it, start to finish, out loud.

He was at the podium for only a half hour, but he stayed in the room, fulfilling what felt like his new purpose, for an hour after that, talking one-on-one to a few of the men who had come. Only half of those who attended signed up to be part of the weekly group he would now lead for Foundations, but that was way more than he'd even hoped for. And perhaps some of the others had heard something that would at least start them on their own journeys home. As Adrian had done for him.

Jake and Rachel sat with Pastor Chris and Pastor Craig for a short time and let the men pray over what Jake was doing. Then Jake took Rachel by the hand and led her quietly to the truck.

"I have one more place I want to go," he said.

Rachel smiled as if she already knew.

A half hour later, they walked side by side. Jake felt Rachel's hand, warm and soft in his, and realized that without that anchor—and his faith, however new and young—he would probably not be able to complete the short walk up the crushed-white-gravel path. She knew to say nothing and he loved her for that.

The air was cool, though the warmth of the early autumn sun was just a few hours away. For a moment it felt a little like walking to a crappy breakfast in Afghanistan. Weird how things unrelated to the war took him there anyway. Jake was learning to live with that instead of fighting it. The war was part of him now, like his DNA. Anyway, there was nothing weird about how easily he'd headed to the war this morning. He guessed, in a way, the path he believed he was back on was taking him right back to Afghanistan.

He stopped at a fork where the path split in two and looked at the black-and-white diagram in his hand with the small star in pen in the middle.

"To the left," Rachel said.

Of course. She had been here before, hadn't she? While he was still far away—in more ways than one.

He nodded and squeezed her hand, not quite able to say anything.

"Do you want me to go with you or would you rather be alone with him?"

Jake adjusted Cal's backpack on his shoulders where it had slipped just a little.

"I don't know," he said honestly.

They continued together along the left path.

As they neared the spot, Jake was surprised at how many wonderful, warm thoughts came to him. He had expected—had feared—that his mind would be full of death and killing, images of firing into the face of that terrorist, of Cal disappearing, and of squirming thumbs. He realized that he hadn't thought of those damn thumbs in quite a long time.

Afghanistan was with him, but his mind was full of other thoughts and images. He remembered Cal laughing with him as he paced nervously on his wedding day. He remembered breakfasts after church and a softball game where Cal broke his wrist. He remembered Cal's quiet calm and strength as he explained, as if to a child, the things he believed while they sat against the berm in the chilly evening air in Afghanistan.

"He's here," Rachel said softly, bringing Jake back to today's mission.

She kissed his cheek and squeezed his hand, then gave him a gentle nudge.

"Tell him I love him," she said with a smile and tear-filled eyes.

Jake swallowed hard and nodded.

He stood before the simple white cross for a moment and then sat in the grass beside it. First, he let his fingers trace Caleb's name on the granite. Then he wiped the tears from his cheeks and forced a smile onto his face—a smile that in some small way felt real. Cal would prefer that, he knew.

"Hey, bro," he said as he unzipped the backpack and pulled Cal's Bible out and into his lap. "Sorry it took me so long, Cal. I'd like to pick our Bible study back up, if you don't mind." The tears that streamed down his cheeks didn't even bother him now, and he let them go instead of wiping them off. He slipped his finger into the pages of the Bible where he had placed a bookmark.

"Rachel found us a great chapter in Ephesians," he began.

He read to Cal for a long time.

ACKNOWLEDGMENTS

When God called me to write this book, I was still far from home myself. There are so many people to thank for helping me find my way back to God's plan for my life, most especially Wendy and our kids, the entire community of Grace Family Church, Mario Martin, with whom I launched the Men's Military Group at Grace—to help ourselves as much as others—and Pastor Jerry Batista, who supported that vision.

This book would not have been possible without the patient guidance of my close friend and faith mentor, Pastor Chris Bonham. In helping me with this book, he helped me on my journey, and I will be eternally grateful for both. Pastor Craig Altman shared so much of his time with me, and lent me both his name and his larger-than-life presence to share with the world on the pages of this book. By doing so, he helped me show a real face and the true heart of a man of God. Thanks also to Pastor Mike Moore for his friendship and creative genius in bringing the story to you by building a multimedia platform for both the book and the resources we hope to bring with it. I owe you way more than a dinner, my friend.

Last, but far from least, thank you to my agent, Gina Panettieri, for supporting my passion for this project when I still had *plenty* of other deadlines on my plate, and to my amazing editor, Caitlin Alexander, whose incredible talent and eye for detail has taken this, and all my books, from story to novel. And of course, my partner and coauthor in the Andrews and Wilson brand, Brian Andrews, for his unconditional support of the time I needed to make this novel a reality. Thanks, brother!

Isaiah 6:8

ABOUT THE AUTHOR

Navy veteran and *Wall Street Journal* and Amazon bestselling thriller author Jeffrey Wilson is a vascular surgeon who was completing his training when terrorists attacked America on 9/11. Already having served, Jeff immediately rejoined the active duty Navy and served as a combat surgeon with the Marines and then with an East Coast–based SEAL team and a Joint Special Operations Task Force, making multiple deployments. His experiences there—seeing things that cannot be unseen—sent him on his own journey exploring, and at times questioning, his faith, and are the inspiration for this novel. Jeff has also worked as an actor, a firefighter, a paramedic, a jet pilot, and a diving instructor.

Together with fellow Navy veteran Brian Andrews, Jeff writes the Amazon #1 bestselling Tier One series of military thrillers and (under the pseudonym Alex Ryan) the Nick Foley thriller series. Jeff is also the author of three award-winning supernatural thrillers.

Jeff and his wife, Wendy, are Virginia natives who, with their four children, Ashley, Emma, Jack, and Connor, call southwest Florida home. When not writing his next novel, Jeff still practices medicine and leads the Men's Military Ministry at his church, where Wendy leads the Beautiful Moms Ministry, Emma sings on the praise and worship team, Jack works on the AV team, and Connor has volunteered in the children's ministry.

Learn more at www.wartornnovel.com and www.andrews-wilson.com.

Made in the USA
Columbia, SC
25 October 2018